Tree-House Comix Proudly Presents

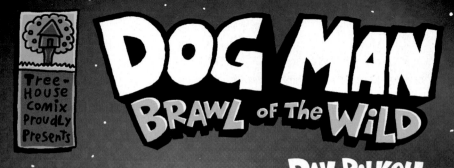

DOG MAN
BRAWL of The WILD

WRITTEN AND ILLUSTRATED BY DAV PILKEY
AS GEORGE BEARD AND HAROLD HUTCHINS
WITH COLOR BY JOSE GARIBALDI

D

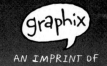

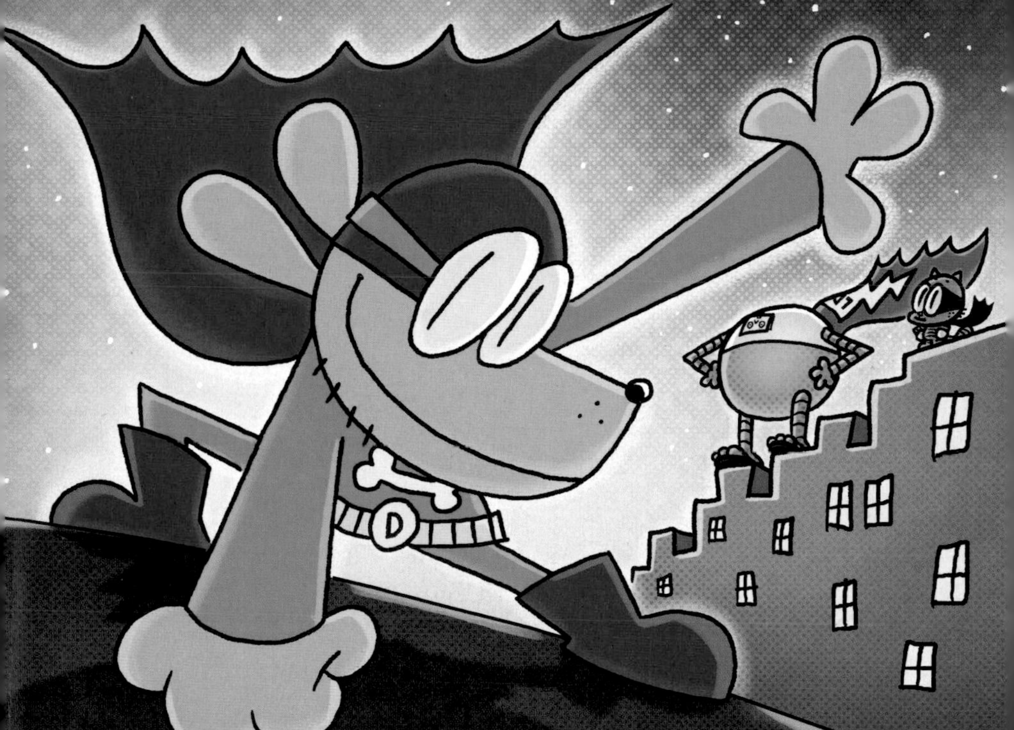

graphix
AN IMPRINT OF
SCHOLASTIC

FOR LIZETTE SERRANO
THANK YOU FOR YOUR STRENGTH,
COMPASSION, AND DEVOTION
TO LIBRARIES AND KIDS

Library of Congress Control Number 2018945989

978-1-338-23657-6 (POB)
978-1-338-29092-9 (Library)

10 9 8 7 6 5 4 3 2 1   19 20 21 22 23

Printed in China   62
First edition, January 2019

Edited by Ken Geist
Book design by Dav Pilkey and Phil Falco
Color by Jose Garibaldi
Color flatting by Rachel Polk
Creative Director: David Saylor

CHAPTERS

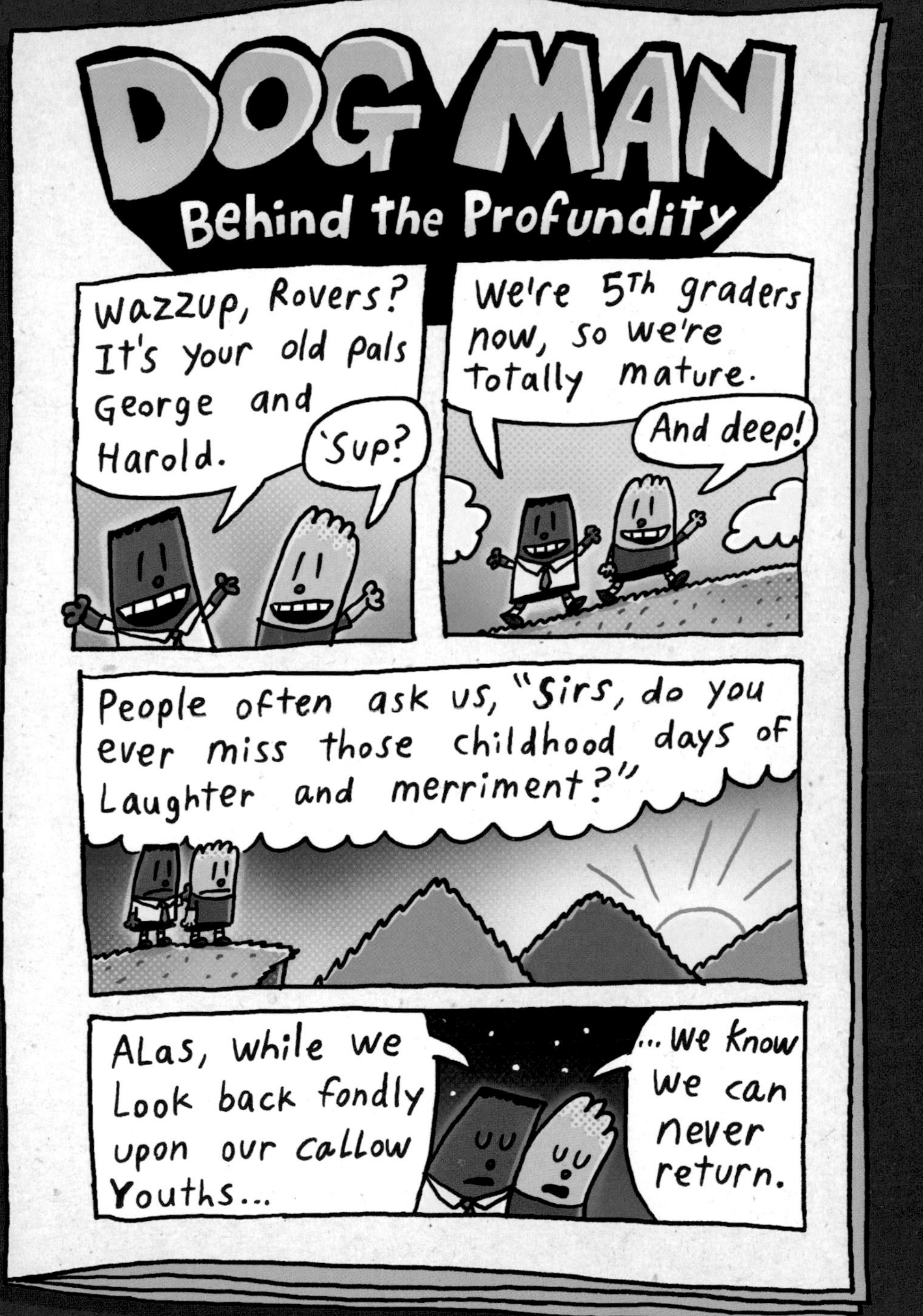
DOG MAN
Behind the Profundity
Wazzup, Rovers? It's your old pals George and Harold.
'Sup?
We're 5th graders now, so we're totally mature.
And deep!
People often ask us, "Sirs, do you ever miss those childhood days of laughter and merriment?"
Alas, while we look back fondly upon our callow youths...
...we know we can never return.

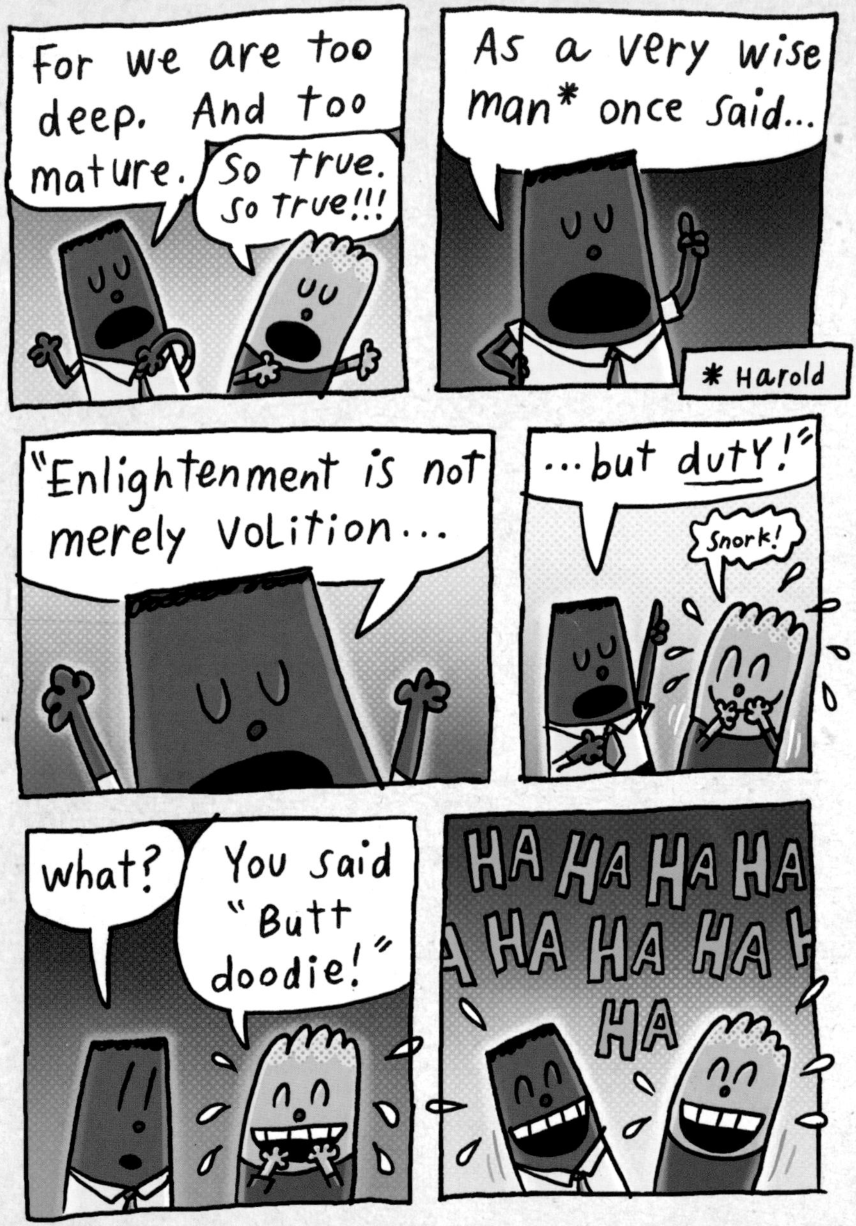
For we are too deep. And too mature.
So true. So true!!!
As a very wise man* once said...
* Harold
"Enlightenment is not merely volition...
...but duty!"
Snork!
what?
You said "Butt doodie!"
HA HA HA HA HA HA HA HA HA

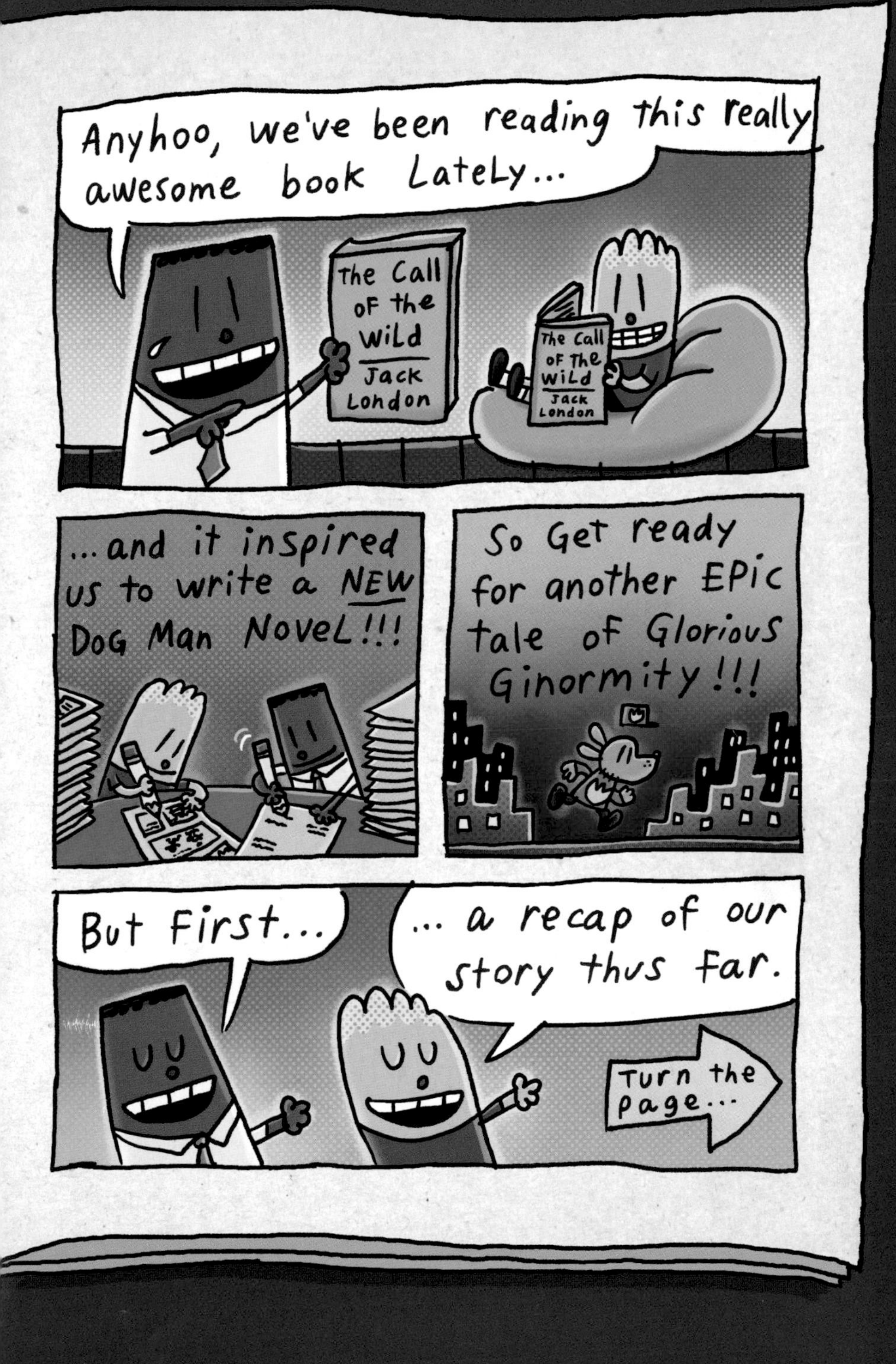

Anyhoo, we've been reading this really awesome book Lately...
The Call of the Wild
Jack London
The Call of The Wild
Jack London
...and it inspired us to write a NEW Dog Man Novel!!!
So Get ready for another EPic tale of Glorious Ginormity!!!
But First...
... a recap of our story thus far.
Turn the page...

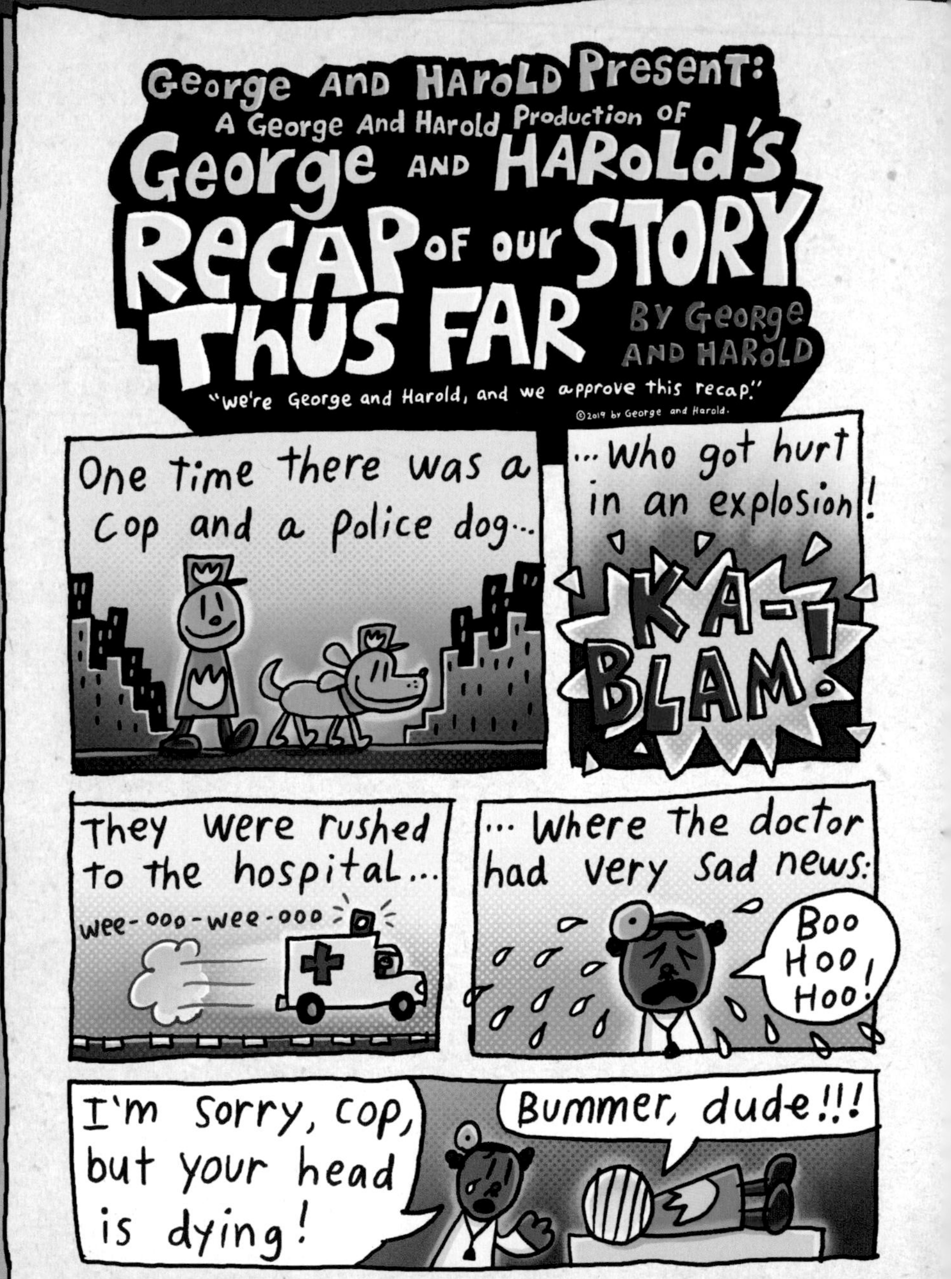
George and Harold Present:
A George and Harold Production of
George and Harold's
Recap of our Story Thus Far
By George and Harold
"We're George and Harold, and we approve this recap."
©2019 by George and Harold.
One time there was a cop and a police dog...
...who got hurt in an explosion!
KA-BLAM!
They were rushed to the hospital...
wee-ooo-wee-ooo
...where the doctor had very sad news:
Boo Hoo Hoo!
I'm sorry, cop, but your head is dying!
Bummer, dude!!!

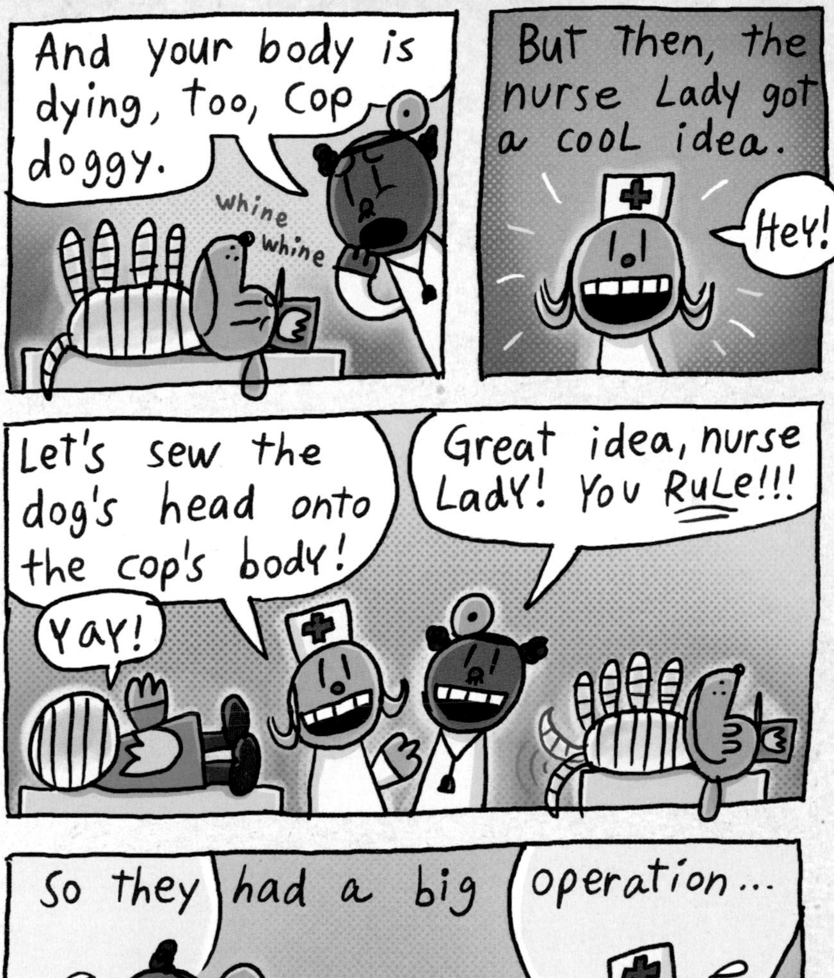

And your body is dying, too, Cop doggy.
whine whine
But Then, the nurse Lady got a cooL idea.
Hey!
Let's sew the dog's head onto the cop's body!
Yay!
Great idea, nurse Lady! You RuLe!!!
So they had a big operation...

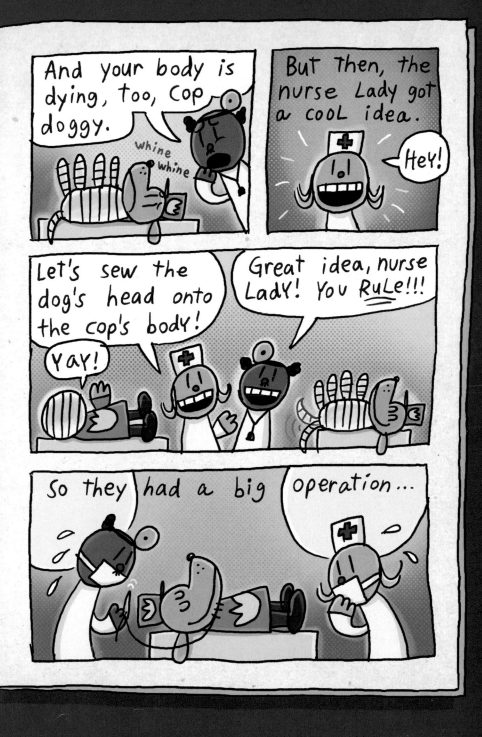

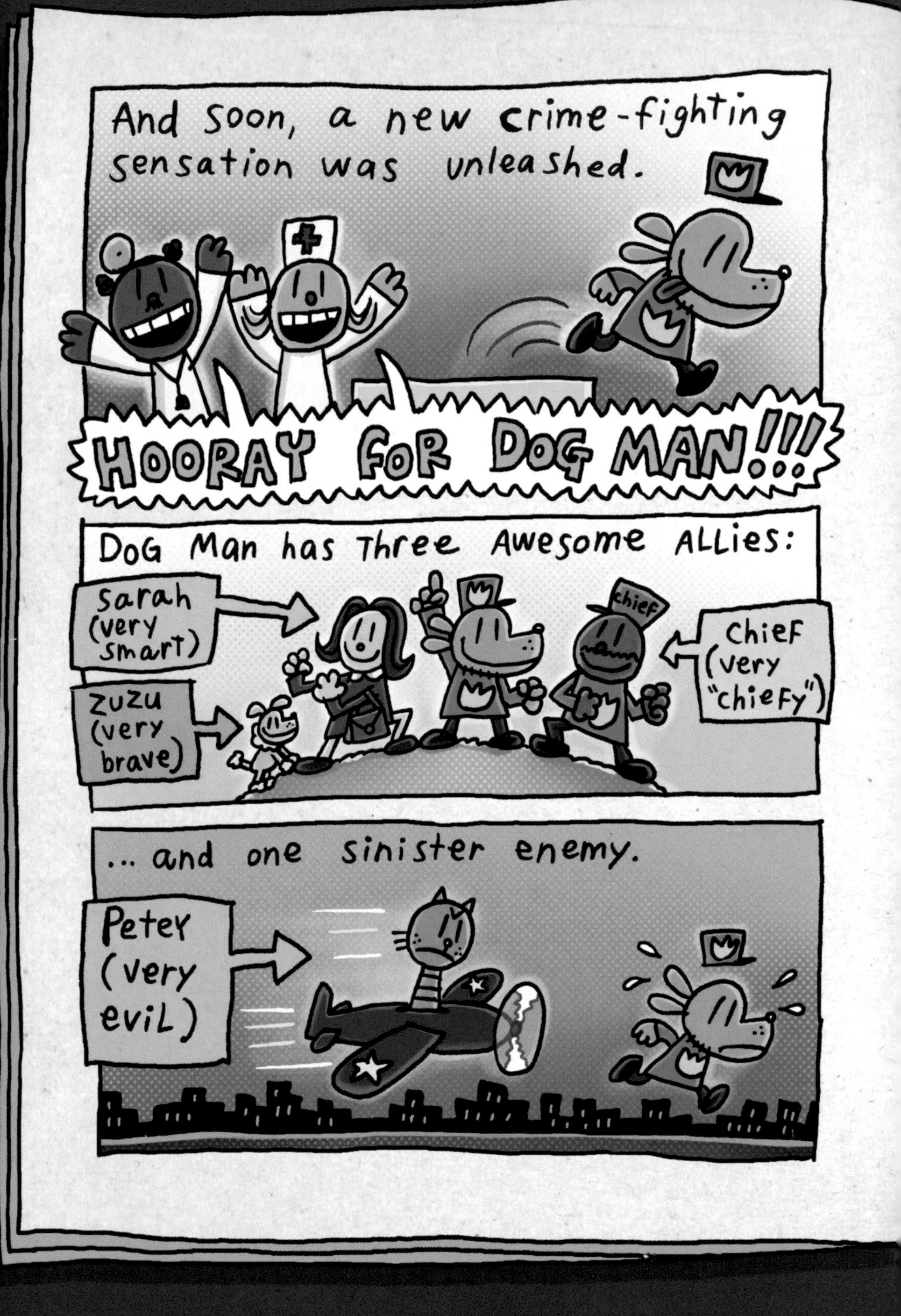

And soon, a new crime-fighting sensation was unleashed.
HOORAY FOR DOG MAN!!!
Dog Man has three awesome allies:
Sarah (very smart)
Zuzu (very brave)
Chief
Chief (very "chiefy")
...and one sinister enemy.
Peter (very evil)

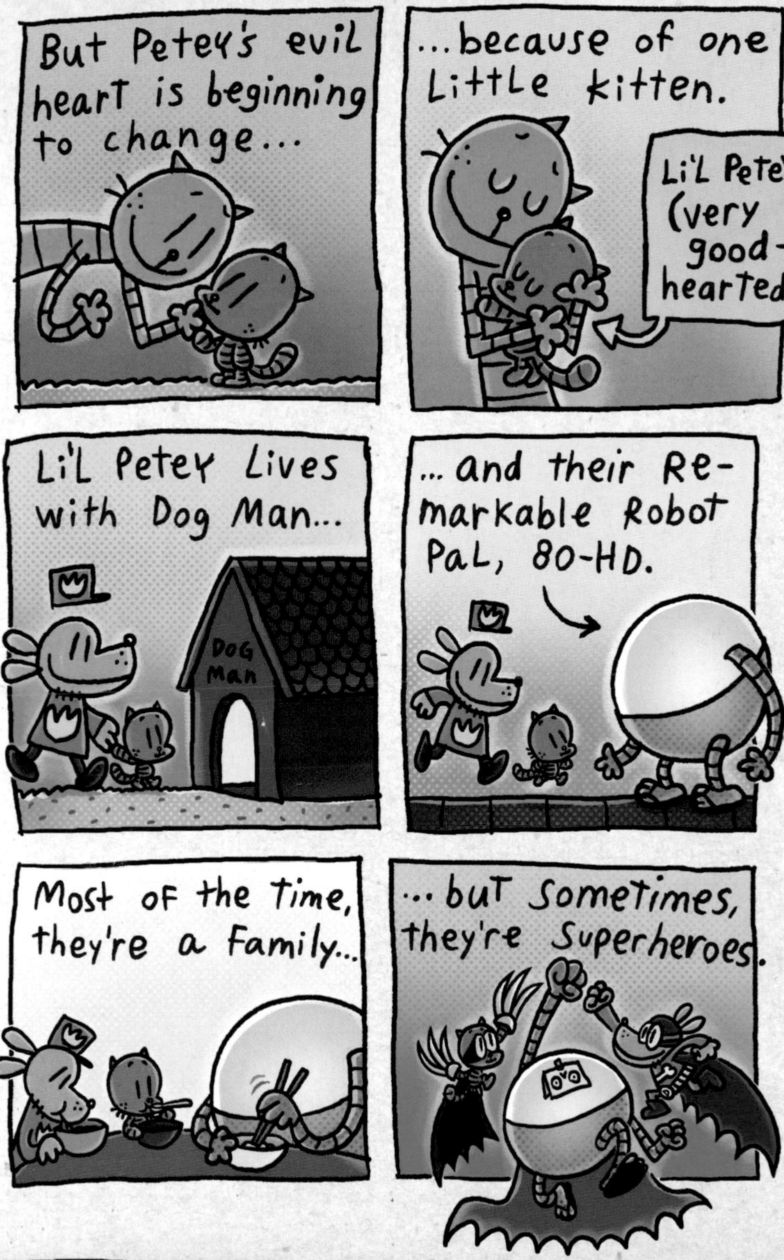
But Petey's evil heart is beginning to change...
...because of one little kitten.
Li'l Petey (very good-hearted)
Li'l Petey lives with Dog Man...
DOG MAN
...and their Re-markable Robot Pal, 80-HD.
Most of the time, they're a family...
...but sometimes, they're Superheroes.

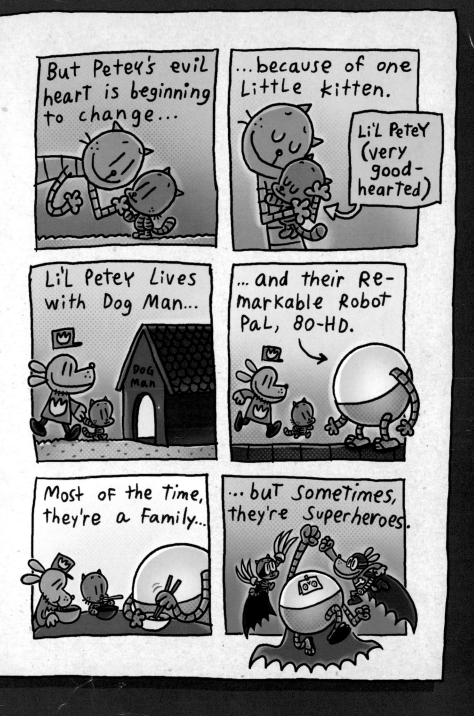

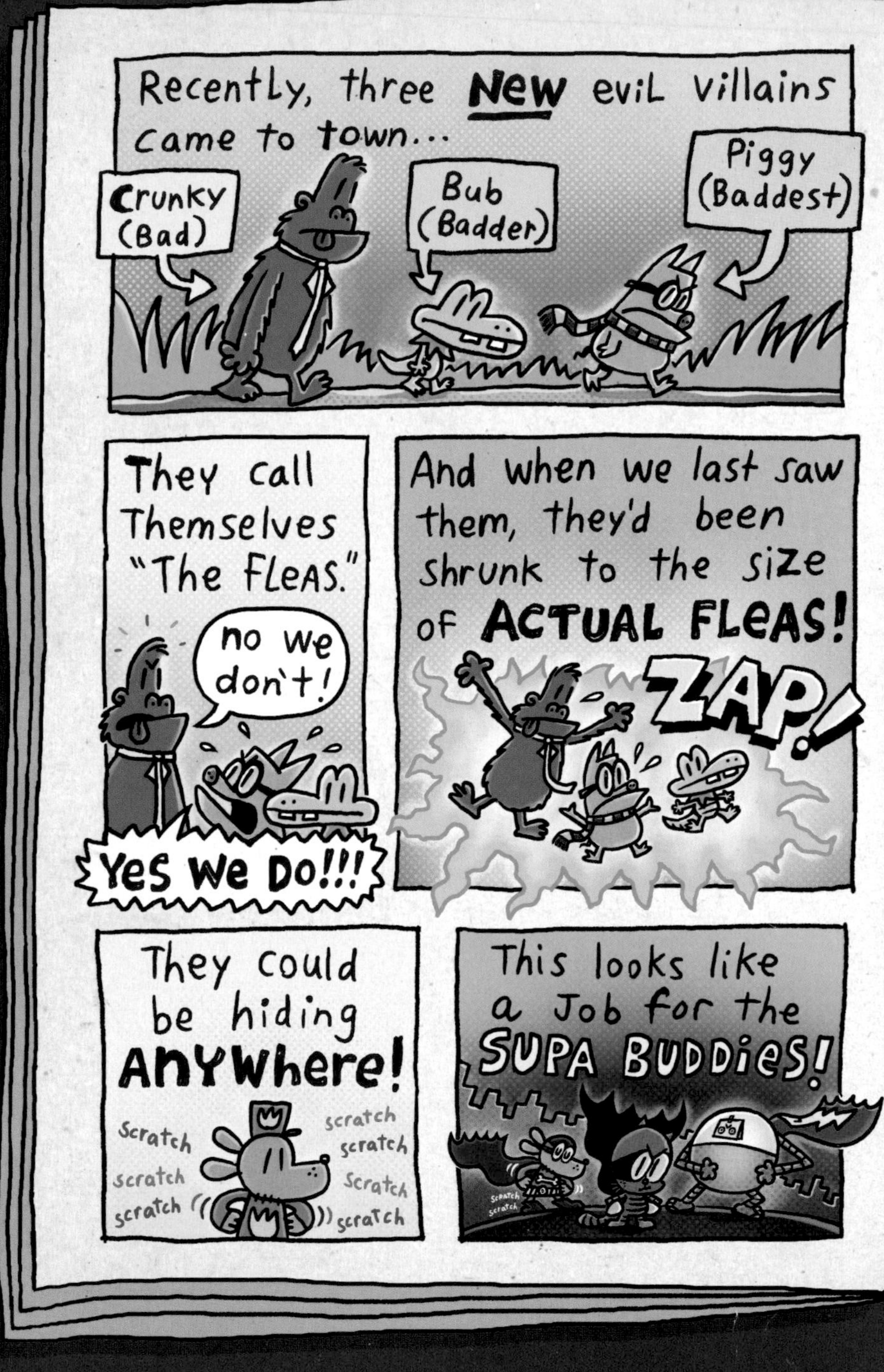

Recently, three NEW evil villains came to town...
Crunky (Bad)
Bub (Badder)
Piggy (Baddest)
They call Themselves "The FLEAS."
no we don't!
YES WE DO!!!
And when we last saw them, they'd been shrunk to the size of ACTUAL FLEAS!
ZAP!
They could be hiding ANYWhere!
scratch
scratch
scratch
scratch
scratch
scratch
scratch
scratch
This looks like a Job for the SUPA BUDDIES!

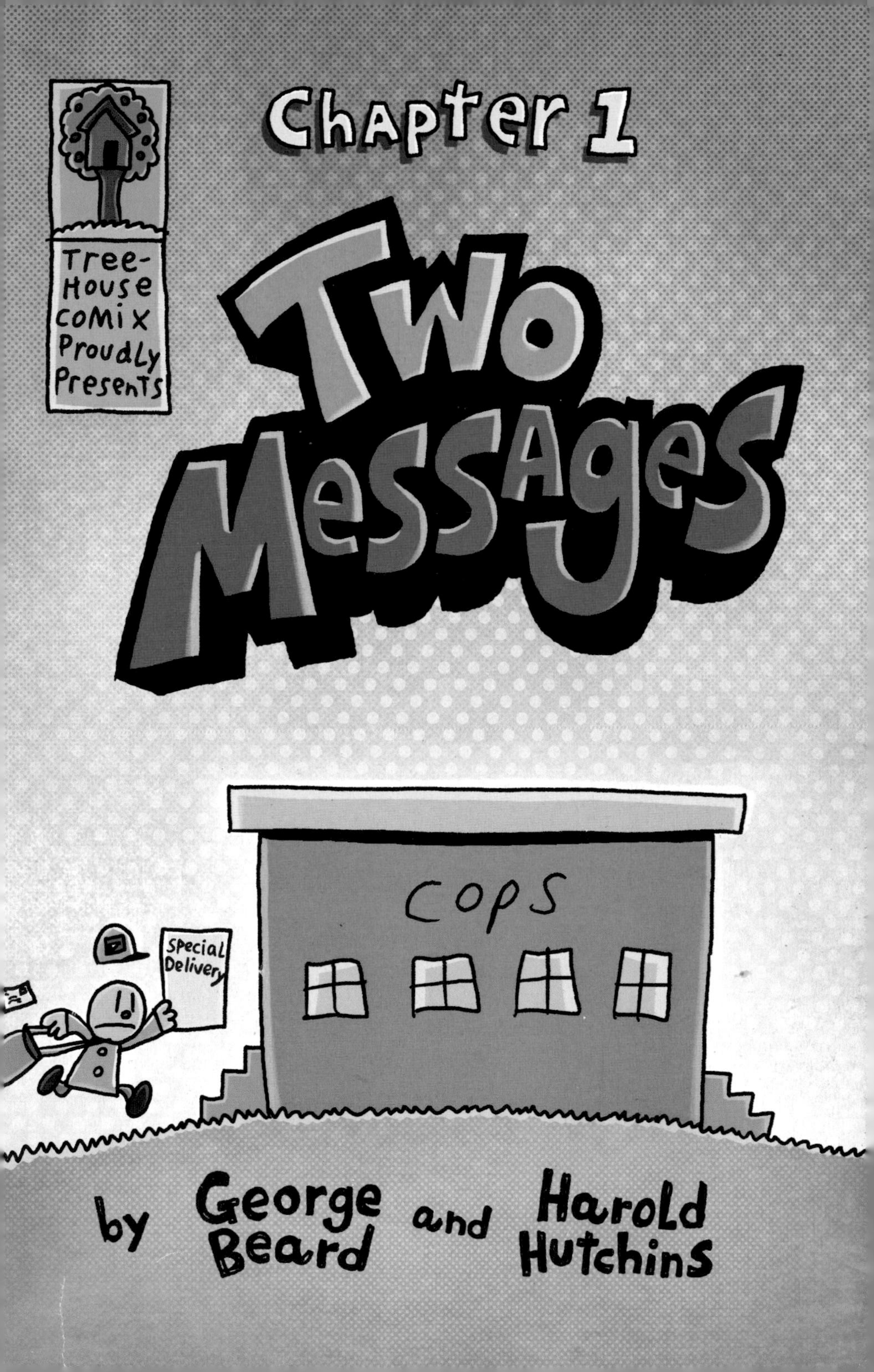
Tree-House Comix Proudly Presents
Chapter 1
Two Messages
COPS
Special Delivery
by George Beard and Harold Hutchins

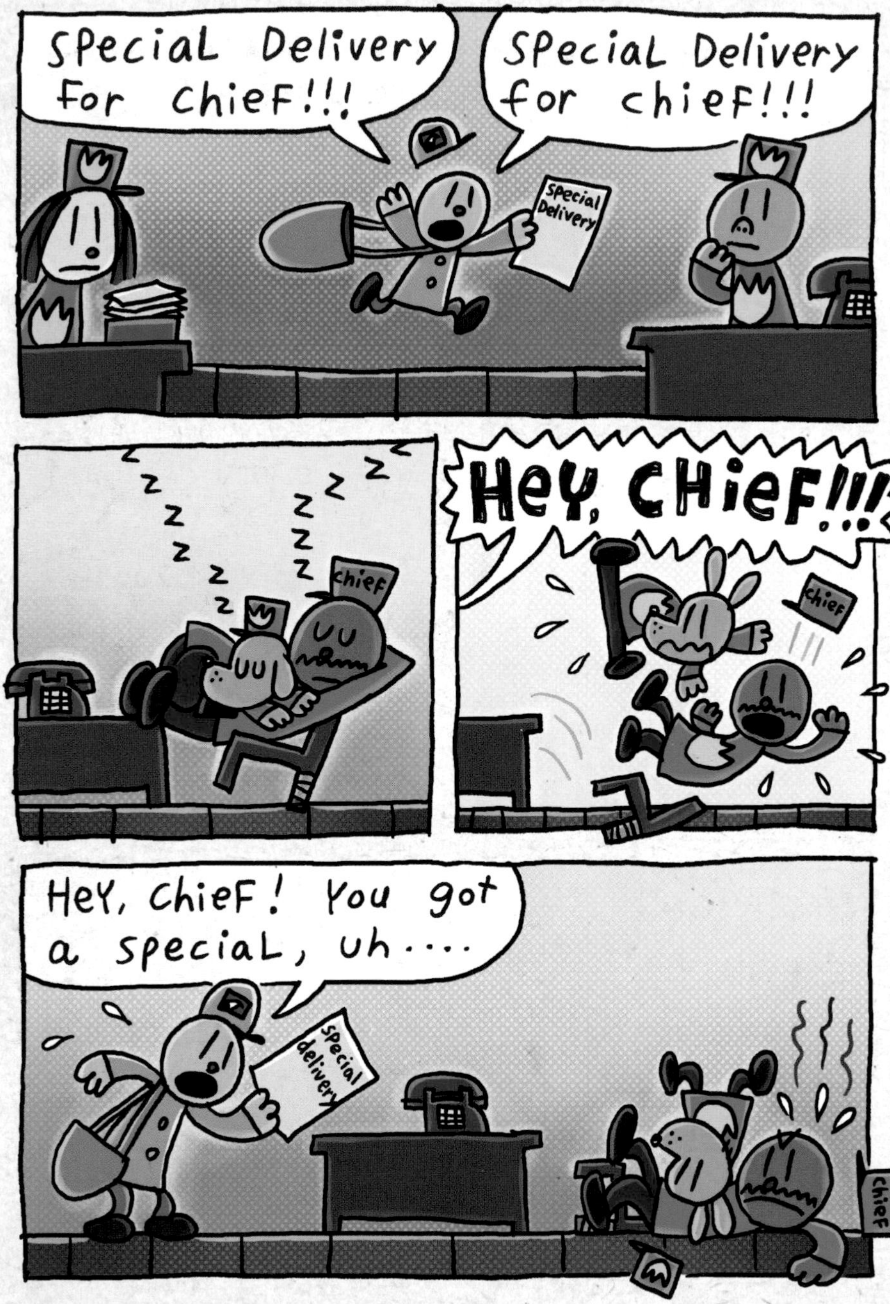

Special Delivery for Chief!!!
Special Delivery for chief!!!
Special Delivery
chief
HEY, CHIEF!!!
chief
Hey, Chief! You got a special, uh....
Special delivery
chief

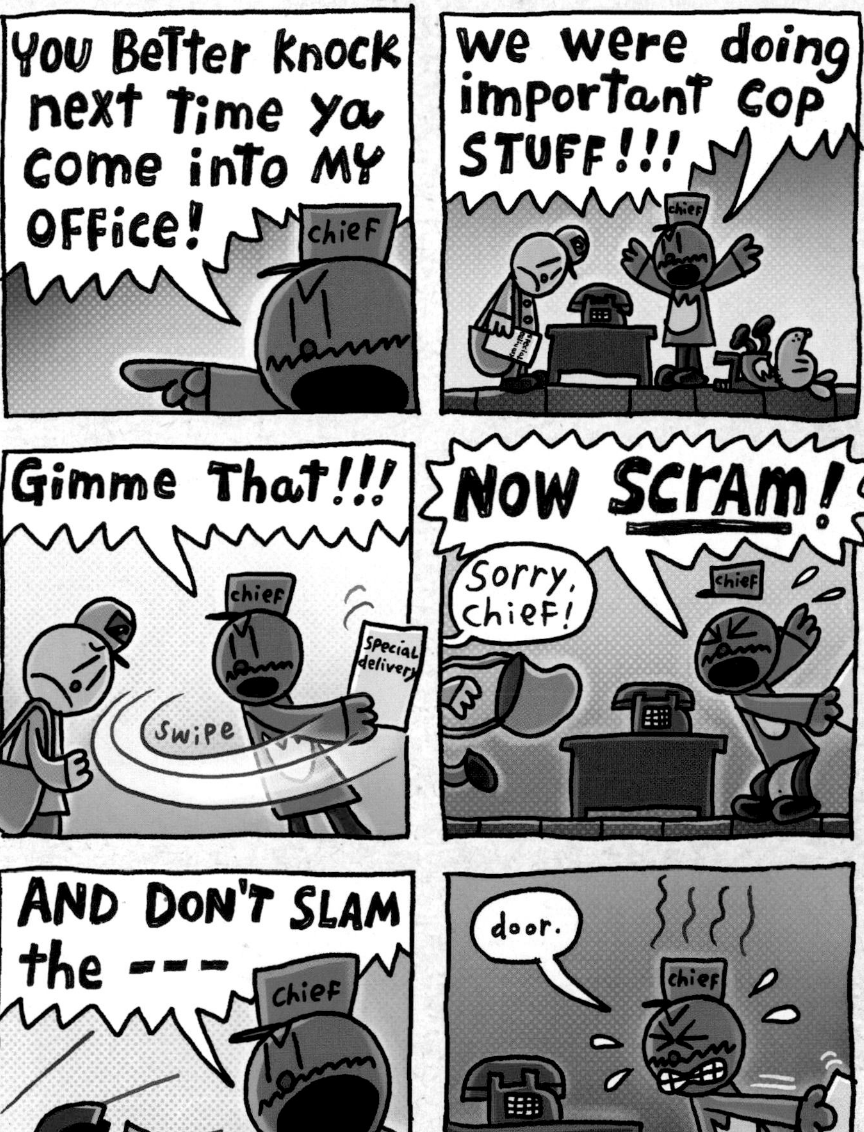
YOU BeTTer Knock next Time ya come into MY OFFice!
chieF
we were doing important cop STUFF!!!
chieF
Special delivery
Gimme That!!!
chieF
Special delivery
Swipe
NOW SCRAM!
Sorry, chieF!
chieF
AND DON'T SLAM the ---
chieF
SLAM!
door.
chieF

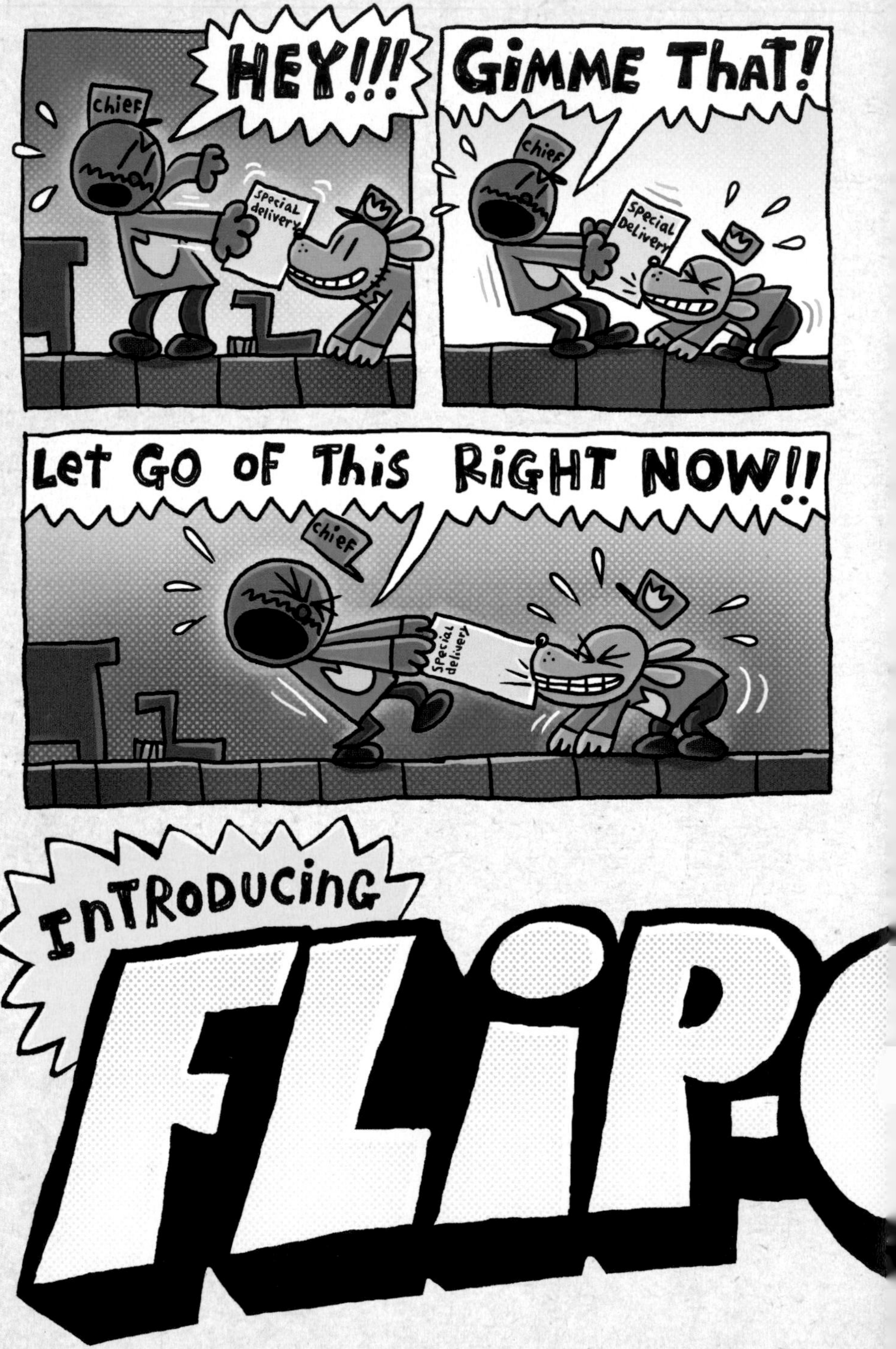
HEY!!!
chief
special delivery
GiMME ThAT!
chief
Special Delivery
Let GO OF This RiGHT NOW!!
chief
Special delivery
InTRODUCinG
FLiP

STEP 1.
First, Place your Left hand inside the dotted Lines marked "Left hand here." HoLd The book open *FLAT*!

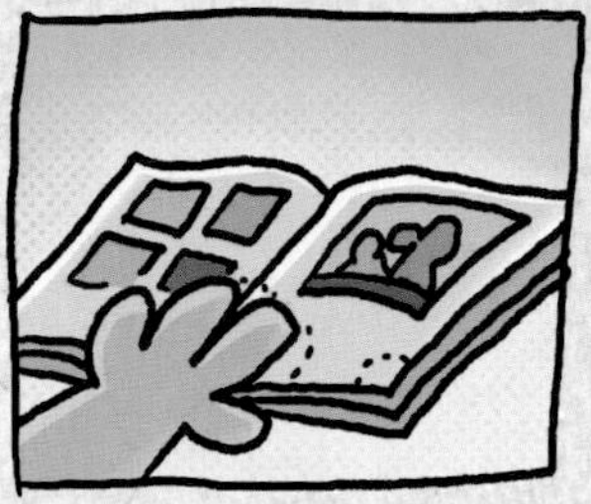

STEP 2:
Grasp the right-hand Page with your Thumb and index finger (inside the dotted Lines marked "Right Thumb Here").

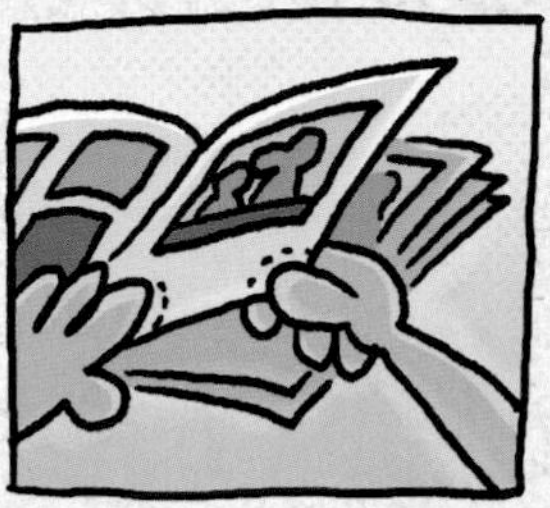

STEP 3:
Now *QUICKLY* fLip the right-hand Page back and forth until the Picture appears to be *Animated*.

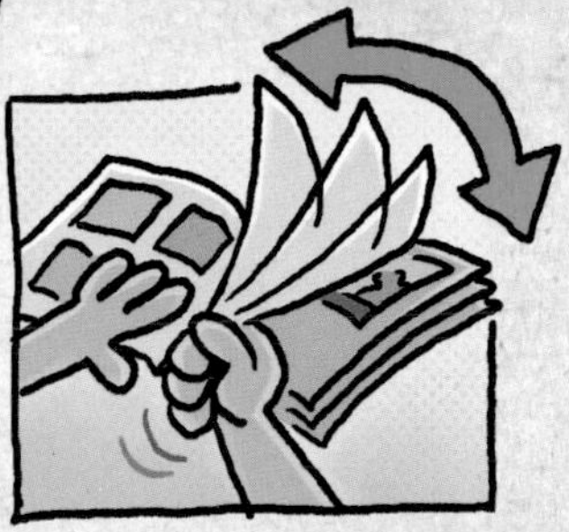

(For extra fun, try adding your own sound-effects!)

RAMA

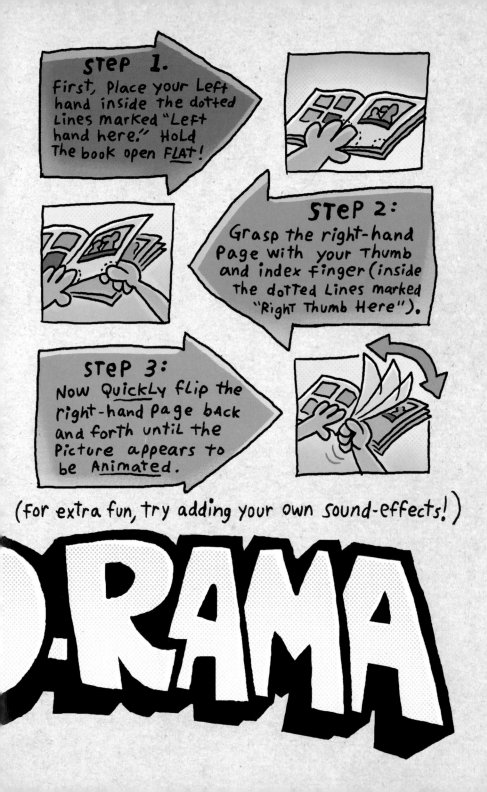

Remember,

while you are flipping,
be sure you can see
the image on page 19
AND the image on page 21.

If you flip quickly,
the two pictures will
start to look like
one **Animated** cartoon!

Don't forget to
add your own
sound-effects!

Left
hand here.

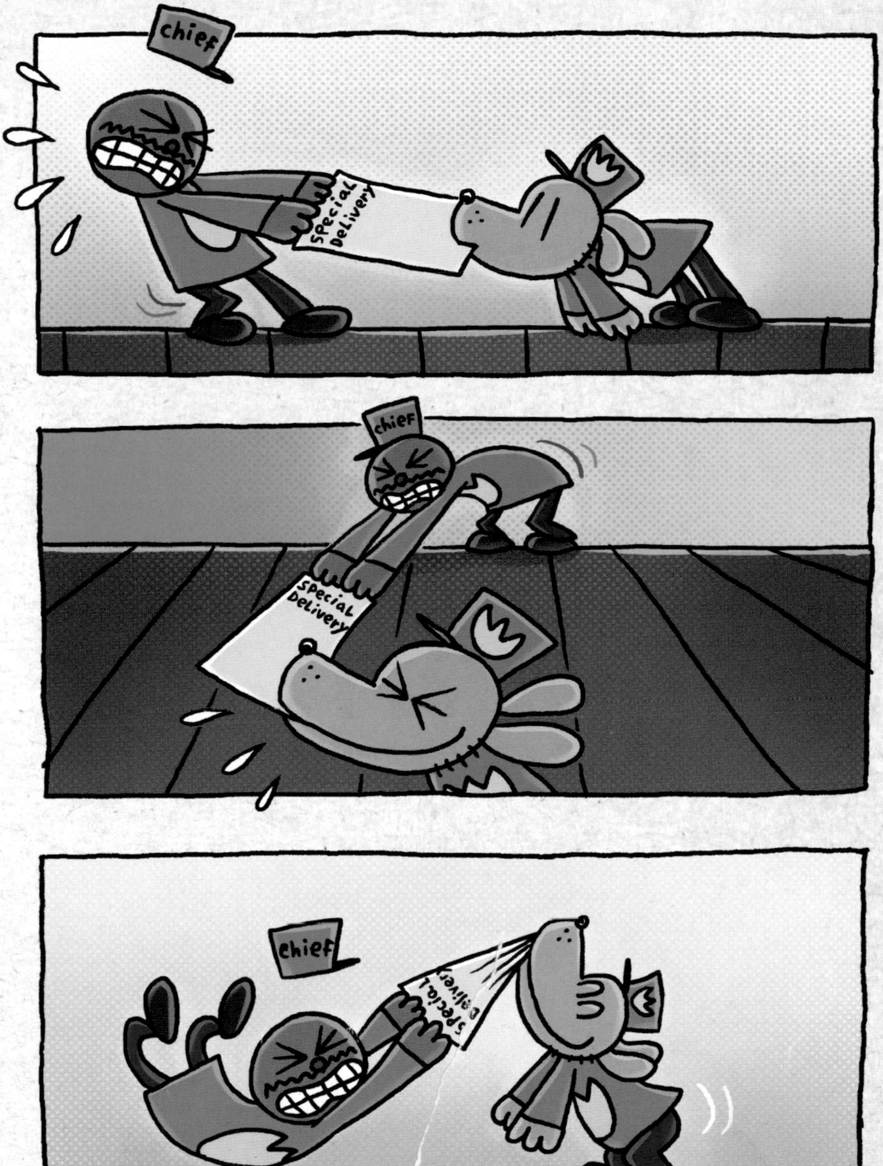
chief
Special Delivery
chief
Special Delivery
chief
Special Delivery

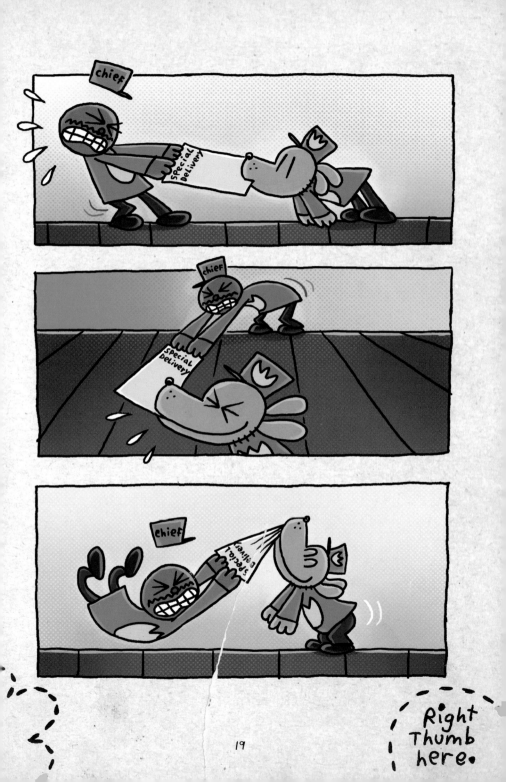

Right Thumb here.

21

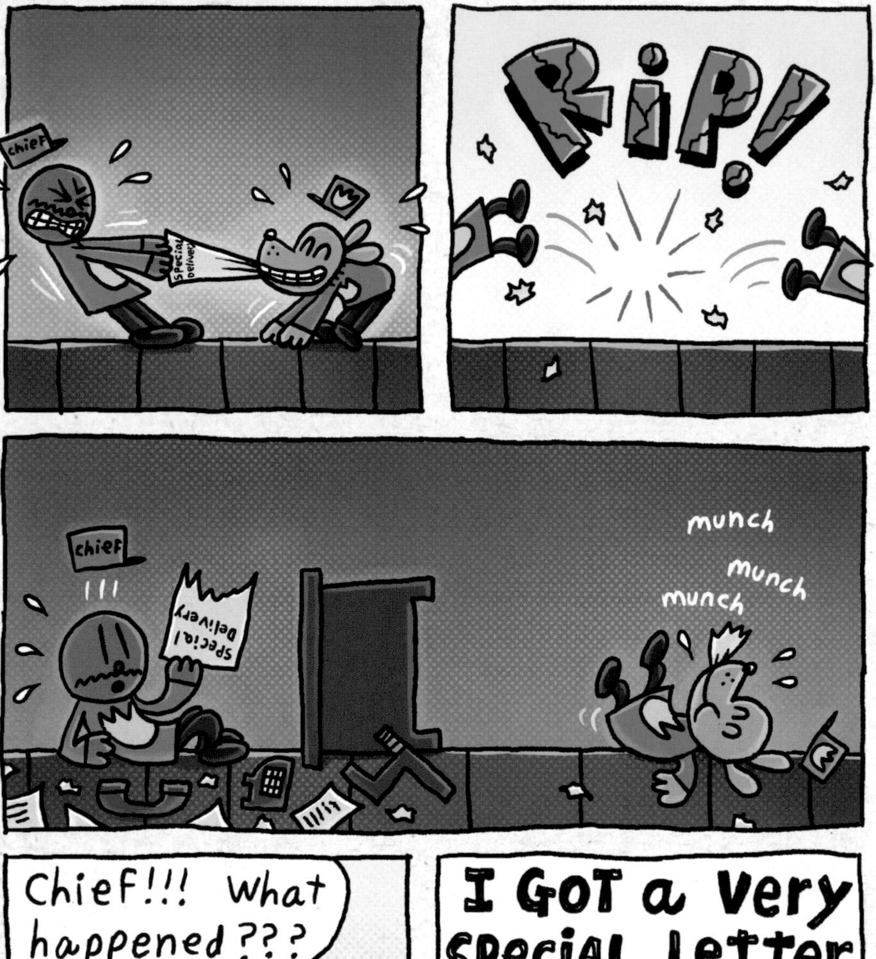
chief
Special Delivery
RIP!
chief
Special Delivery
munch
munch
munch
Chief!!! What happened???
chief
Special Delivery
I GOT a Very SPECIAL Letter And DOG MAN DESTROYED IT!
Special delivery

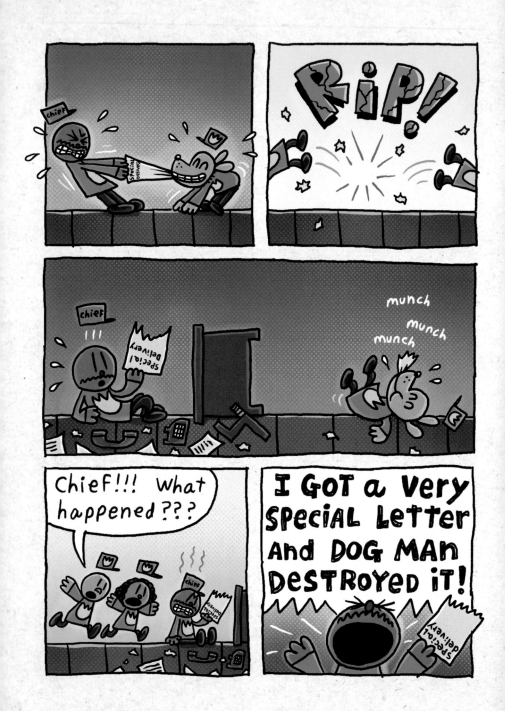

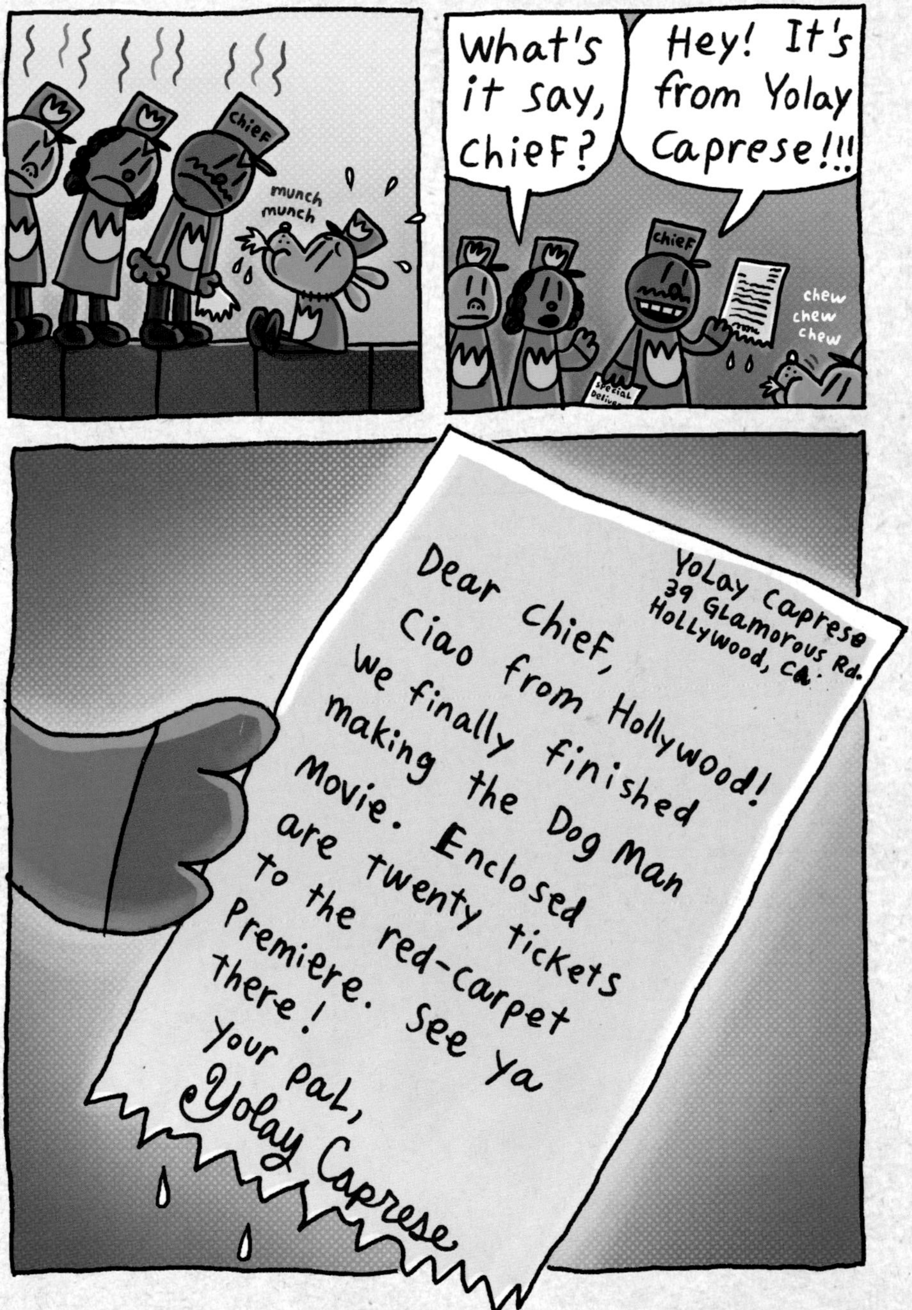
chief
munch munch
What's it say, chief?
Hey! It's from Yolay Caprese!!!
chief
chew chew chew
Special Delivery
YoLay Caprese
39 GLamorous Rd.
HoLLywood, CA.
Dear Chief,
Ciao from Hollywood!
We finally finished making the Dog Man Movie. Enclosed are twenty tickets to the red-carpet Premiere. See ya there!
Your paL,
Yolay Caprese

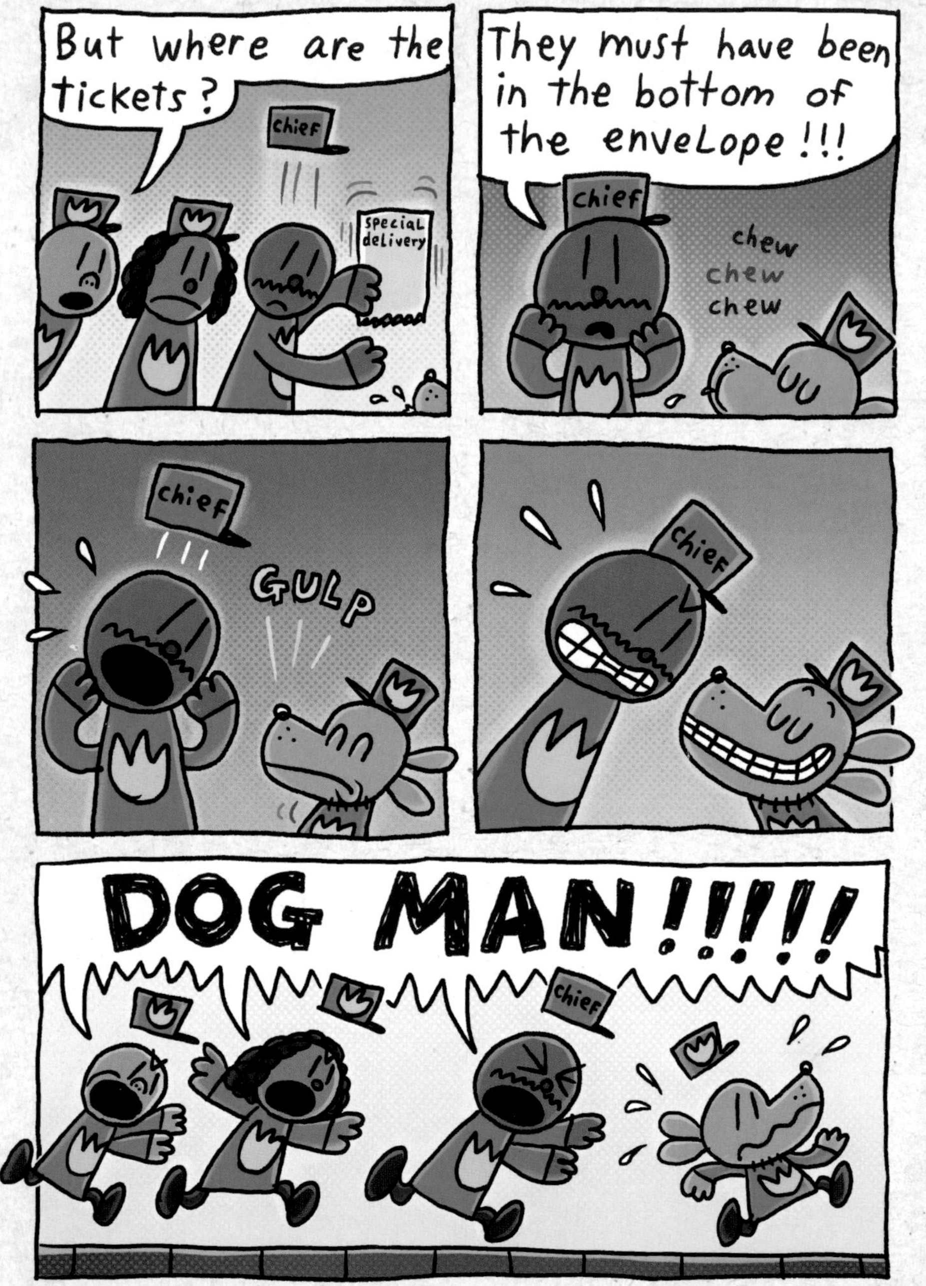
But where are the tickets?
chief
Special delivery
They must have been in the bottom of the envelope!!!
chief
chew chew chew
chief
GULP
chief
DOG MAN!!!!!
chief

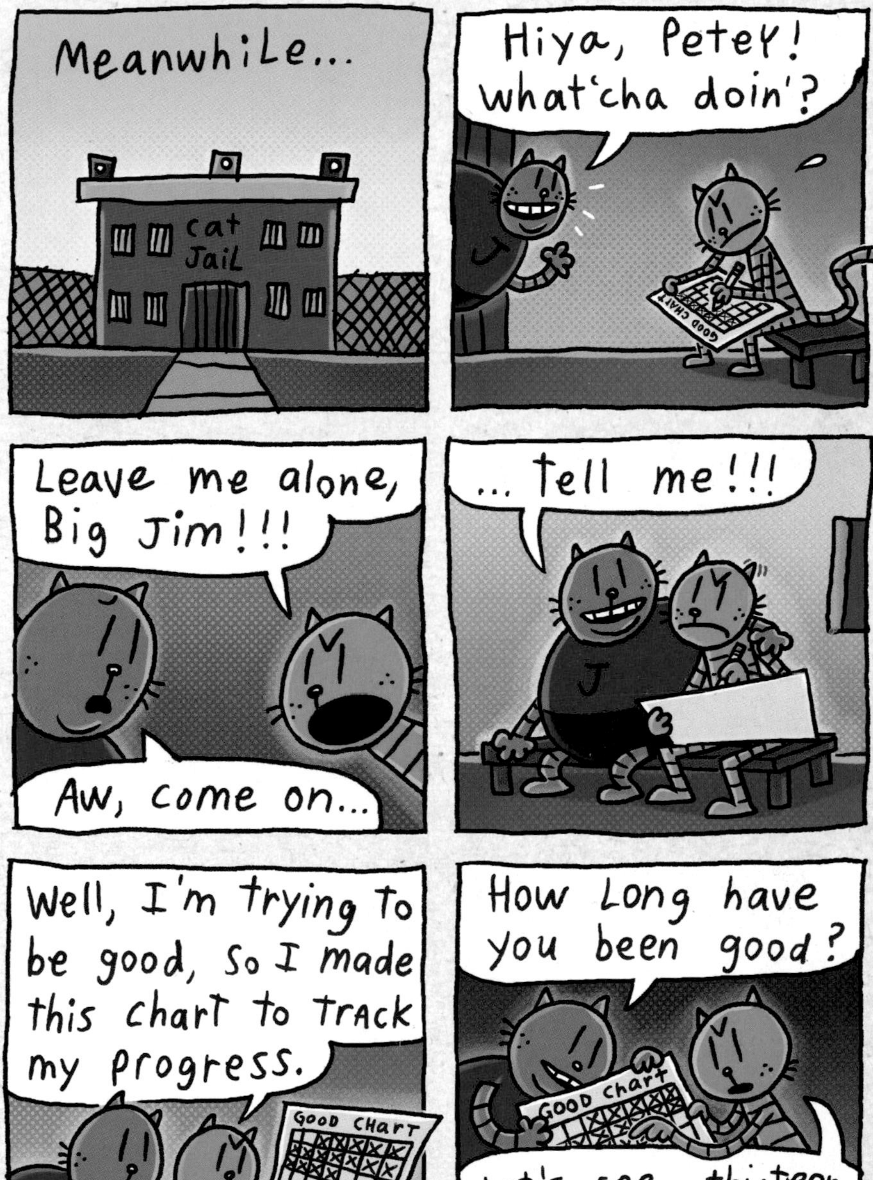
Meanwhile...
Cat Jail
Hiya, Petey! what'cha doin'?
GOOD CHART
Leave me alone, Big Jim!!!
Aw, come on...
... Tell me!!!
Well, I'm trying to be good, so I made this chart to track my progress.
GOOD CHART
How long have you been good?
GOOD CHART
Let's see... thirteen, fourteen, fifteen...

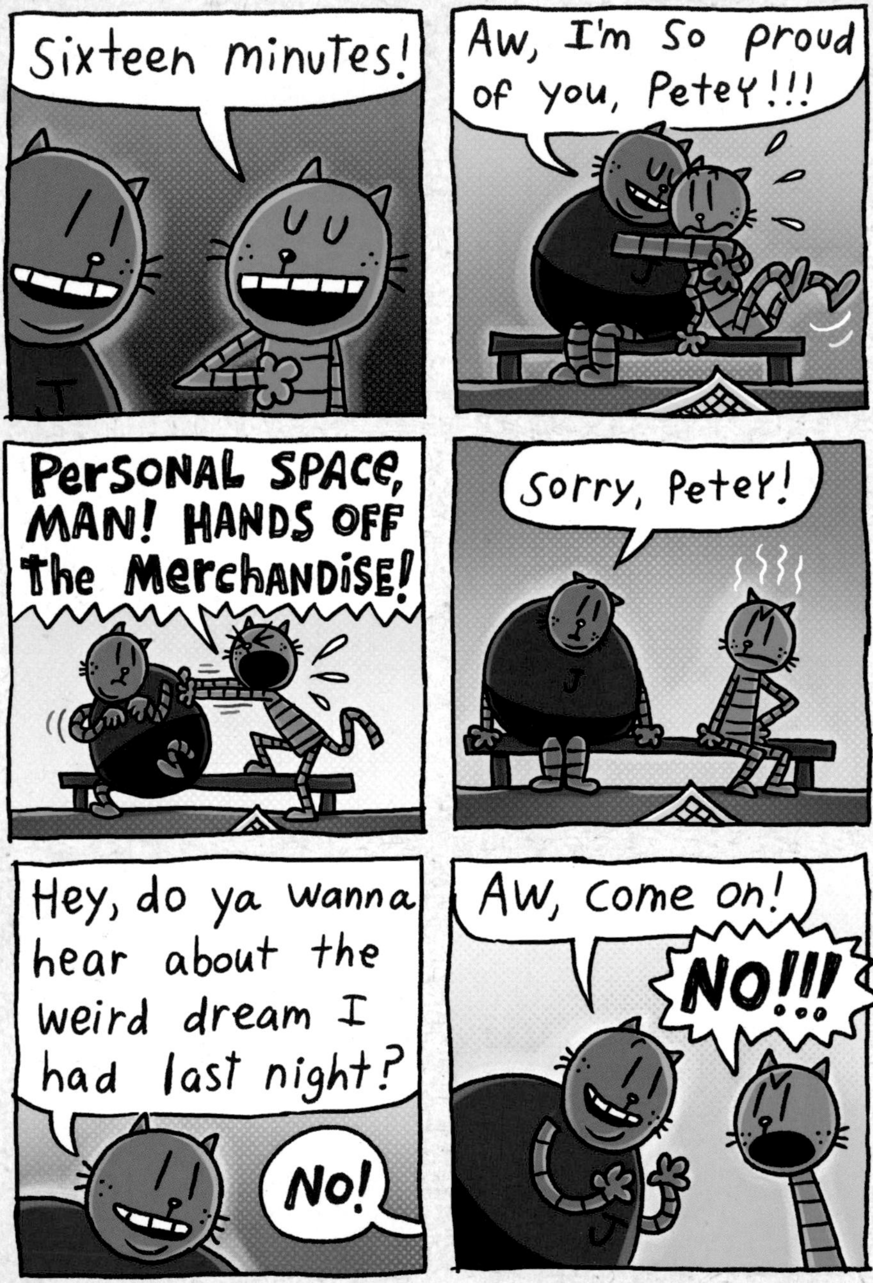

Sixteen minutes!
Aw, I'm so proud of you, Petey!!!
PERSONAL SPACE, MAN! HANDS OFF the MERCHANDISE!
Sorry, Petey!
Hey, do ya wanna hear about the weird dream I had last night?
NO!
Aw, come on!
NO!!!

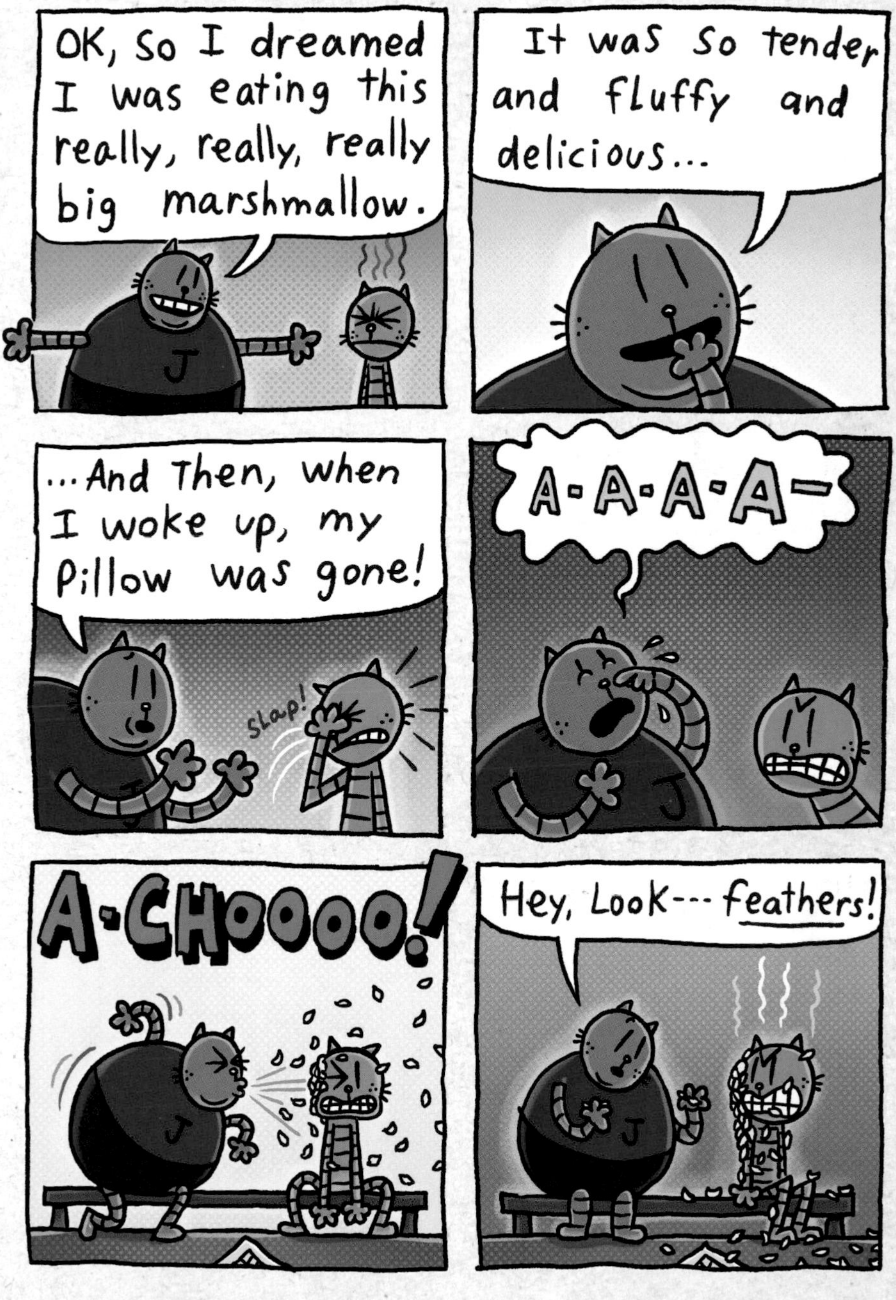
OK, So I dreamed I was eating this really, really, really big marshmallow.
It was so tender and fluffy and delicious...
...And Then, when I woke up, my Pillow was gone!
Slap!
A-A-A-A-
A-CHOOOO!
Hey, Look--- feathers!

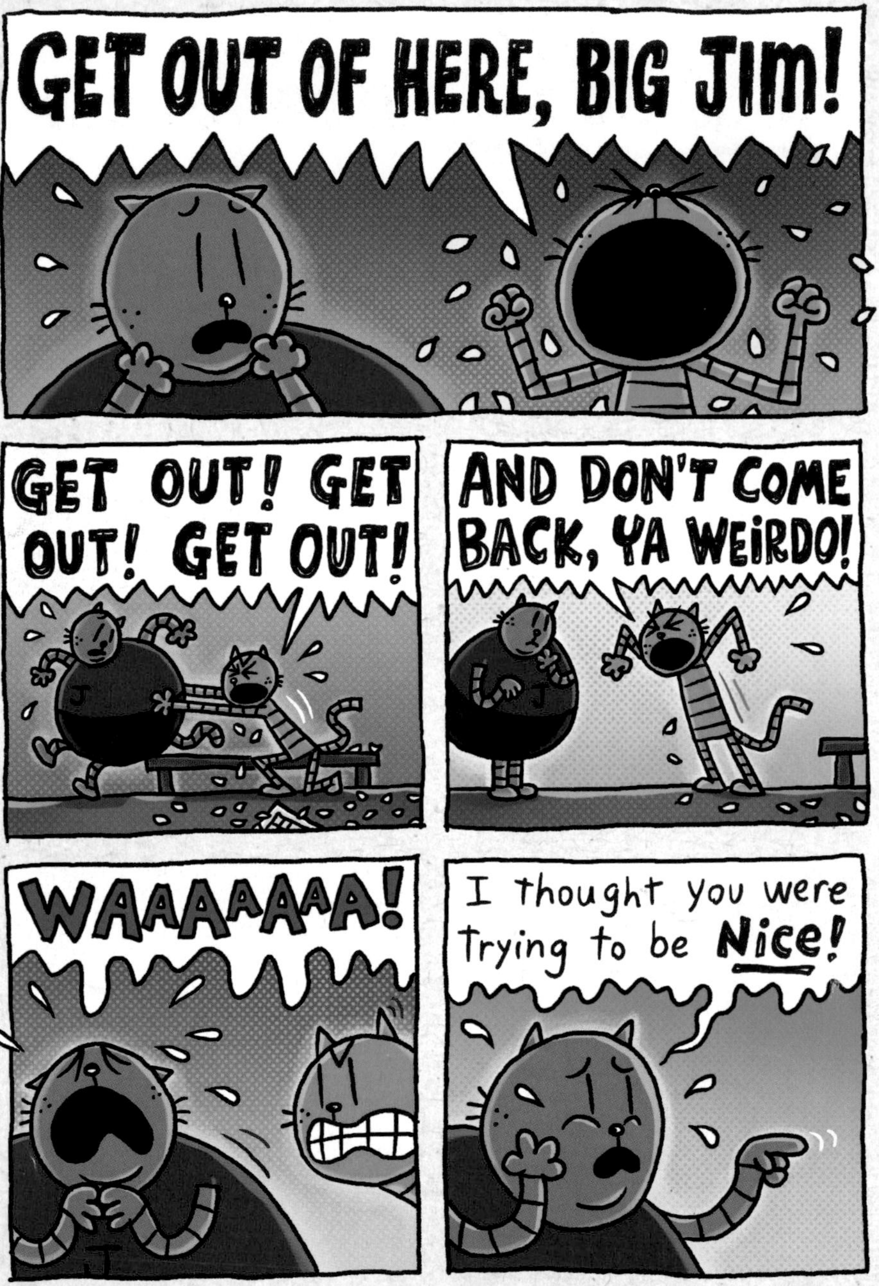
GET OUT OF HERE, BIG JIM!
GET OUT! GET OUT! GET OUT!
AND DON'T COME BACK, YA WEIRDO!
J
J
WAAAAAAA!
I thought you were trying to be Nice!

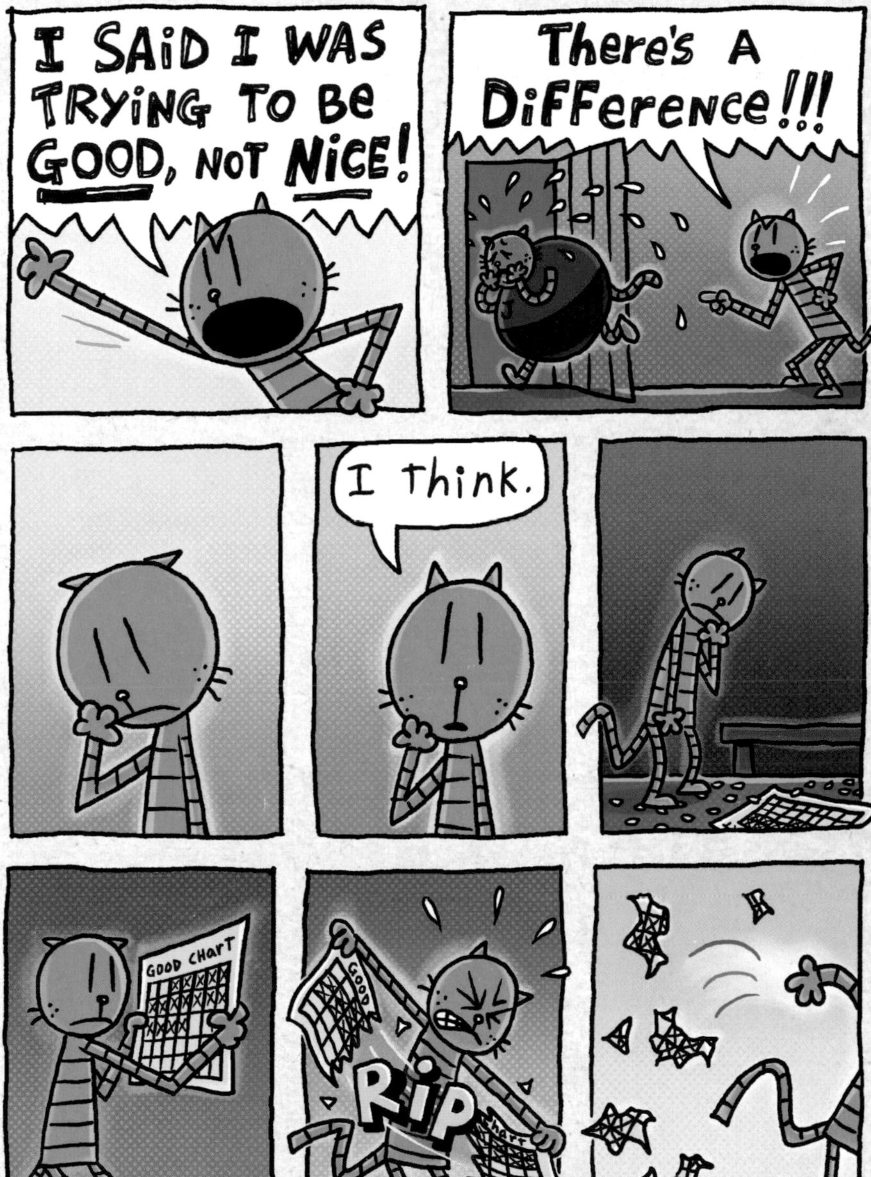
I SAID I WAS TRYING TO BE GOOD, NOT NICE!
There's A DIFFERENCE!!!
I think.
GOOD CHART
GOOD
RIP
CHART

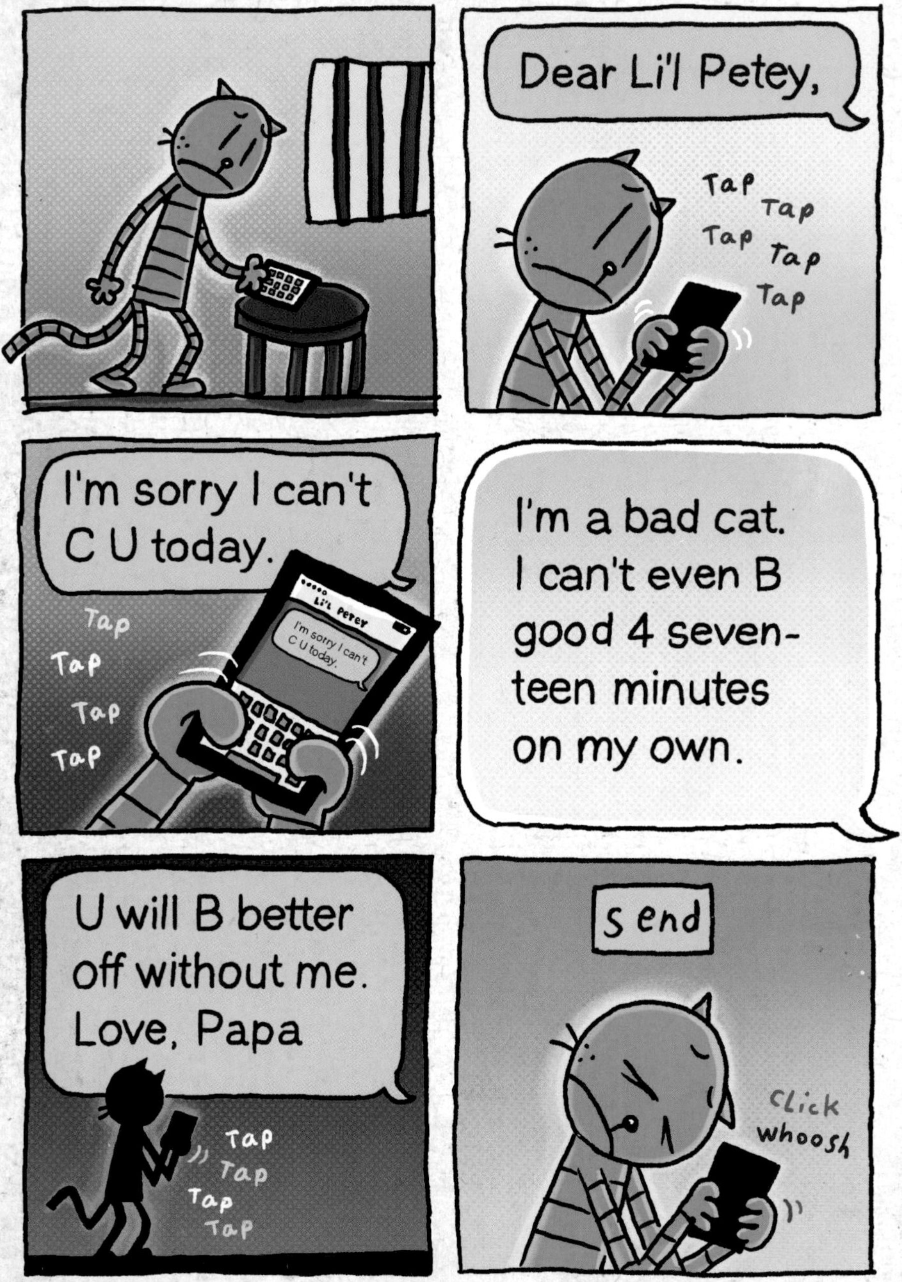

Dear Li'l Petey,
Tap Tap Tap Tap Tap
I'm sorry I can't C U today.
Li'l Petey
I'm sorry I can't C U today.
Tap Tap Tap Tap
I'm a bad cat. I can't even B good 4 seven-teen minutes on my own.
U will B better off without me. Love, Papa
Tap Tap Tap Tap
Send
Click whoosh

Chapter 2

The Sad Guys

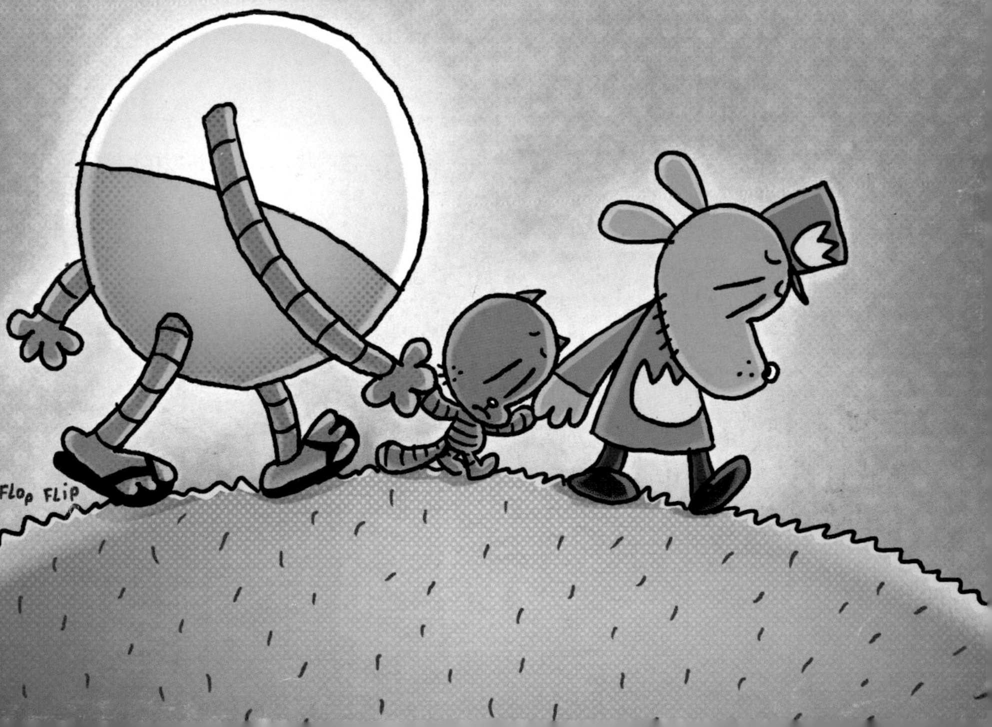
FLOP FLIP

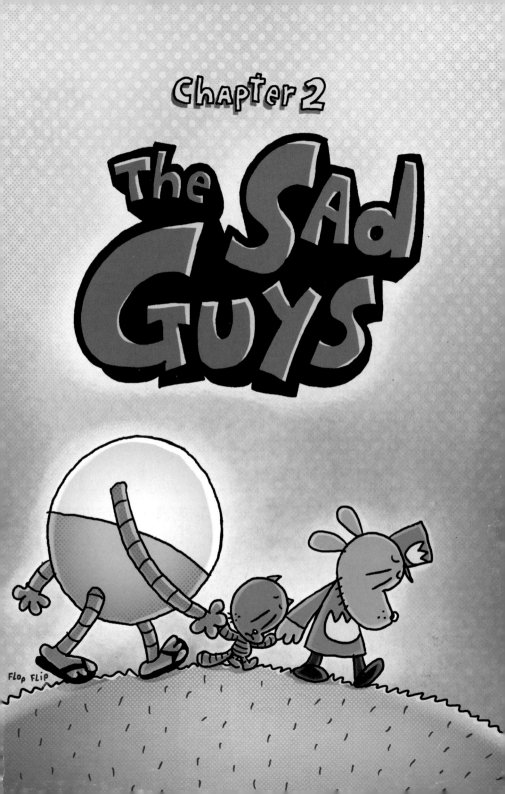

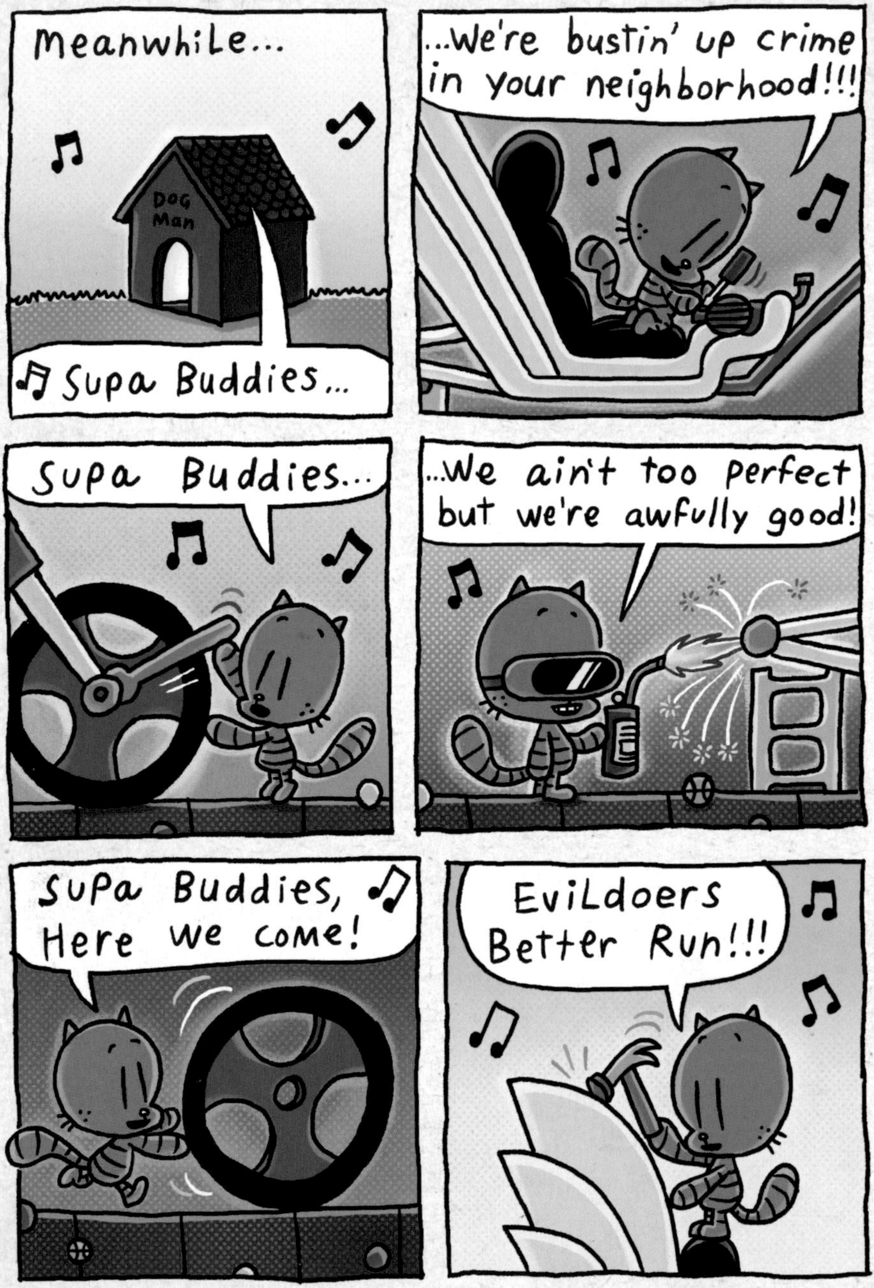
Meanwhile...
DOG Man
♫ Supa Buddies...
...We're bustin' up crime in your neighborhood!!!
Supa Buddies...
...We ain't too perfect but we're awfully good!
Supa Buddies, ♫ Here we come!
Evildoers Better Run!!!

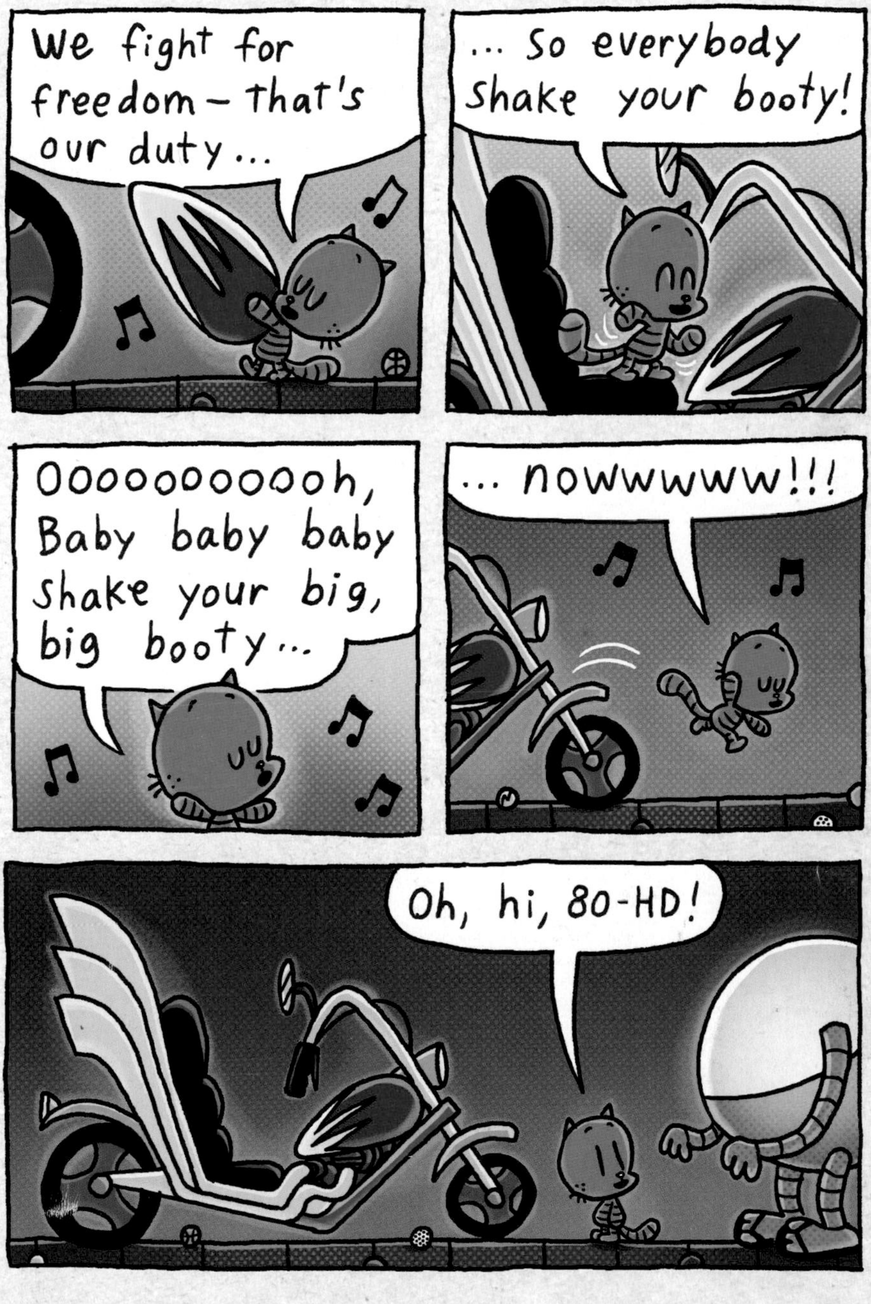
We fight for freedom — that's our duty...
... So everybody shake your booty!
Ooooooooooh, Baby baby baby shake your big, big booty...
... nowwwwww!!!
Oh, hi, 80-HD!

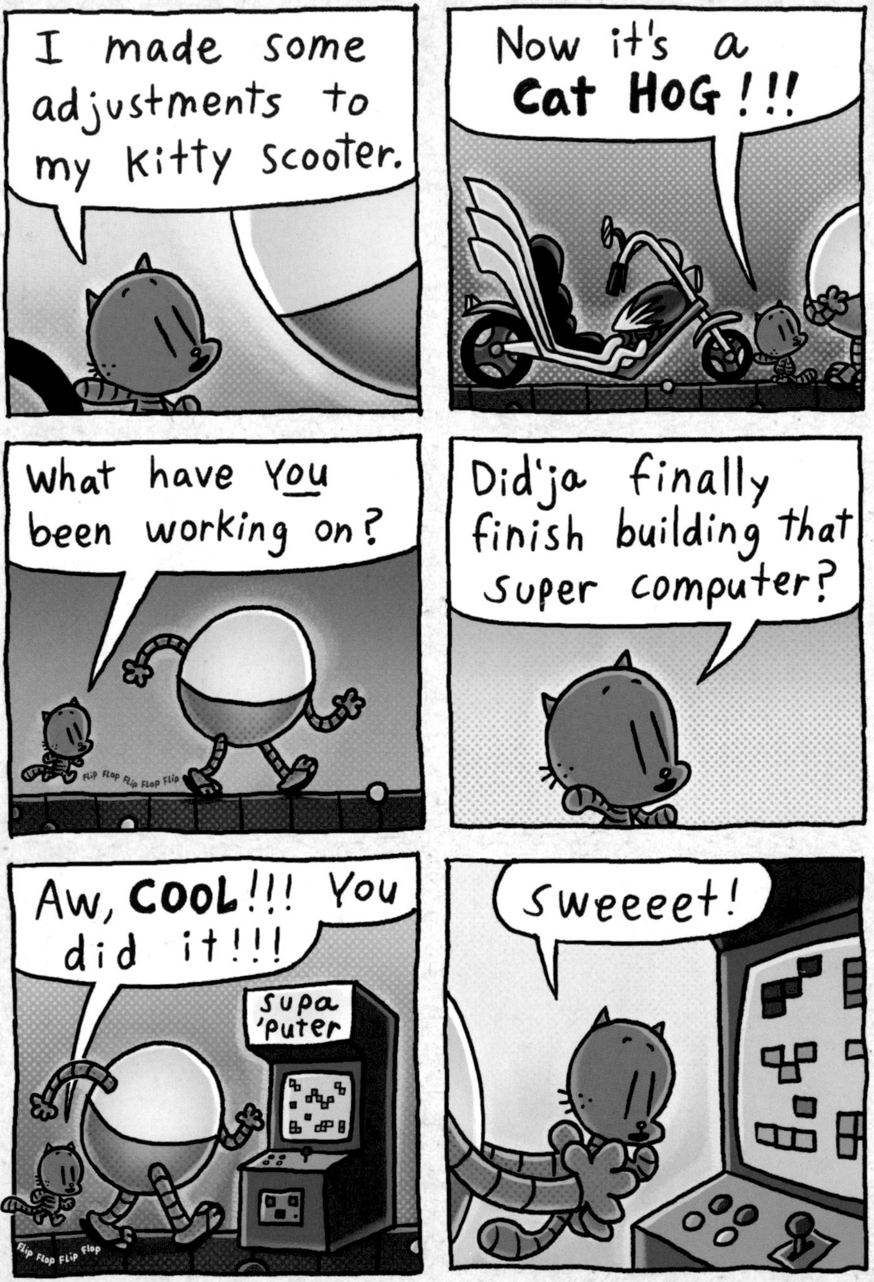
I made some adjustments to my kitty scooter.
Now it's a Cat HOG!!!
What have YOU been working on?
Flip Flop Flip Flop Flip
Did'ja finally finish building that super computer?
Aw, COOL!!! You did it!!!
Supa 'puter
Flip Flop Flip Flop
Sweeeet!

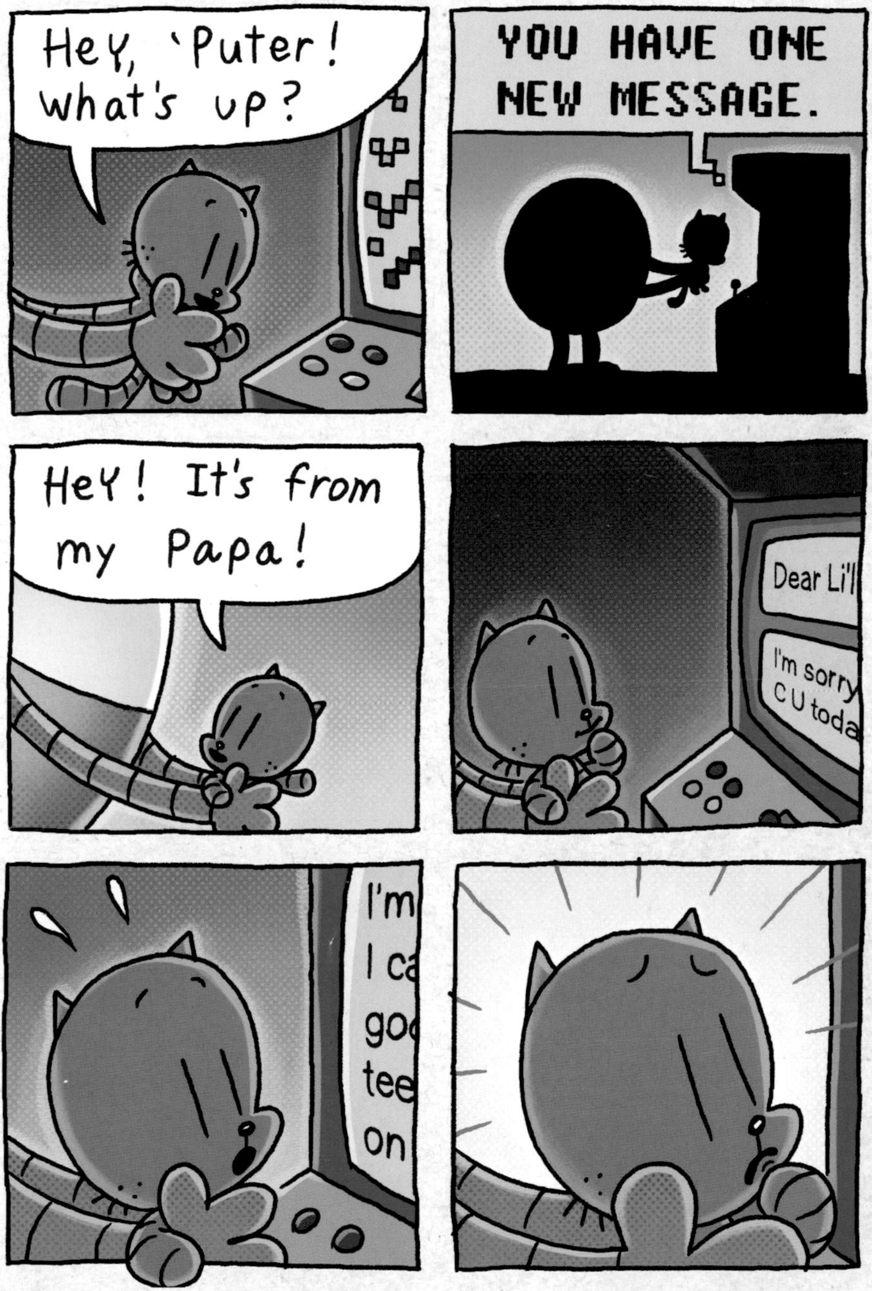
Hey, 'Puter! what's up?
YOU HAVE ONE NEW MESSAGE.
Hey! It's from my Papa!
Dear Li'l
I'm sorry

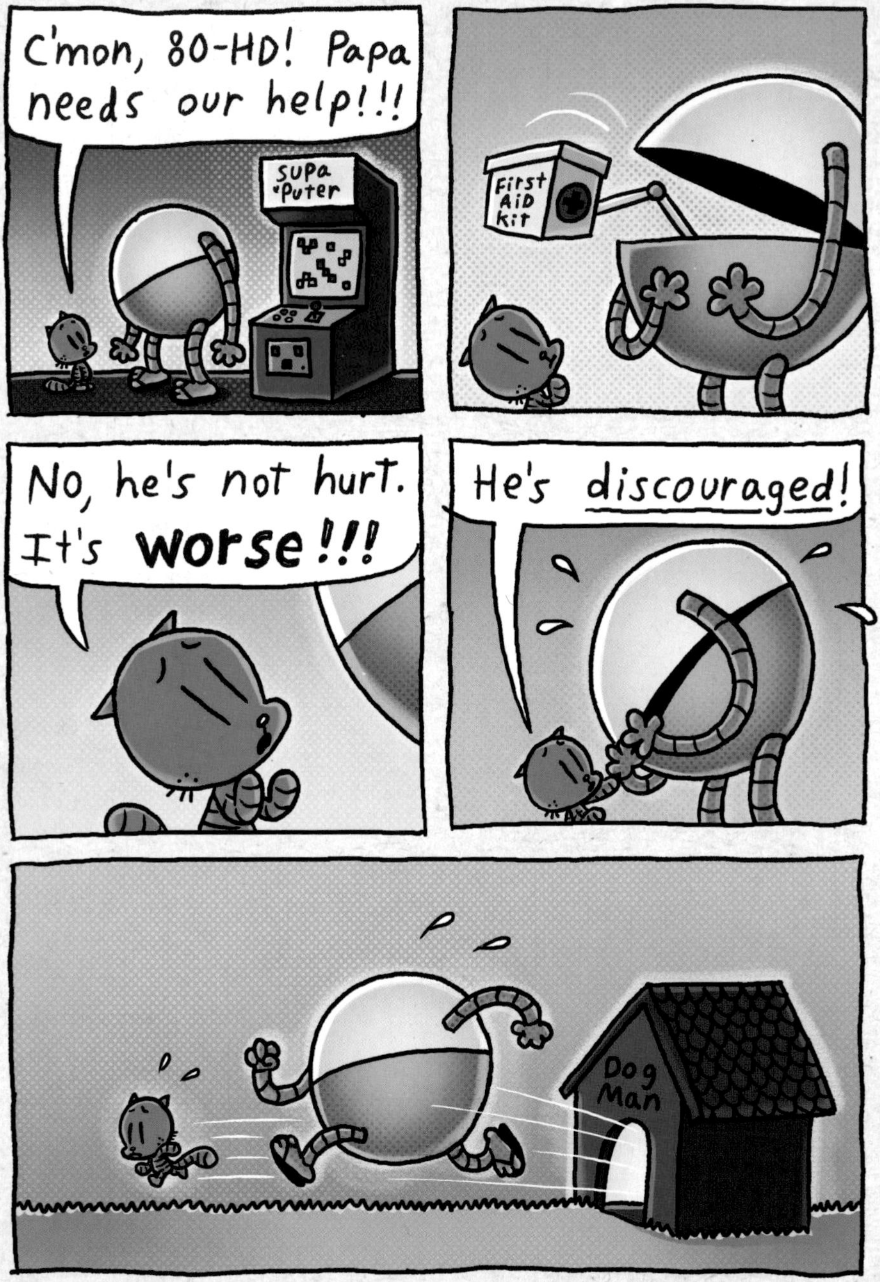
C'mon, 80-HD! Papa needs our help!!!
SUPA 'PUTER
First AID Kit
No, he's not hurt. It's **worse**!!!
He's discouraged!
Dog Man

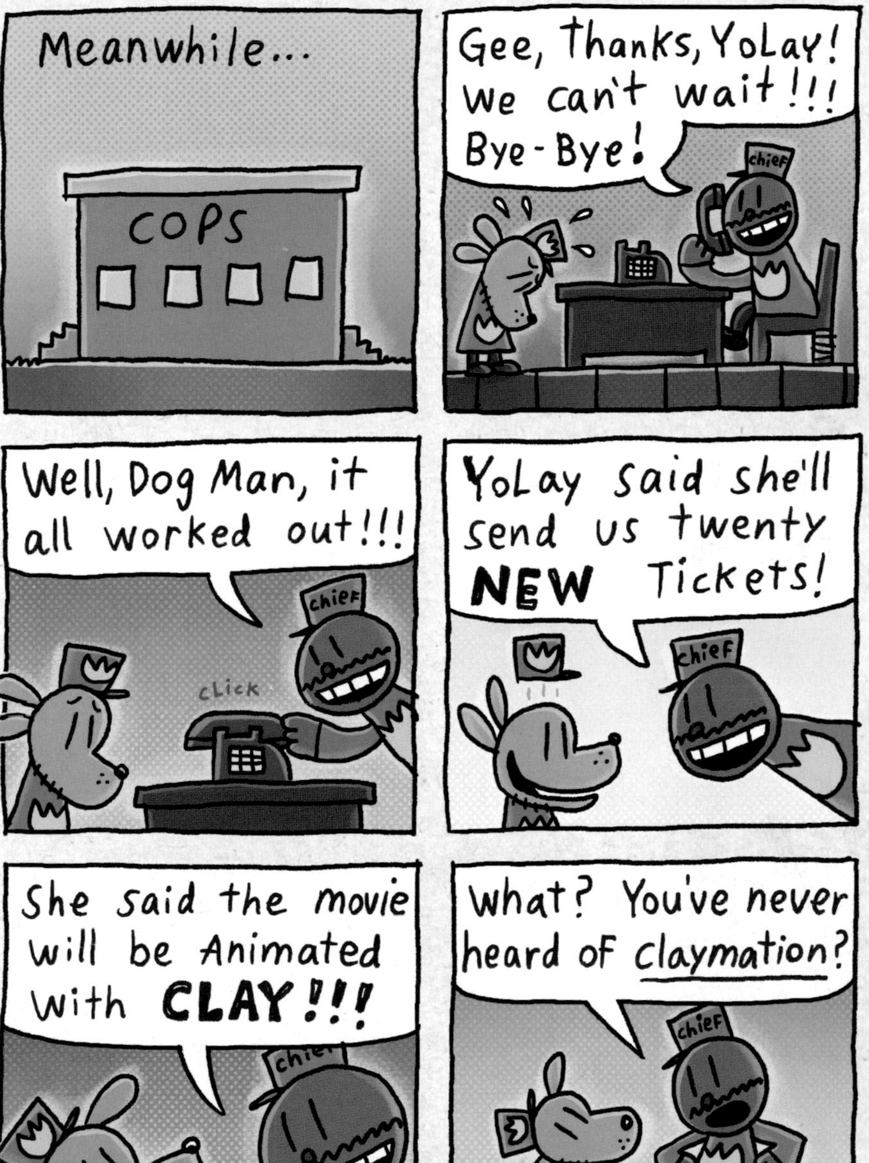
Meanwhile...
COPS
Gee, Thanks, YoLay! We can't wait!!! Bye-Bye!
chief
Well, Dog Man, it all worked out!!!
chief
CLICK
YoLay said she'll send us twenty NEW Tickets!
chief
She said the movie will be Animated with CLAY!!!
What? You've never heard of claymation?
chief

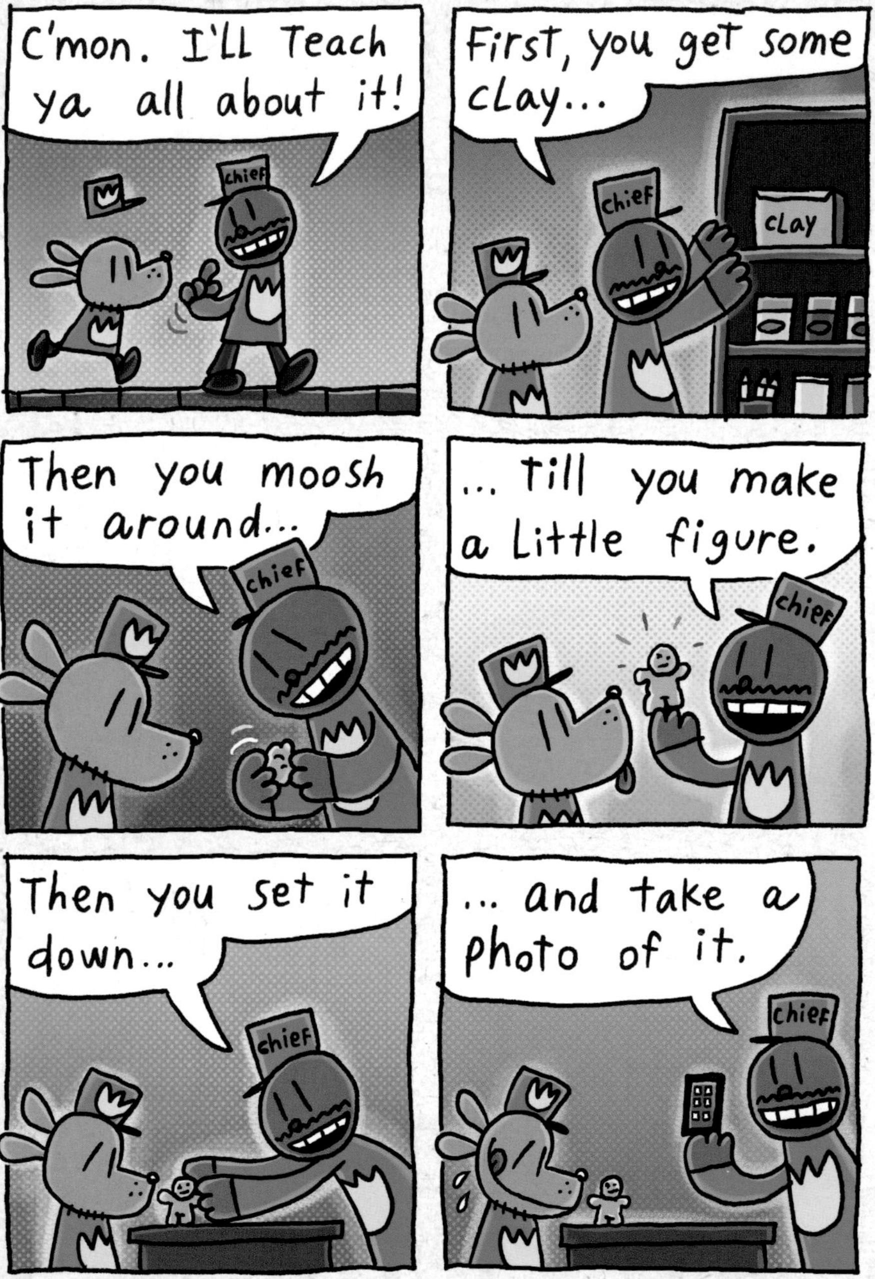
C'mon. I'LL Teach ya all about it!
chief
First, you get some cLay...
chief
cLay
Then you moosh it around...
chief
... Till you make a Little figure.
chief
Then you set it down...
chief
... and take a photo of it.
chief

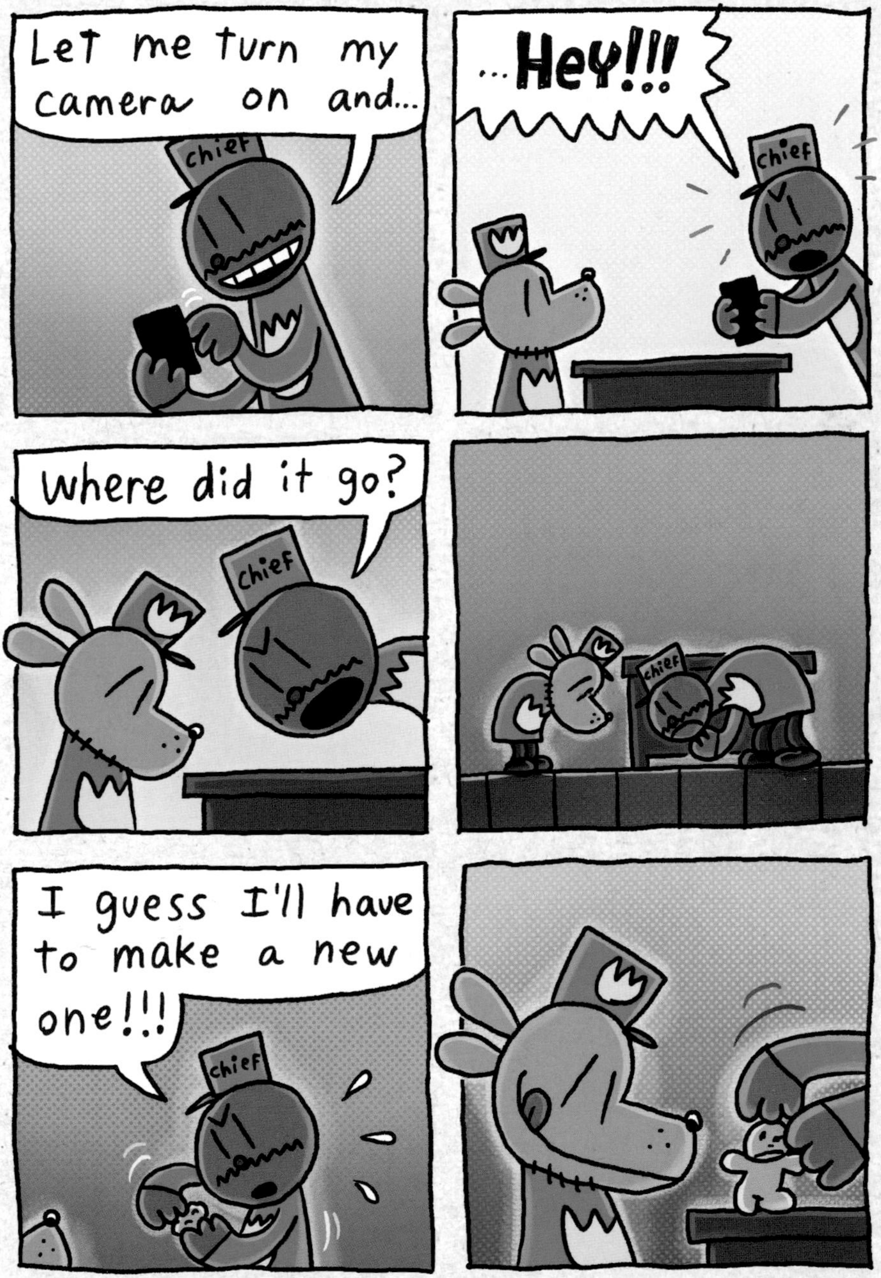
Let me turn my camera on and...
chief
...Hey!!!
chief
Where did it go?
chief
chief
I guess I'll have to make a new one!!!
chief

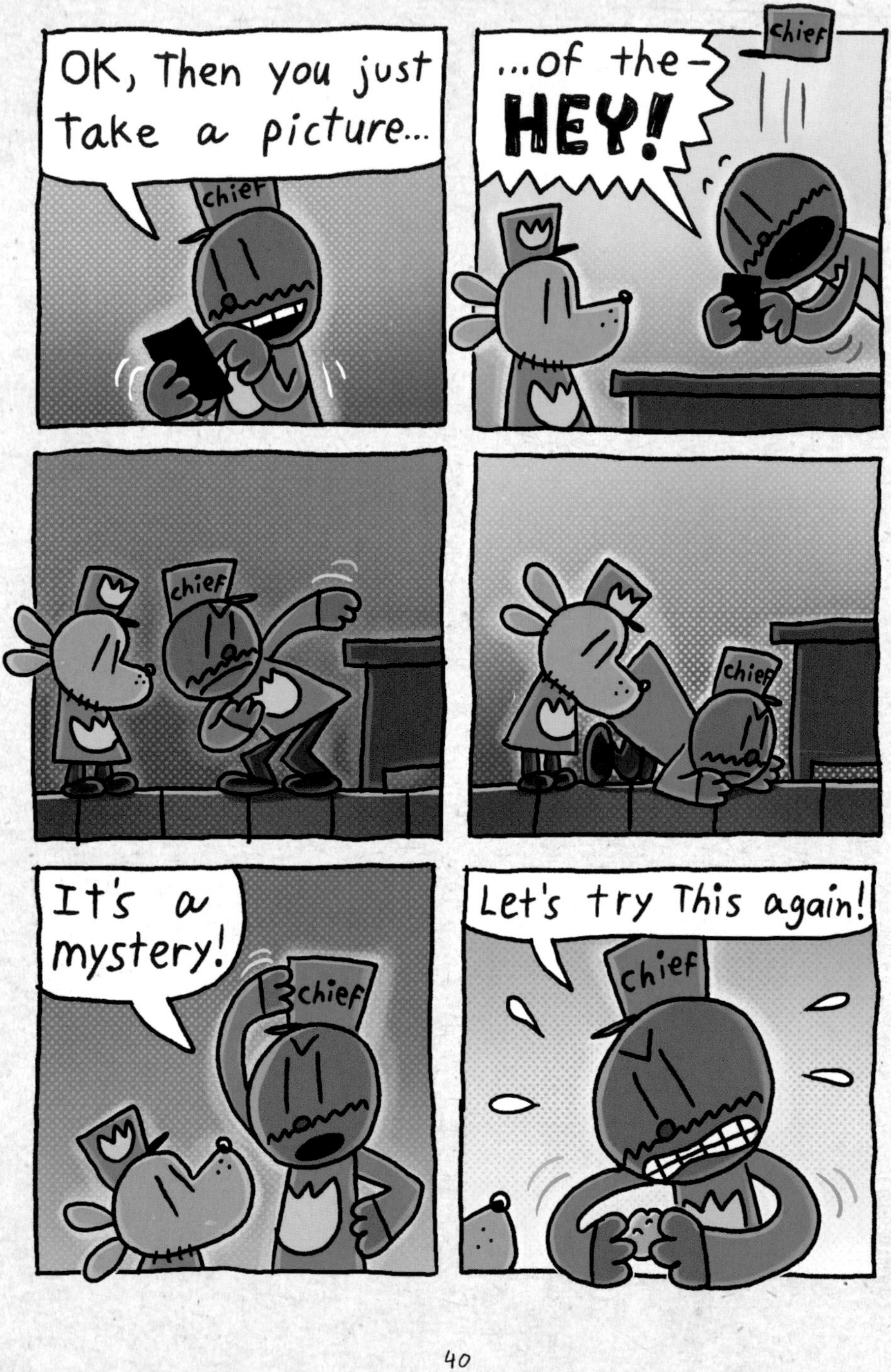
OK, Then you just take a picture...
chief
chief
...of the—
HEY!
chief
chief
It's a mystery!
chief
Let's try This again!
chief

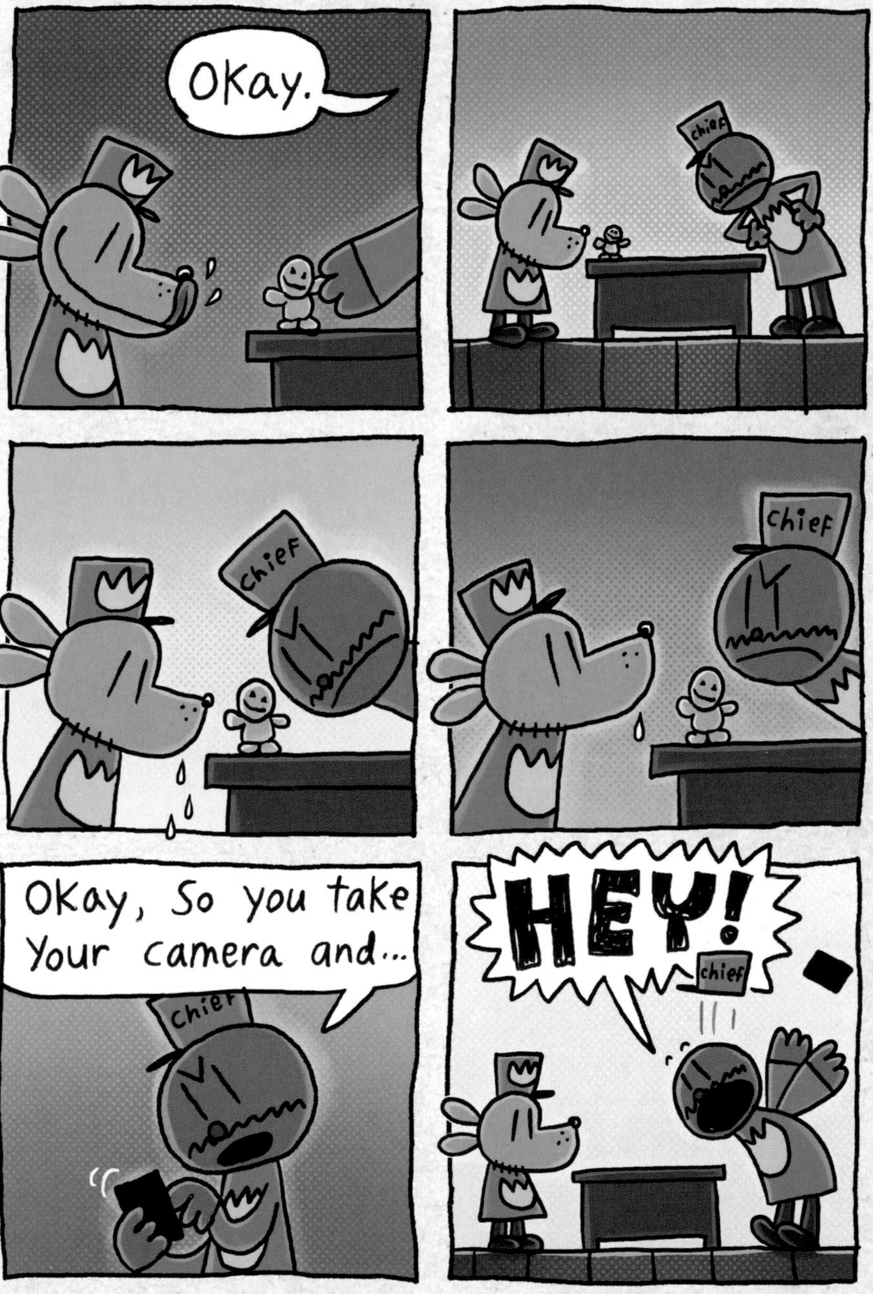
Okay.
chief
chief
chief
Okay, So you take Your camera and...
chief
HEY!
chief

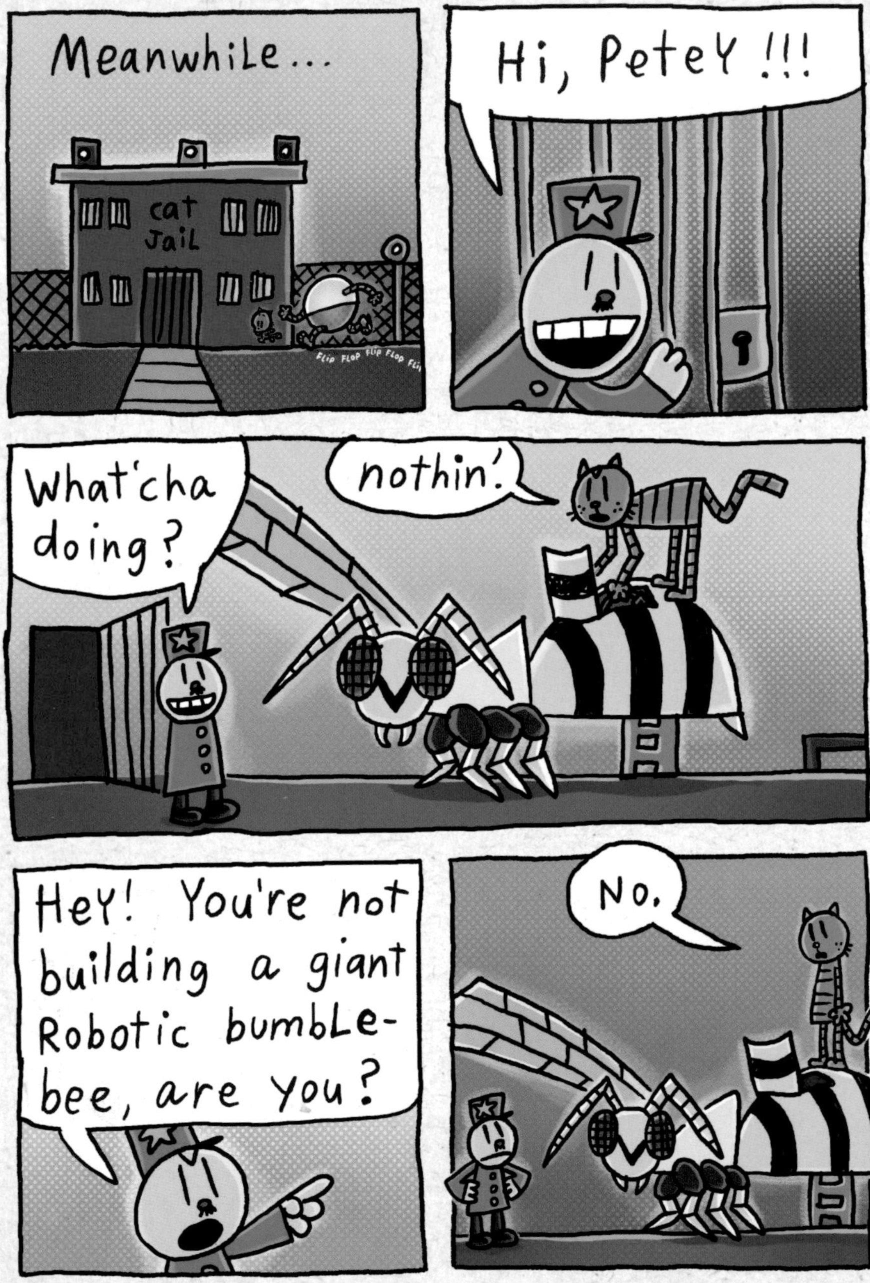
Meanwhile...
cat Jail
Flip Flop Flip Flop Fli
Hi, Petey !!!
What'cha doing?
nothin'.
Hey! You're not building a giant Robotic bumble-bee, are you?
No.

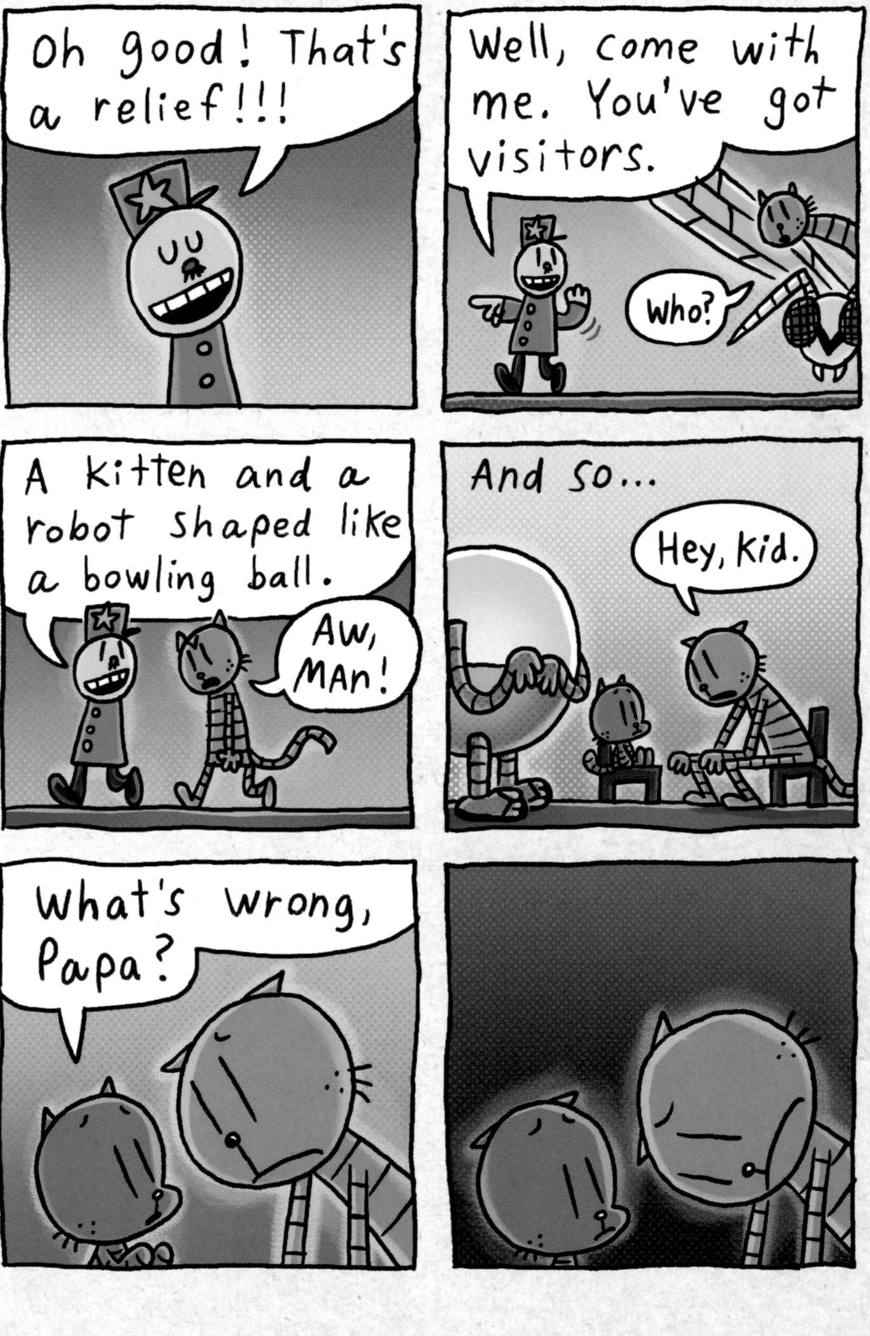
Oh good! That's a relief!!!
Well, come with me. You've got visitors.
Who?
A kitten and a robot shaped like a bowling ball.
AW, MAN!
And so...
Hey, Kid.
What's wrong, Papa?

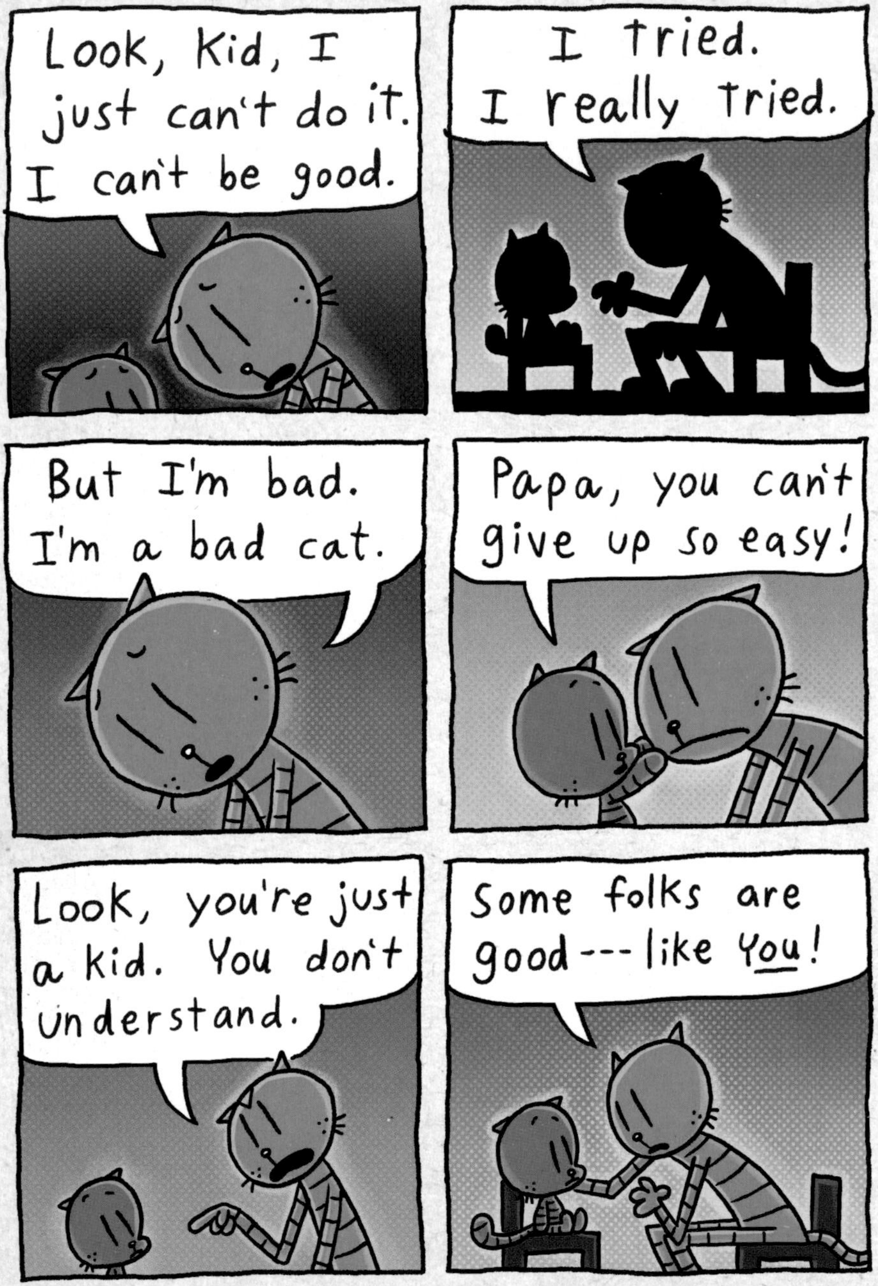
LOOK, KID, I just can't do it. I can't be good.
I tried. I really tried.
But I'm bad. I'm a bad cat.
Papa, you can't give up so easy!
Look, you're just a kid. You don't understand.
Some folks are good---like YOU!

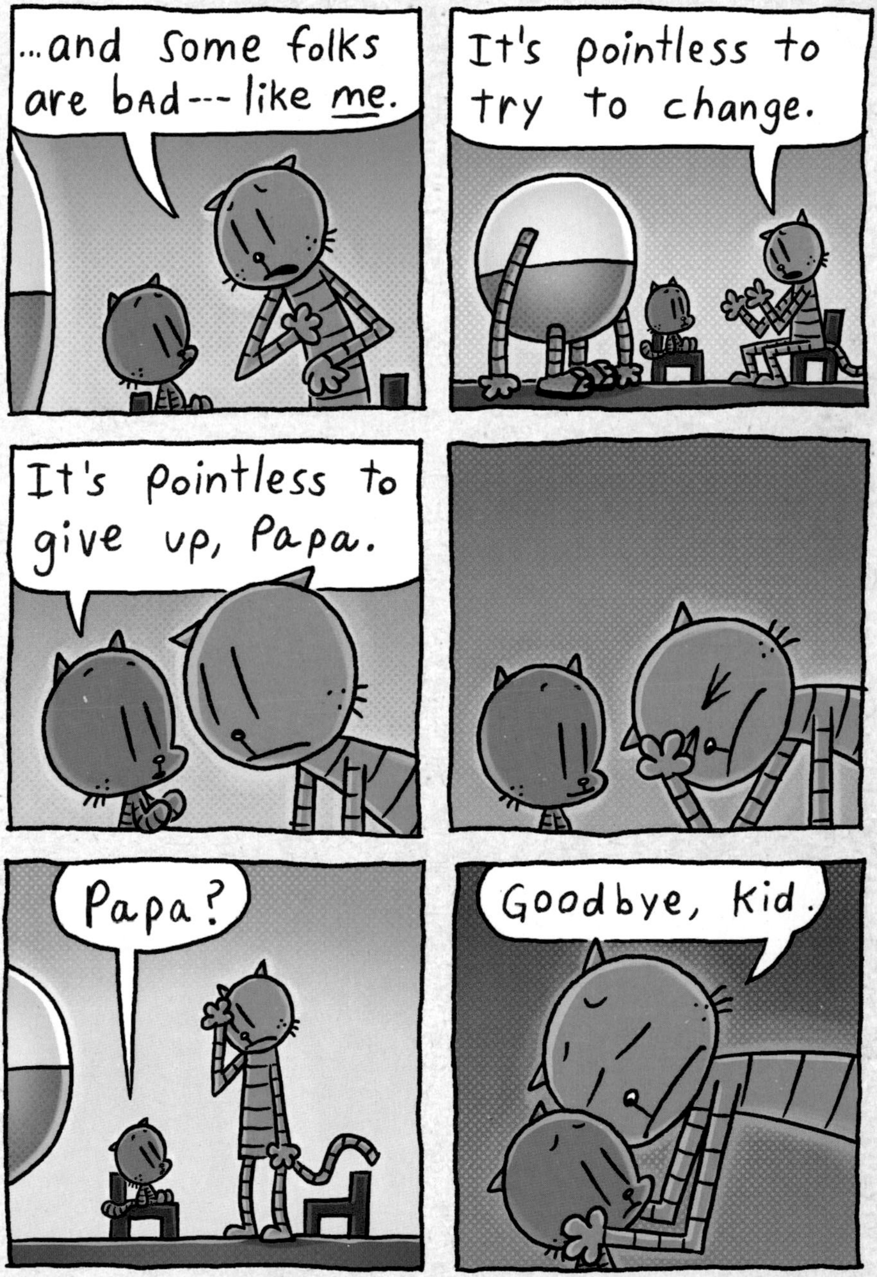
...and some folks are BAD--- like me.
It's pointless to try to change.
It's pointless to give up, Papa.
Papa?
Goodbye, kid.

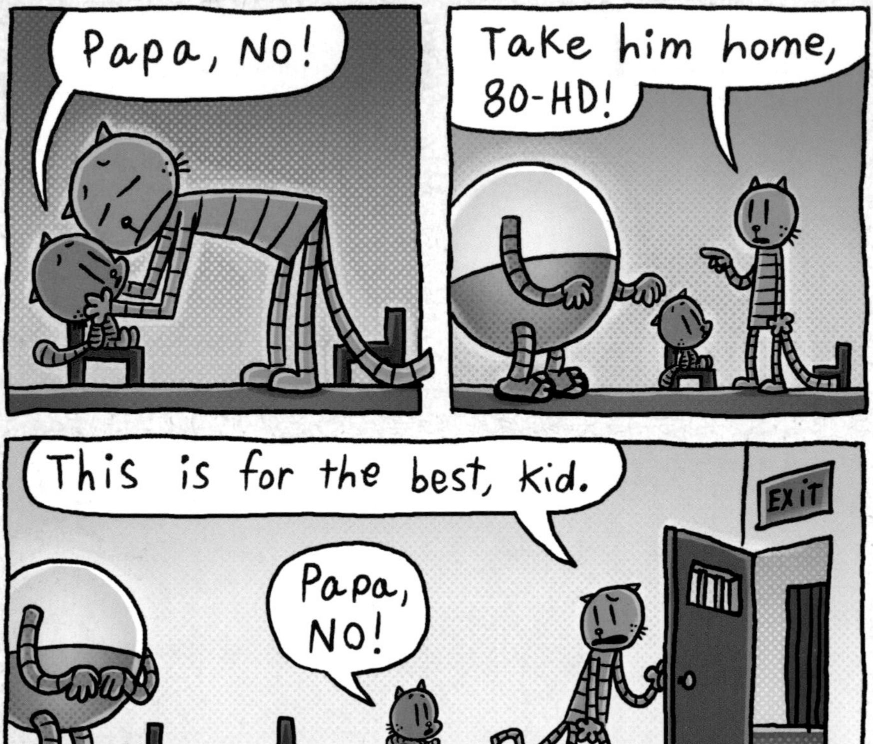
Papa, No!
Take him home, 80-HD!
This is for the best, kid.
EXIT
Papa, NO!
TAKE HIM HOME, 80-HD!
Papa.
Exit

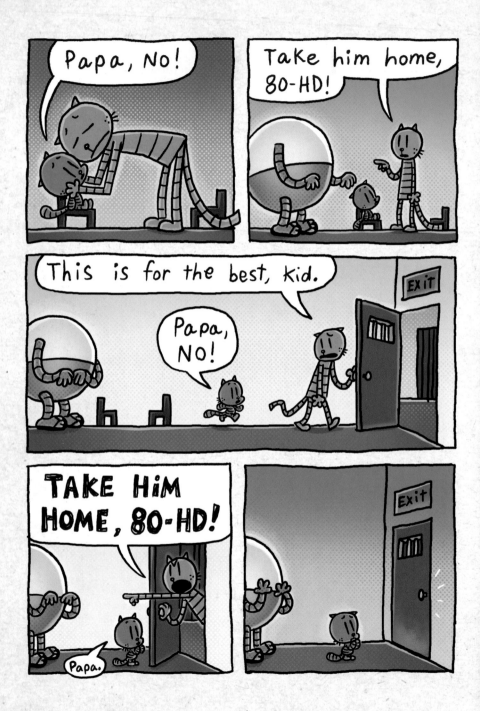

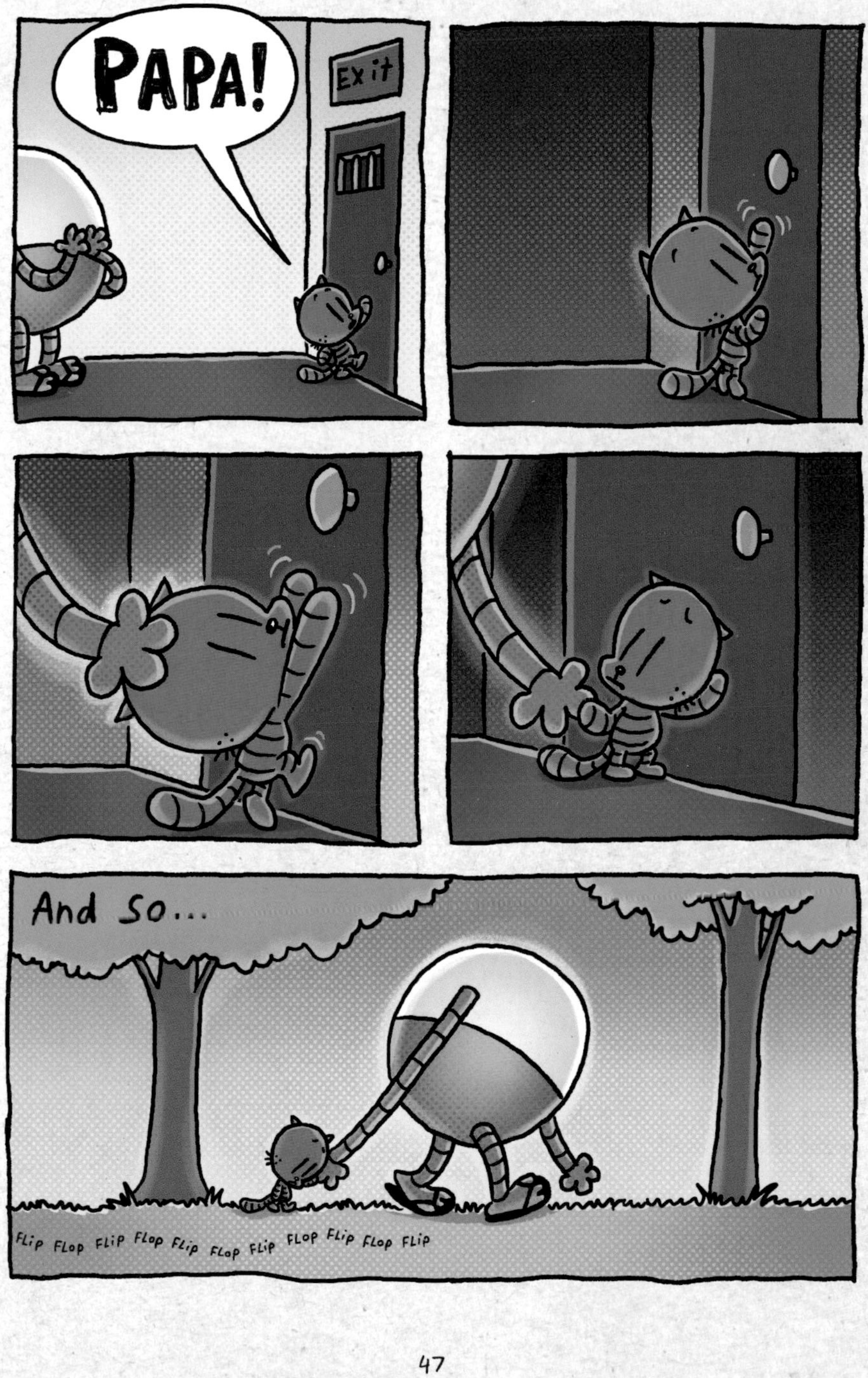
PAPA!
Ex it
And so...
FLip FLop FLip FLop FLip FLop FLip FLOP FLip FLop FLip

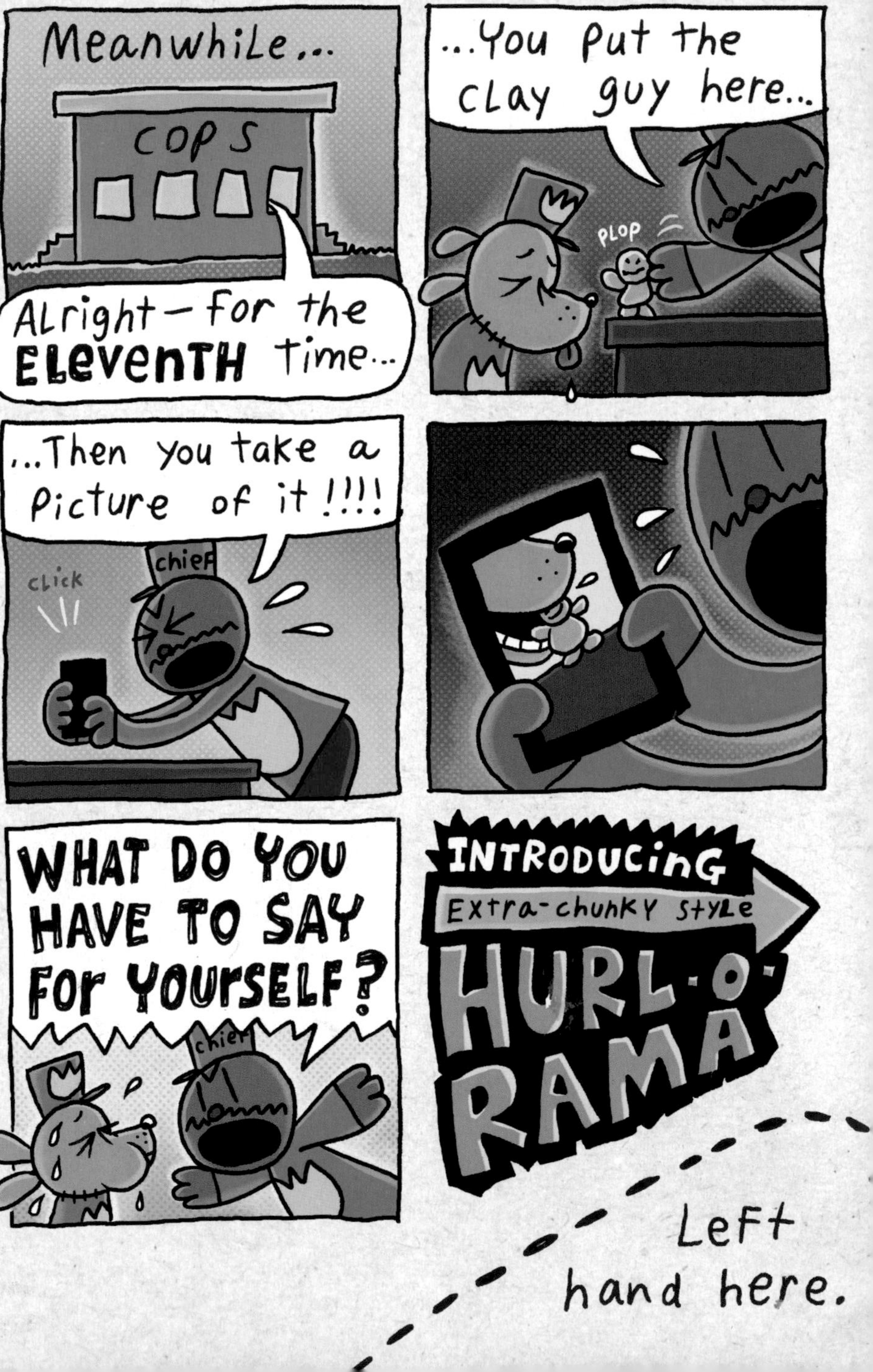
Meanwhile...
COPS
Alright—for the ELEVENTH time...
...You put the clay guy here...
PLOP
...Then you take a picture of it!!!!
chief
CLICK
WHAT DO YOU HAVE TO SAY FOR YOURSELF?
chief
INTRODUCING
Extra-chunky style
HURL-O-RAMA
Left hand here.

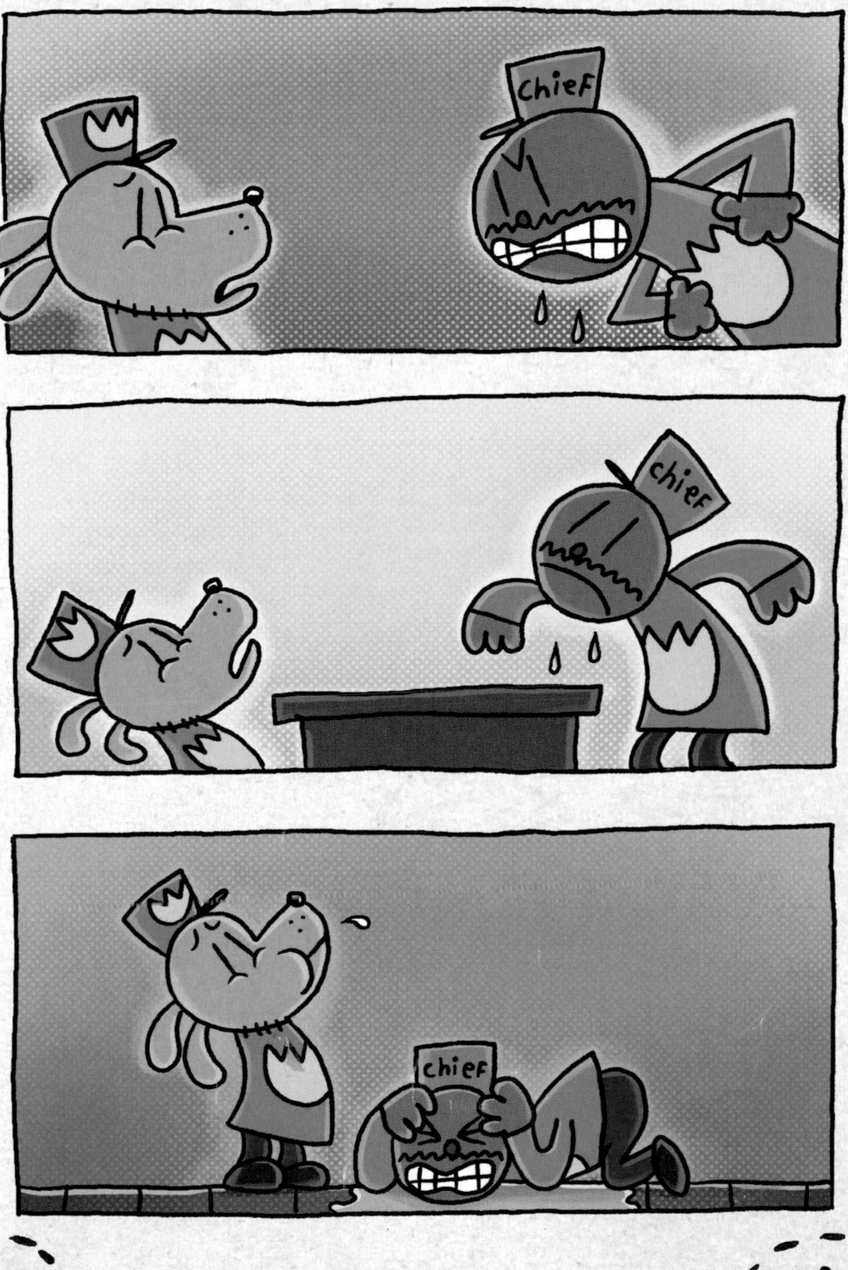
chief
chief
chief

Right Thumb here.

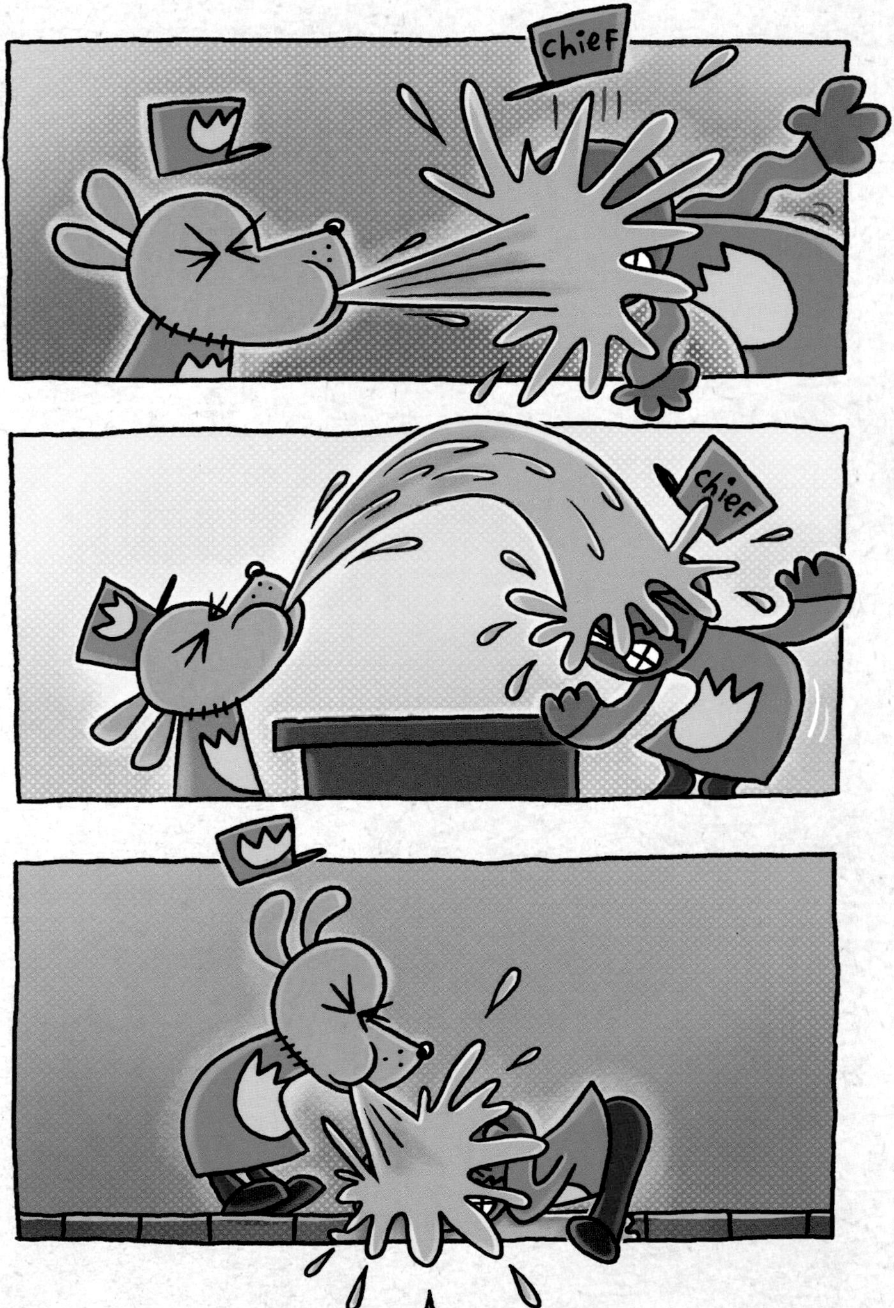
chief
chief

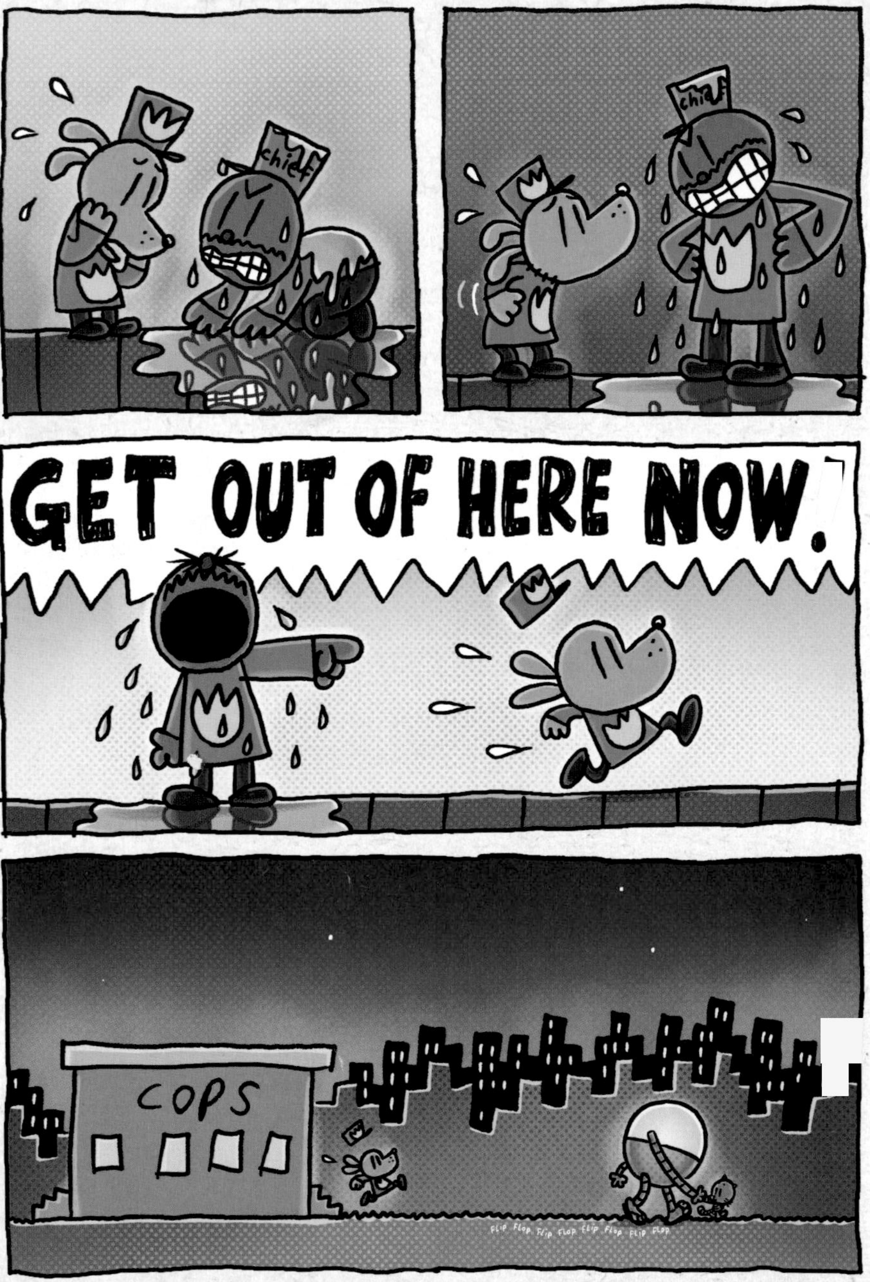
chief
chief
GET OUT OF HERE NOW!
COPS
FLIP FLOP FLIP FLOP FLIP FLOP FLIP FLOP

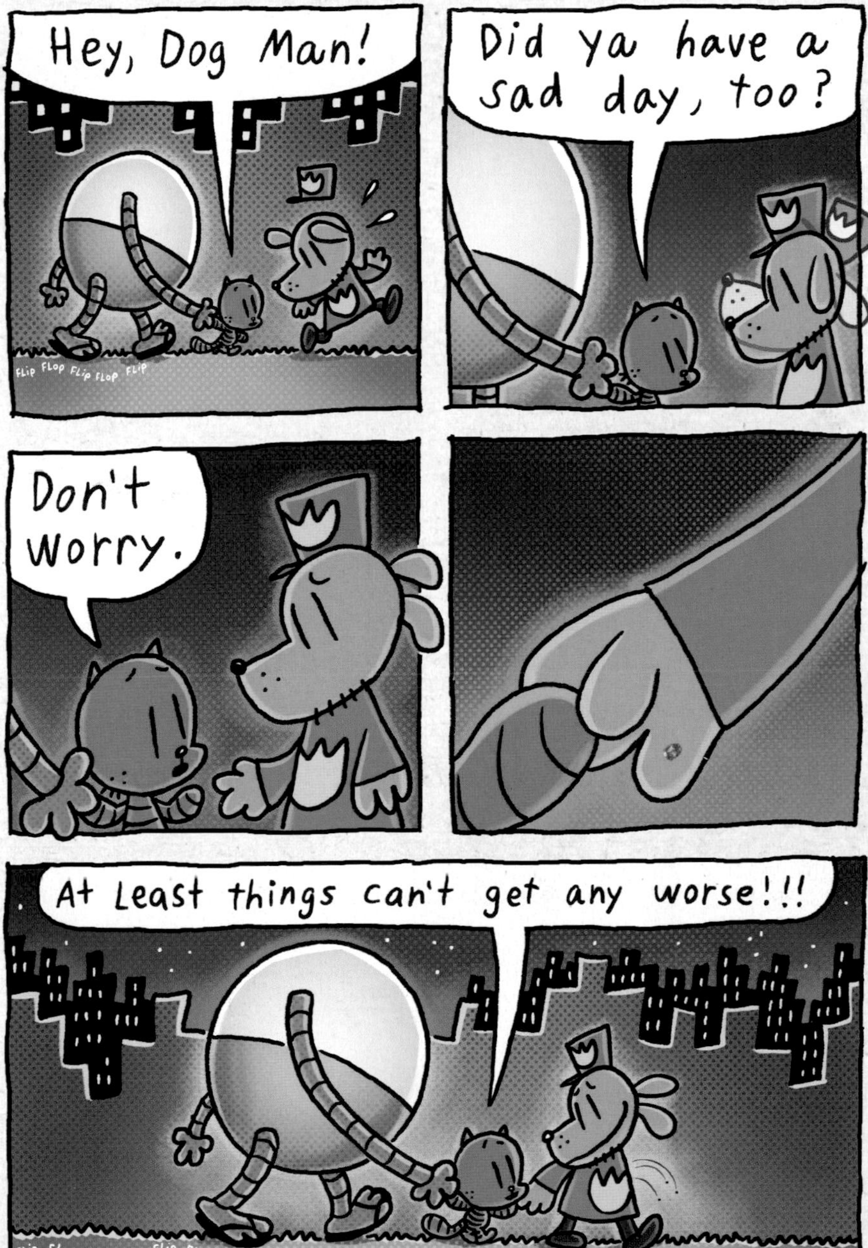
Hey, Dog Man!
FLIP FLOP FLIP FLOP FLIP
Did ya have a sad day, too?
Don't worry.
At Least things can't get any worse!!!
FLIP FLOP FLIP FLOP FLIP FLOP FLIP

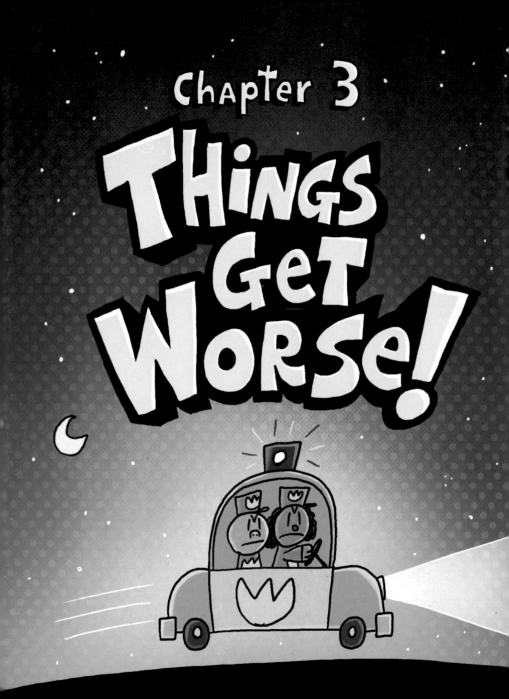

Chapter 3

Things Get Worse!

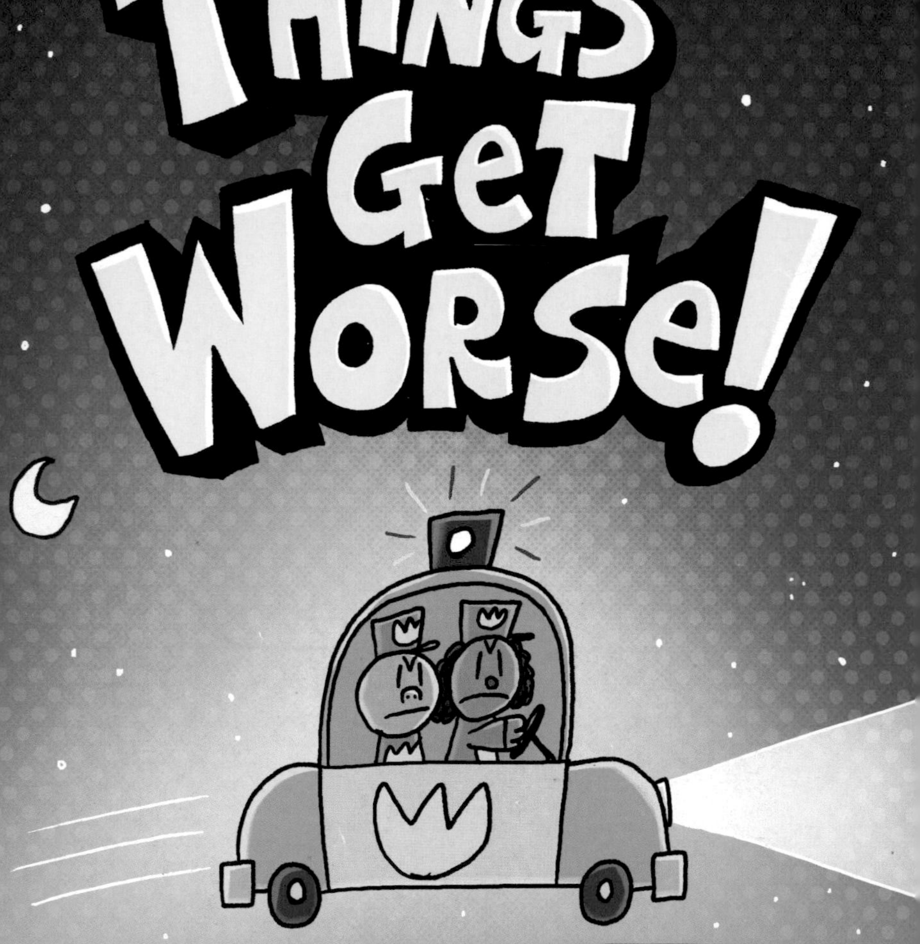

By George Beard and Harold Hutchins

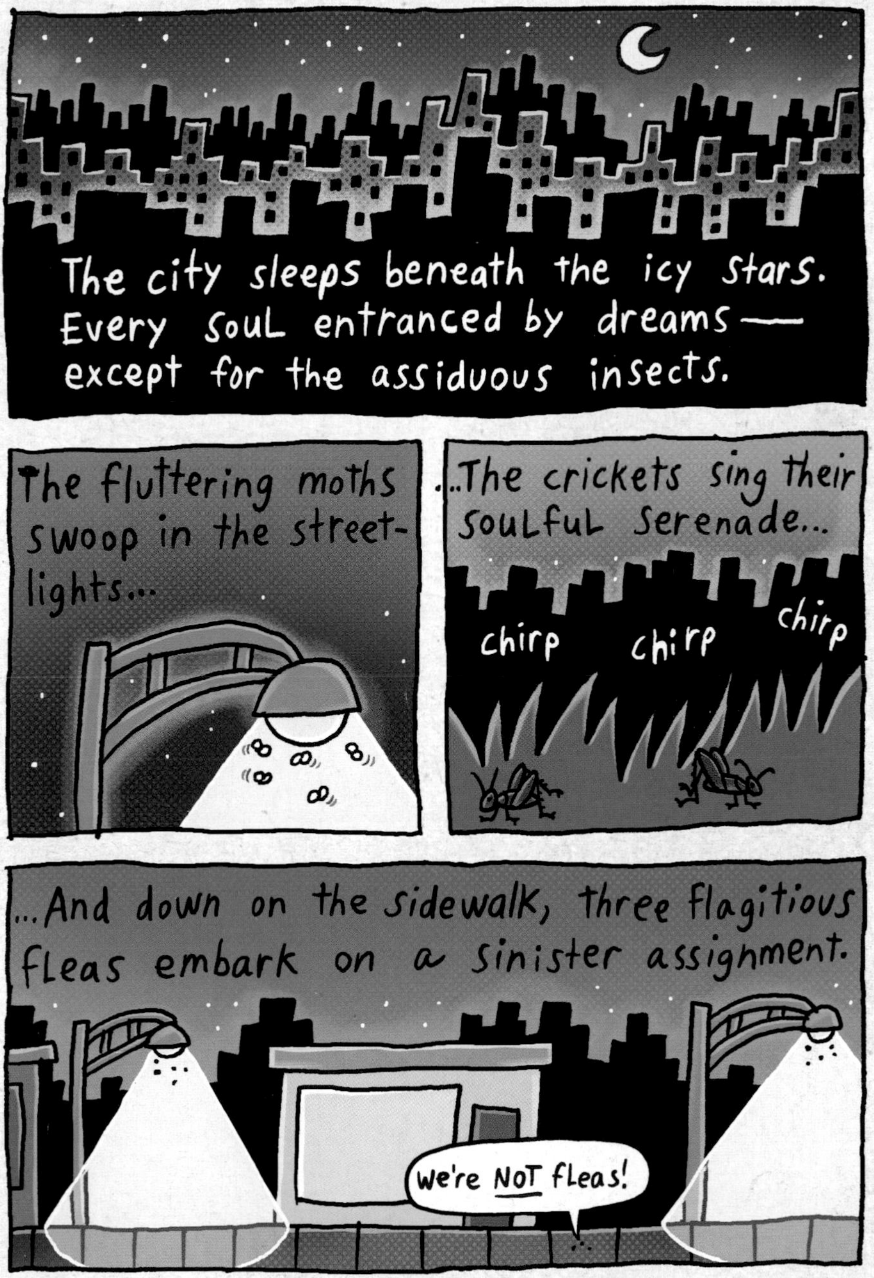
The city sleeps beneath the icy stars. Every soul entranced by dreams—except for the assiduous insects.
The fluttering moths swoop in the street-lights...
...The crickets sing their soulful serenade...
chirp
chirp
chirp
...And down on the sidewalk, three flagitious fleas embark on a sinister assignment.
We're NOT fleas!

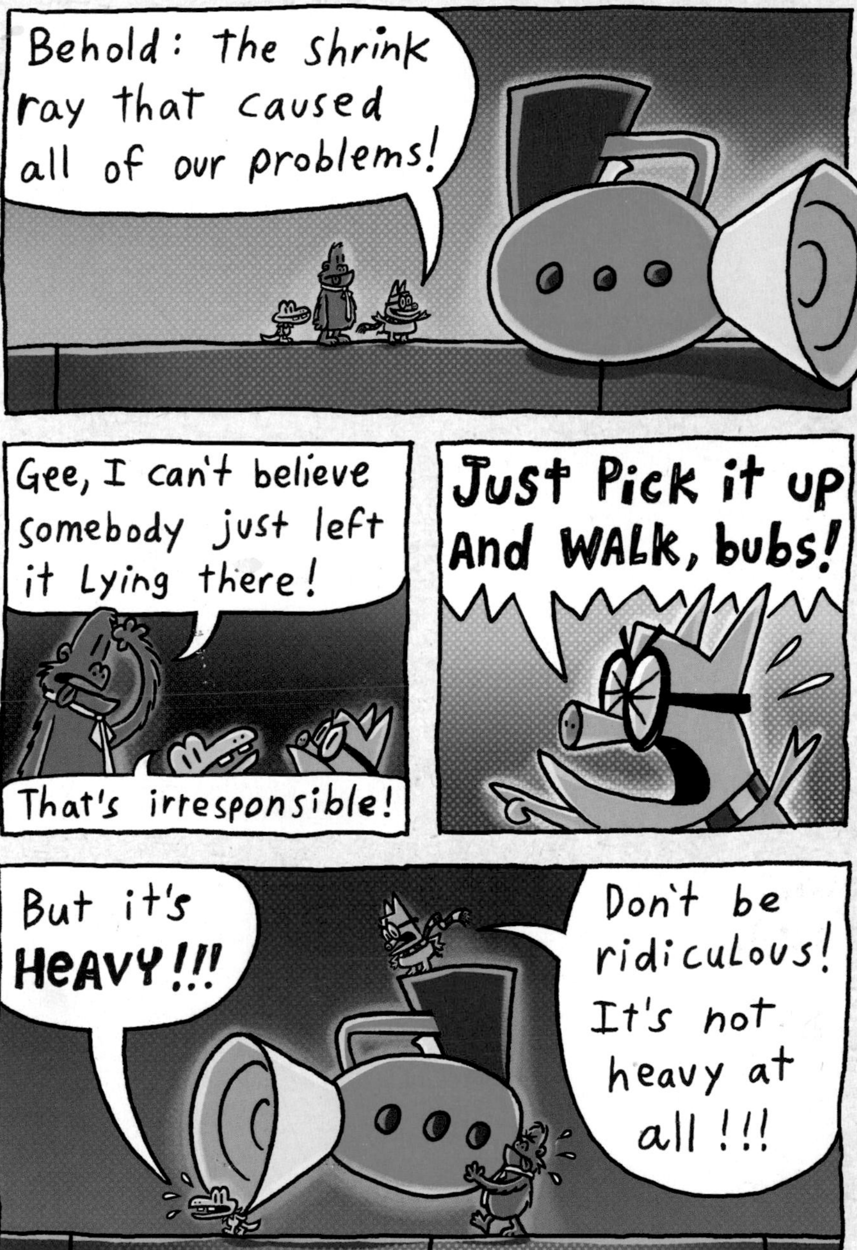
Behold: the shrink ray that caused all of our problems!
Gee, I can't believe somebody just left it Lying there!
That's irresponsible!
Just Pick it up And WALK, bubs!
But it's HEAVY!!!
Don't be ridiculous! It's not heavy at all!!!

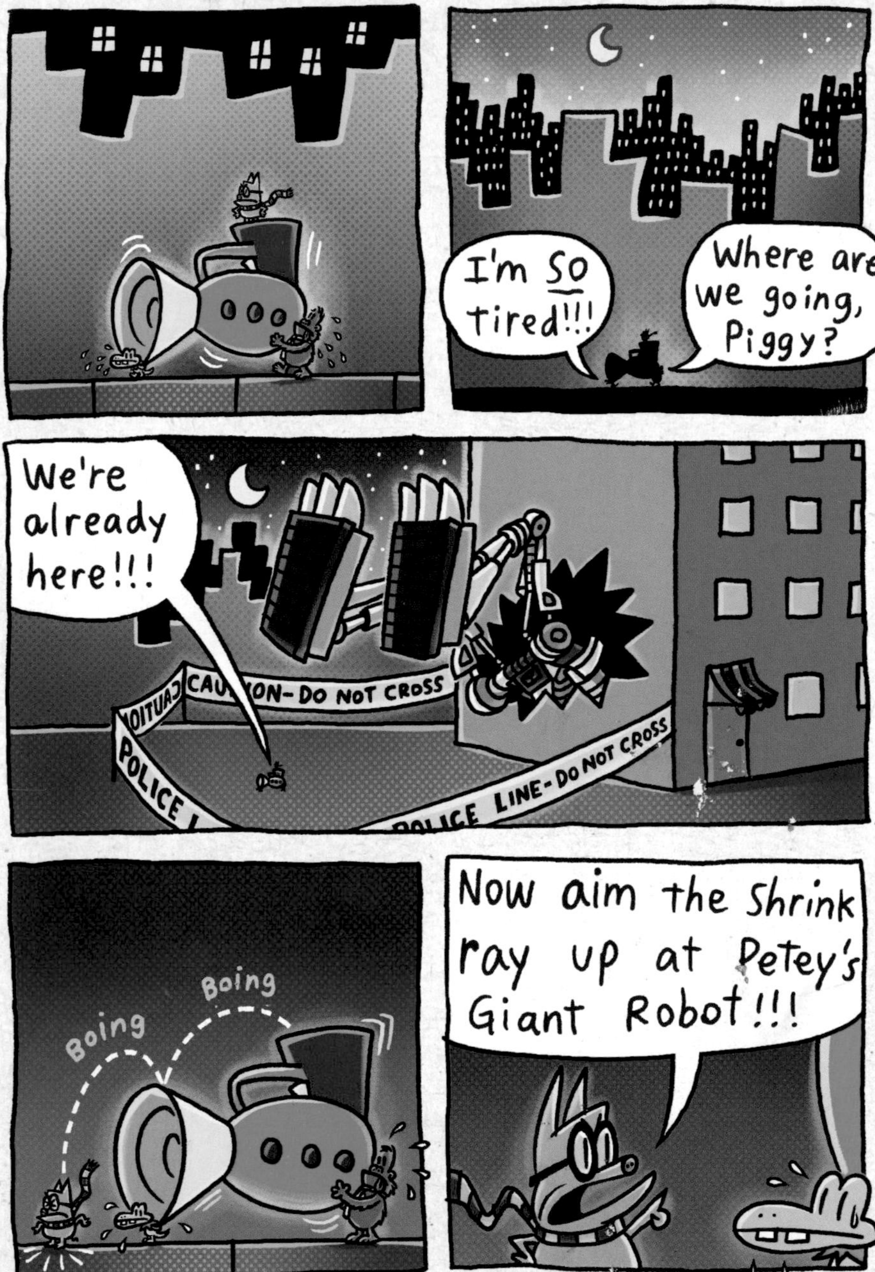

I'm SO tired!!!
Where are we going, Piggy?
We're already here!!!
CAUTION-DO NOT CROSS
POLICE LINE-DO NOT CROSS
Boing
Boing
Now aim the Shrink ray up at Petey's Giant Robot!!!

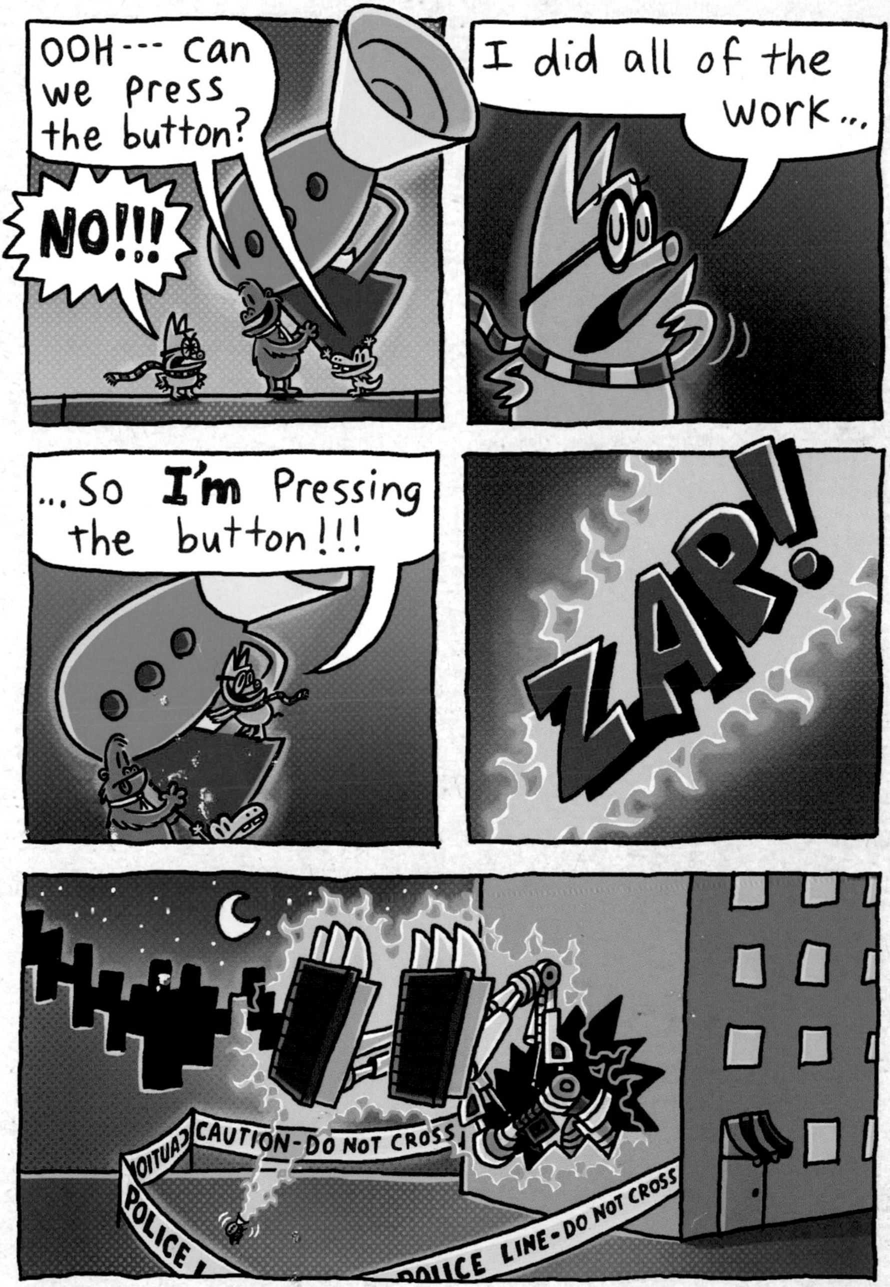
OOH--- can we press the button?
NO!!!
I did all of the work...
...So I'm Pressing the button!!!
ZAP!
CAUTION-DO NOT CROSS
POLICE LINE-DO NOT CROSS

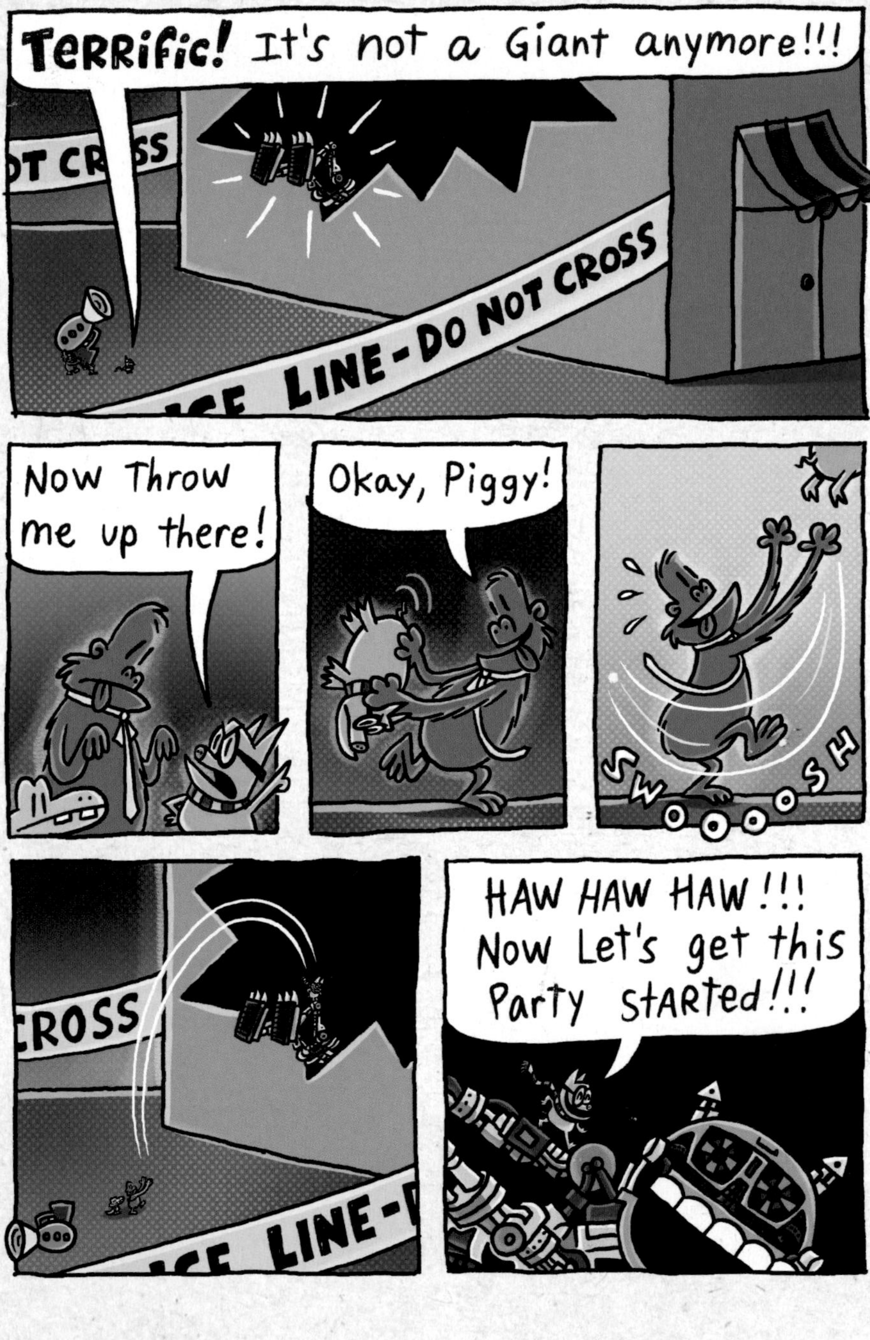
TERRIFIC! It's not a Giant anymore!!!
OT CROSS
LINE-DO NOT CROSS
Now Throw me up there!
Okay, Piggy!
SWOOOOOOSH
CROSS
LINE-
HAW HAW HAW!!! Now Let's get this Party STARTED!!!

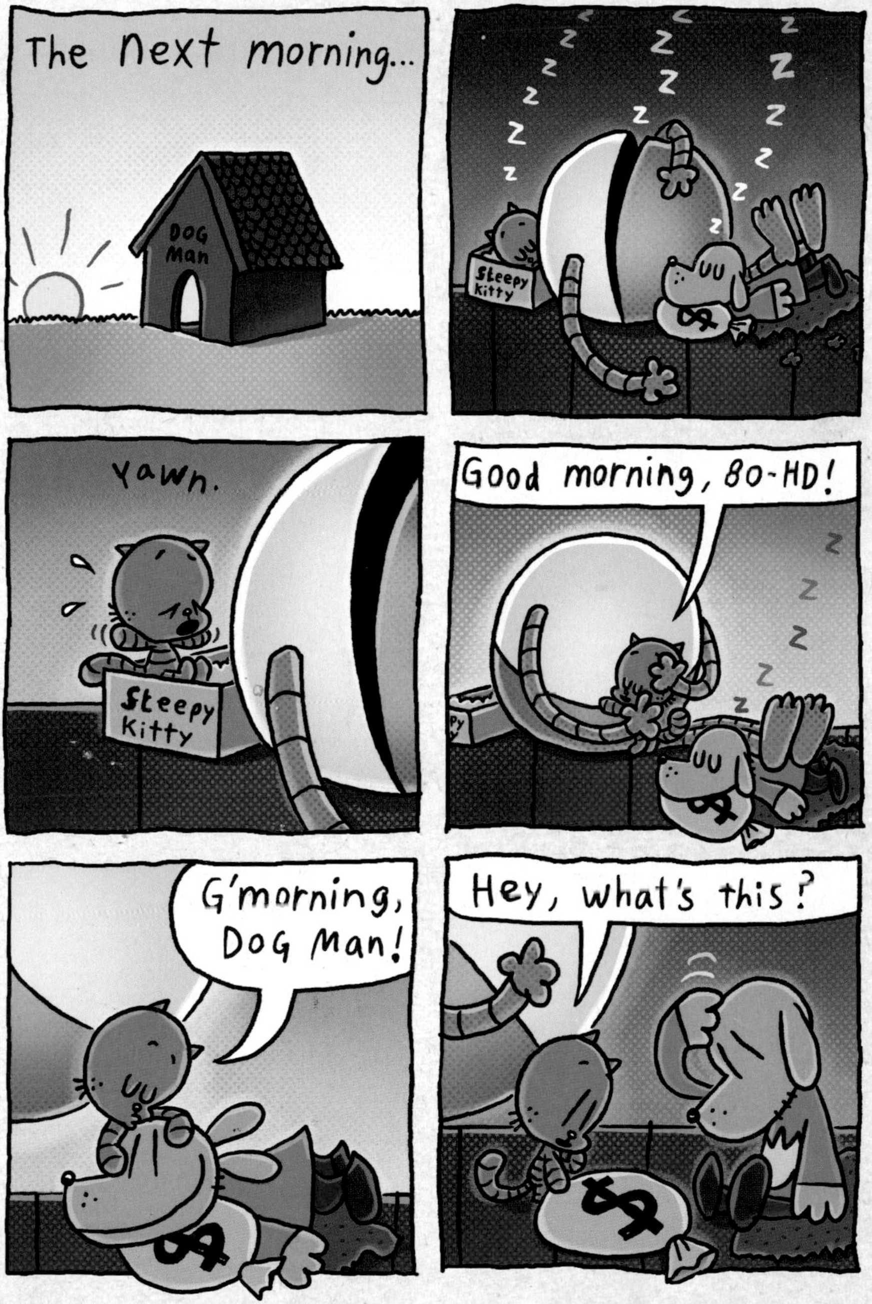
The next morning...
DOG Man
Sleepy Kitty
Yawn.
Sleepy Kitty
Good morning, 80-HD!
G'morning, DOG Man!
Hey, what's this?

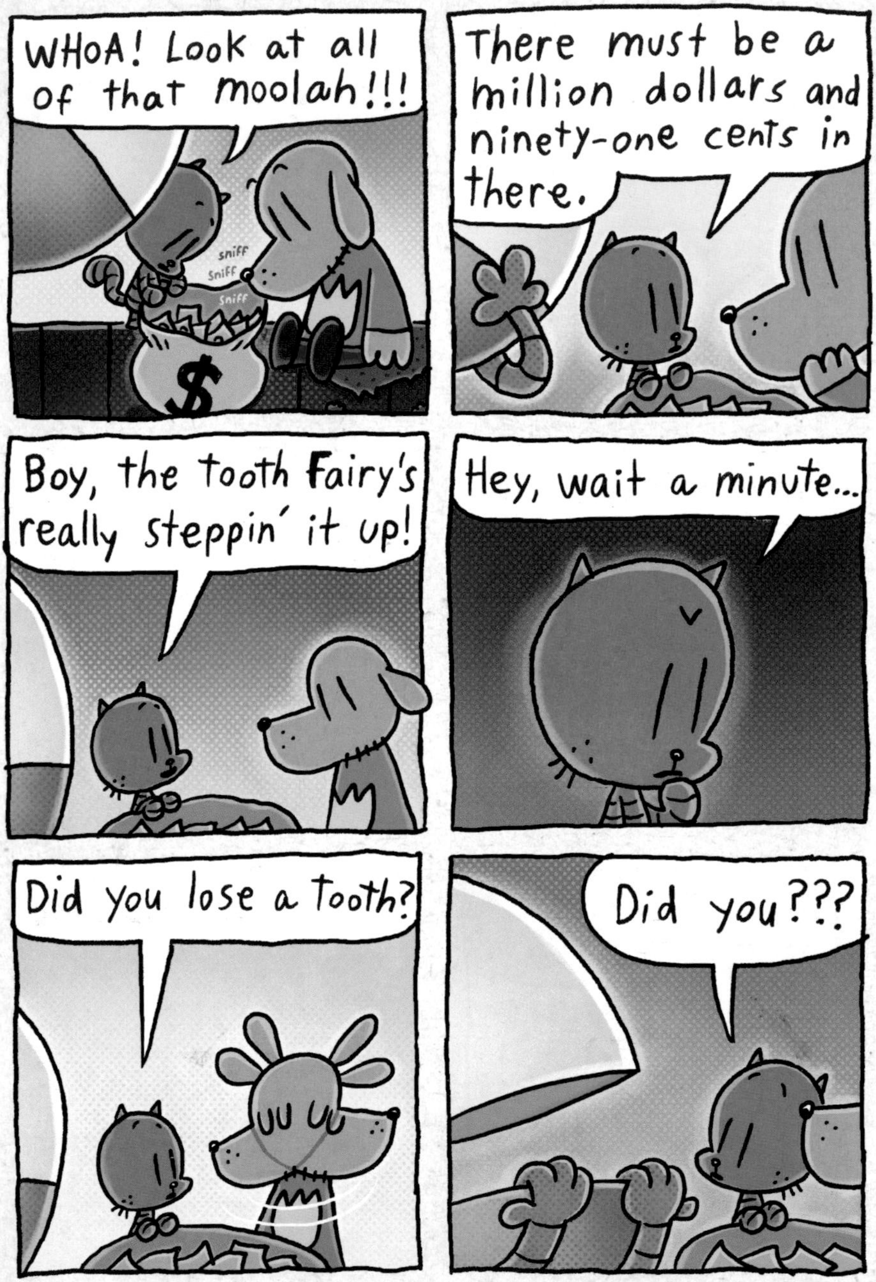
WHOA! Look at all of that moolah!!!
sniff
sniff
sniff
There must be a million dollars and ninety-one cents in there.
Boy, the tooth Fairy's really steppin' it up!
Hey, wait a minute...
Did you lose a tooth?
Did you???

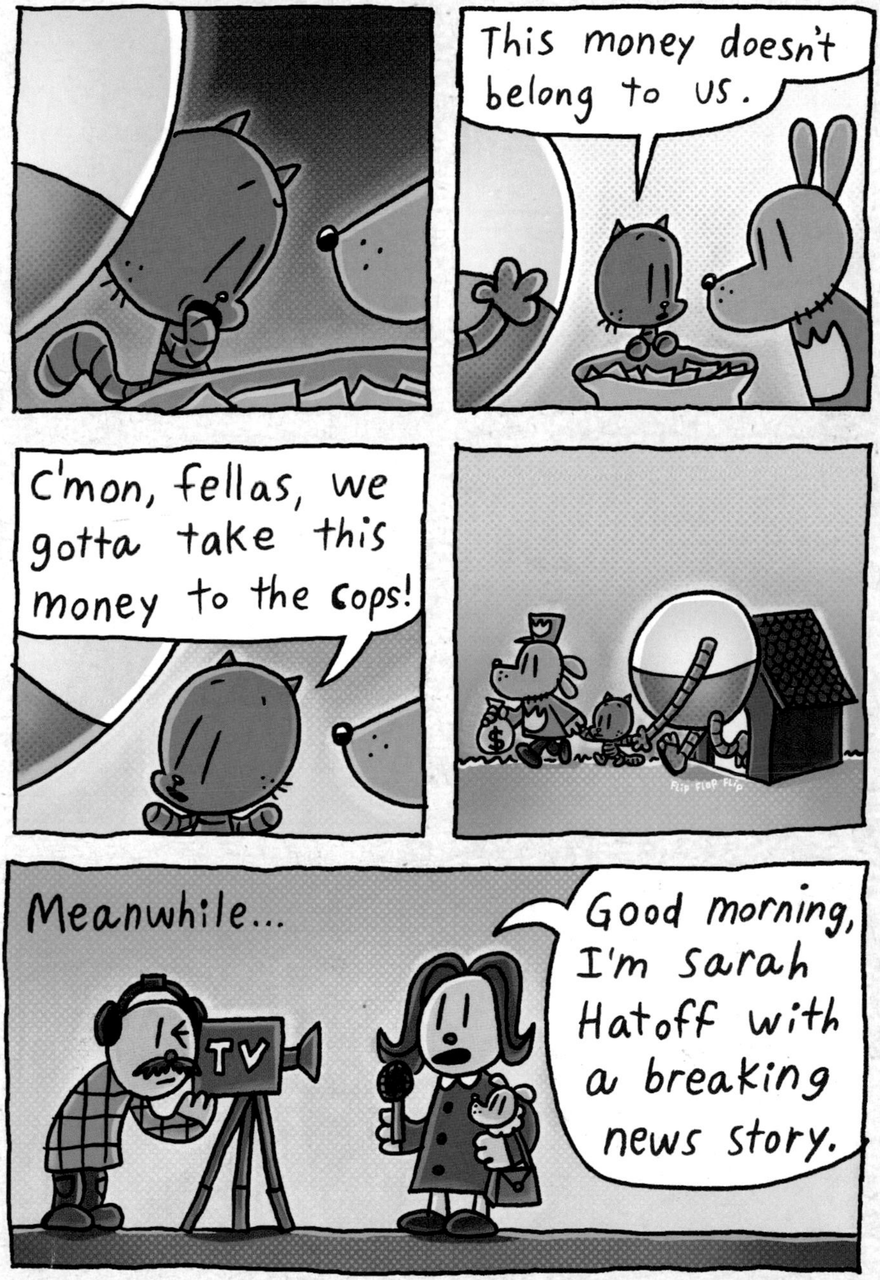
This money doesn't belong to us.
C'mon, fellas, we gotta take this money to the cops!
Flip Flop Flip
Meanwhile...
Good morning, I'm Sarah Hatoff with a breaking news story.
TV

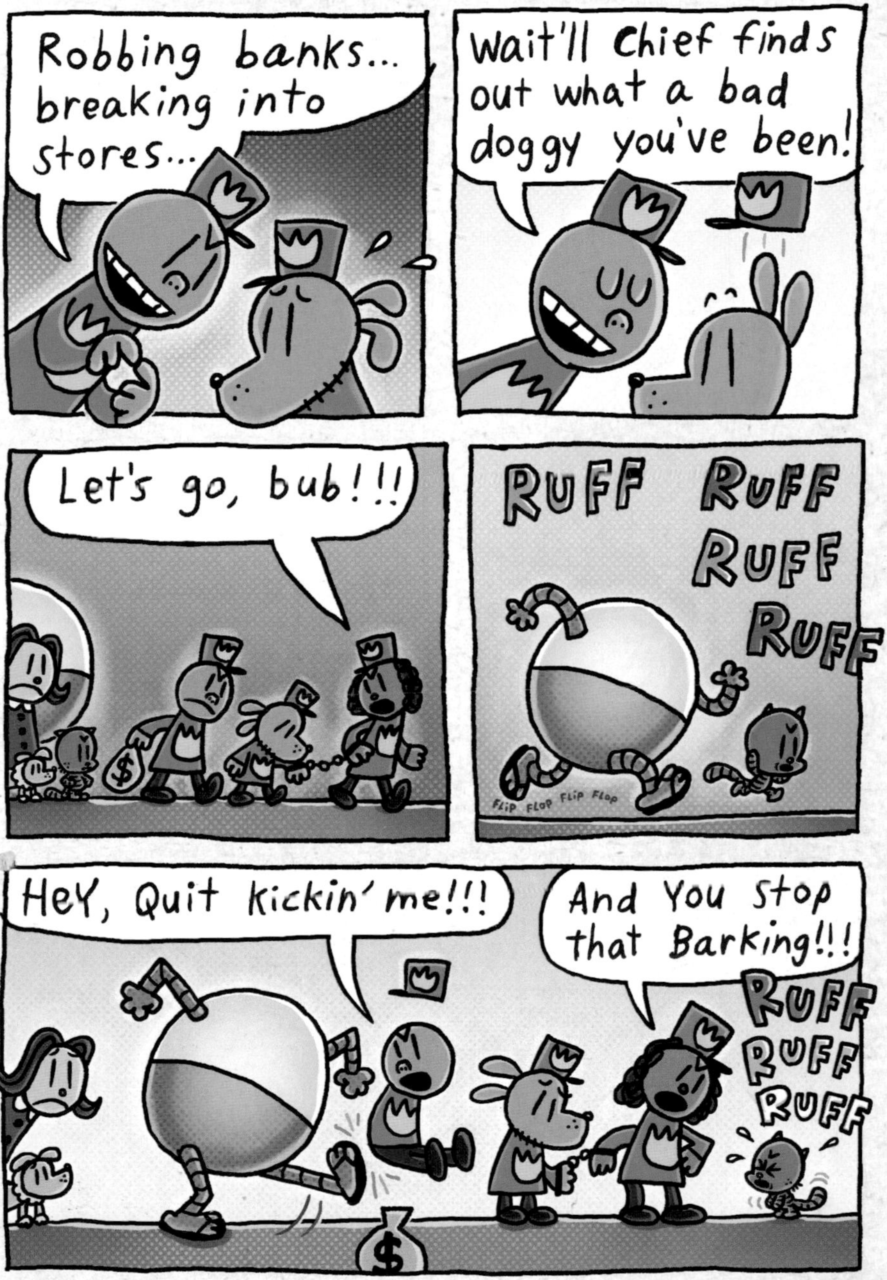
Robbing banks... breaking into stores...
Wait'll Chief finds out what a bad doggy you've been!
Let's go, bub!!!
RUFF RUFF RUFF RUFF
FLIP FLOP FLIP FLOP
HEY, Quit kickin' me!!!
And You Stop that Barking!!!
RUFF RUFF RUFF

CHAPTER 4

A Buncha Stuff That Happened Next

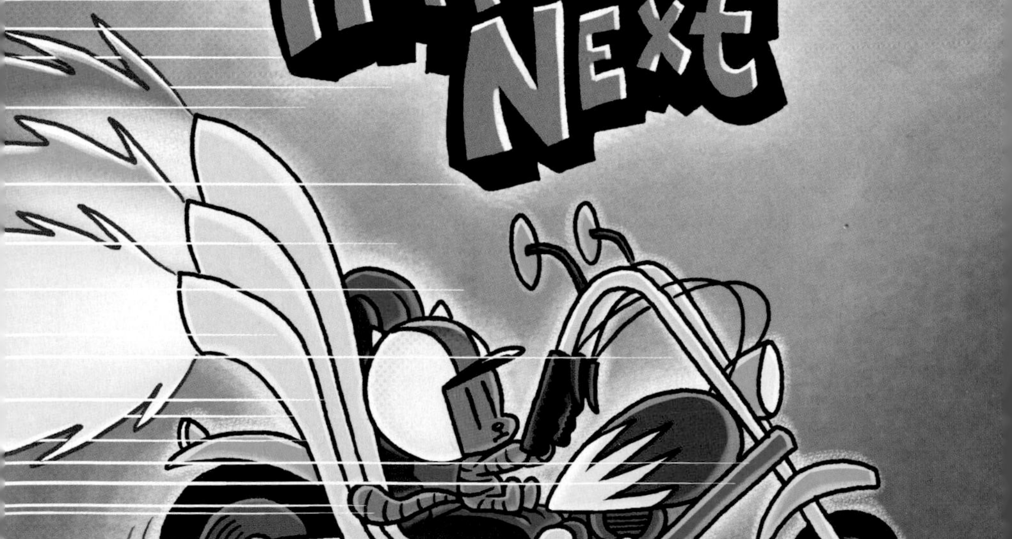

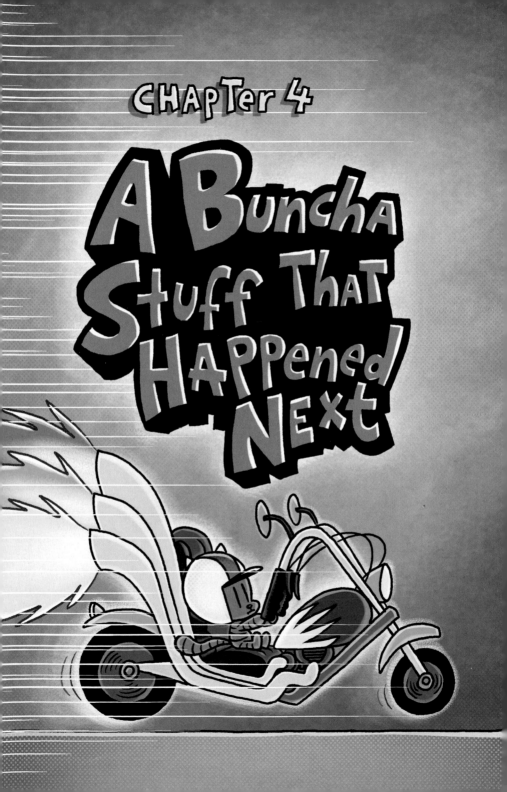

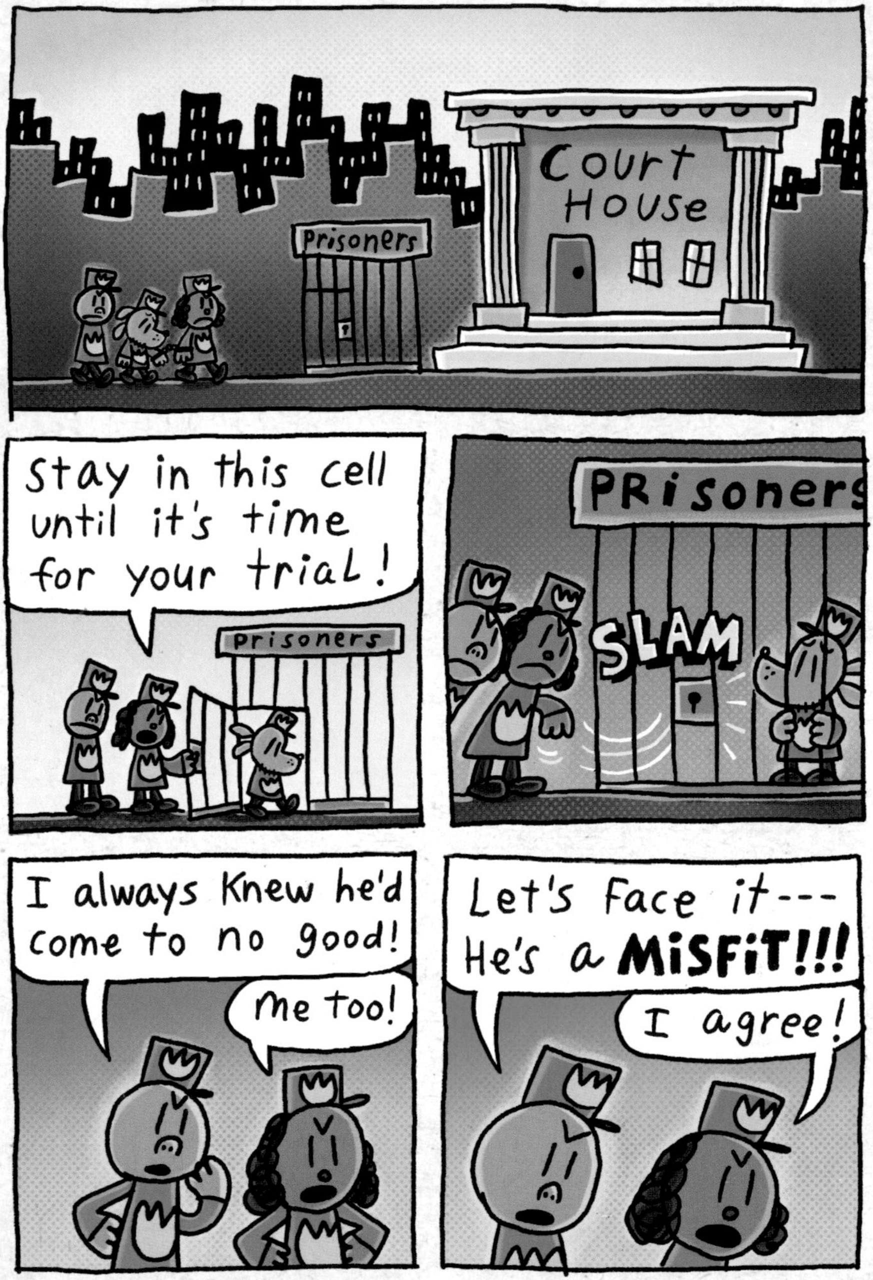
Court House
Prisoners
Stay in this cell until it's time for your trial!
Prisoners
PRisoners
SLAM
I always Knew he'd come to no good!
Me too!
Let's Face it--- He's a MiSFiT!!!
I agree!

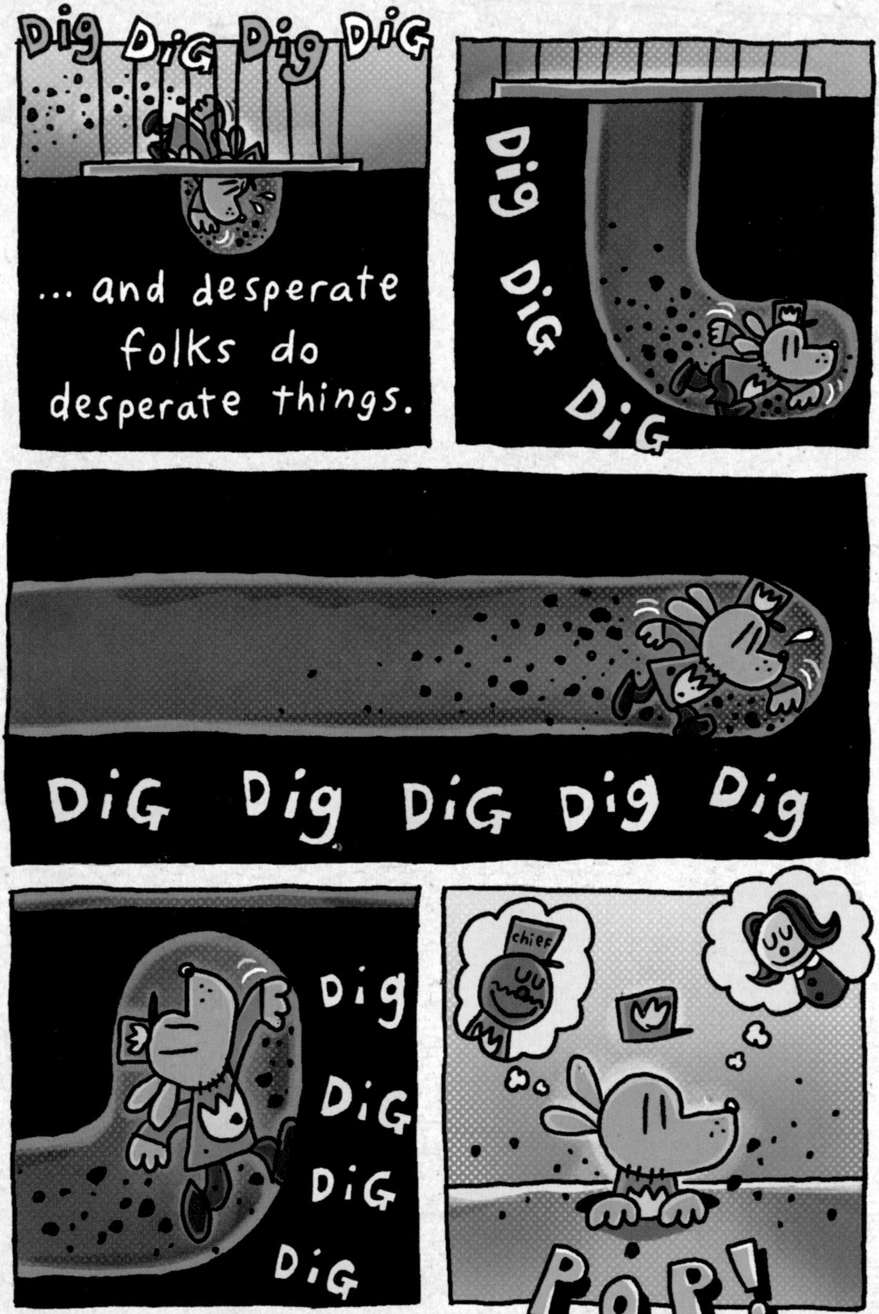
Dig DiG Dig DiG
... and desperate folks do desperate things.
Dig DiG DiG
DiG Dig DiG Dig Dig
Dig DiG DiG DiG
chief
POP!

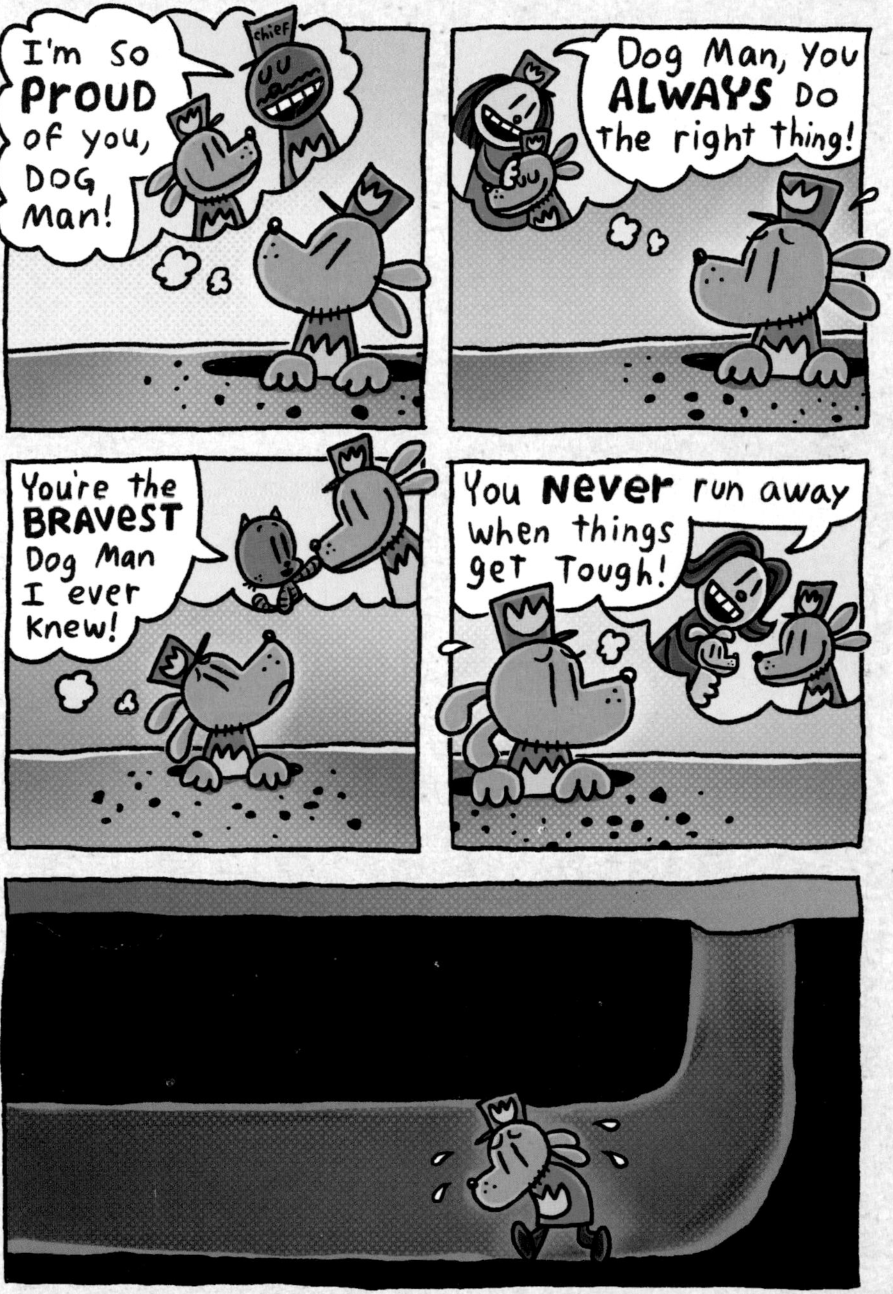
I'm So PROUD of you, DOG Man!
chief
Dog Man, You ALWAYS Do the right thing!
You're the BRAVEST Dog Man I ever Knew!
You NEVER run away when things get Tough!

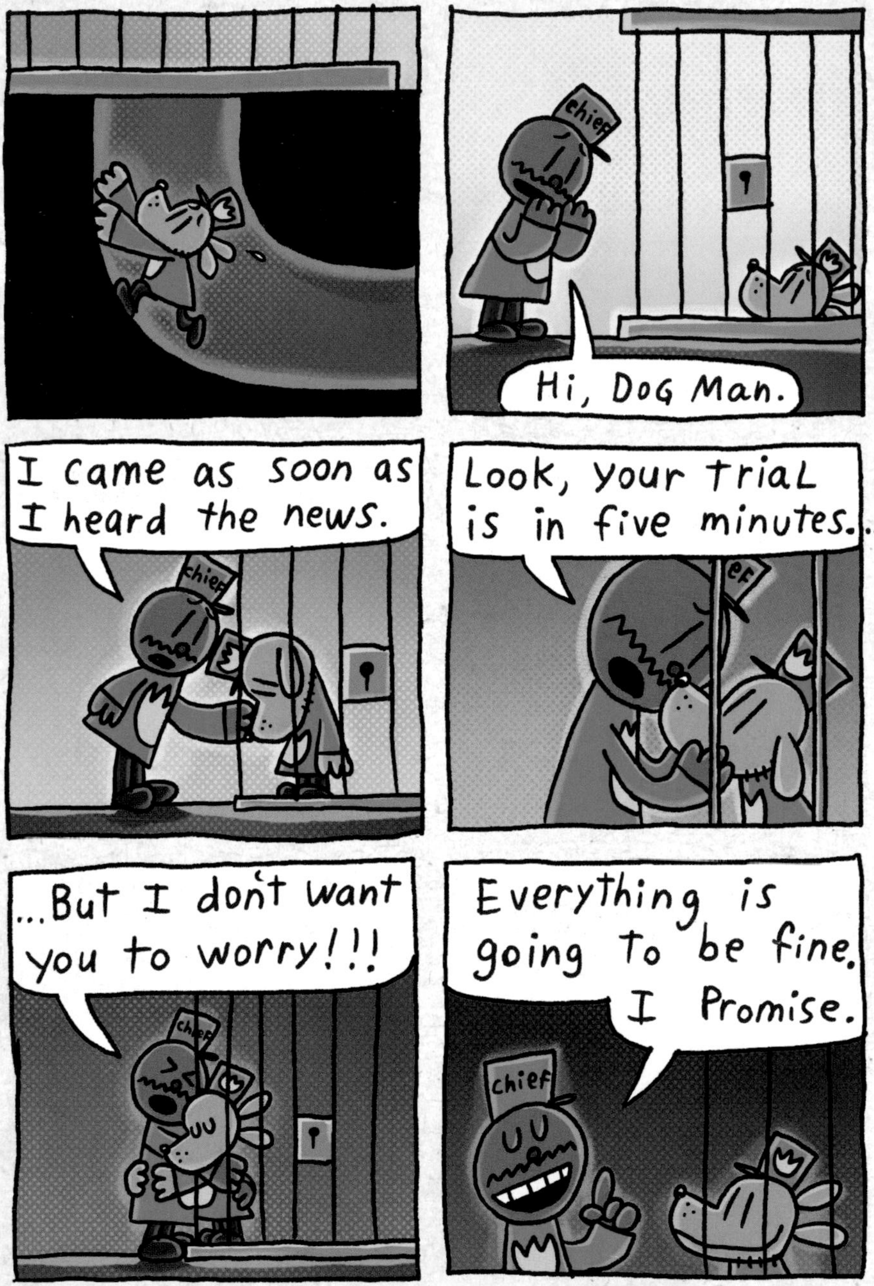
chief
Hi, DOG Man.
I came as soon as I heard the news.
chief
Look, your trial is in five minutes...
...But I don't want you to worry!!!
chief
Everything is going to be fine. I Promise.
chief

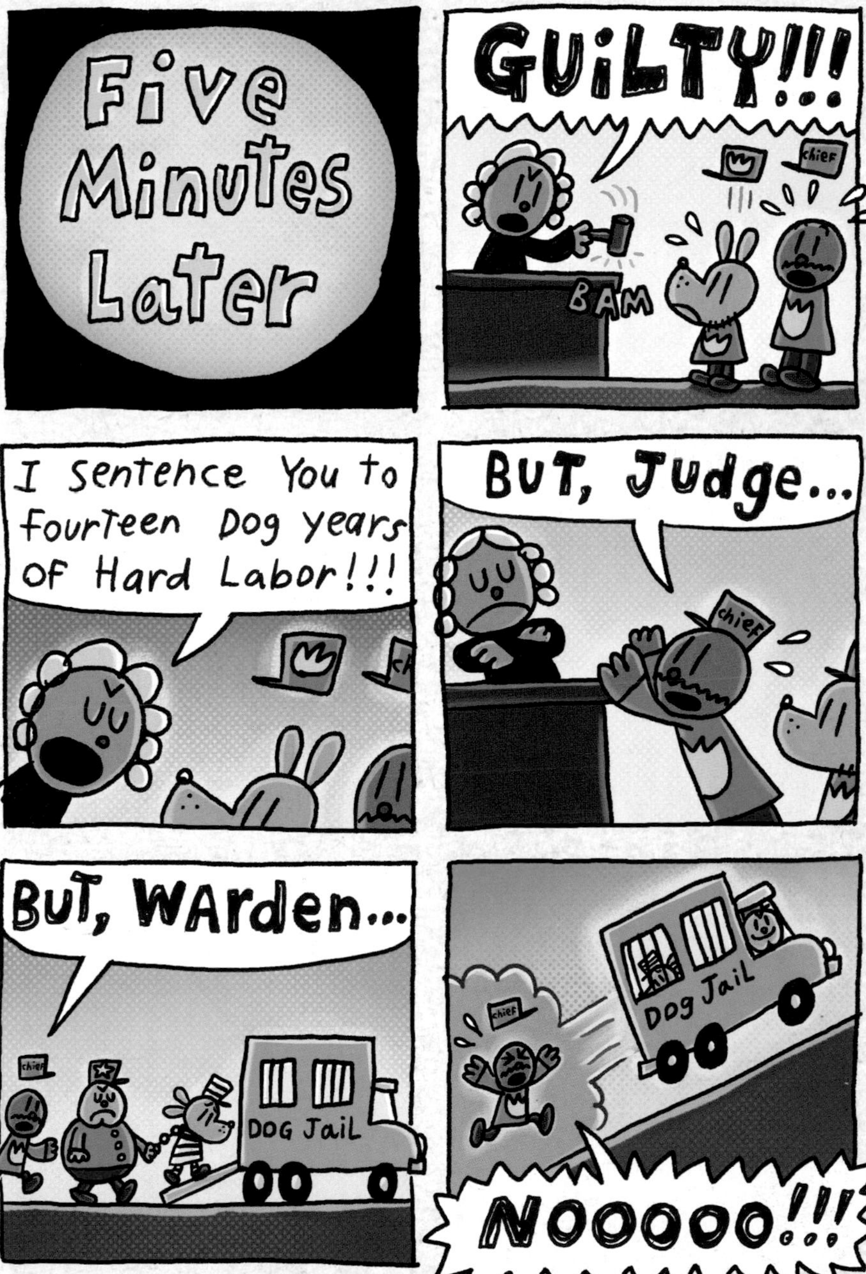
Five Minutes Later
GUILTY!!!
BAM
chief
I sentence You to Fourteen Dog years of Hard Labor!!!
BUT, Judge...
chief
BUT, WArden...
chief
DOG JaiL
chief
Dog Jail
NOOOOO!!!

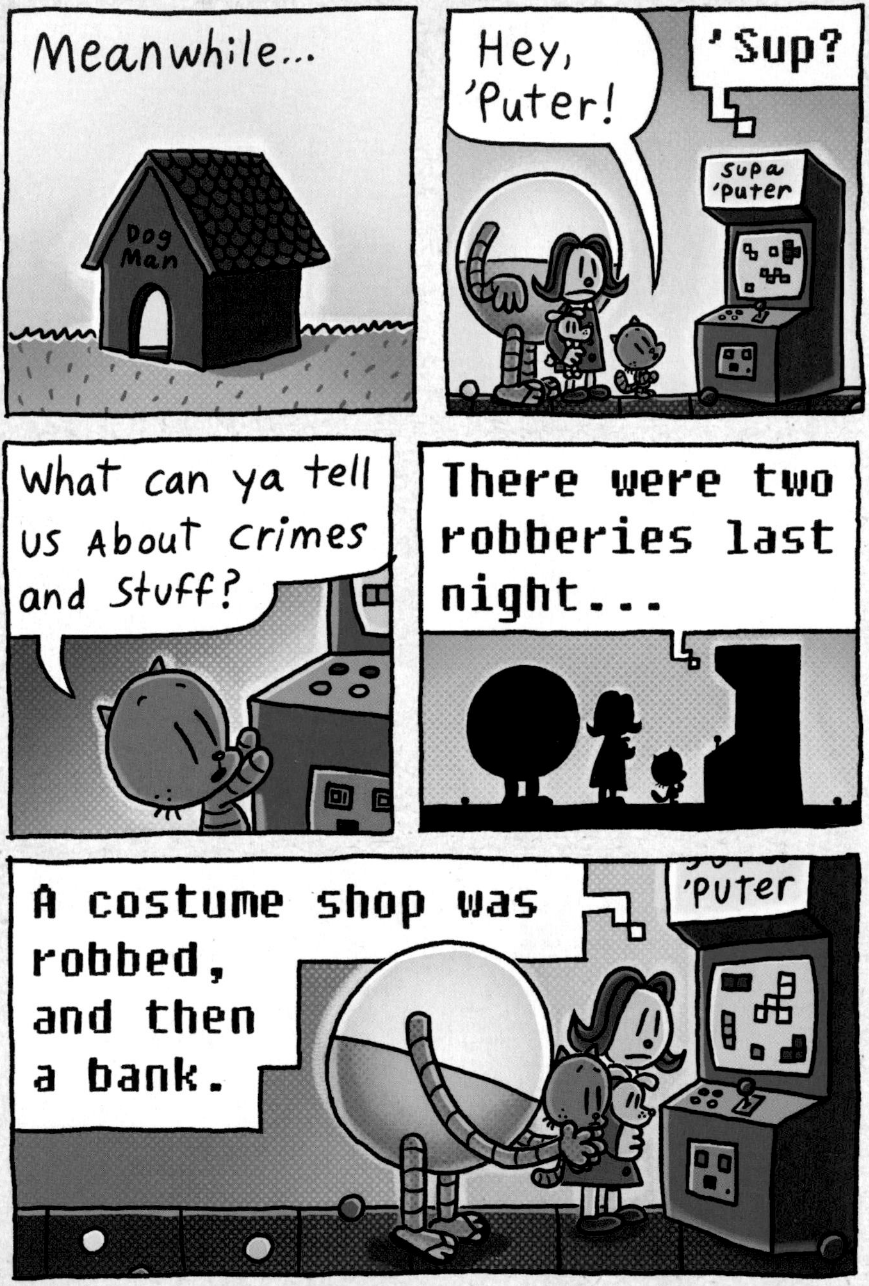
Meanwhile...
Dog Man
Hey, 'Puter!
'Sup?
Supa 'Puter
What can ya tell us About crimes and Stuff?
There were two robberies last night...
A costume shop was robbed, and then a bank.
'Puter

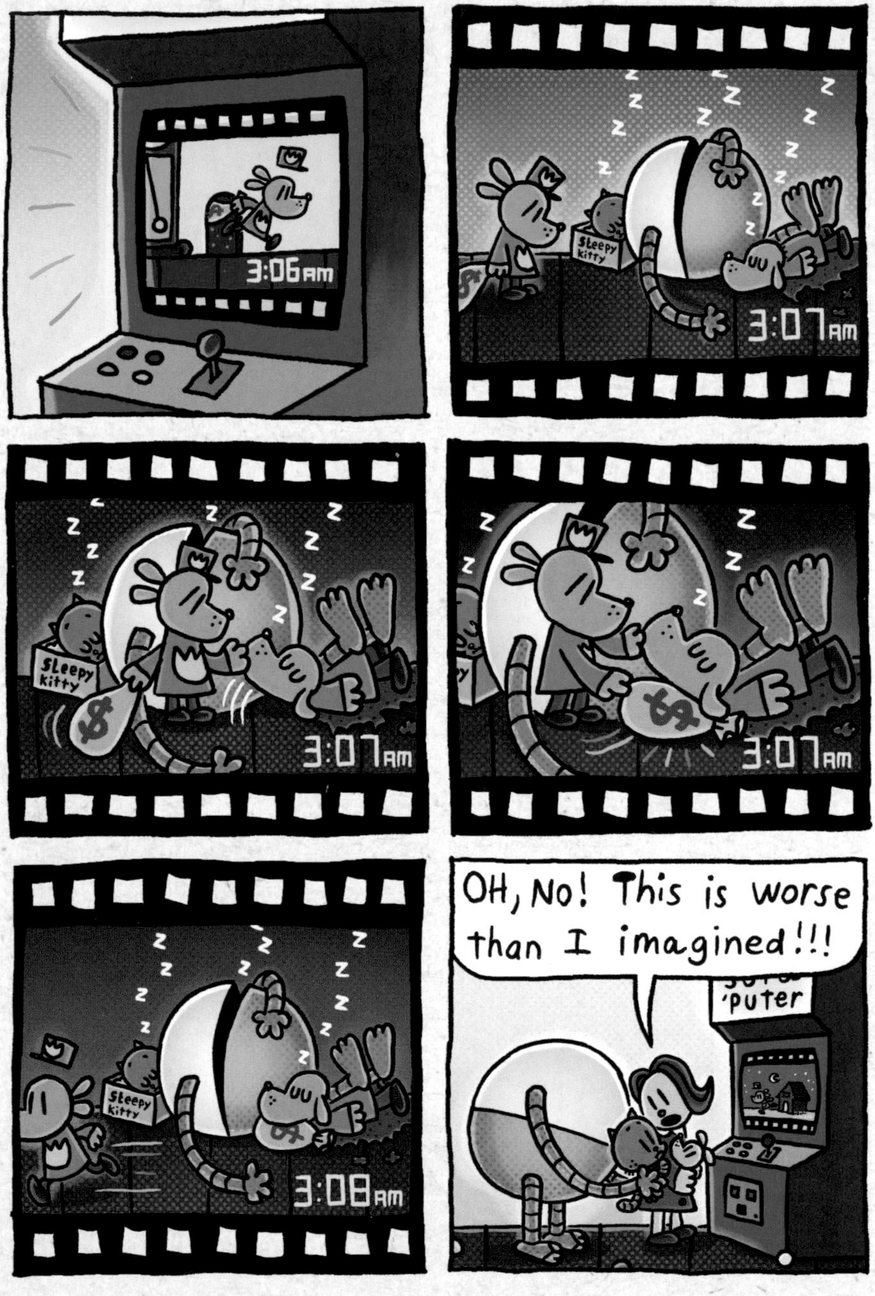
3:06AM
Sleepy kitty
3:07AM
Sleepy kitty
3:07AM
3:07AM
Sleepy kitty
3:08AM
OH, No! This is worse than I imagined!!!
'puter

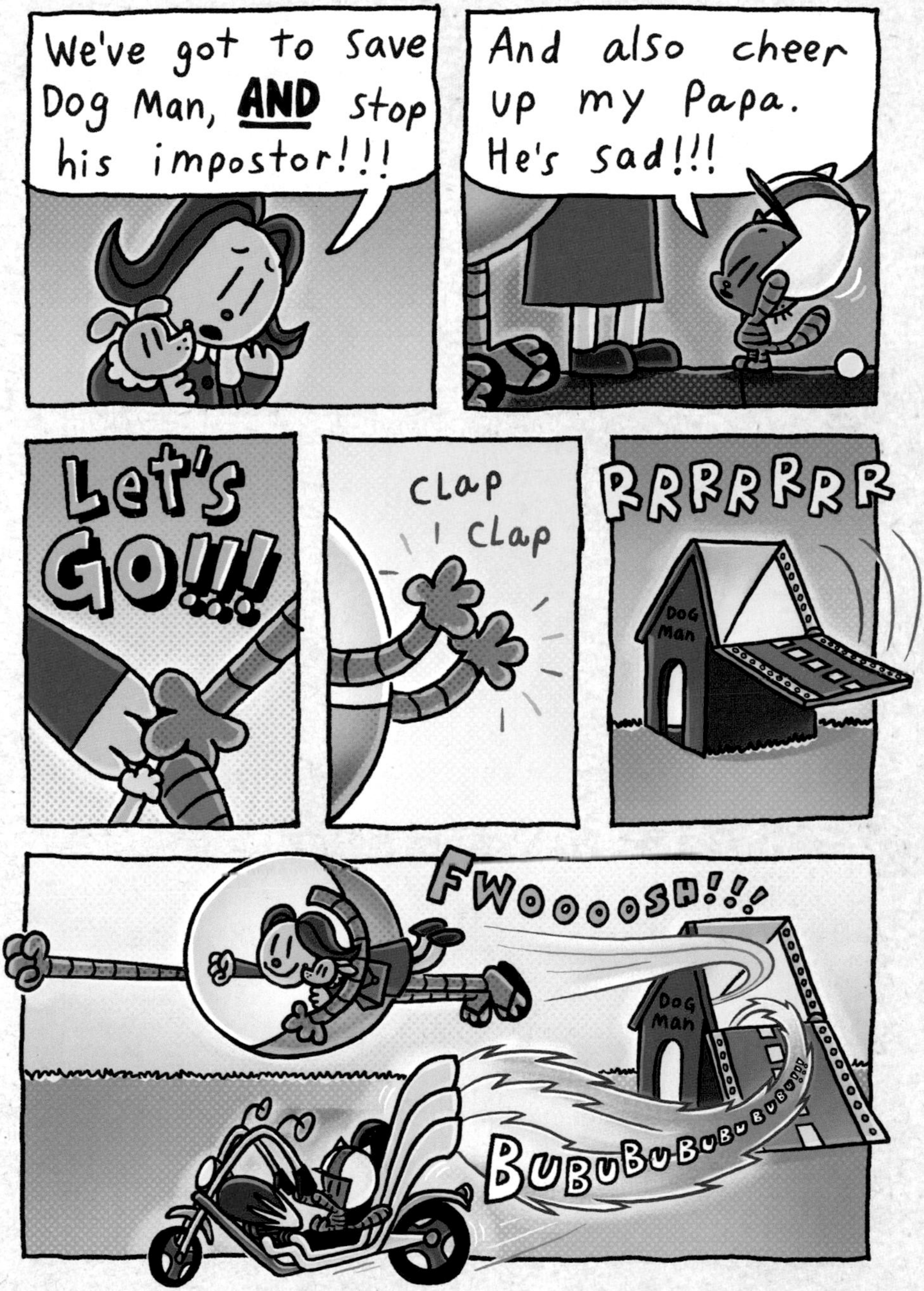

We've got to save Dog Man, **AND** stop his impostor!!!
And also cheer up my Papa. He's sad!!!
Let's GO!!!
CLAP
CLAP
RRRRRRR
DOG Man
FWOOOOOSH!!!
DOG Man
BUBUBUBUBUBUBUBU!!!

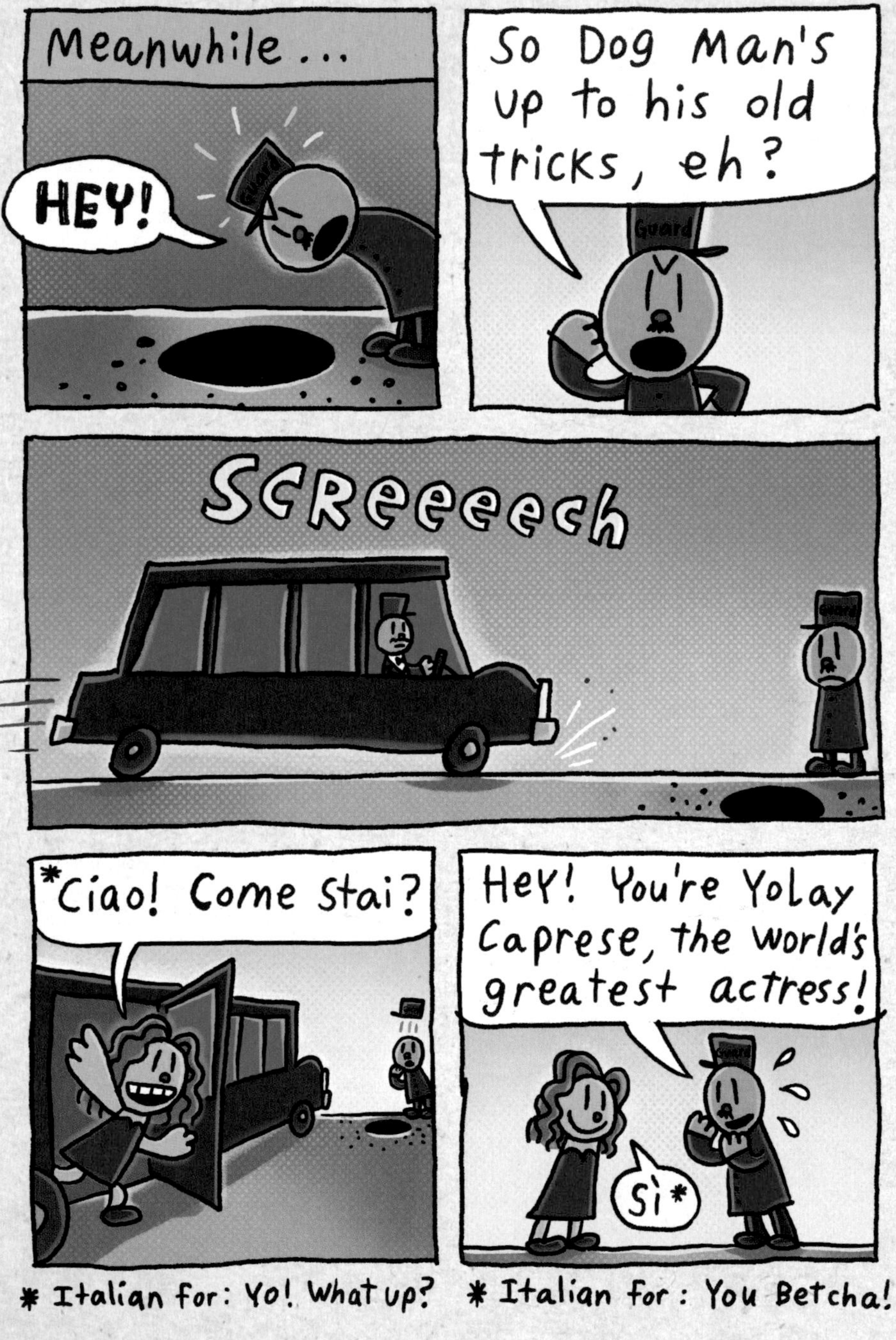
Meanwhile . . .
HEY!
So Dog Man's up to his old tricks, eh?
Guard
SCReeeech
*Ciao! Come Stai?
Hey! You're Yolay Caprese, the world's greatest actress!
Sì*

* Italian for: Yo! What up? * Italian for: You Betcha!

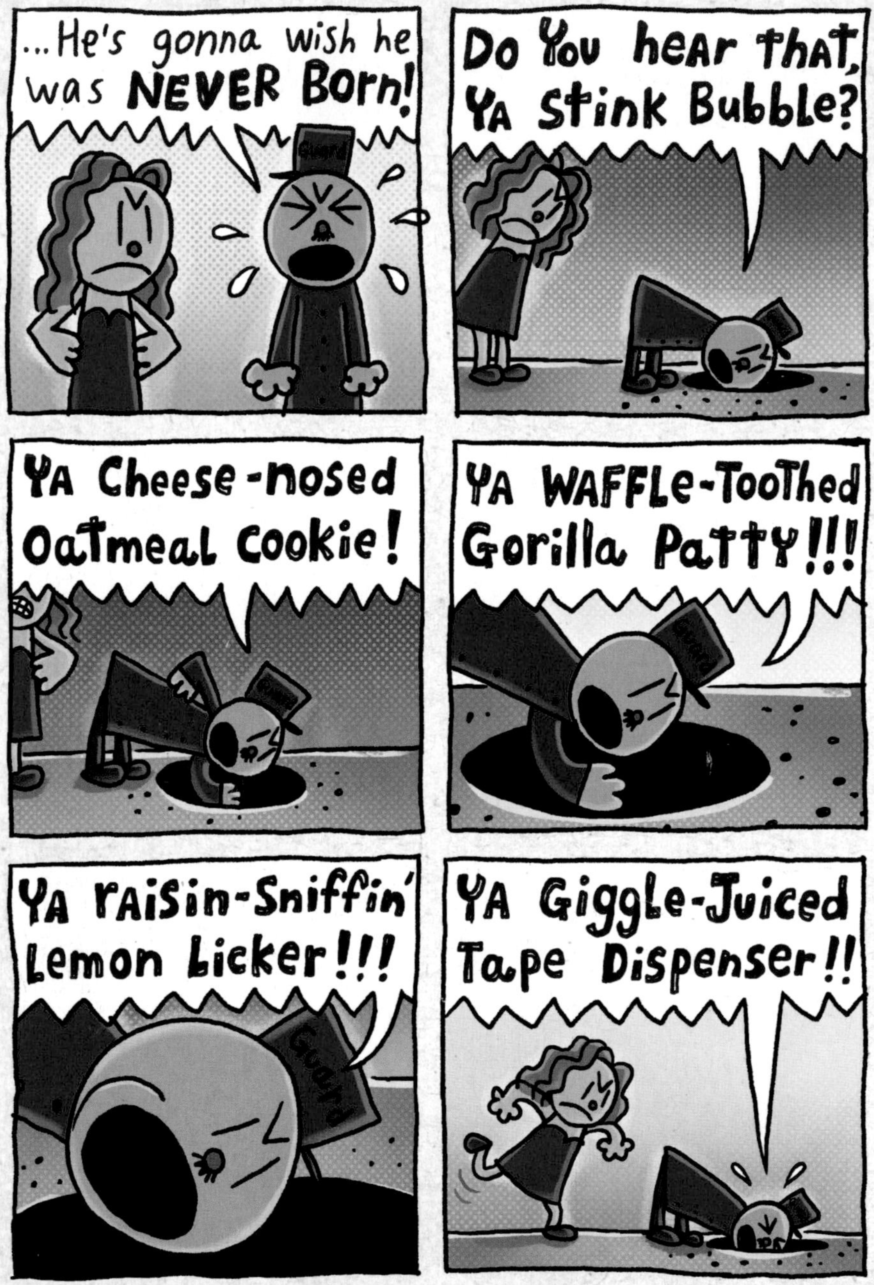
...He's gonna wish he was NEVER Born!
Do You hear that, YA Stink Bubble?
YA Cheese-nosed Oatmeal Cookie!
YA WAFFLE-Toothed Gorilla Patty!!!
YA raisin-Sniffin' Lemon Licker!!!
YA Giggle-Juiced Tape Dispenser!!

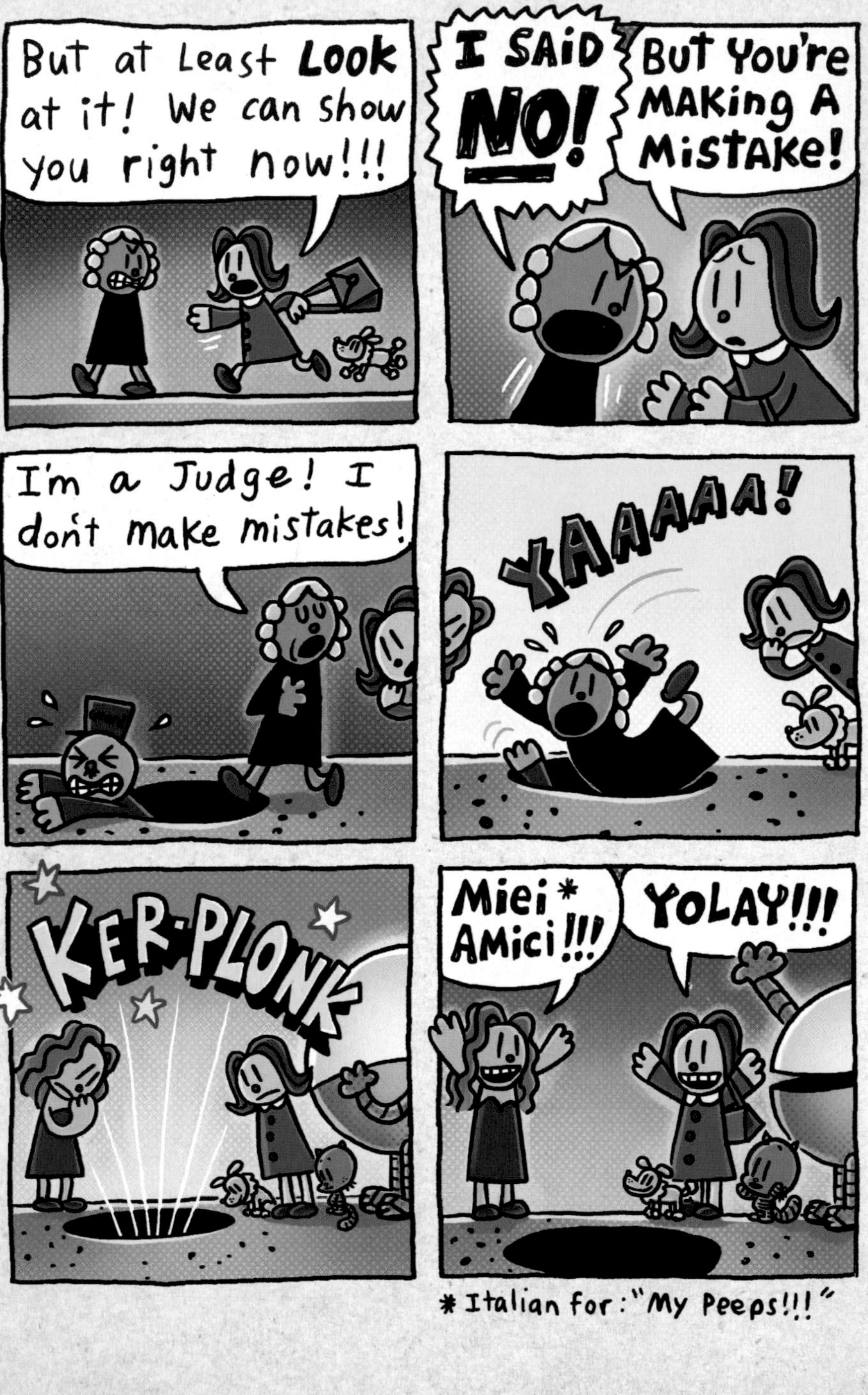
But at Least LOOK at it! We can show you right now!!!
I SAID NO!
But You're MAKING A MISTAKE!
I'm a Judge! I don't make mistakes!
YAAAAAA!
KER-PLONK
Miei* AMici!!!
YOLAY!!!

* Italian for: "My Peeps!!!"

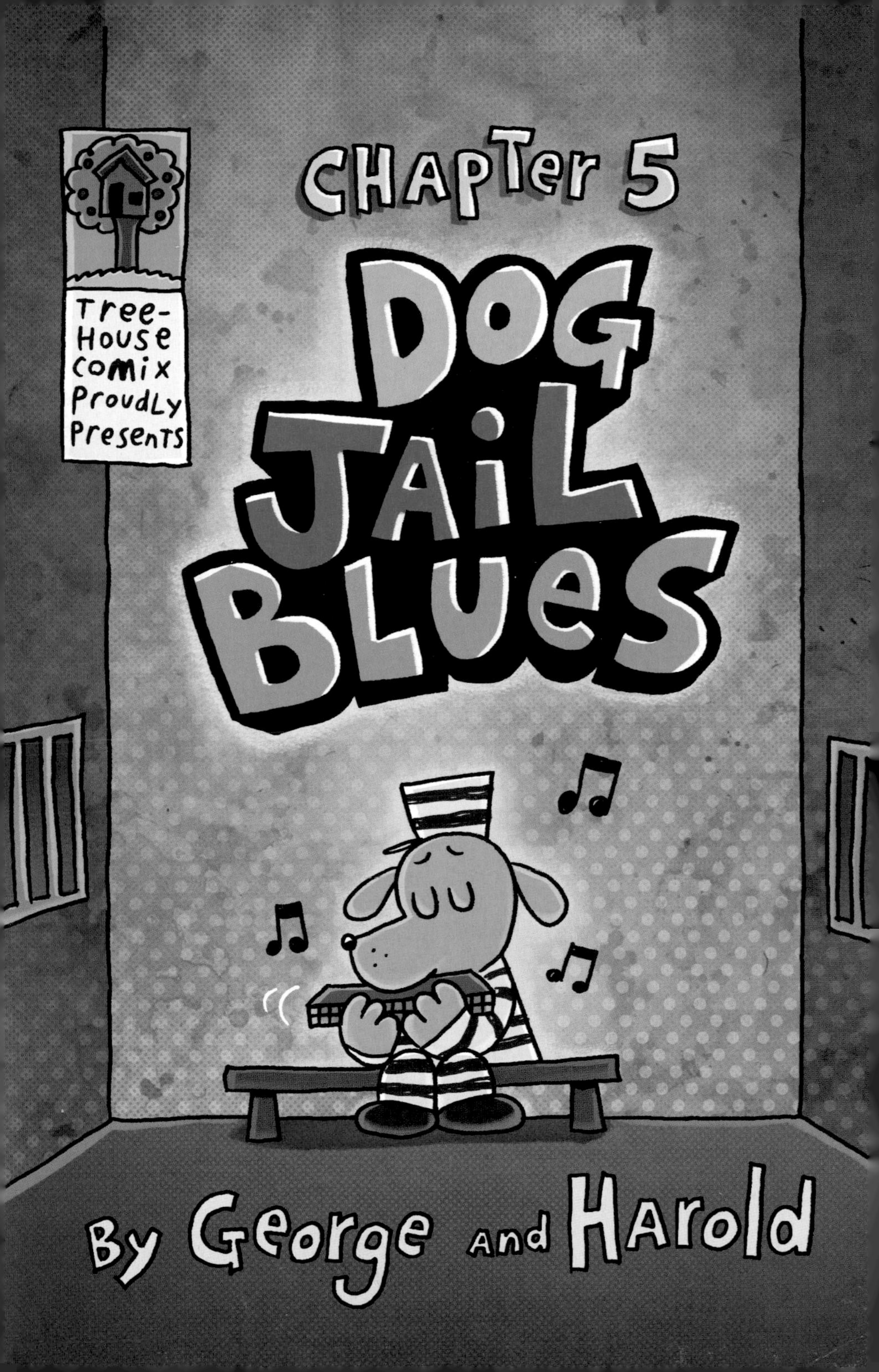
Tree-House Comix Proudly Presents
CHAPTER 5
DOG JAIL BLUES
By George and Harold

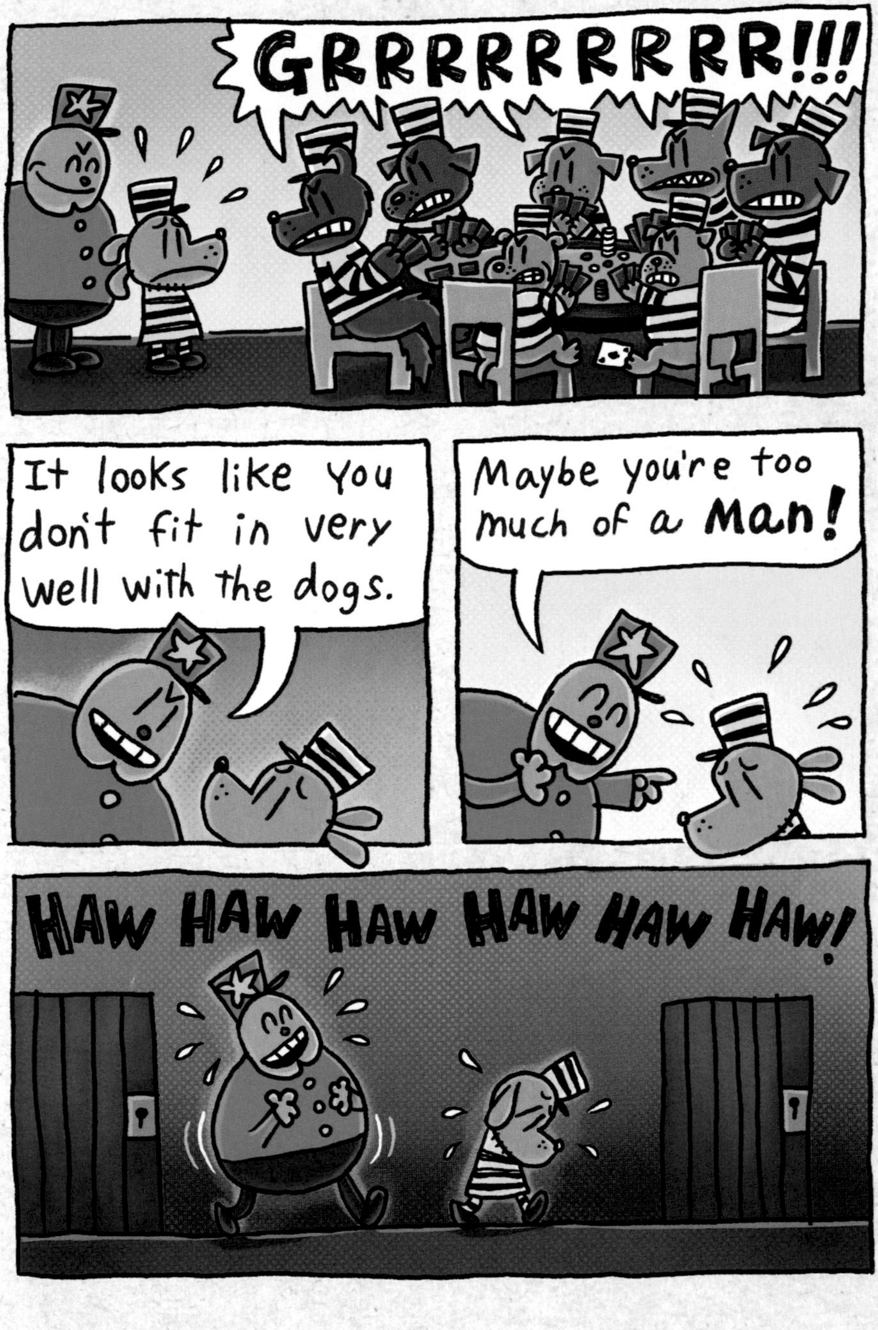
GRRRRRRRRR!!!
It looks like you don't fit in very well with the dogs.
Maybe you're too much of a Man!
HAW HAW HAW HAW HAW HAW!

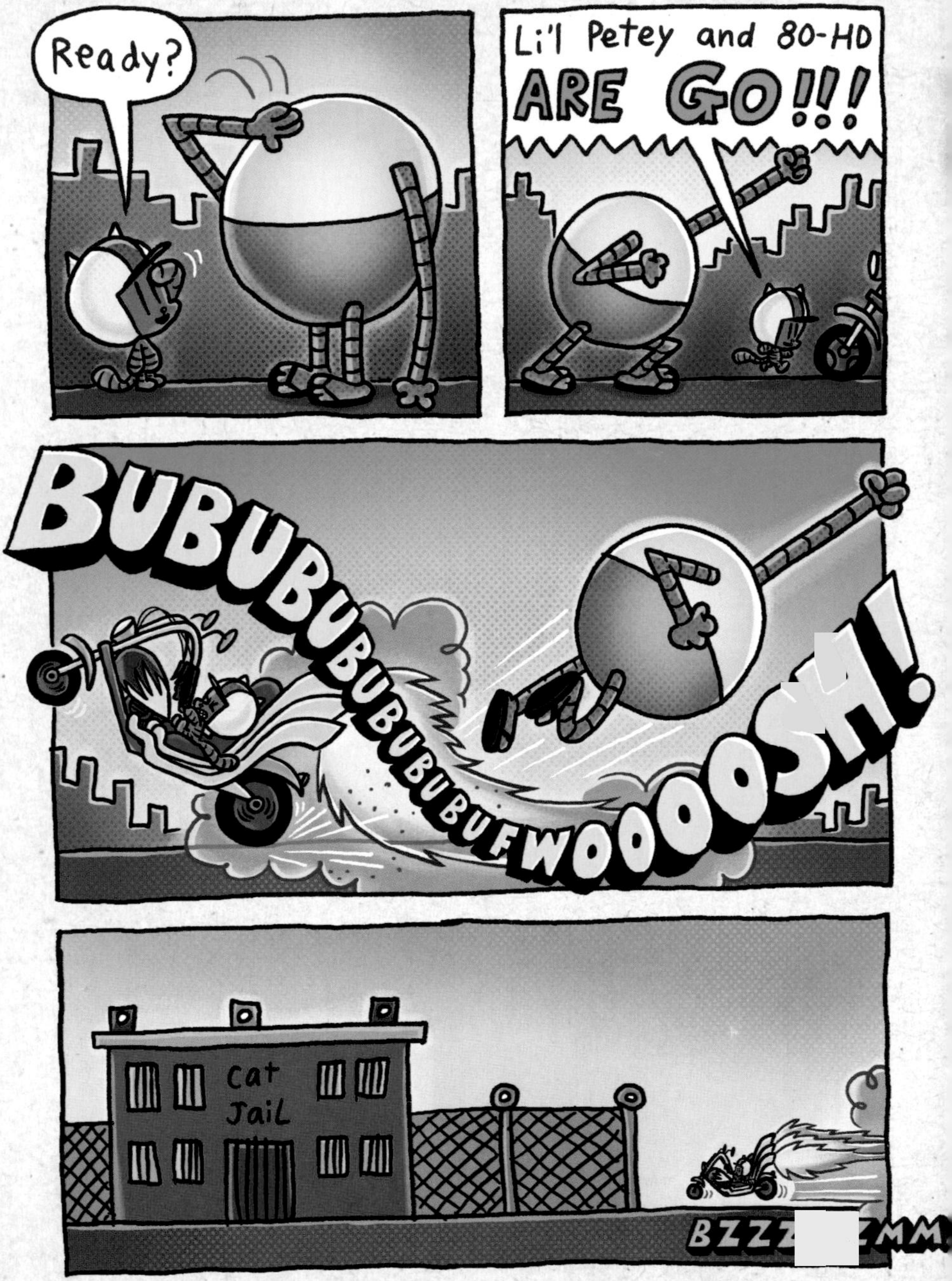
Ready?
Li'l Petey and 80-HD ARE GO!!!
BUBUBUBUBUBUBUBUBUFWOOOOOSH!
Cat Jail
BZZZ ZMM

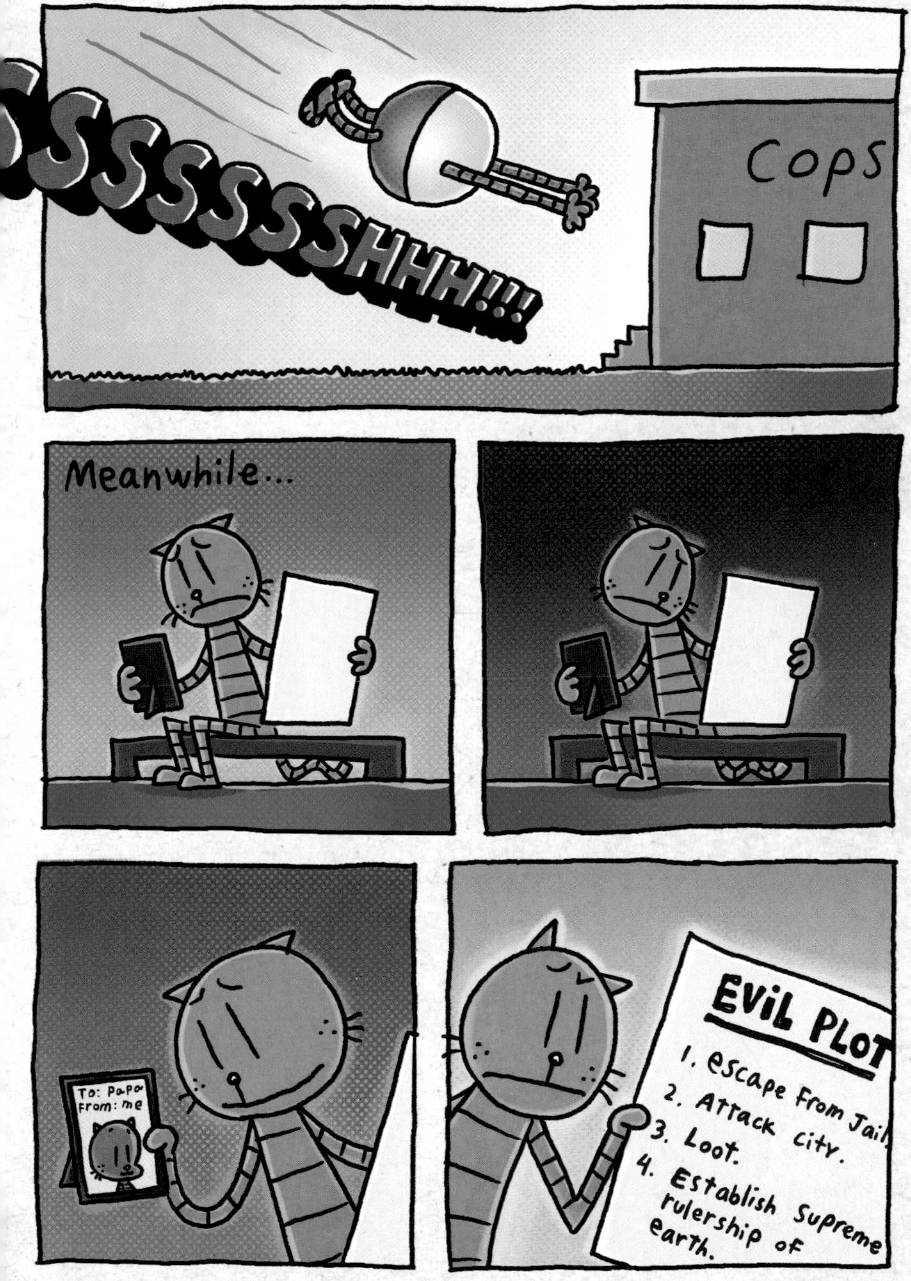
SSSSSSSSHHH!!!
Cops
Meanwhile...
To: Papa
From: me
EVIL PLOT
1. escape from Jail.
2. Attack city.
3. Loot.
4. Establish Supreme rulership of earth.

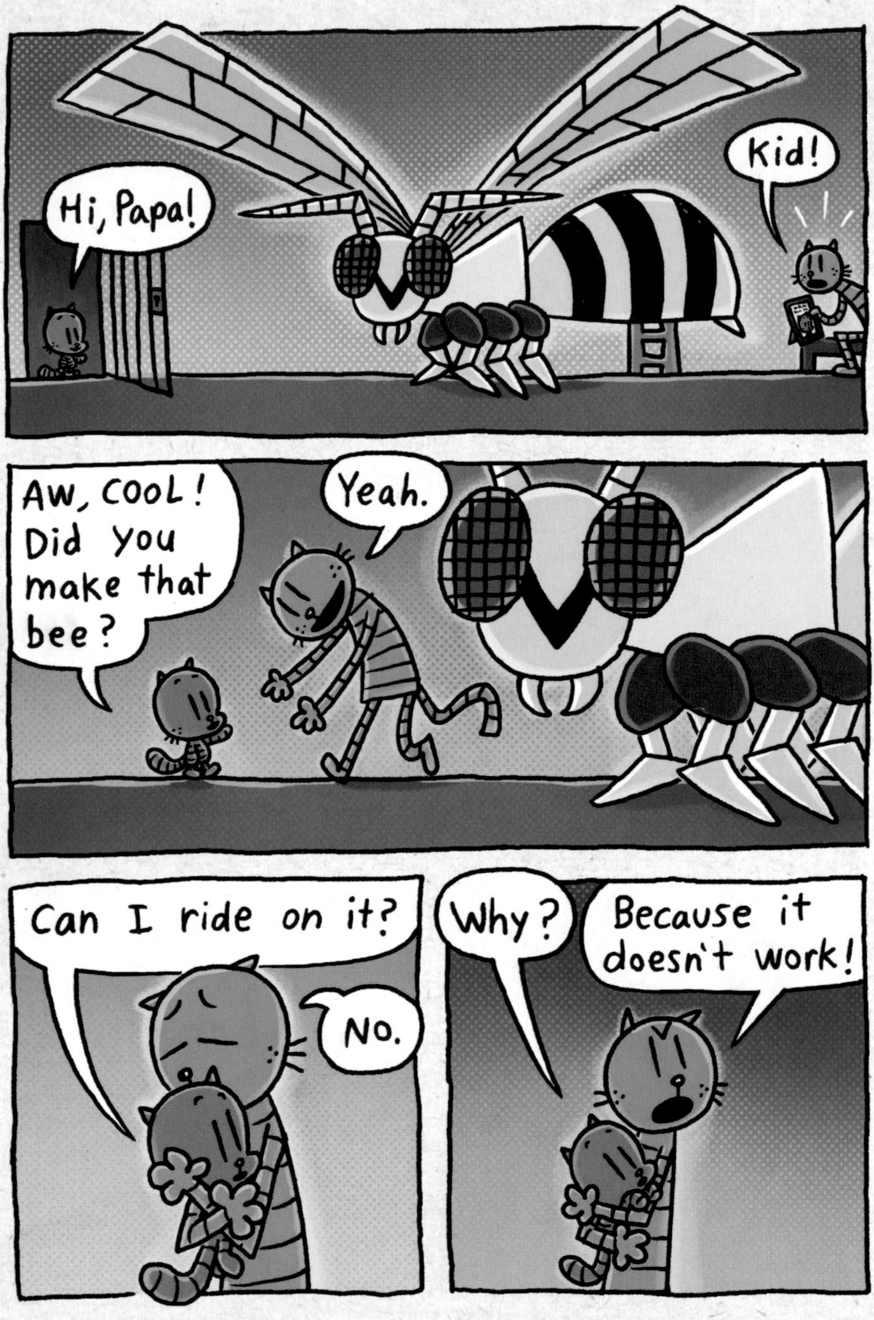
Hi, Papa!
Kid!
AW, COOL! Did you make that bee?
Yeah.
Can I ride on it?
No.
Why?
Because it doesn't work!

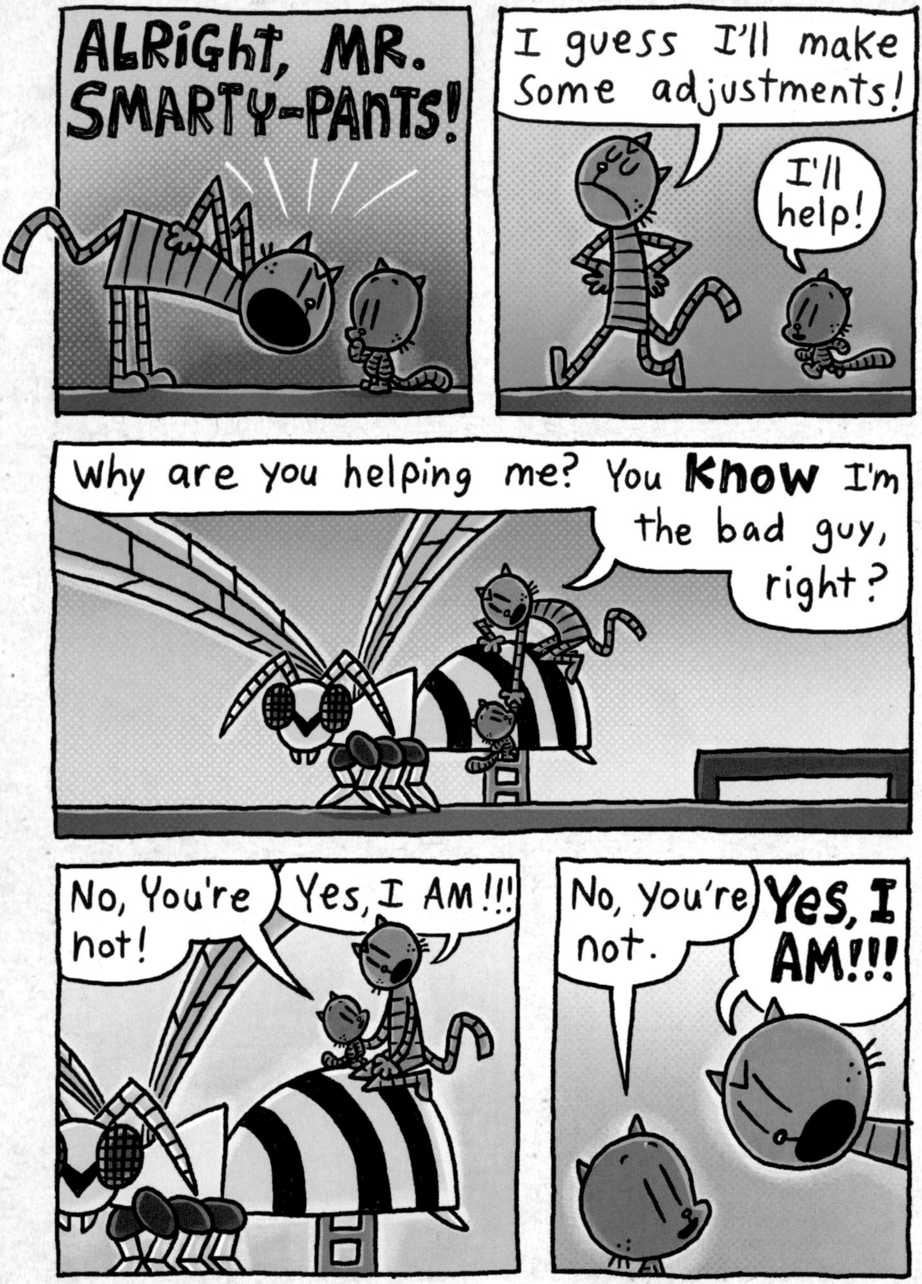
ALRIGHT, MR. SMARTY-PANTS!
I guess I'll make some adjustments!
I'll help!
Why are you helping me? You KNOW I'm the bad guy, right?
No, You're not!
Yes, I AM!!!
No, you're not.
Yes, I AM!!!

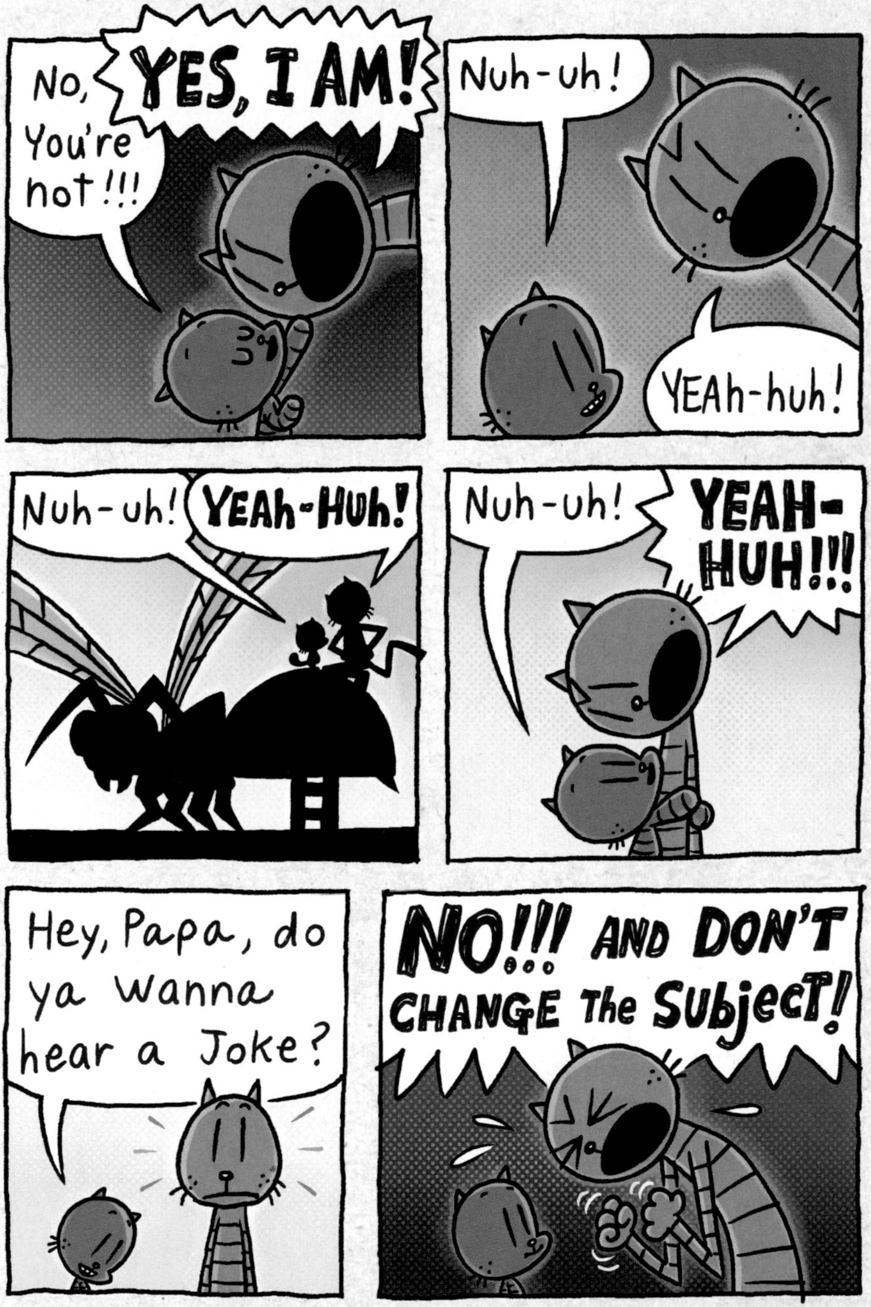
No, You're not!!!
YES, I AM!
Nuh-uh!
YEAh-huh!
Nuh-uh!
YEAh-HUh!
Nuh-uh!
YEAH-HUH!!!
Hey, Papa, do ya wanna hear a Joke?
NO!!! AND DON'T CHANGE The SUbjecT!

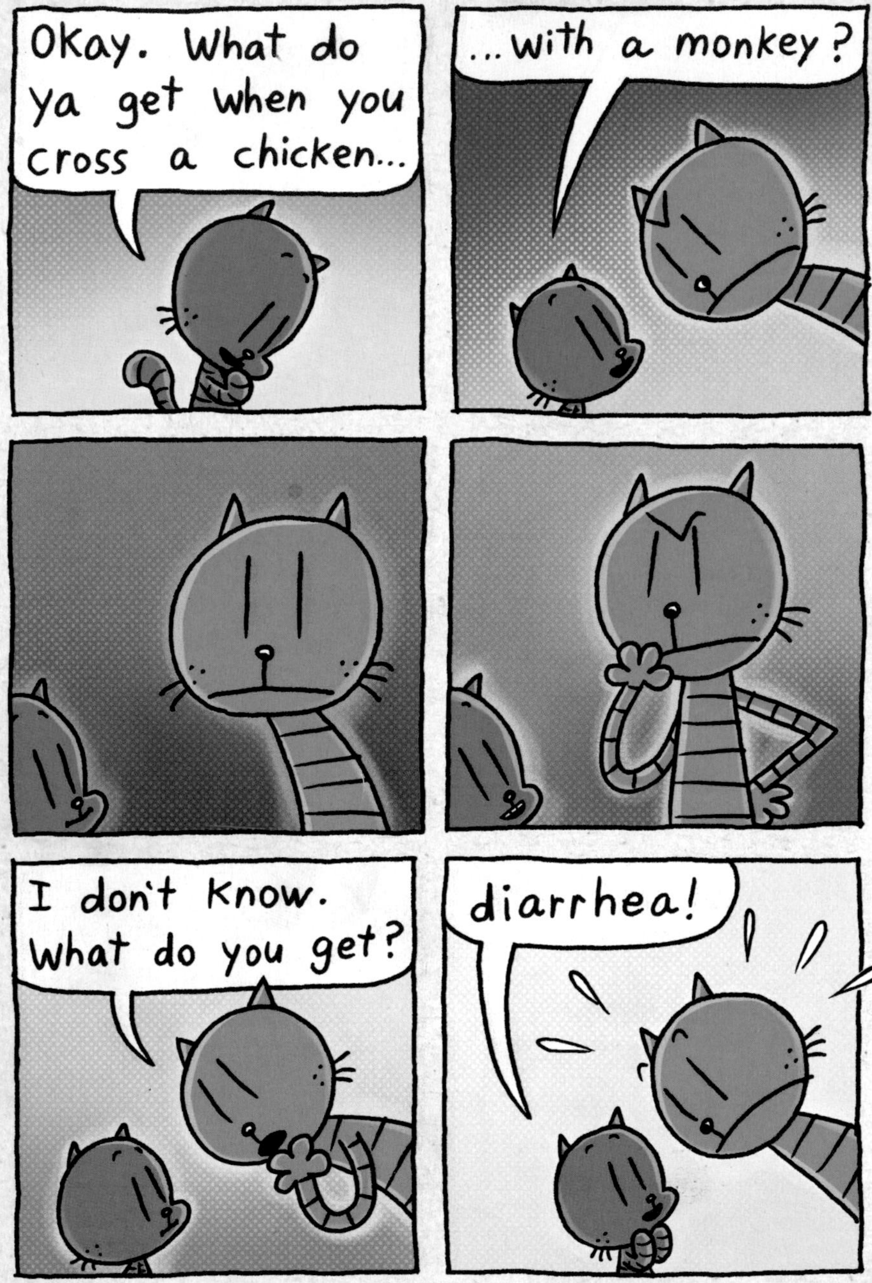
Okay. What do ya get when you cross a chicken...
...with a monkey?
I don't know. What do you get?
diarrhea!

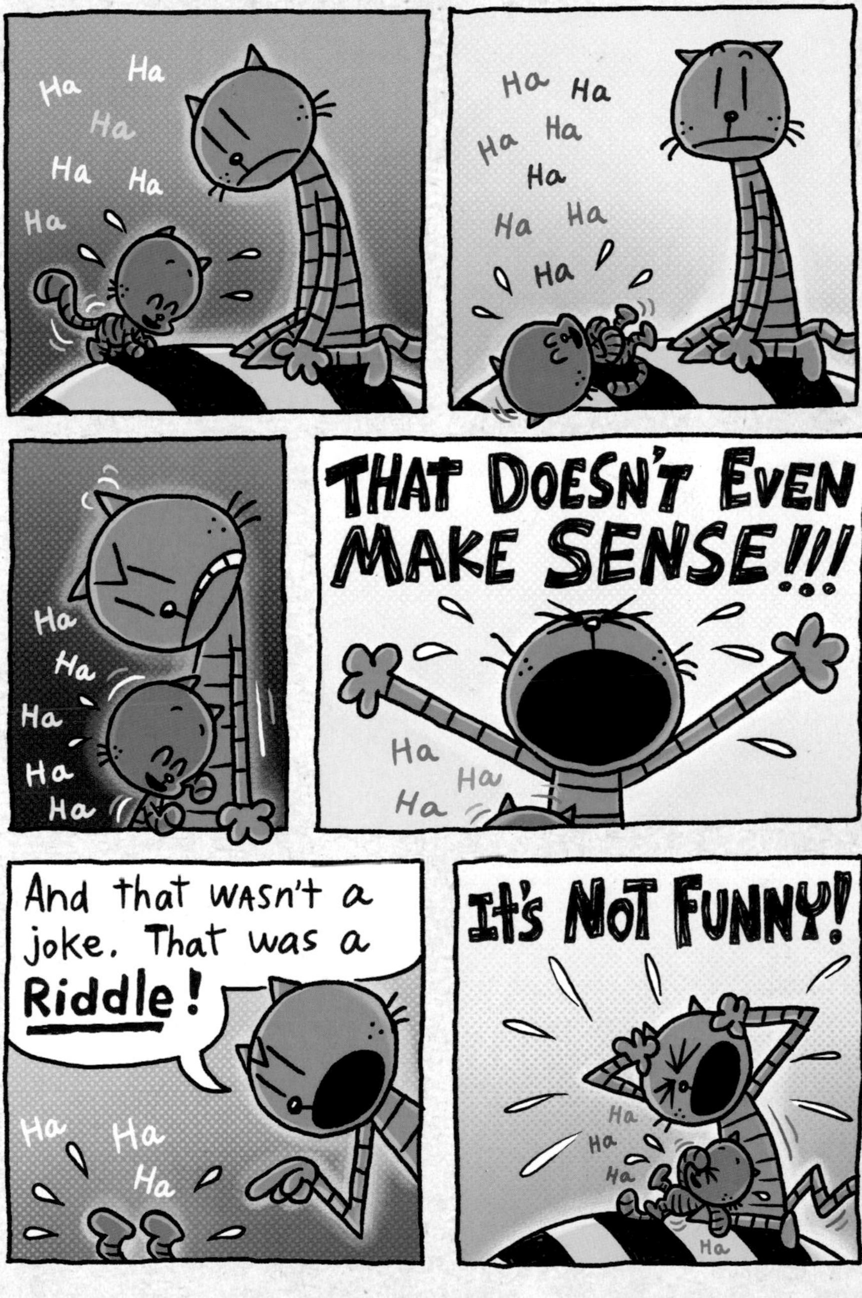

Ha Ha Ha Ha Ha Ha
Ha Ha Ha Ha Ha Ha Ha Ha
Ha Ha Ha Ha Ha
THAT DOESN'T EVEN MAKE SENSE!!!
Ha Ha Ha
And that WASN'T a joke. That was a Riddle!
Ha Ha Ha
IT'S NOT FUNNY!
Ha Ha Ha Ha

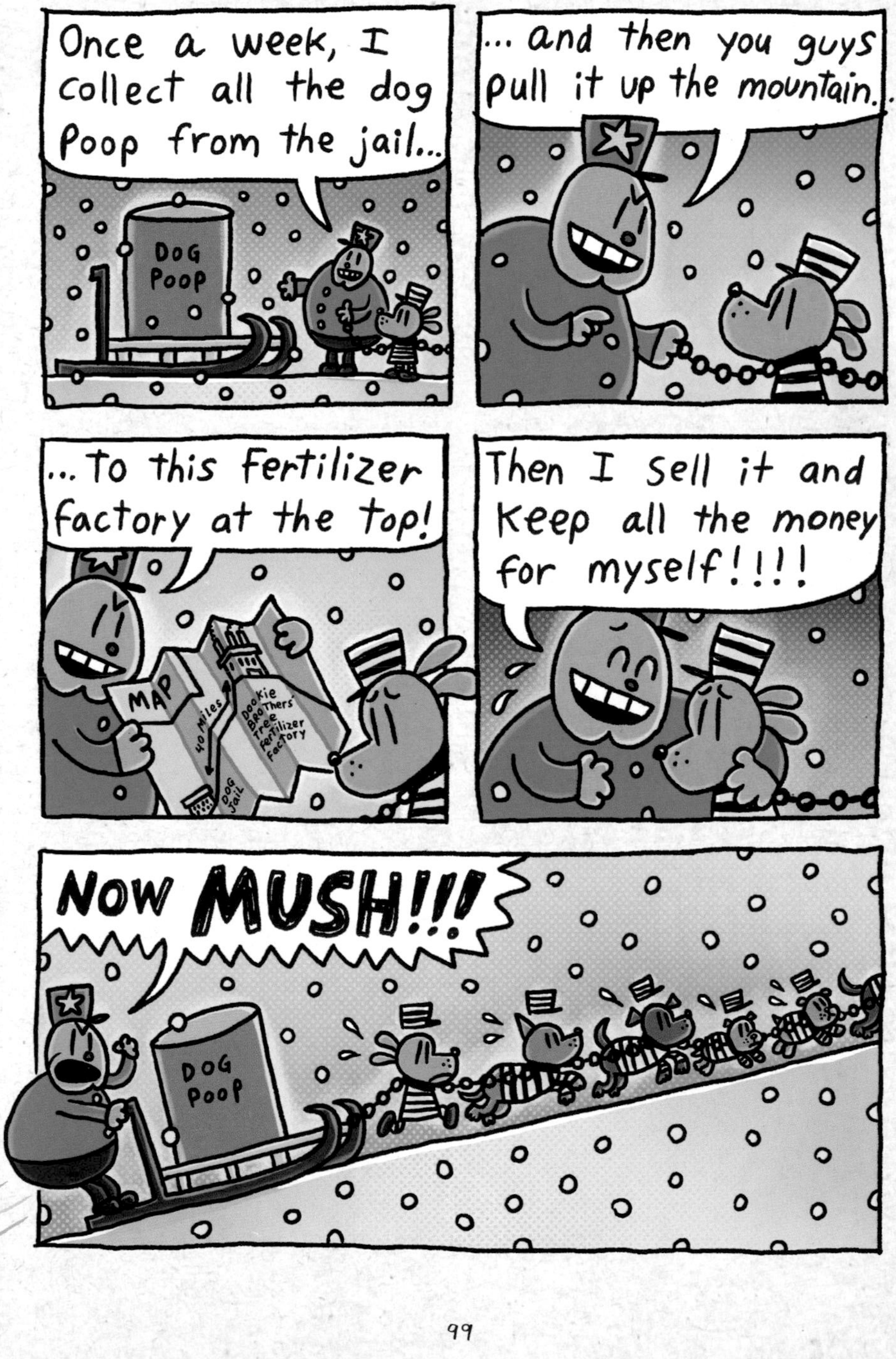
Once a week, I collect all the dog poop from the jail...
DOG POOP
...and then you guys pull it up the mountain...
...to this fertilizer factory at the top!
MAP
40 Miles
Dookie Brothers' Tree Fertilizer Factory
DOG JAIL
Then I sell it and keep all the money for myself!!!!
NOW MUSH!!!
DOG POOP

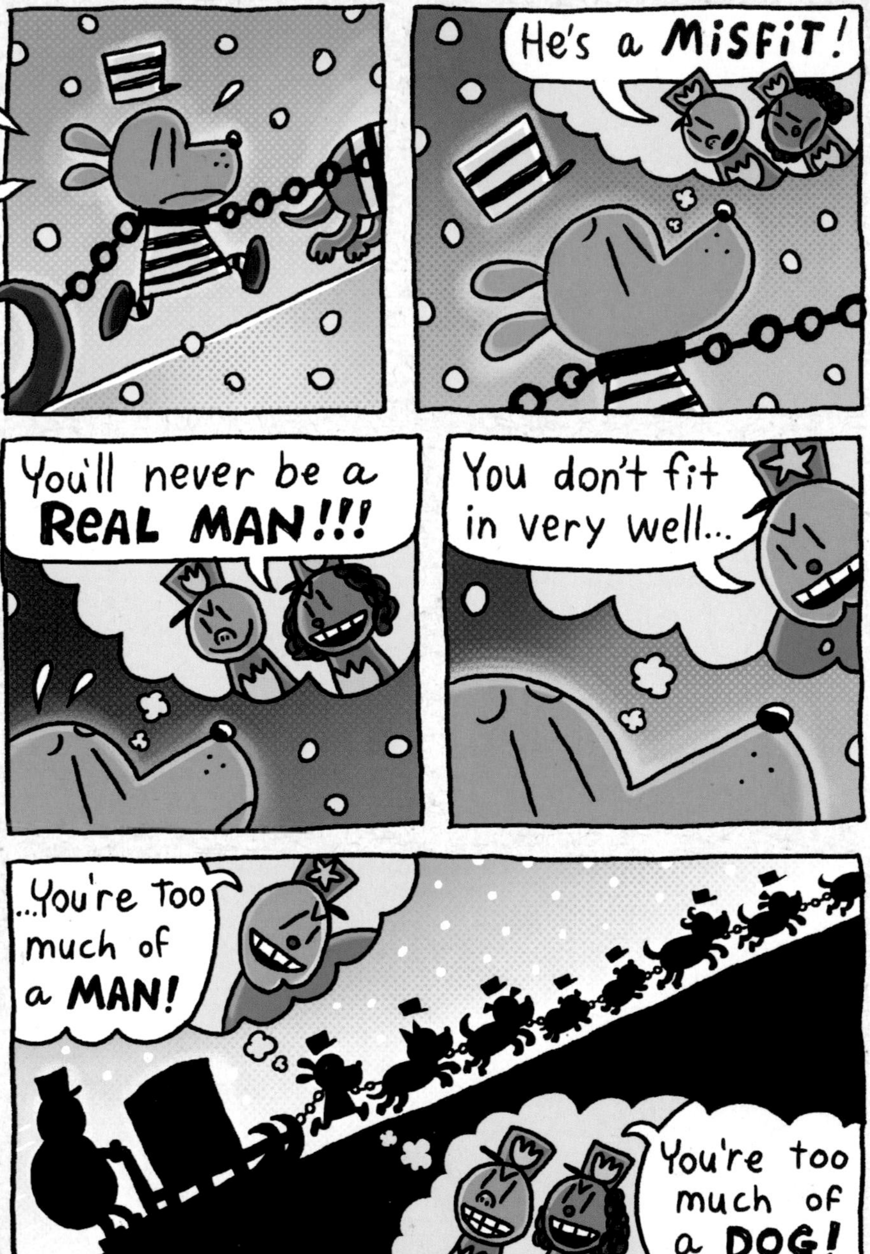
He's a MISFIT!
You'll never be a REAL MAN!!!
You don't fit in very well...
...You're too much of a MAN!
You're too much of a DOG!

Tree-House Comix Proudly Presents

Chapter 6
Even MORE STUFF HAPPENS!

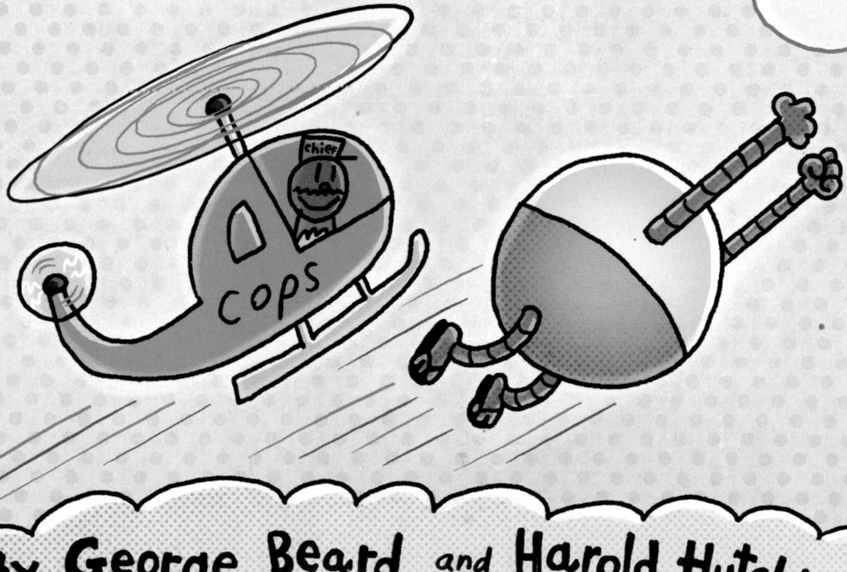
chief
COPS

By George Beard and Harold Hutchins

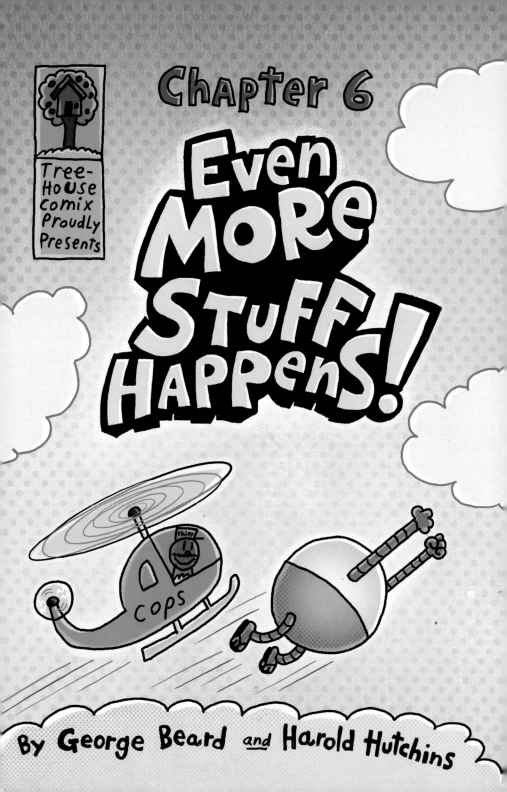

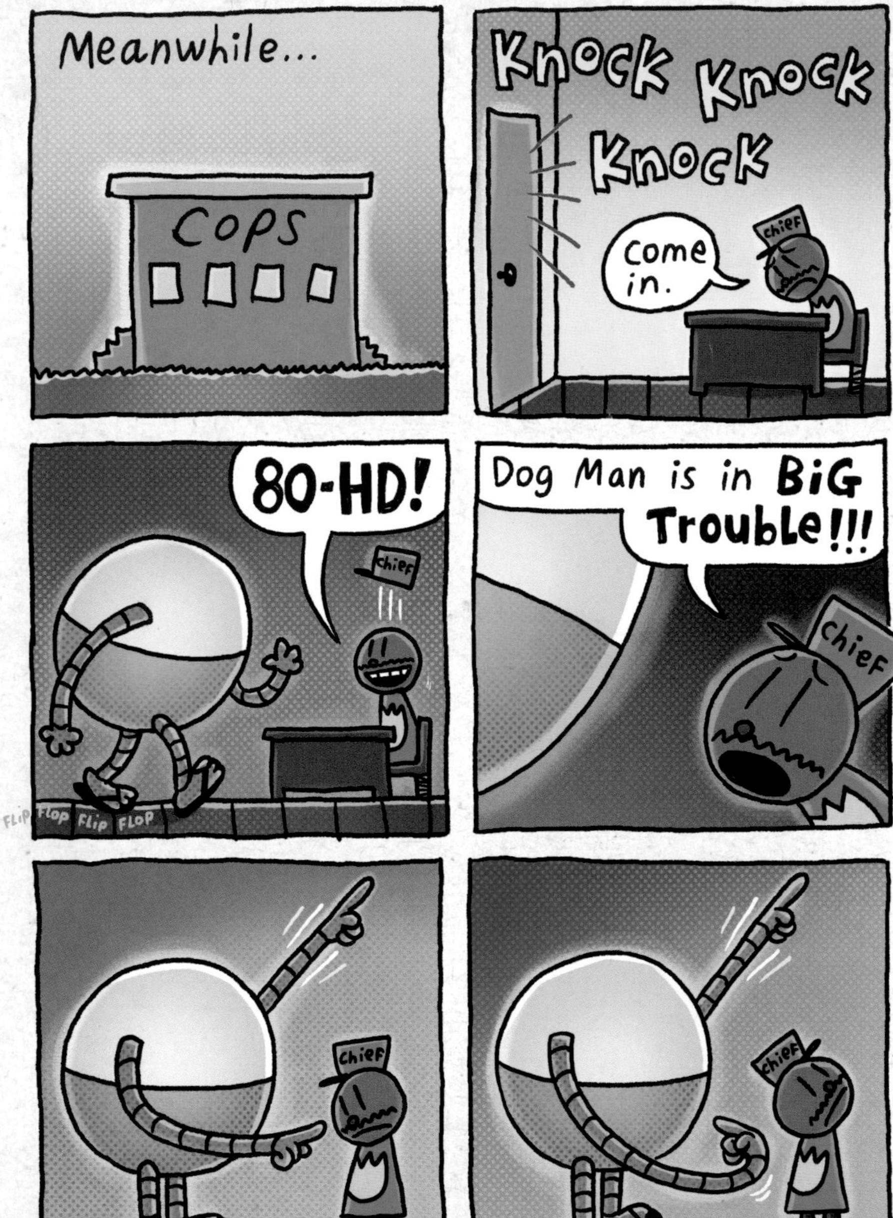
Meanwhile...
COPS
Knock Knock
Knock
Come in.
Chief
80-HD!
chief
FLIP FLOP FLIP FLOP
Dog Man is in BiG Trouble!!!
Chief
Chief
Chief

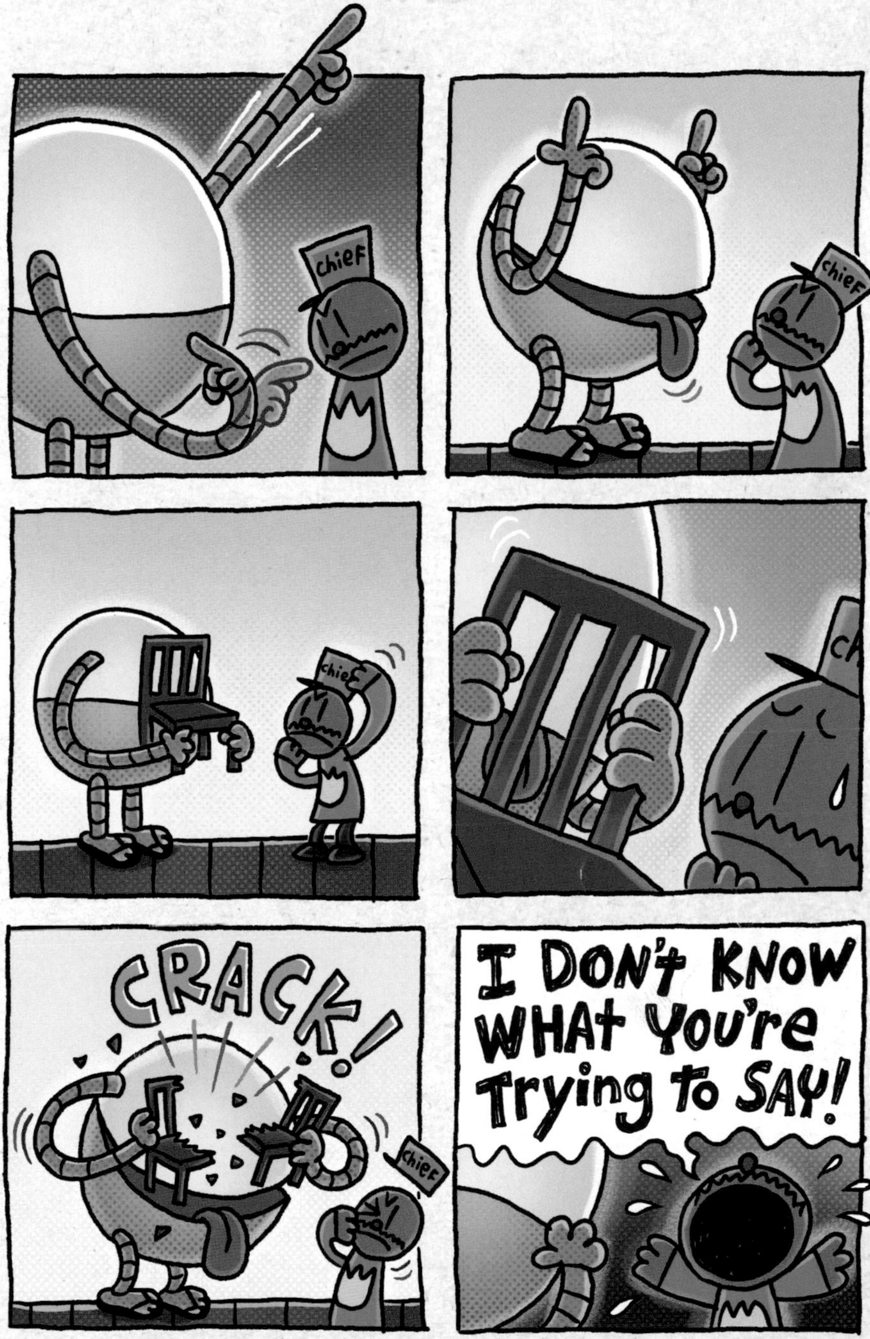
chief
chief
chief
CRACK!
chief
I DON'T KNOW WHAT YOU'RE TRYING TO SAY!

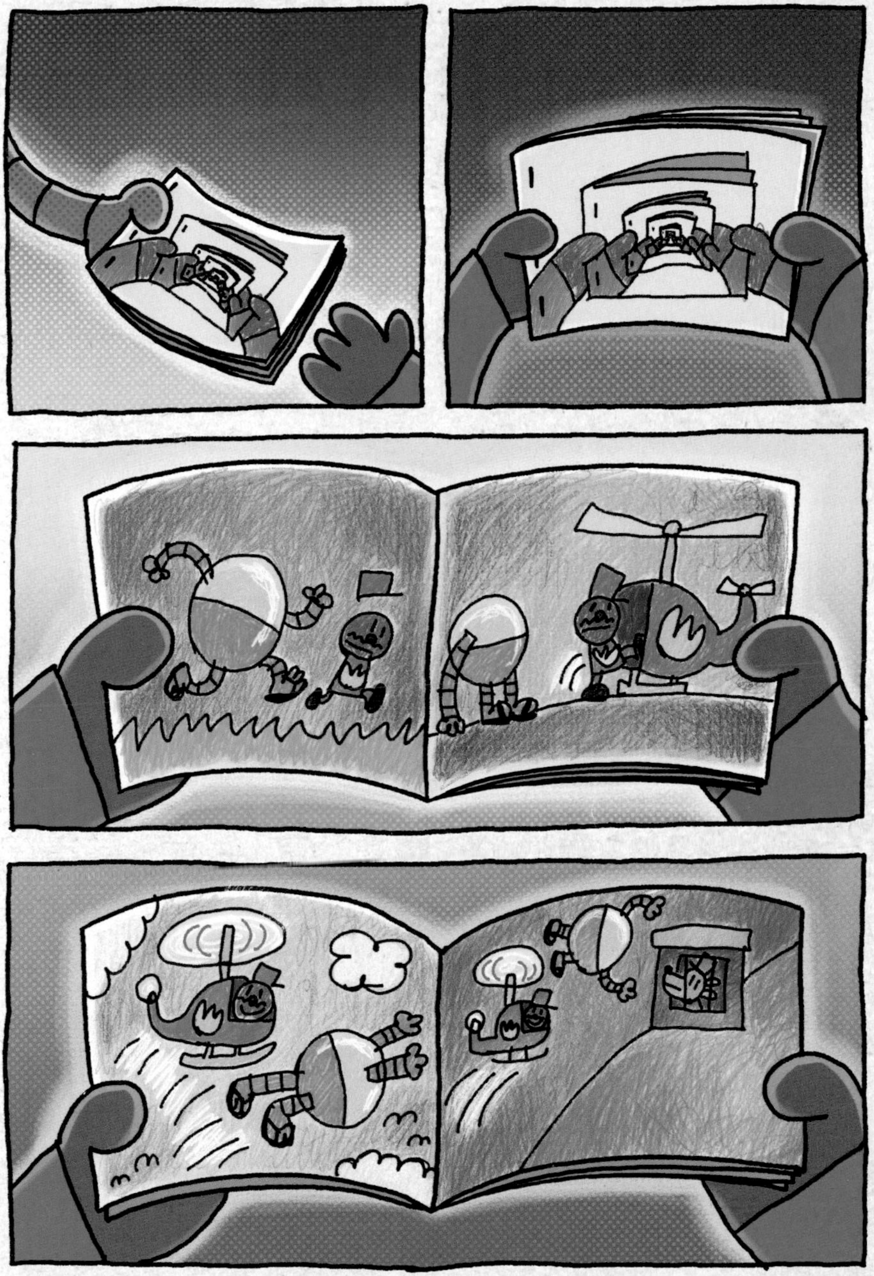

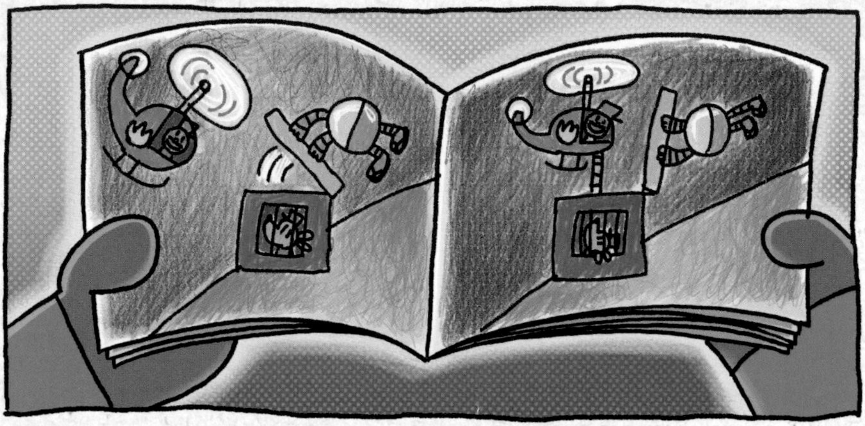

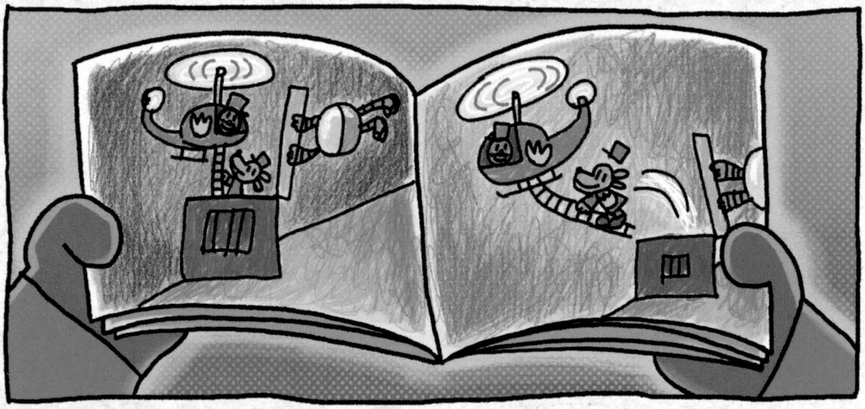

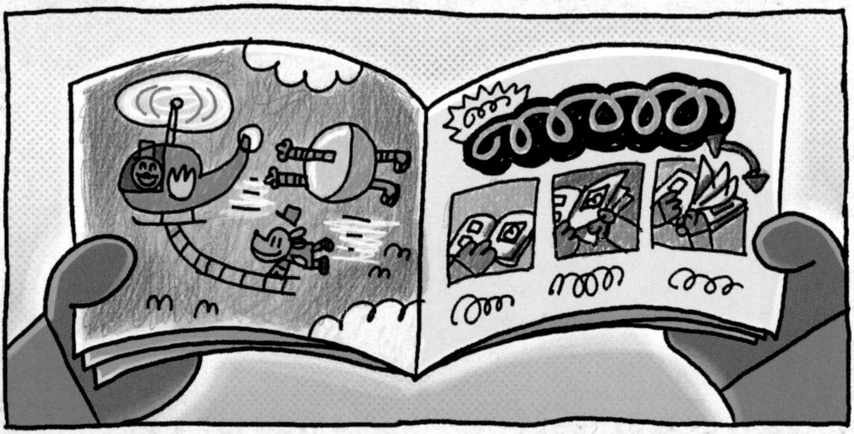

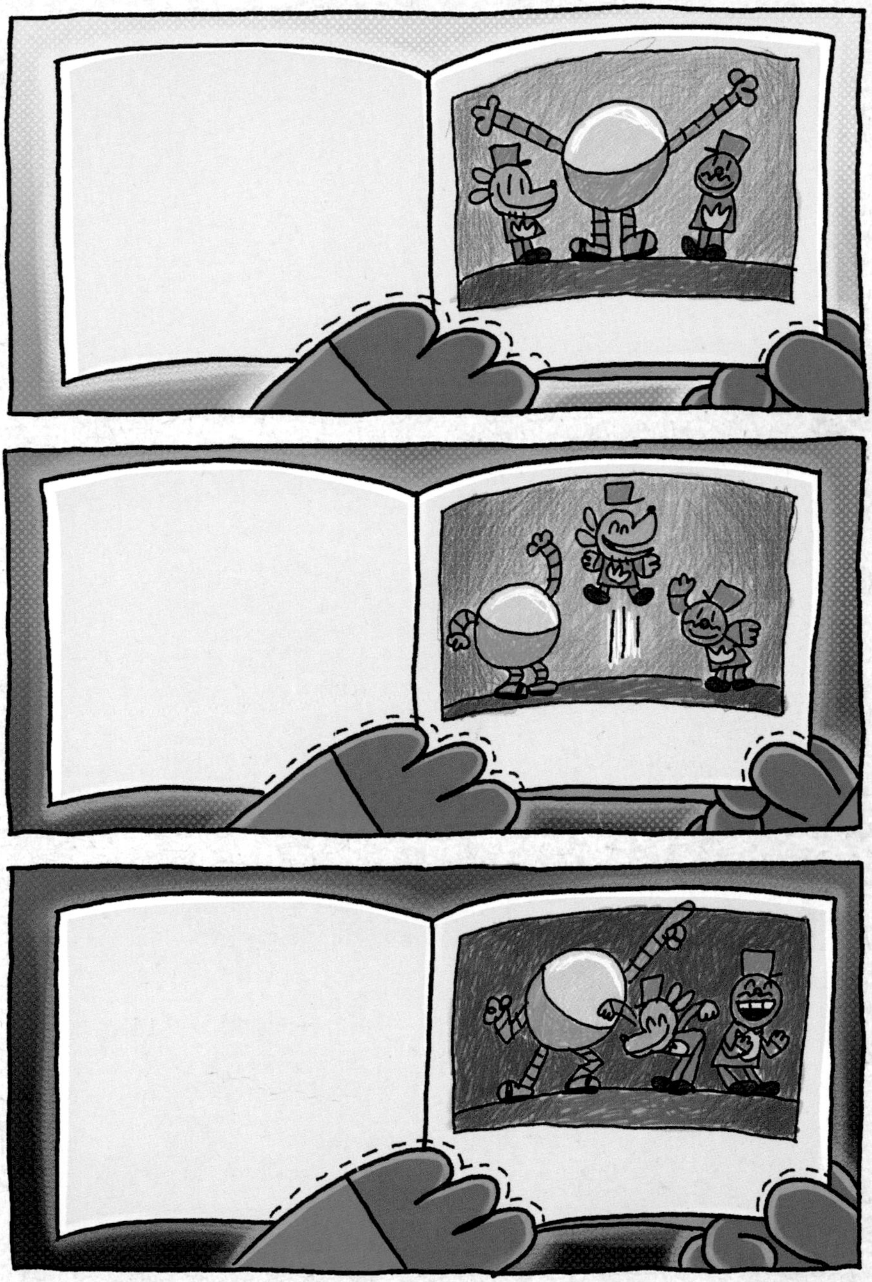

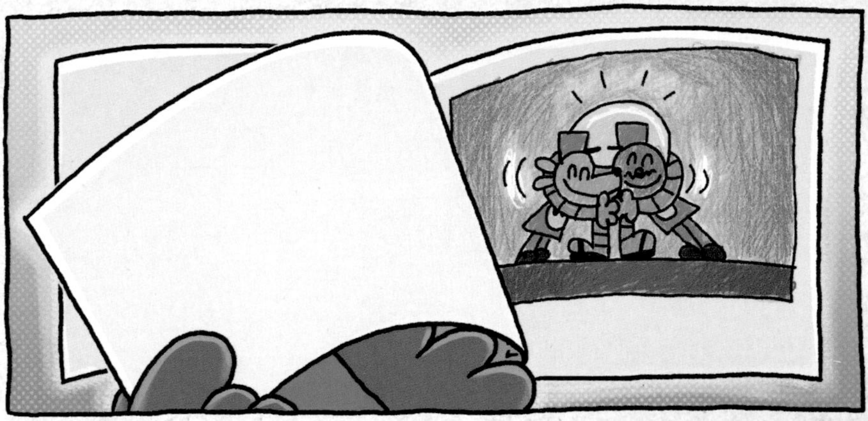

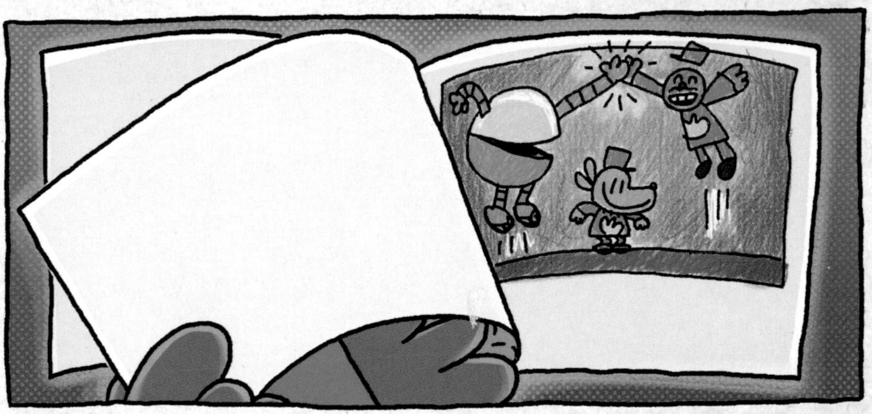

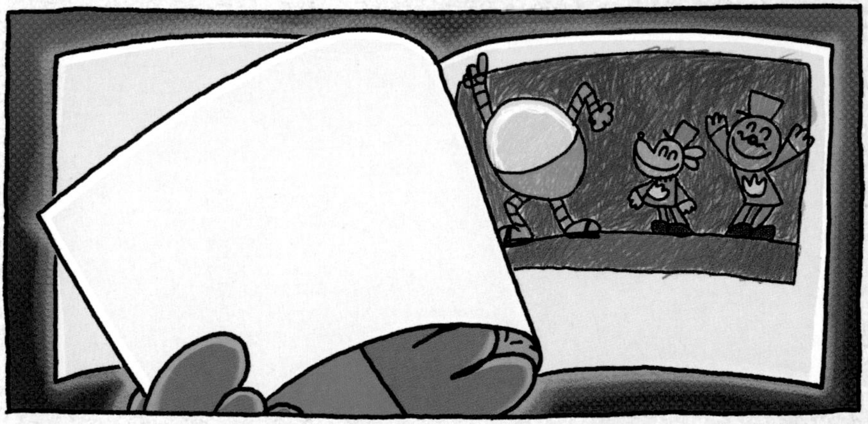

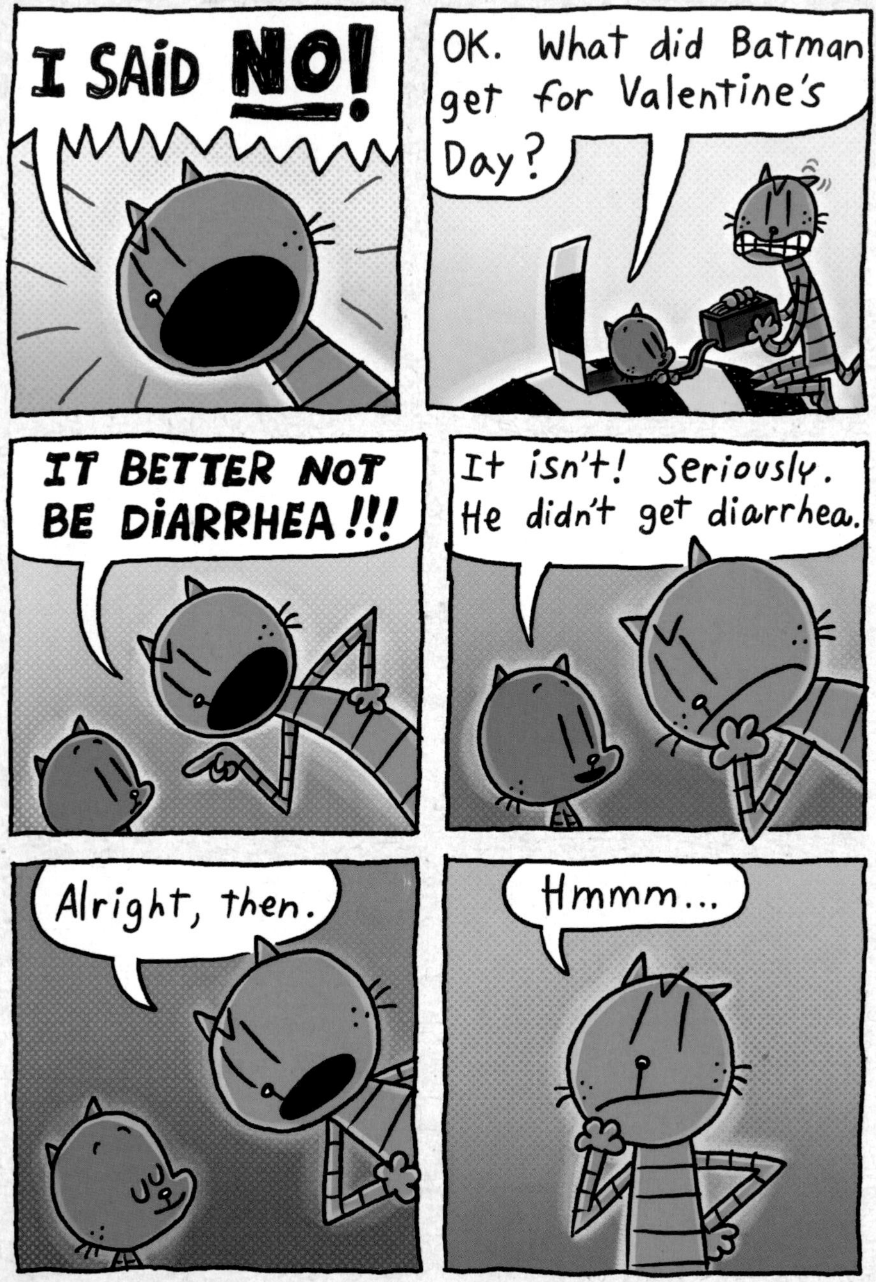
I SAID NO!
OK. What did Batman get for Valentine's Day?
IT BETTER NOT BE DIARRHEA!!!
It isn't! Seriously. He didn't get diarrhea.
Alright, then.
Hmmm...

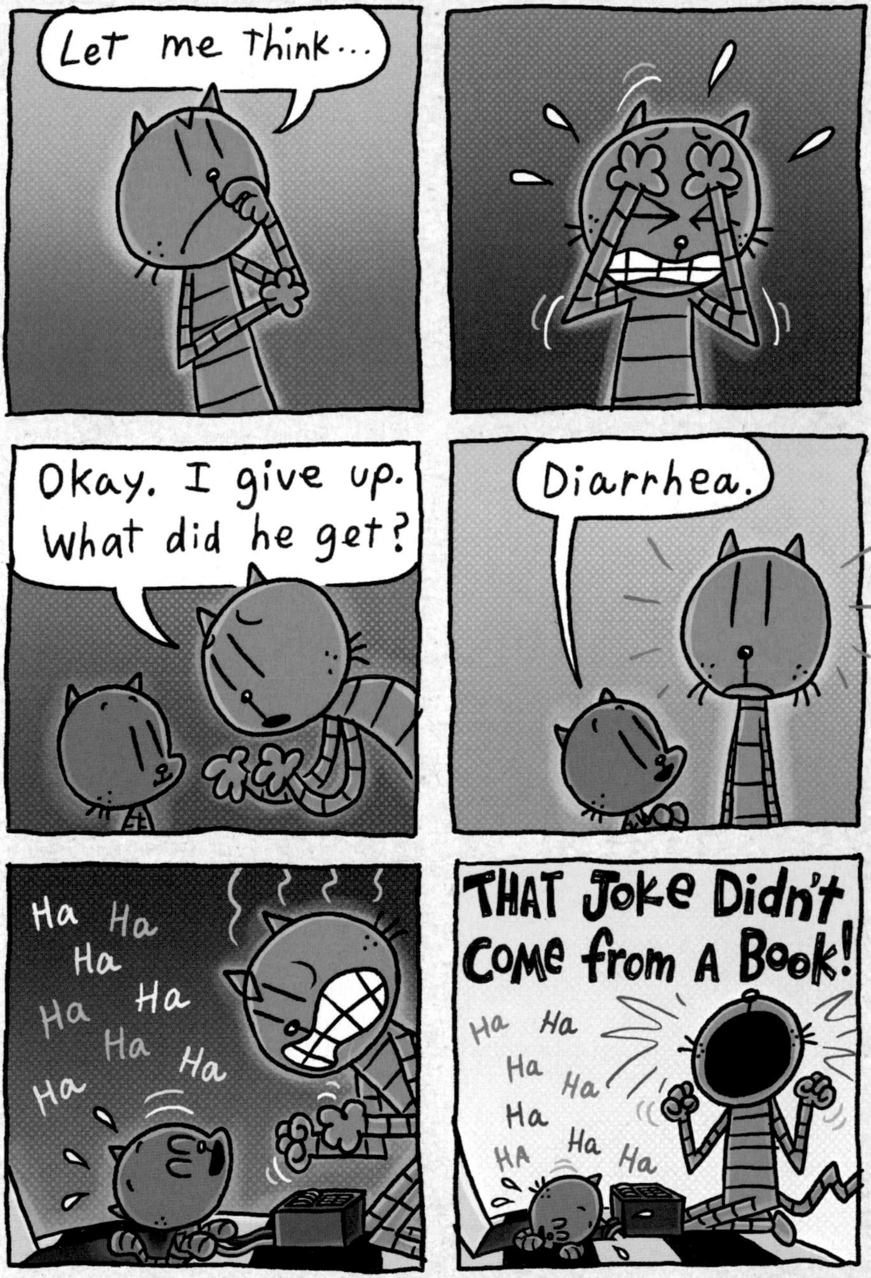
Let me Think...
Okay. I give up. What did he get?
Diarrhea.
Ha Ha Ha Ha Ha Ha Ha Ha
THAT JoKe Didn't Come from A Book!
Ha Ha Ha Ha Ha Ha Ha HA

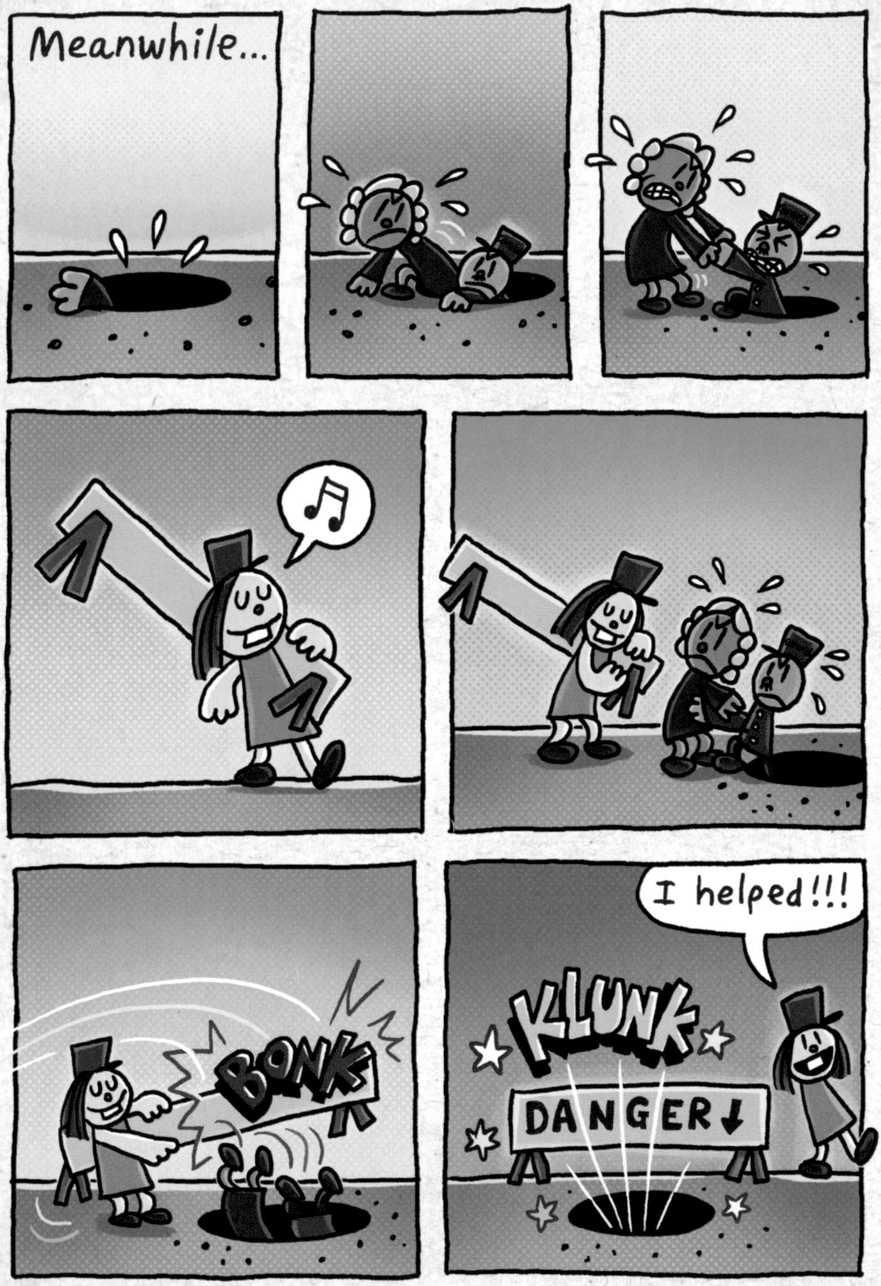
Meanwhile...
BONK
KLUNK
DANGER
I helped!!!

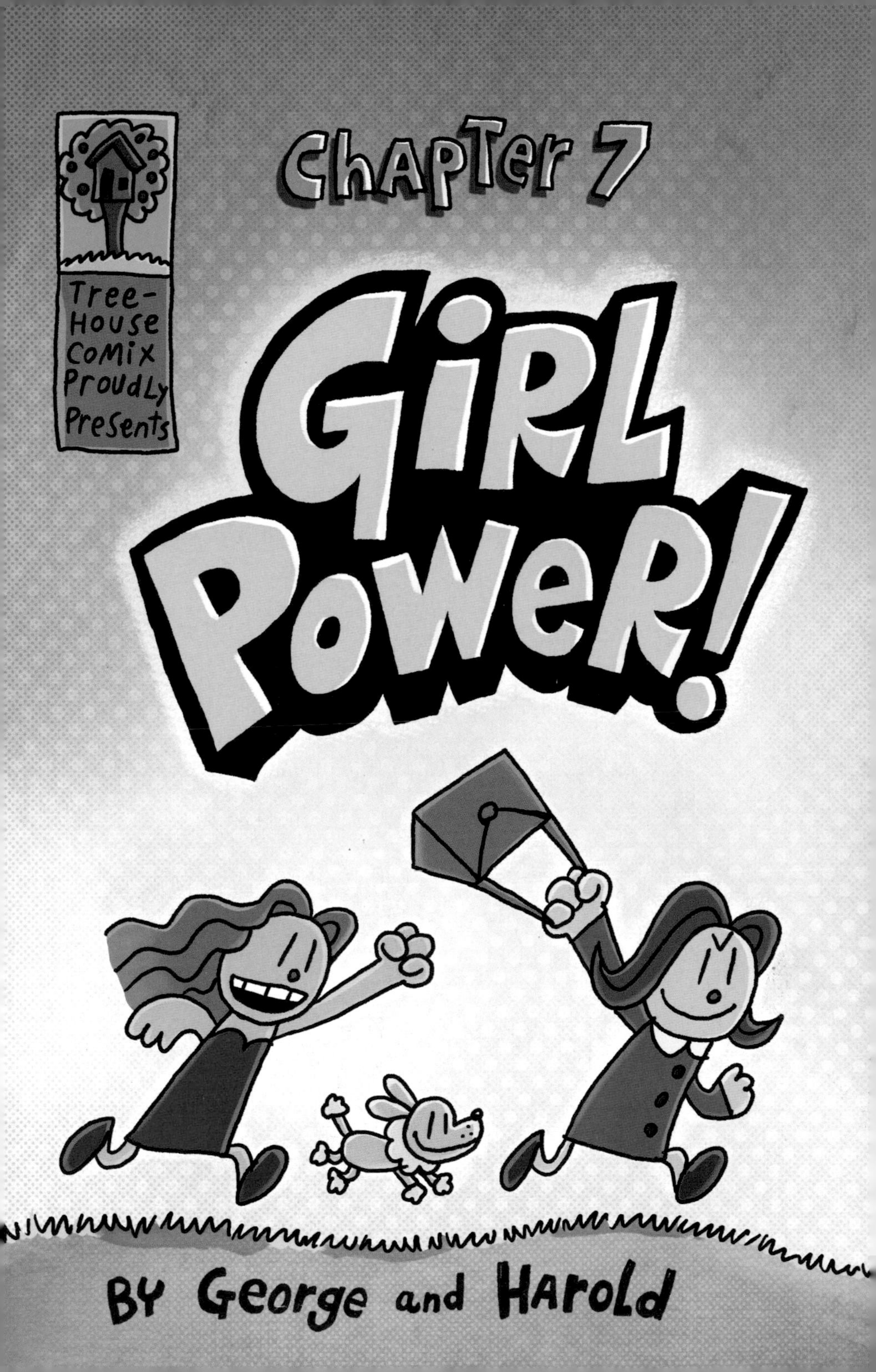
Tree-House Comix Proudly Presents
Chapter 7
Girl Power!
By George and Harold

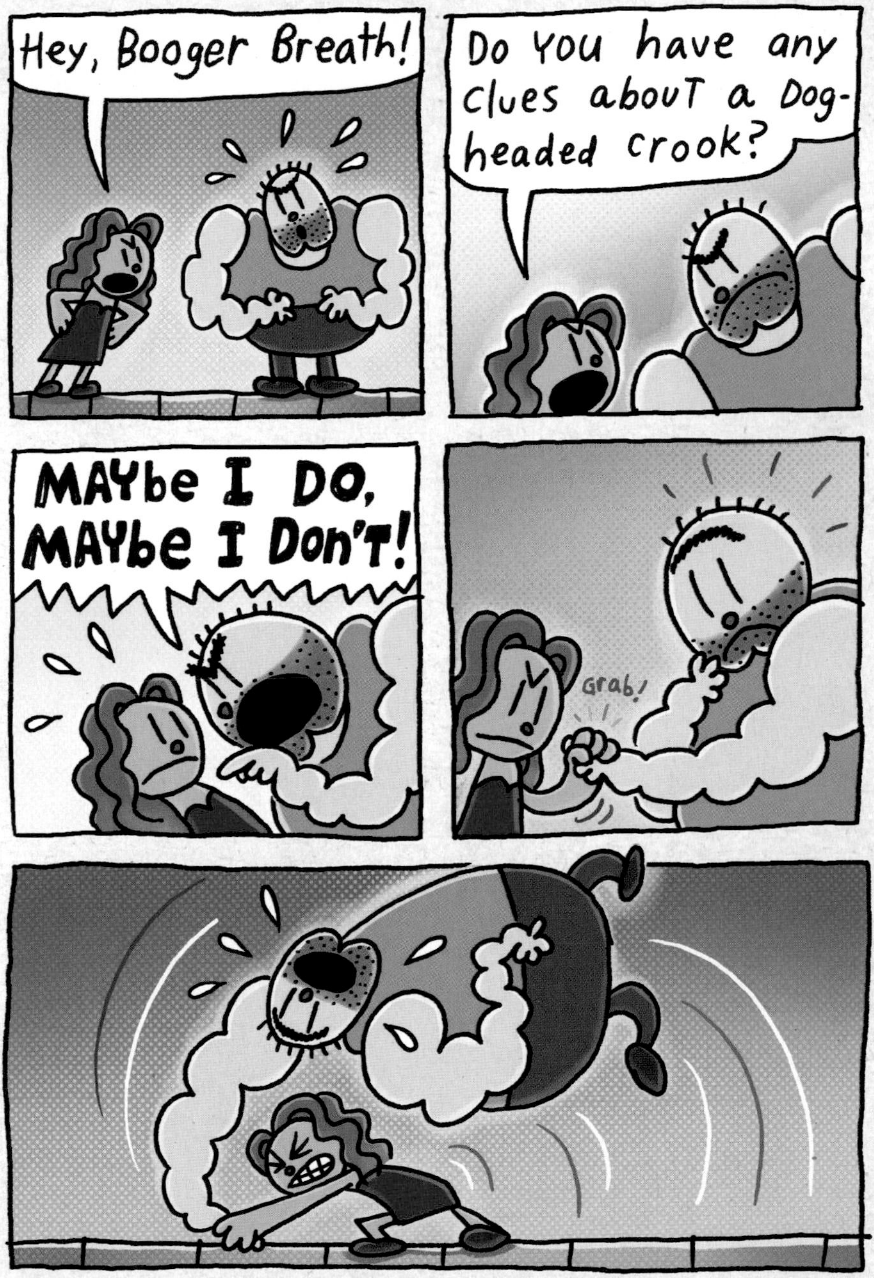
Hey, Booger Breath!
Do you have any clues about a Dog-headed crook?
MAYbe I DO, MAYbe I DON'T!
Grab!

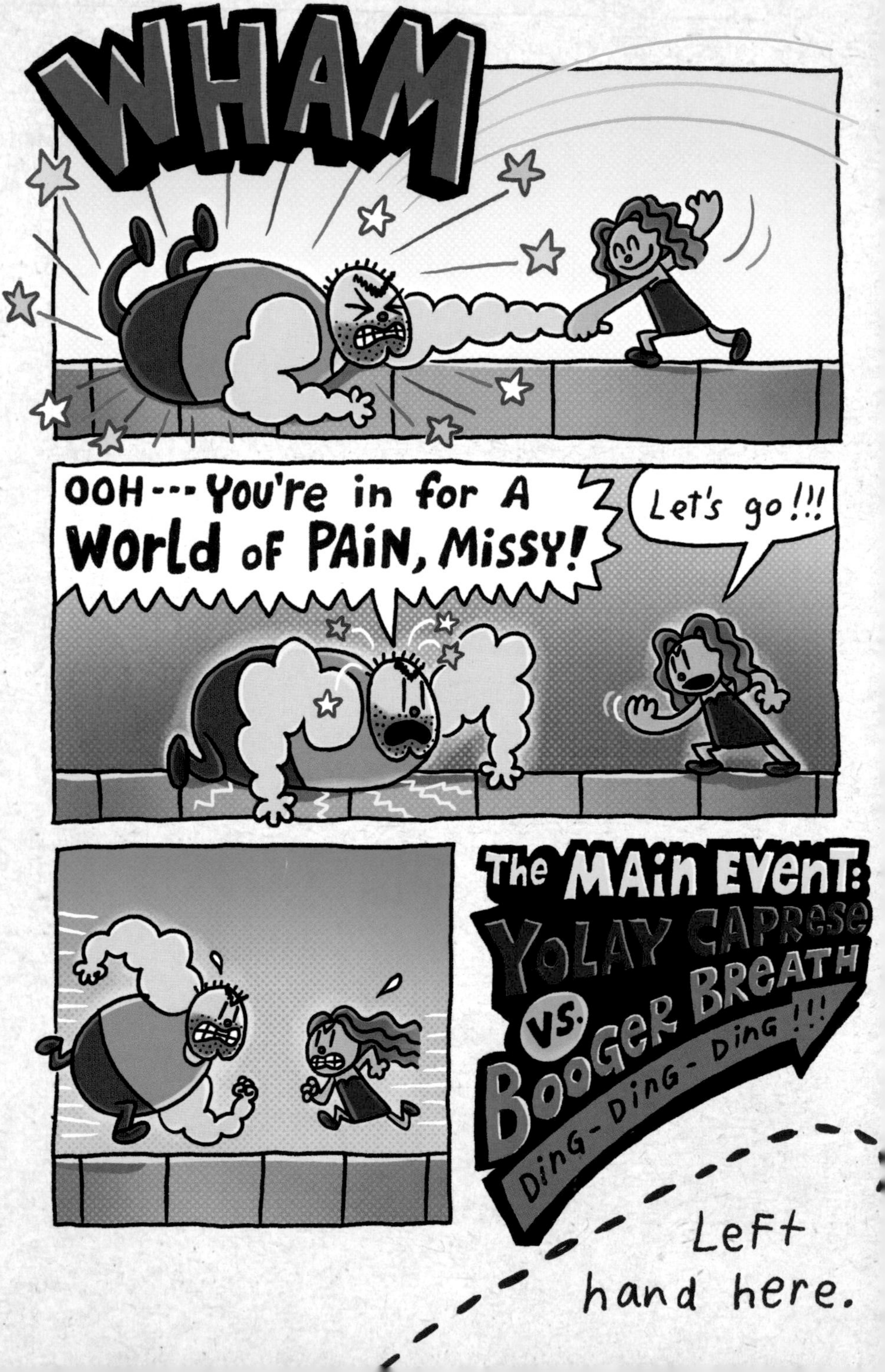
WHAM
OOH --- You're in for A WORLD OF PAIN, MISSY!
Let's go!!!
The MAIN EVENT:
YOLAY CAPRESE
VS.
BOOGER BREATH
DING-DING-DING!!!
Left hand here.

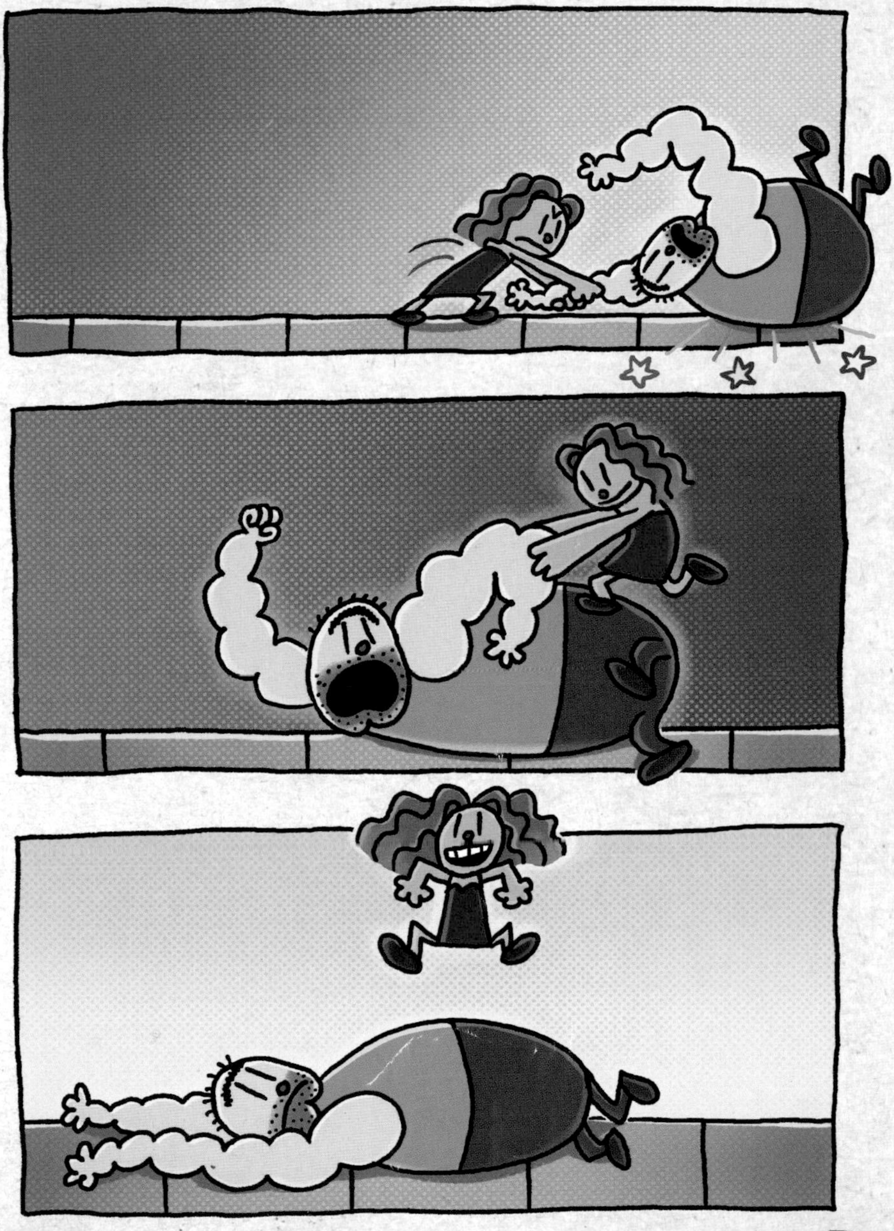

Right
Thumb
here.

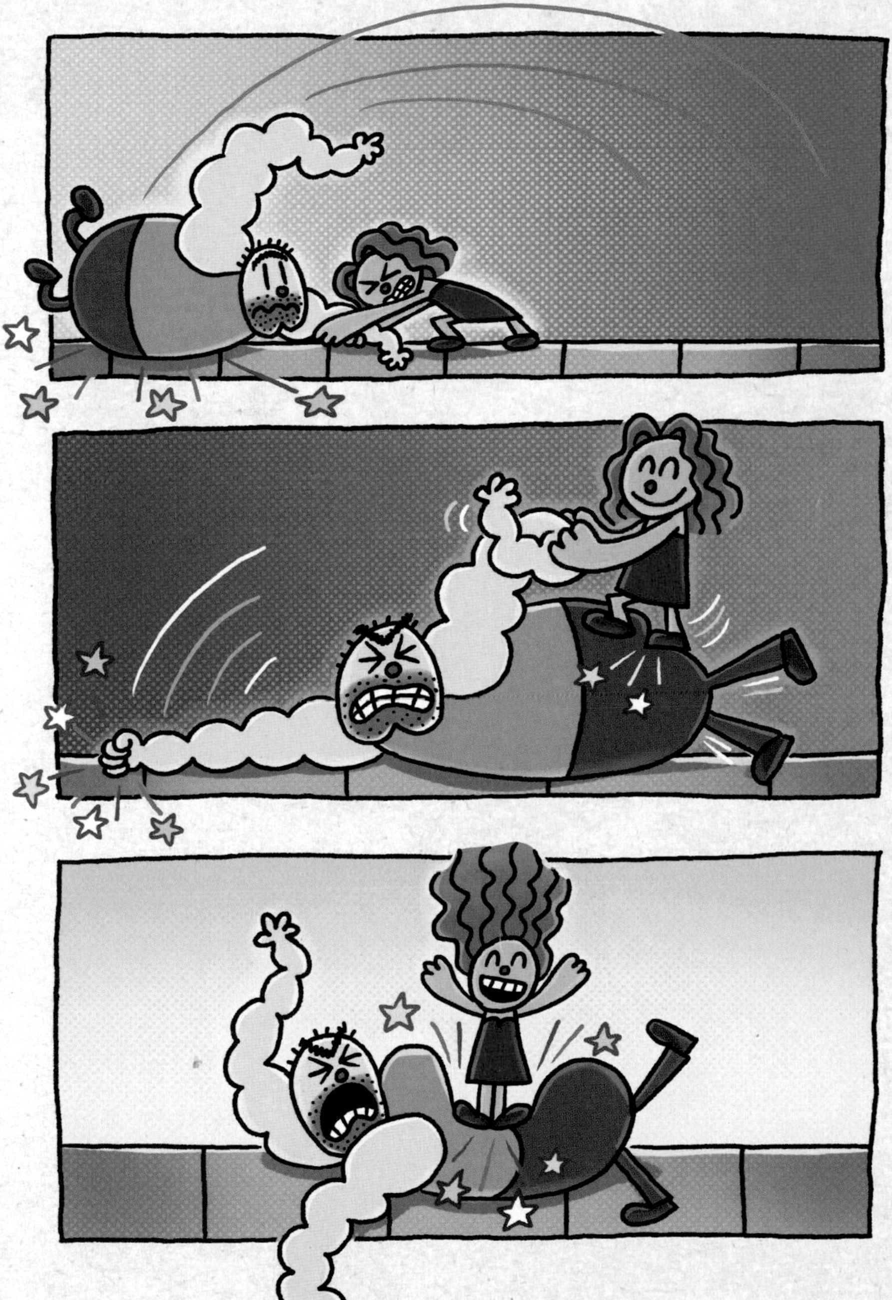

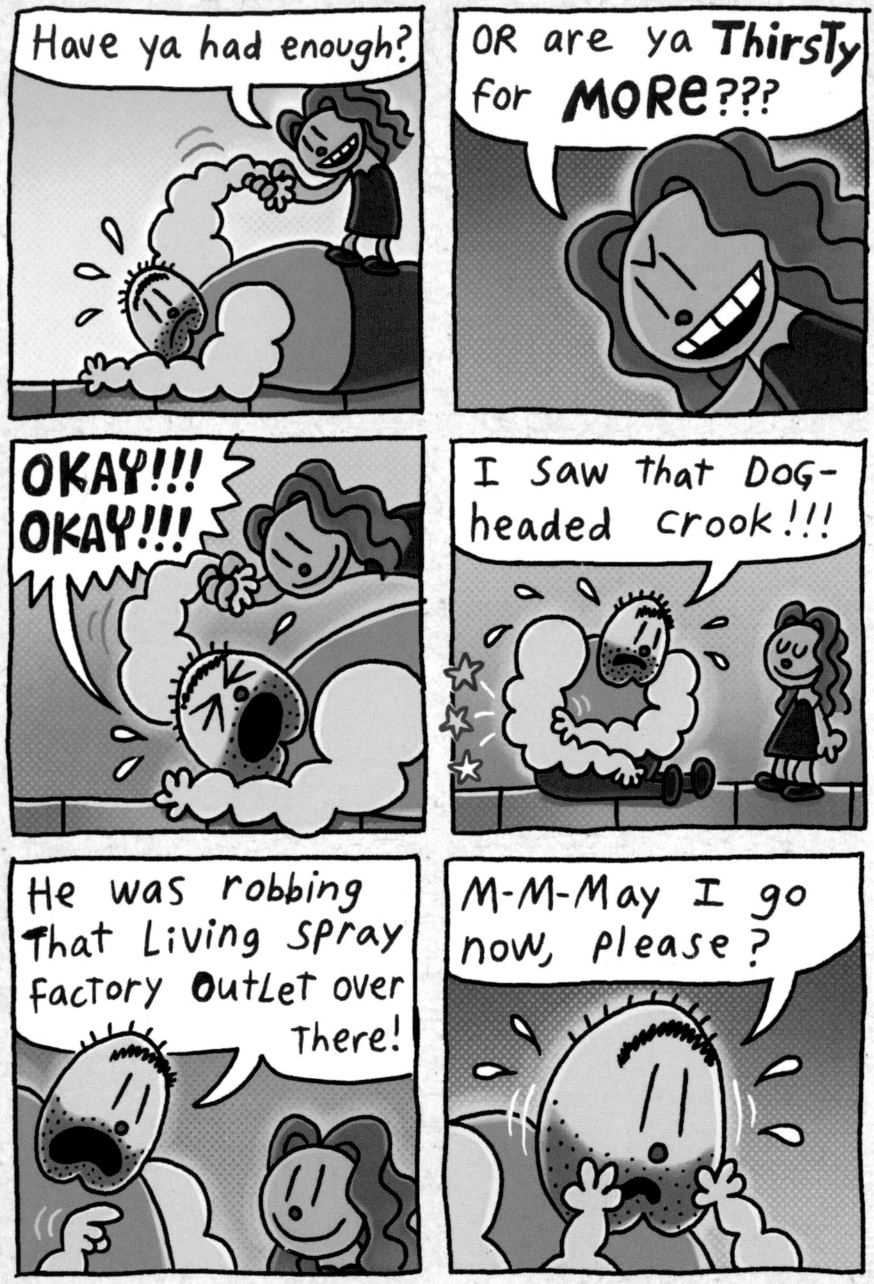
Have ya had enough?
OR are ya ThirsTy for MORE???
OKAY!!! OKAY!!!
I saw that DOG-headed crook!!!
He was robbing That Living Spray Factory OutLet over There!
M-M-May I go now, please?

Chapter 8

Help is on the Way

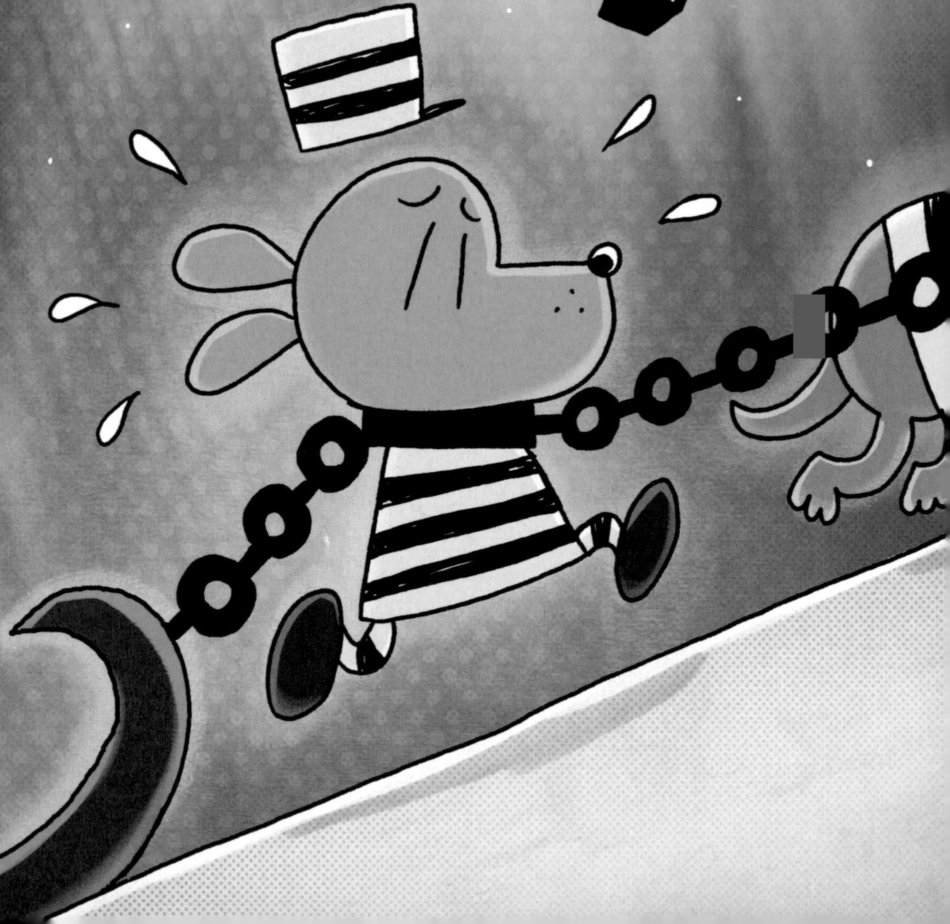

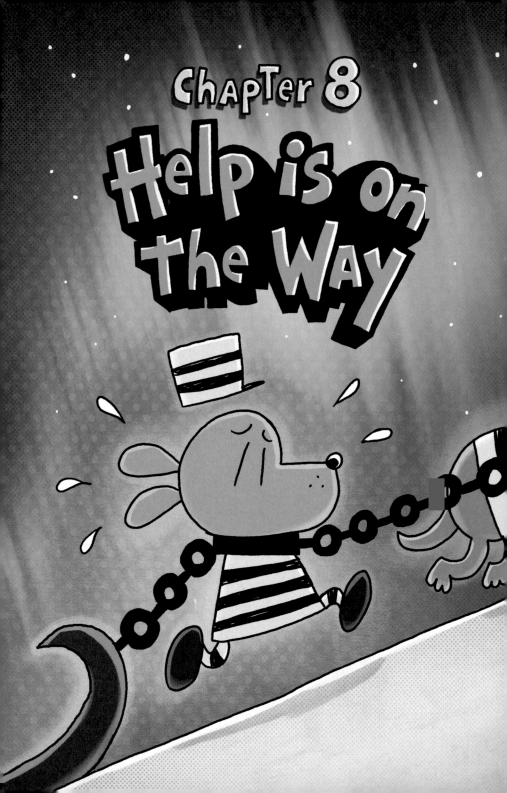

126

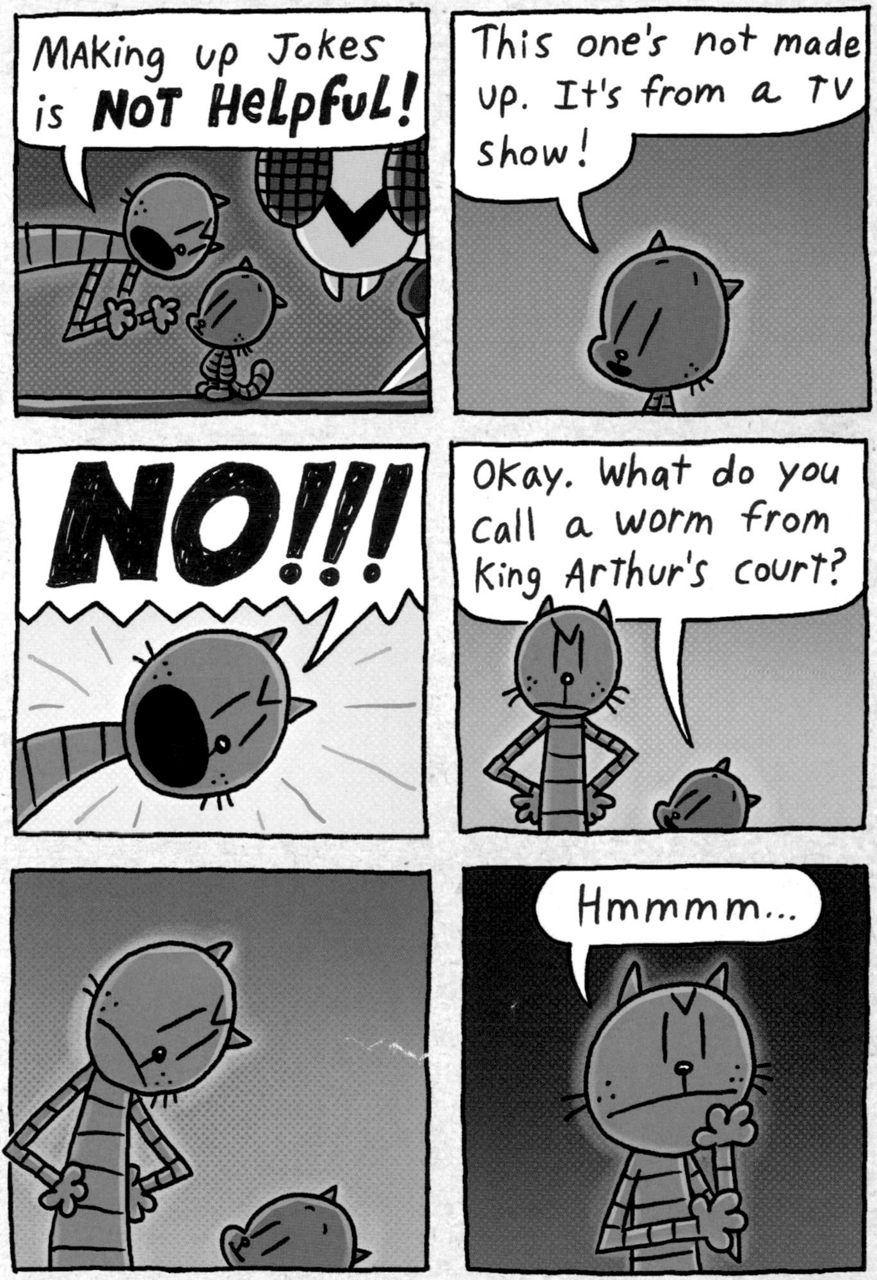
MAKing up Jokes is NOT HeLpfuL!
This one's not made up. It's from a TV show!
NO!!!
OKay. What do you call a worm from King Arthur's court?
Hmmmm...

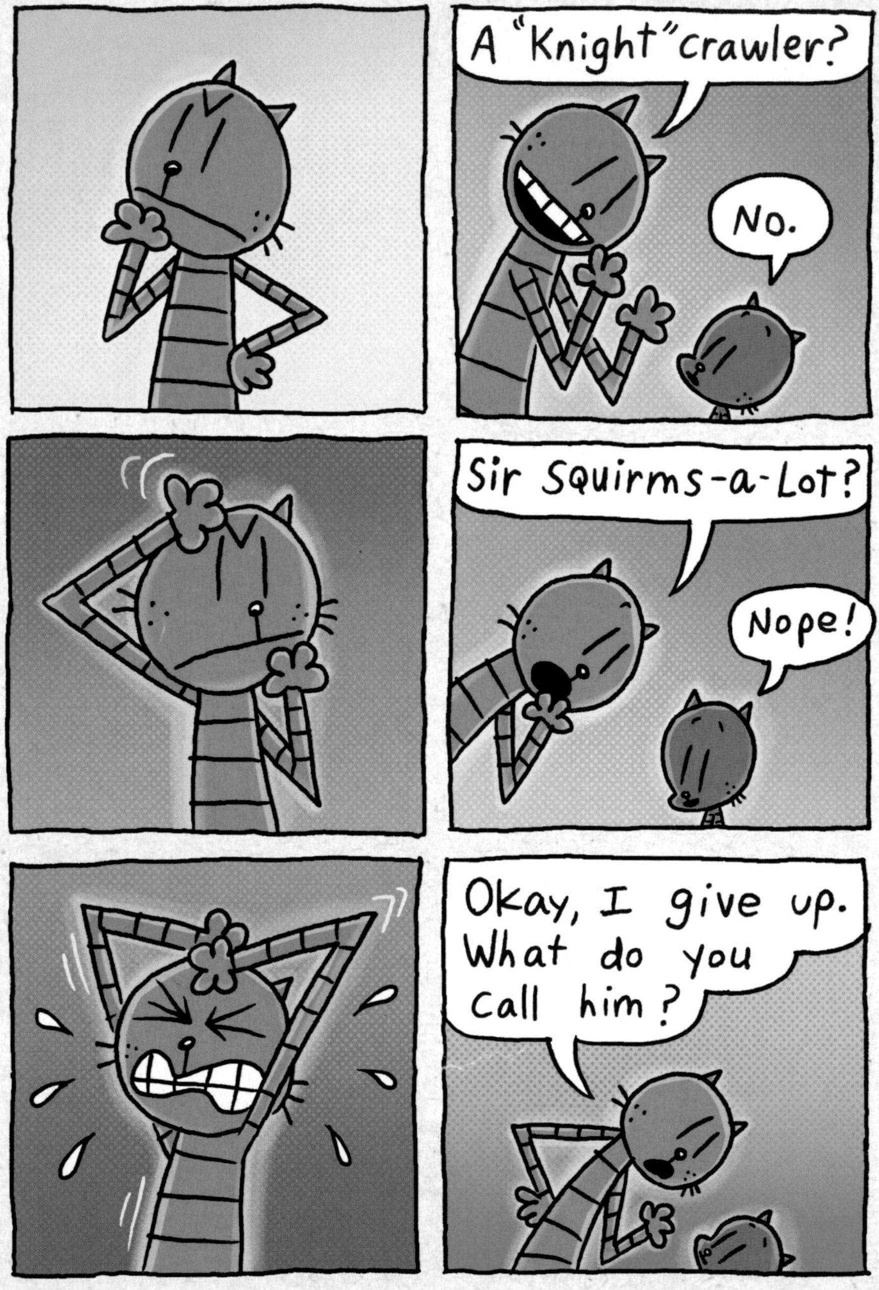
A "Knight" crawler?
No.
Sir Squirms-a-Lot?
Nope!
Okay, I give up. What do you call him?

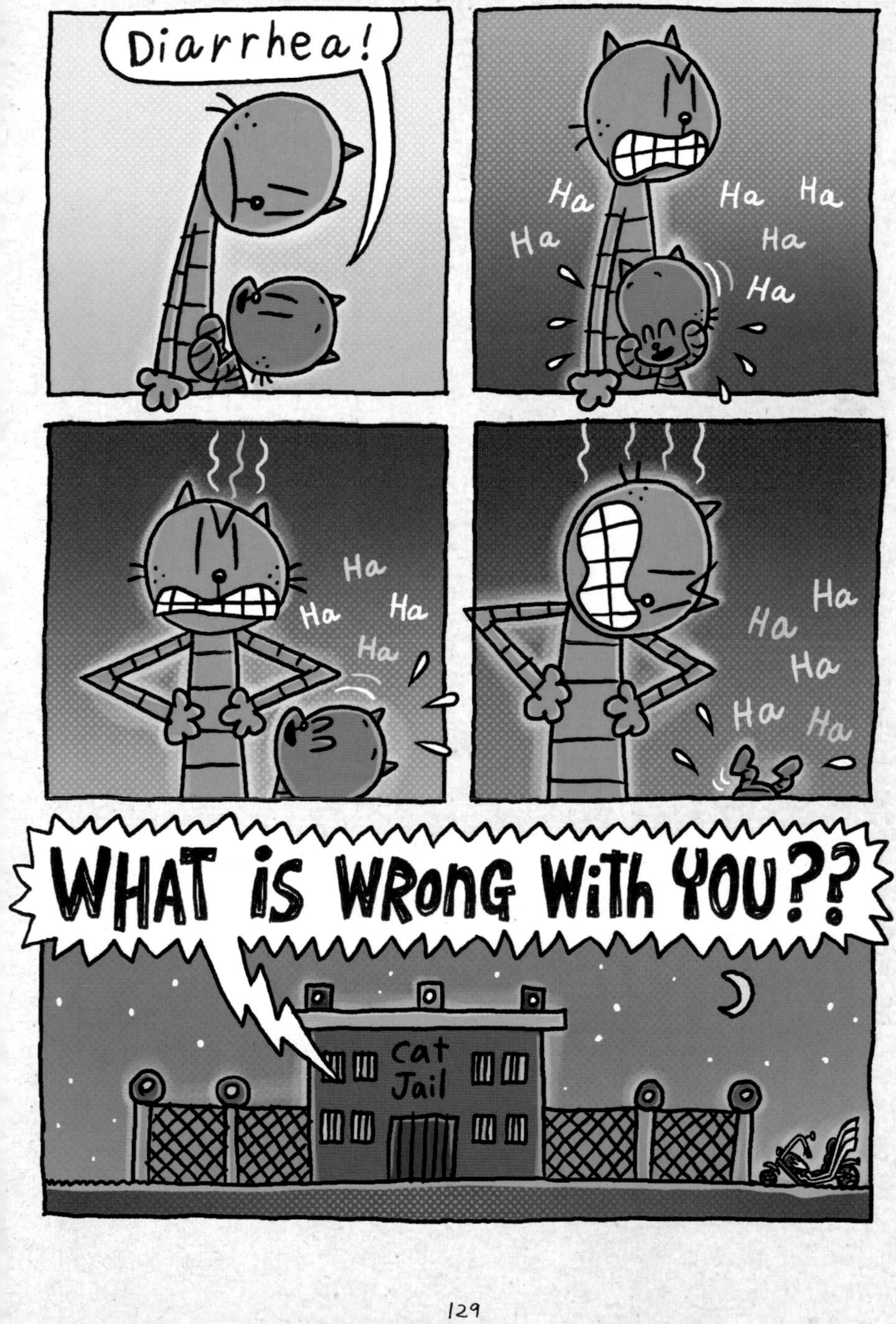
Diarrhea!
Ha
Ha
Ha
Ha
Ha
Ha
Ha
Ha
Ha
Ha
Ha
Ha
Ha
Ha
Ha
WHAT is WRONG With YOU??
Cat Jail

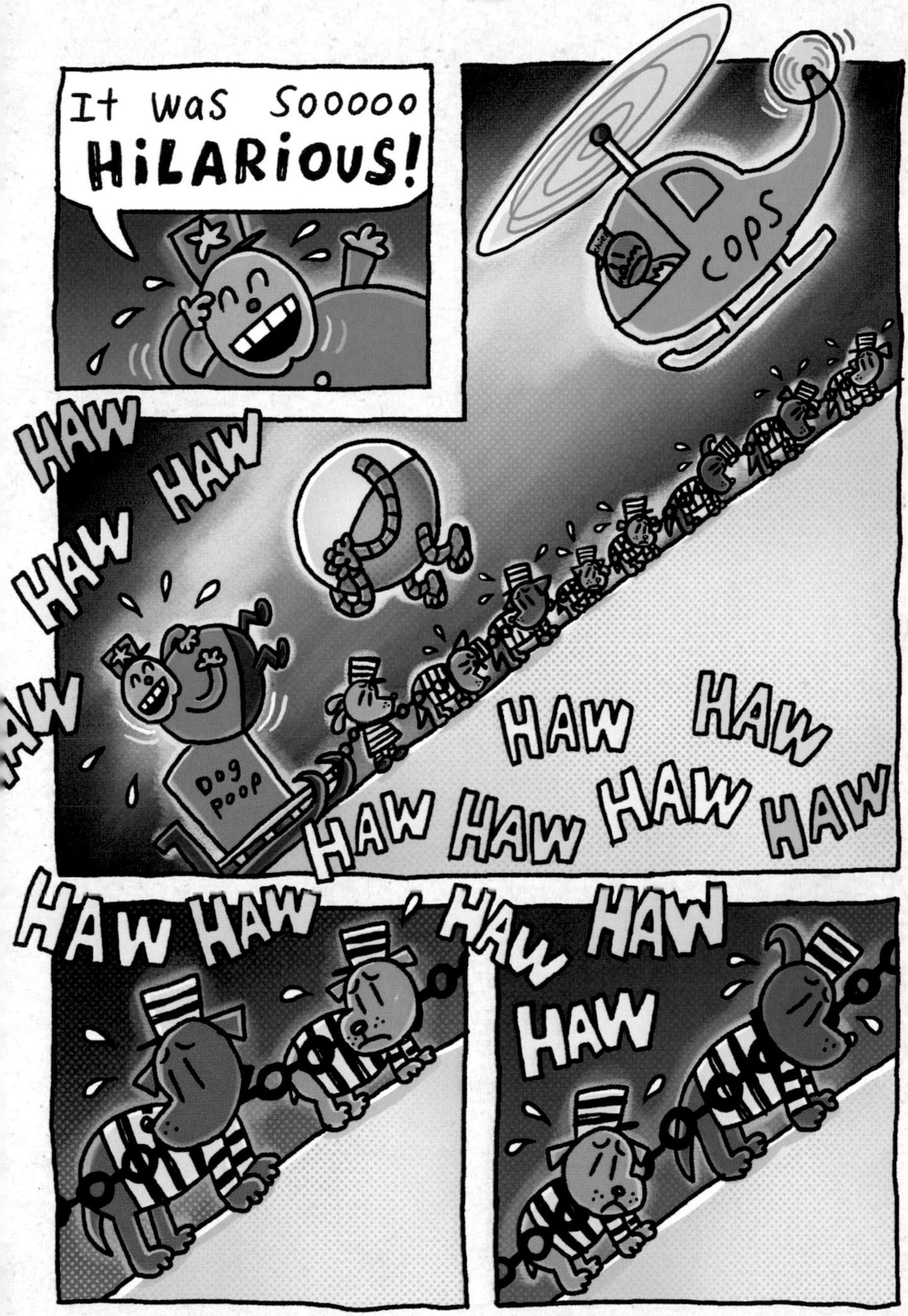

It was Sooooo HiLARiOUS!
COPS
HAW
HAW HAW
HAW
HAW
Dog Poop
HAW HAW
HAW HAW HAW HAW
HAW HAW
HAW HAW
HAW

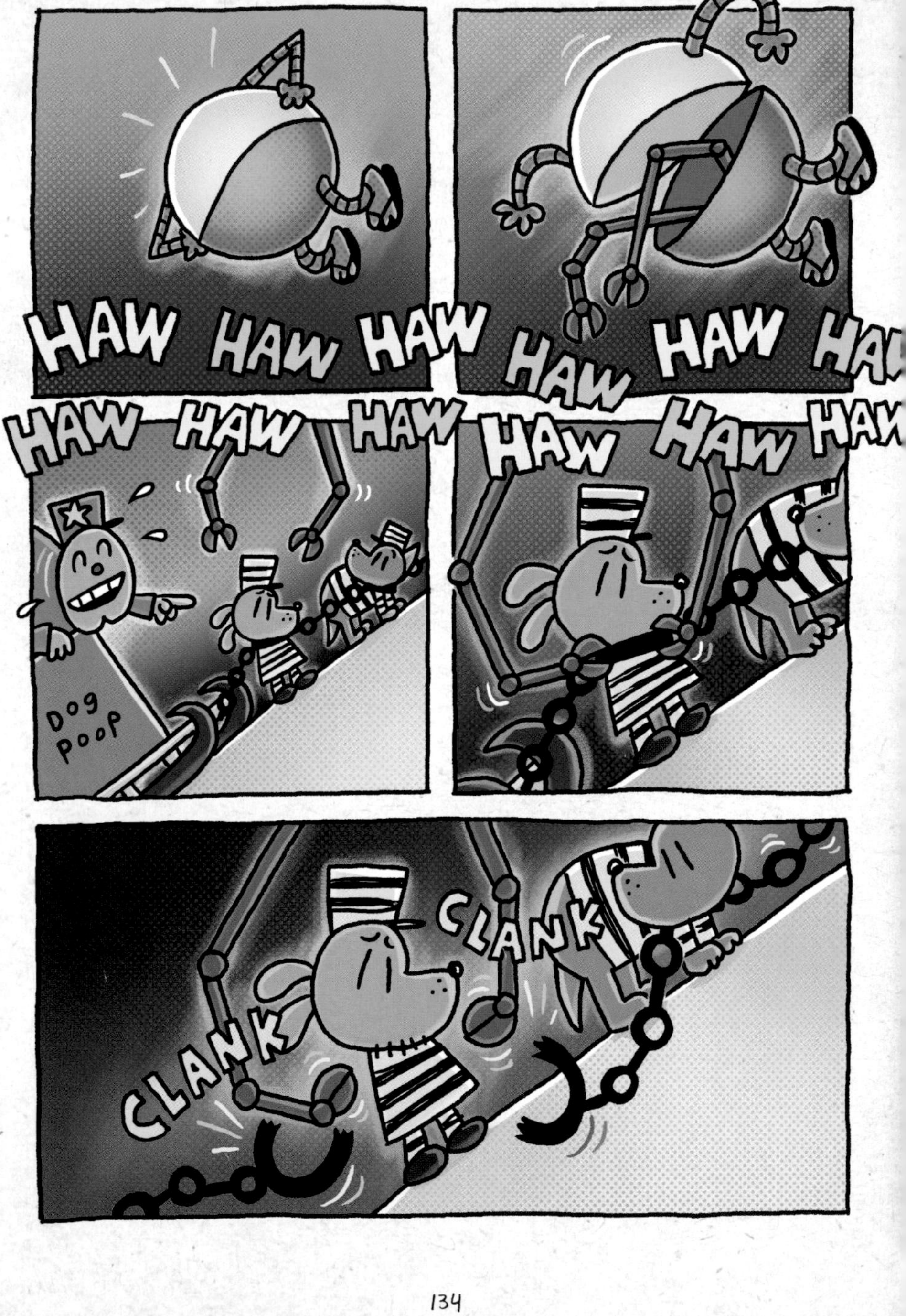
HAW HAW HAW HAW HAW HA
HAW HAW HAW HAW HAW HAW
DOG POOP
CLANK
CLANK

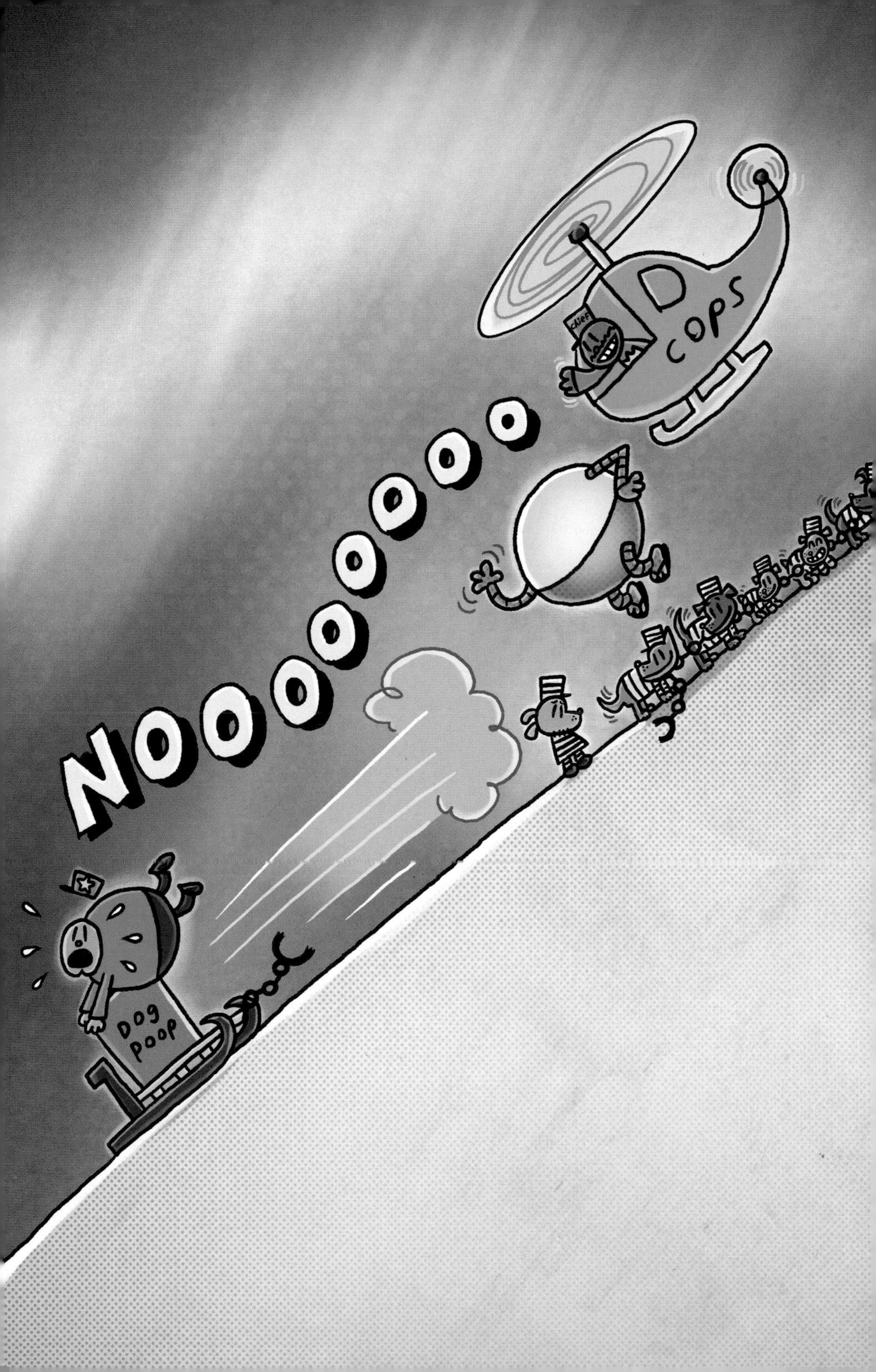

NOOOOOOOOO
CHIEF
COPS
DOG POOP

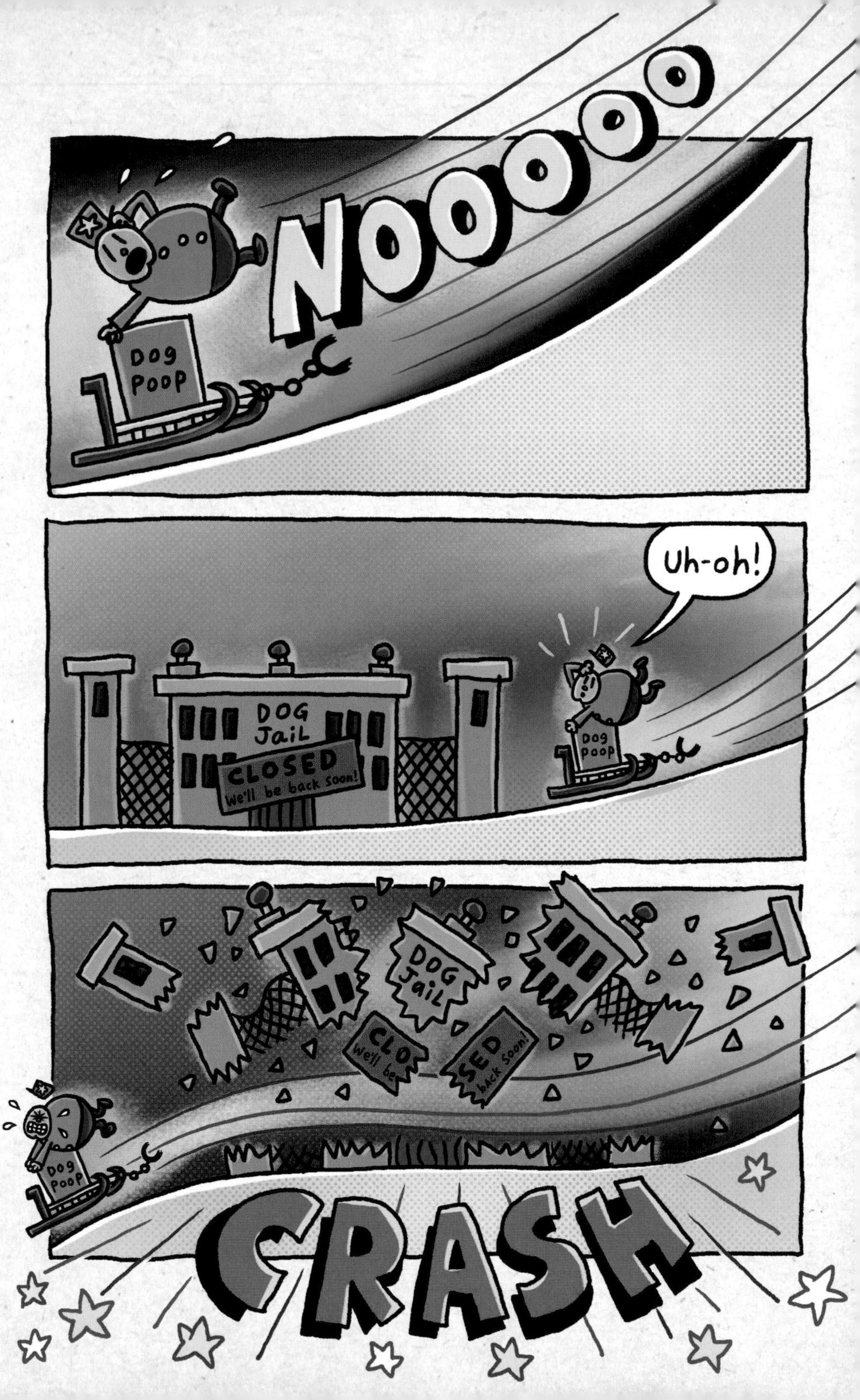

NOOOOOO
DOG POOP
DOG Jail
CLOSED
We'll be back Soon!
Uh-oh!
Dog Poop
DOG Jail
CLO We'll be
SED back Soon!
Dog Poop
CRASH

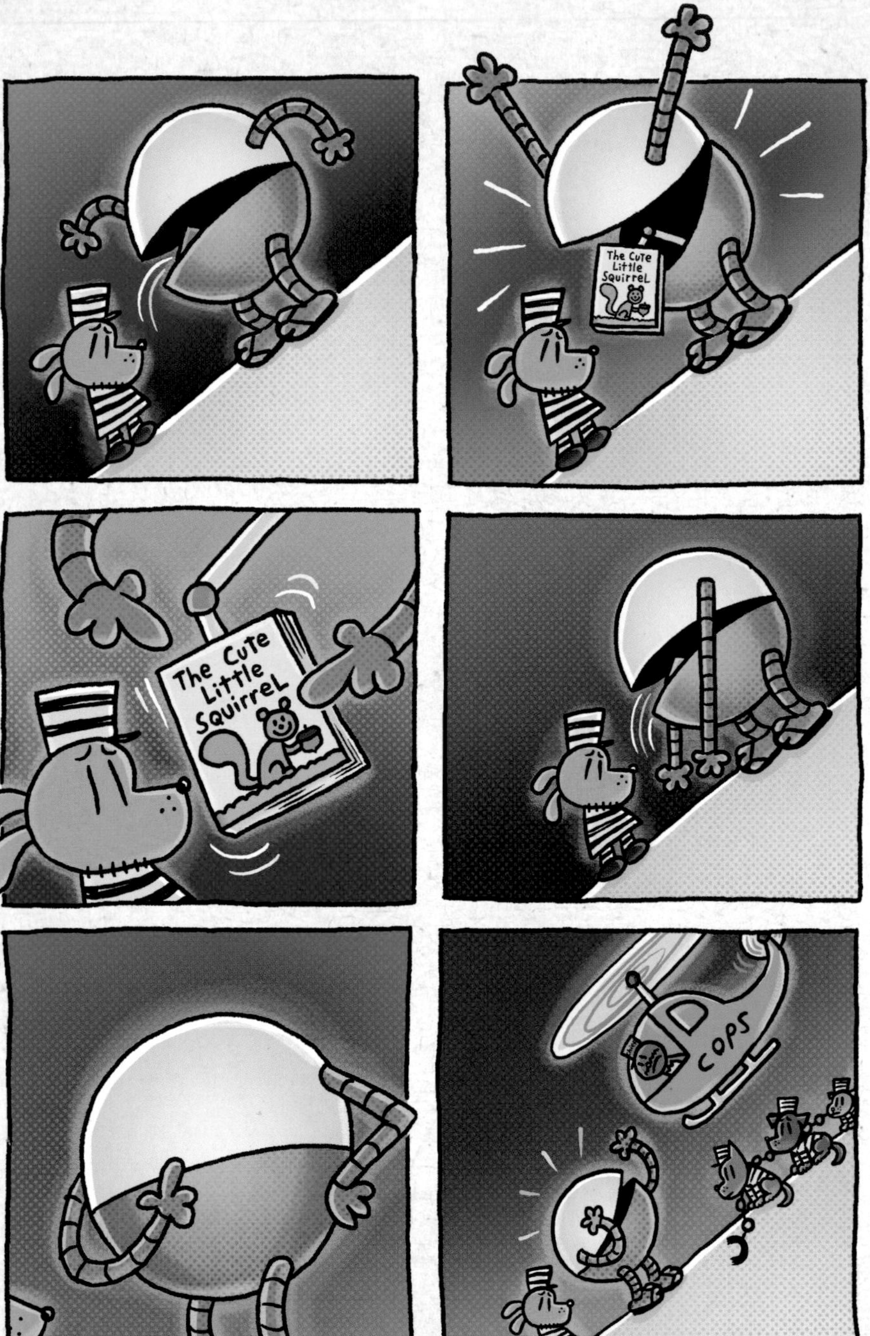

The Cute Little Squirrel
The Cute Little Squirrel
COPS

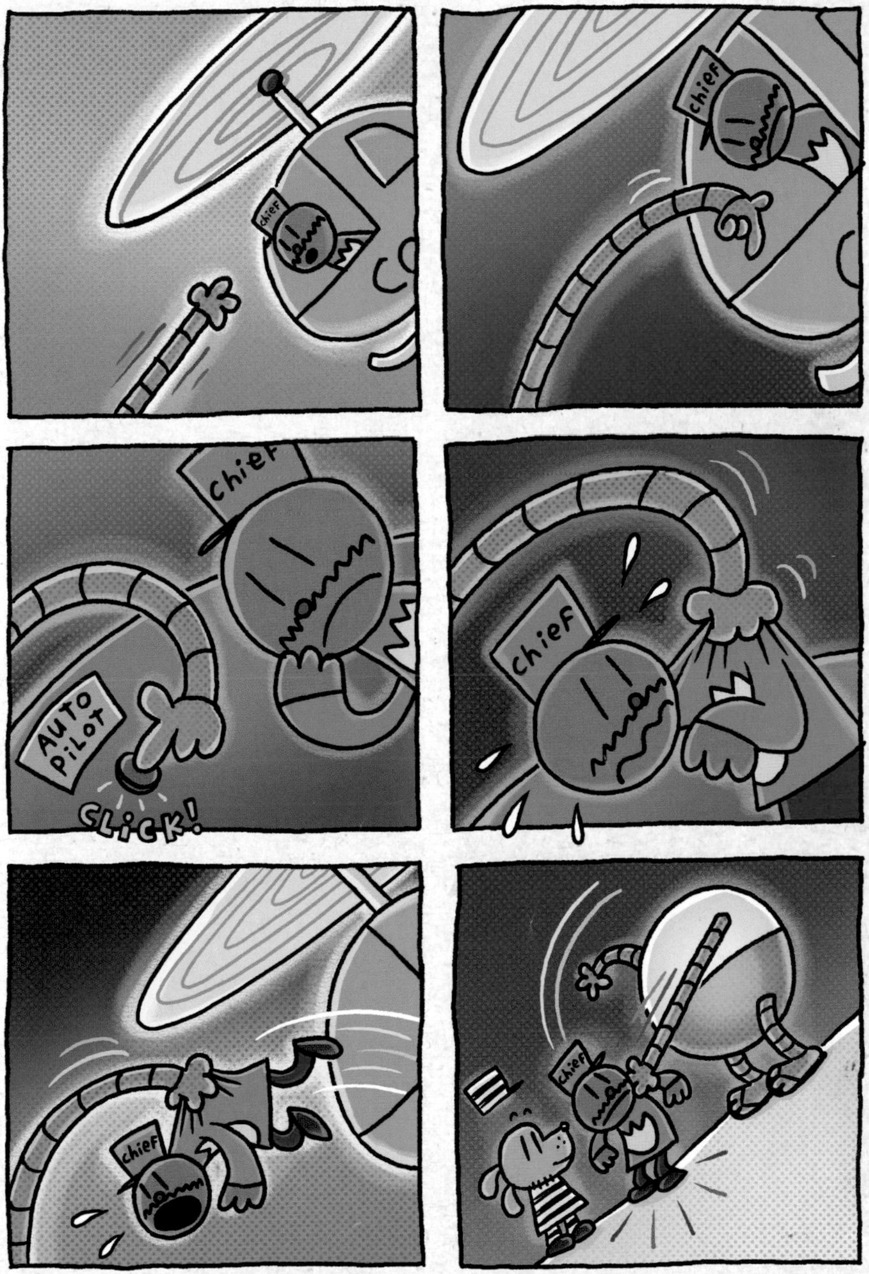
chief
chief
chief
AUTO PiLOT
CLiCK!
chief
chief
chief

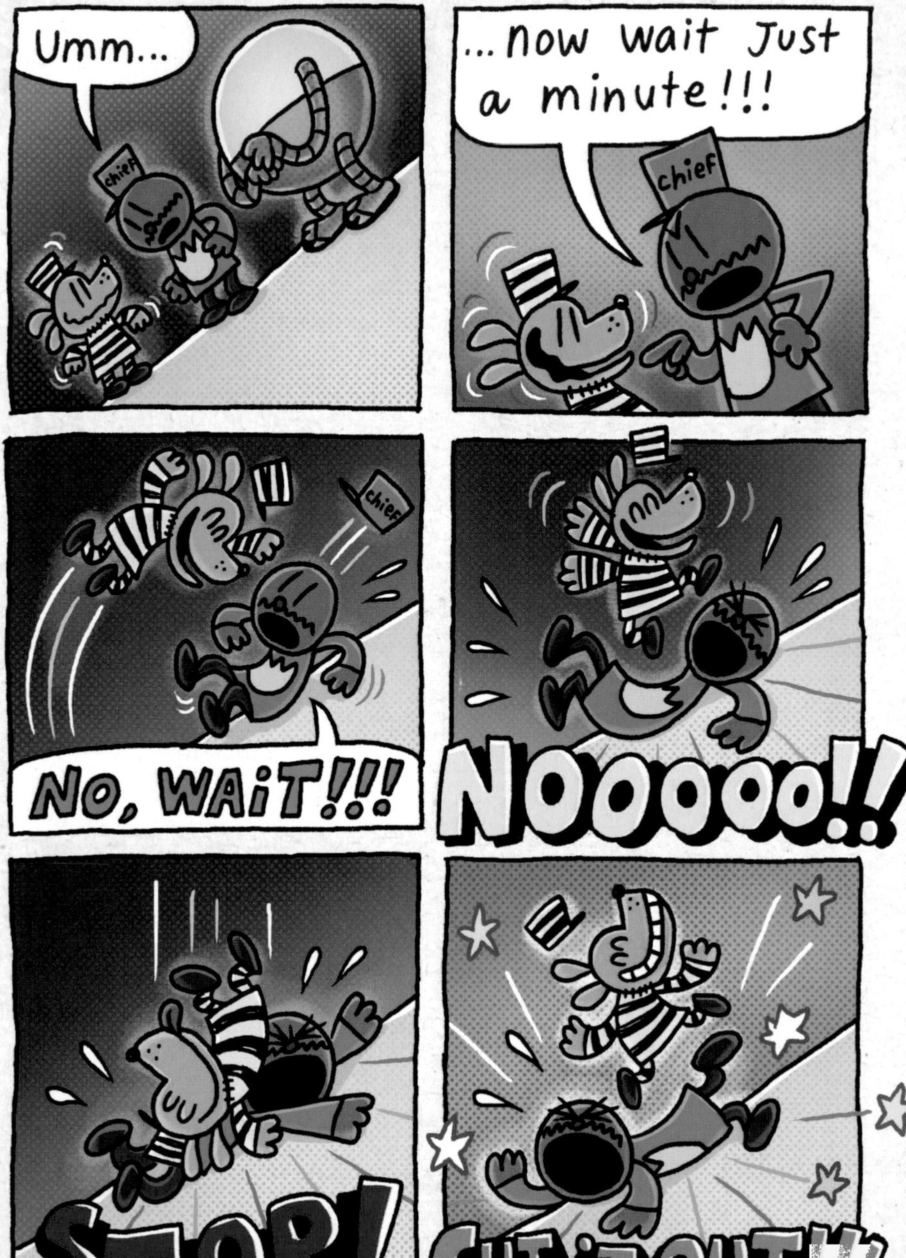
Umm...
chief
...now wait Just a minute!!!
chief
chief
NO, WAiT!!!
NOOOOO!!
STOP!
CUT iT OUT!!

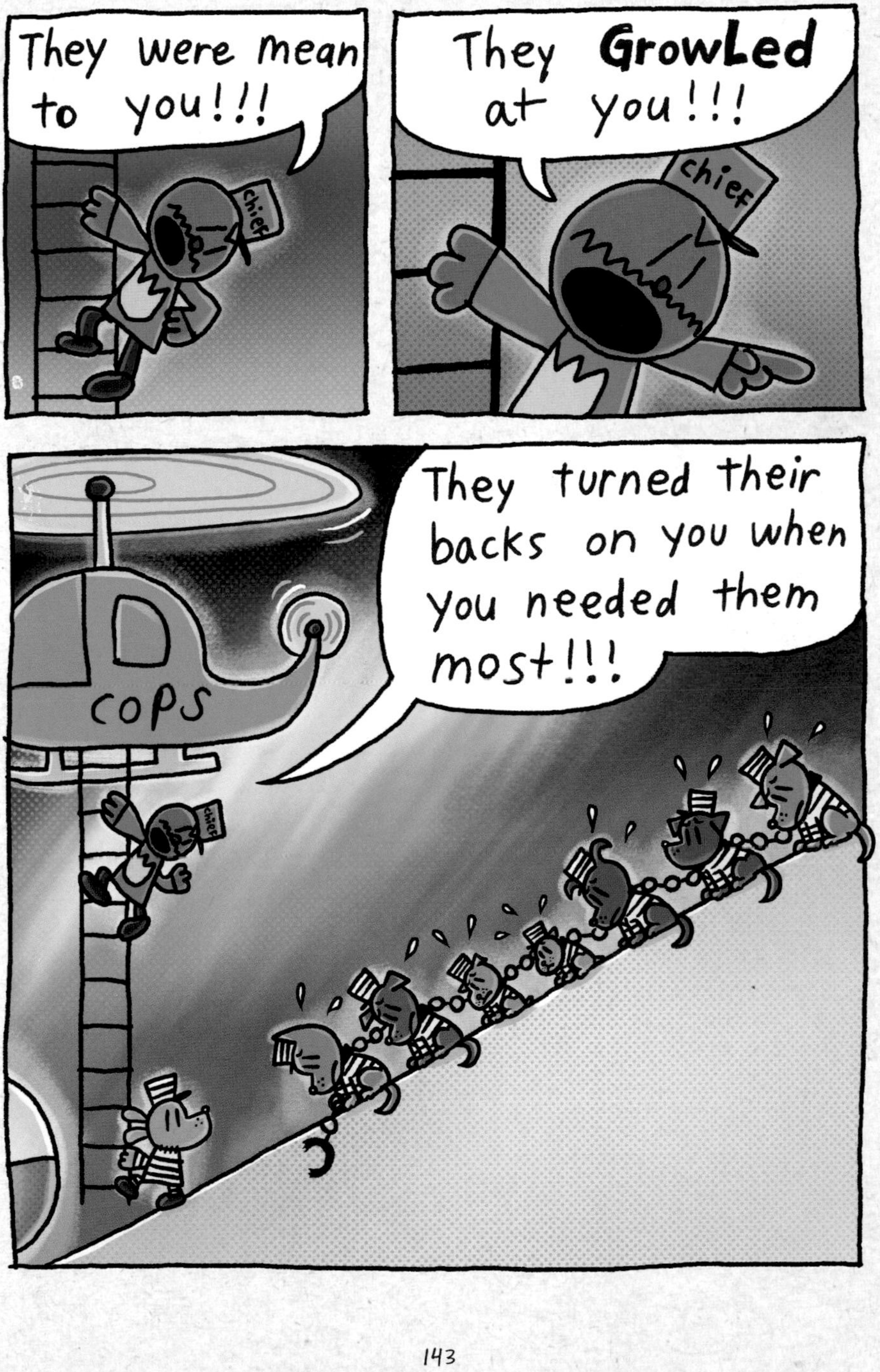
They were mean to you!!!
chief
They GrowLed at you!!!
chief
They turned their backs on you when you needed them most!!!
cops
chief

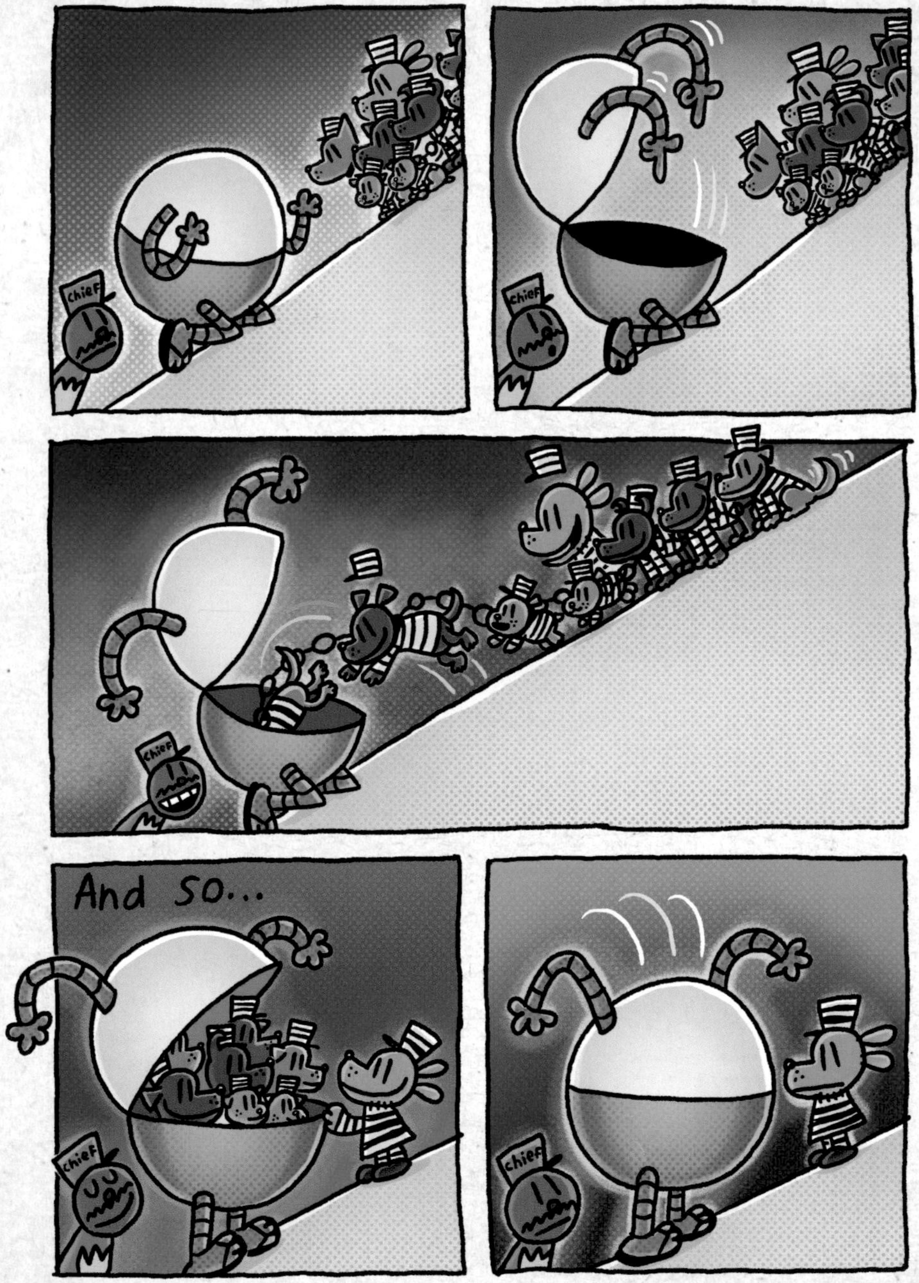
CHIEF
CHIEF
CHIEF
And so...
CHIEF
CHIEF

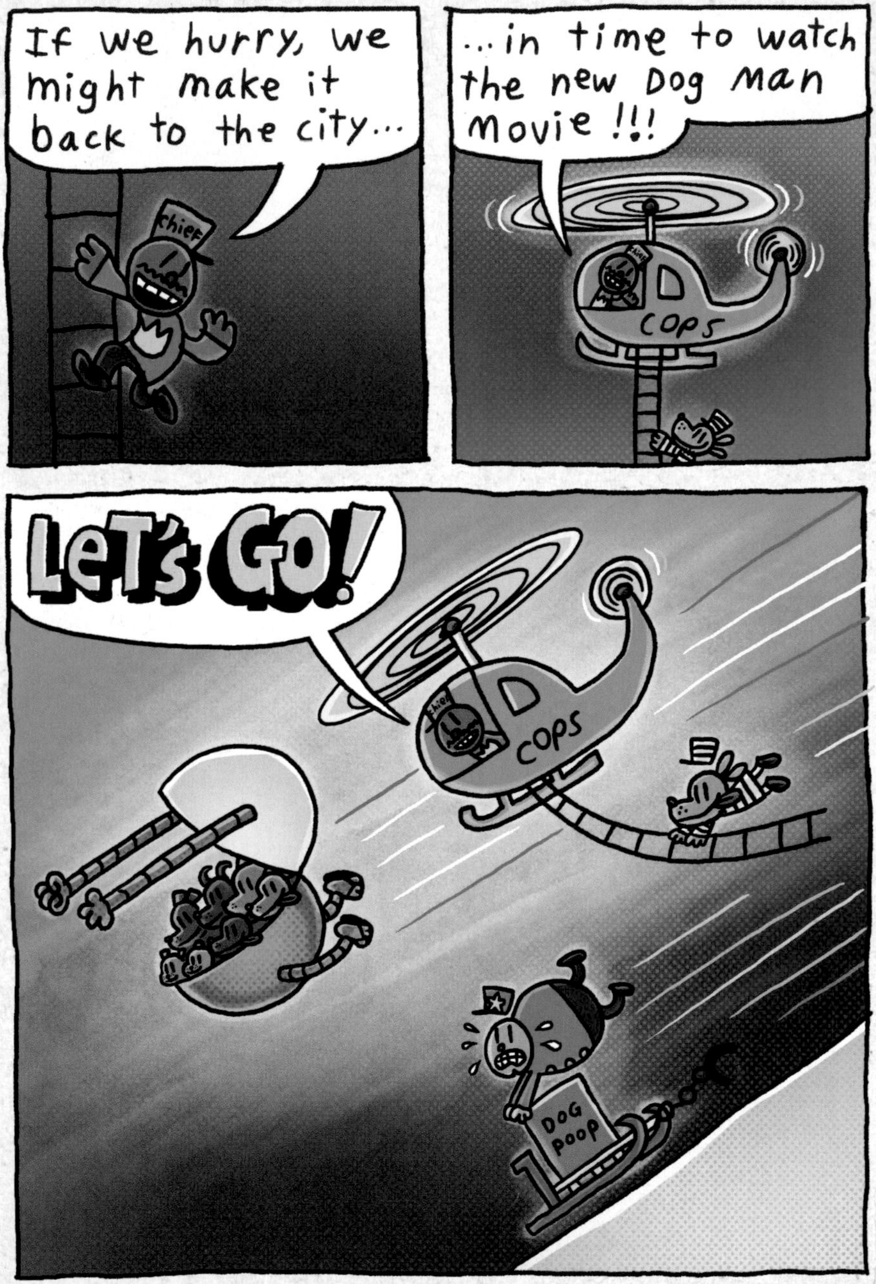
If we hurry, we might make it back to the city...
...in time to watch the new Dog Man movie!!!
LET'S GO!
COPS
CHIEF
COPS
DOG POOP

Chapter 9

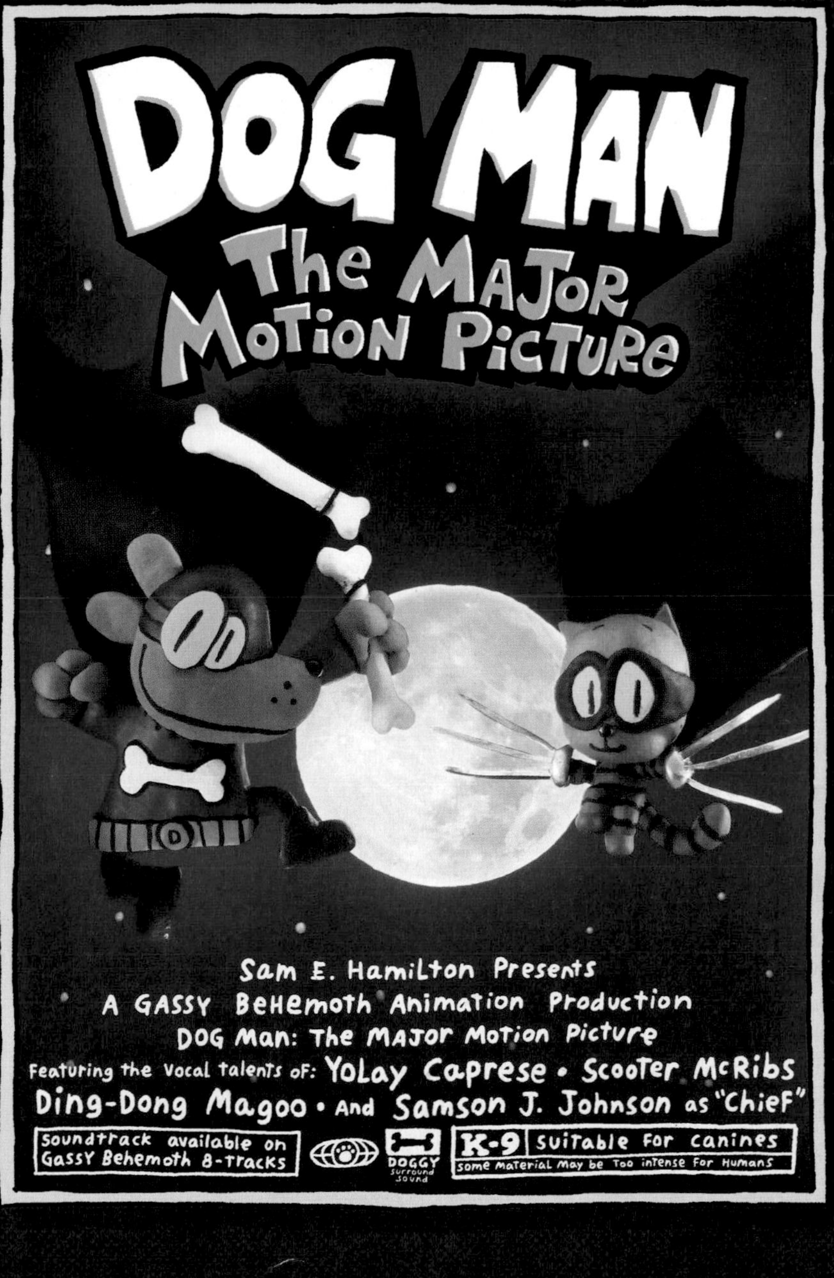
DOG MAN
The Major Motion Picture
Sam E. Hamilton Presents
A GASSY Behemoth Animation Production
DOG Man: The MAJOR Motion Picture
Featuring the vocal talents of: YoLay Caprese • Scooter McRibs
Ding-Dong Magoo • And Samson J. Johnson as "Chief"
Soundtrack available on Gassy Behemoth 8-Tracks
DOGGY Surround Sound
K-9 Suitable for canines
Some material may be too intense for Humans

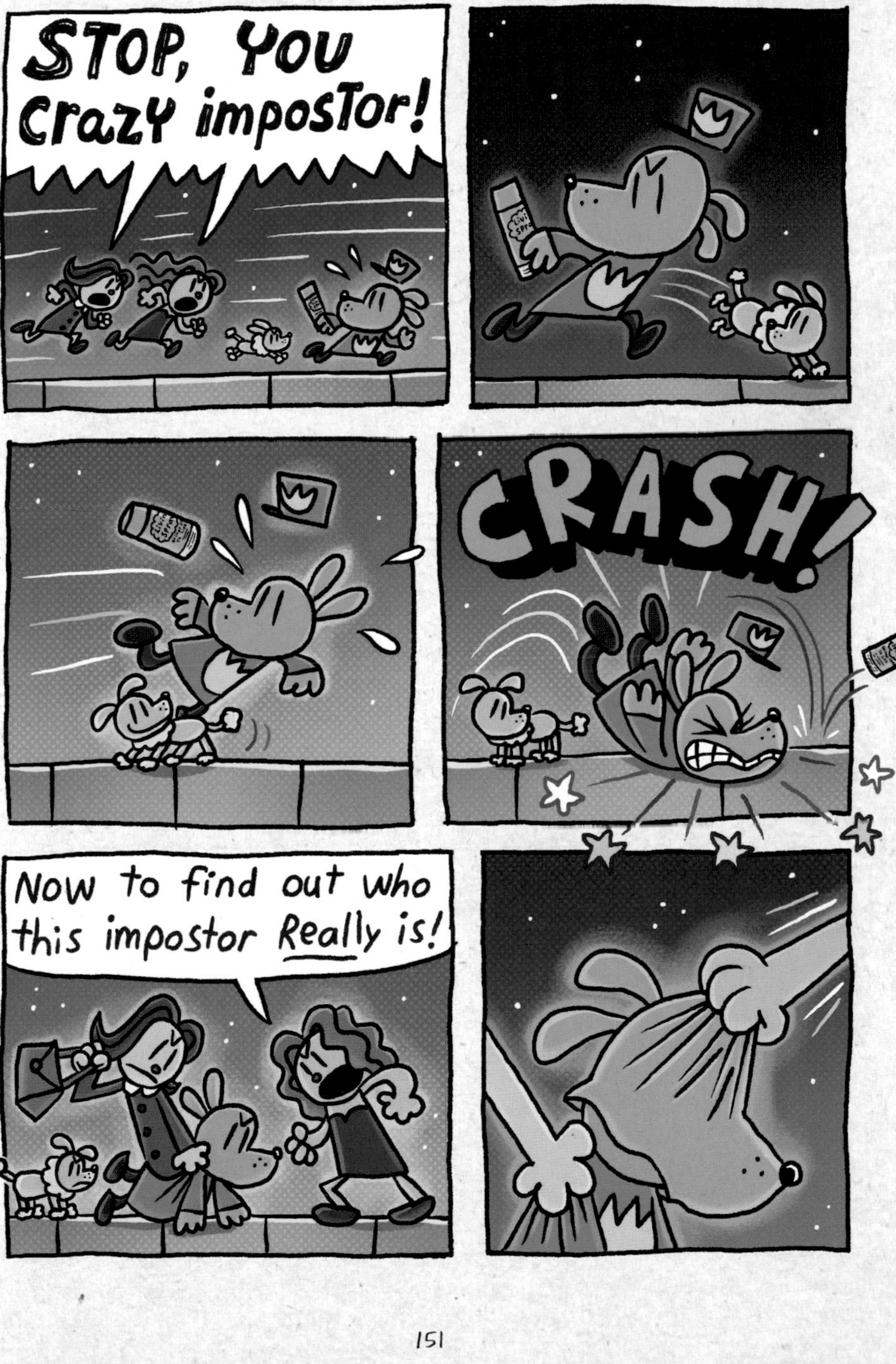
STOP, YOU Crazy impostor!
CRASH!
Now to find out who this impostor Really is!

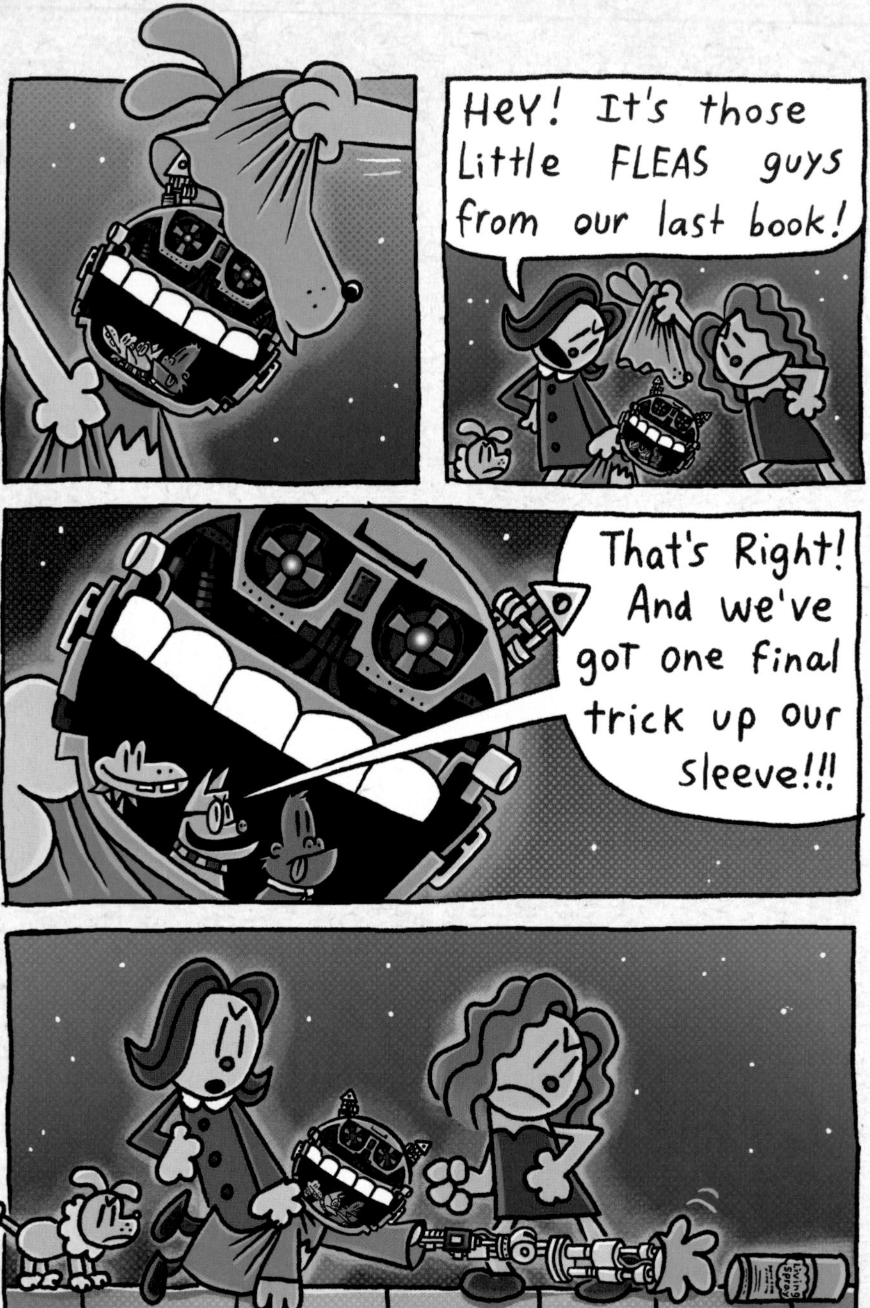
HEY! It's those Little FLEAS guys from our last book!
That's Right! And we've got one final trick up our sleeve!!!
Living Spray

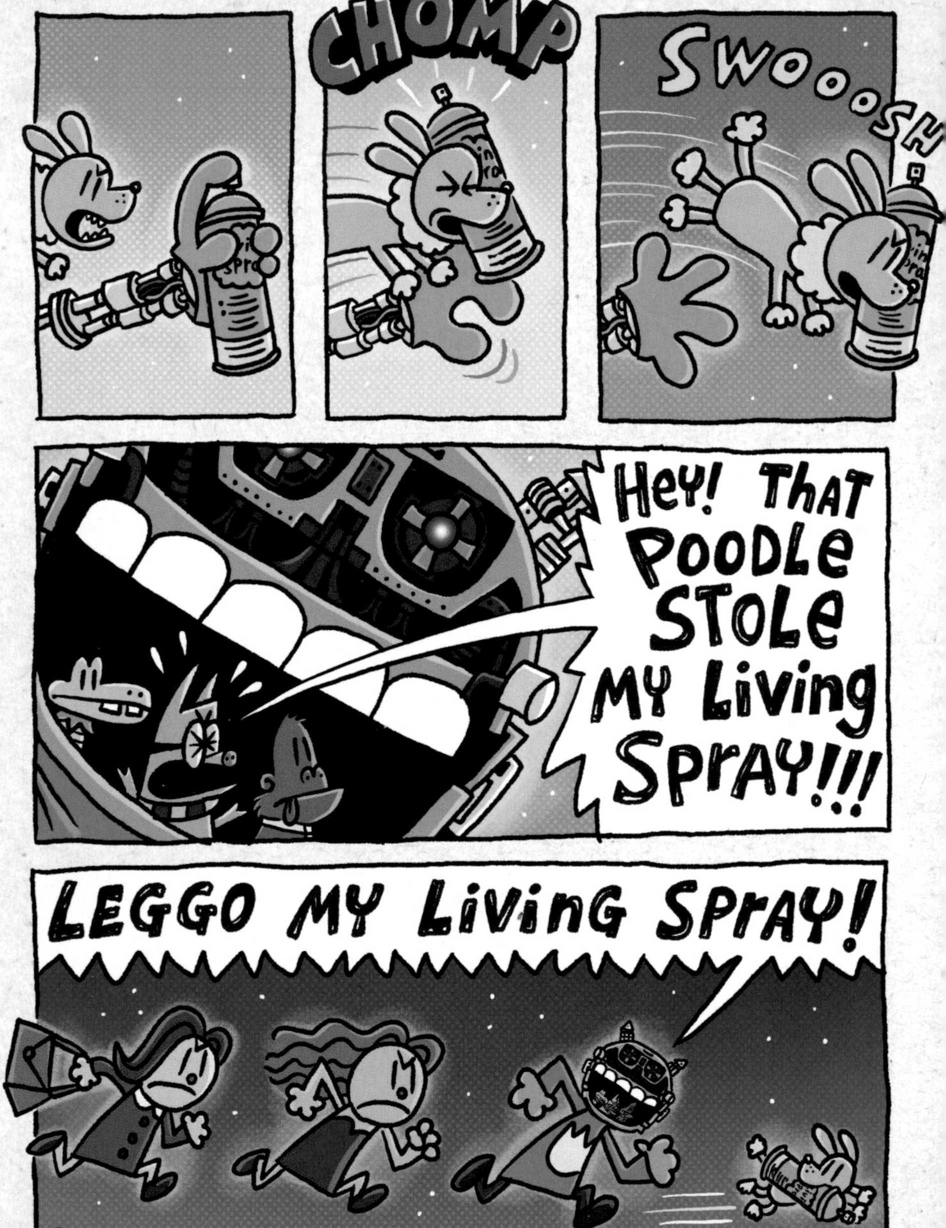
CHOMP
SWOOOOSH
HEY! THAT POODLE STOLE MY LIVING SPRAY!!!
LEGGO MY LIVING SPRAY!

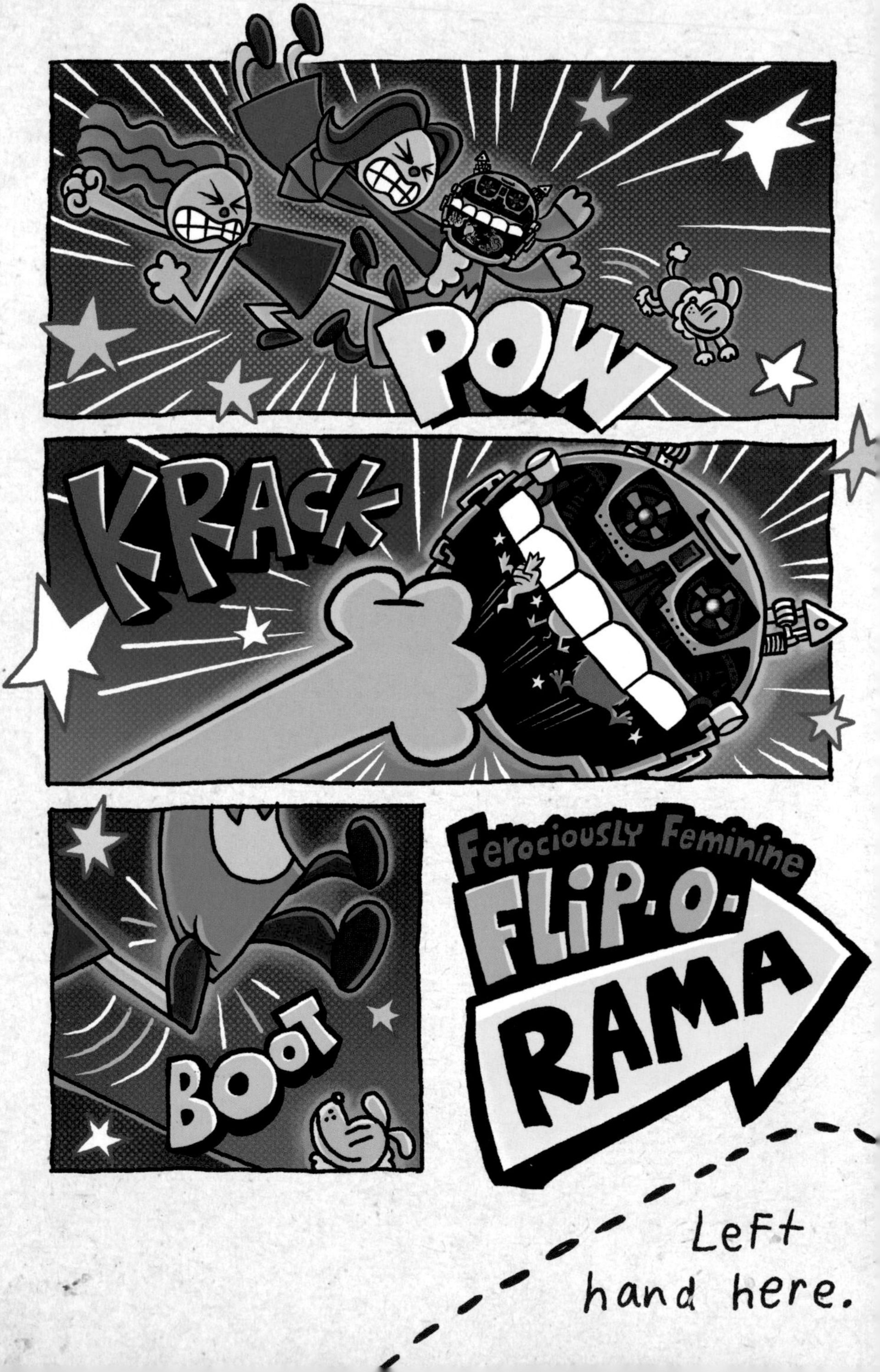
POW
KRACK
BOOT
Ferociously Feminine
FLIP-O-RAMA
Left hand here.

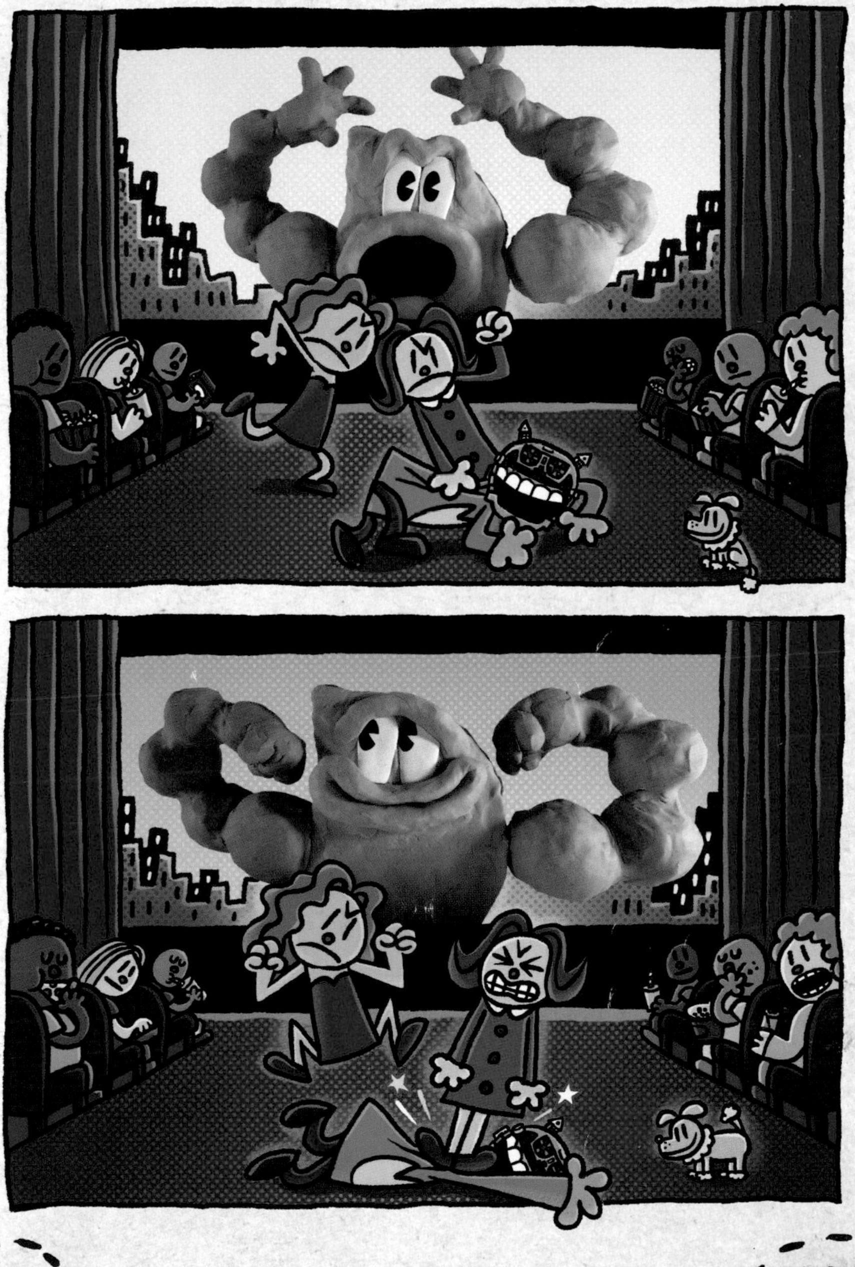

Right Thumb here.

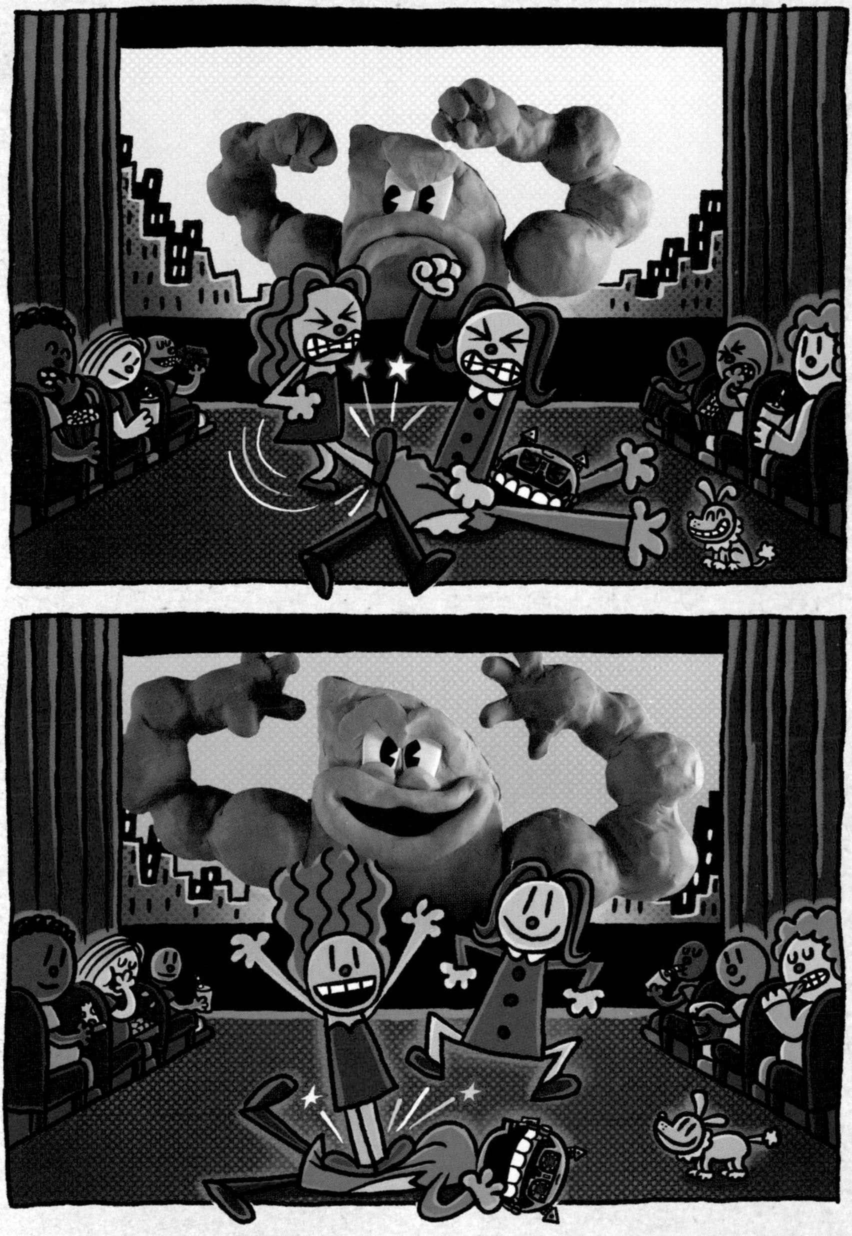

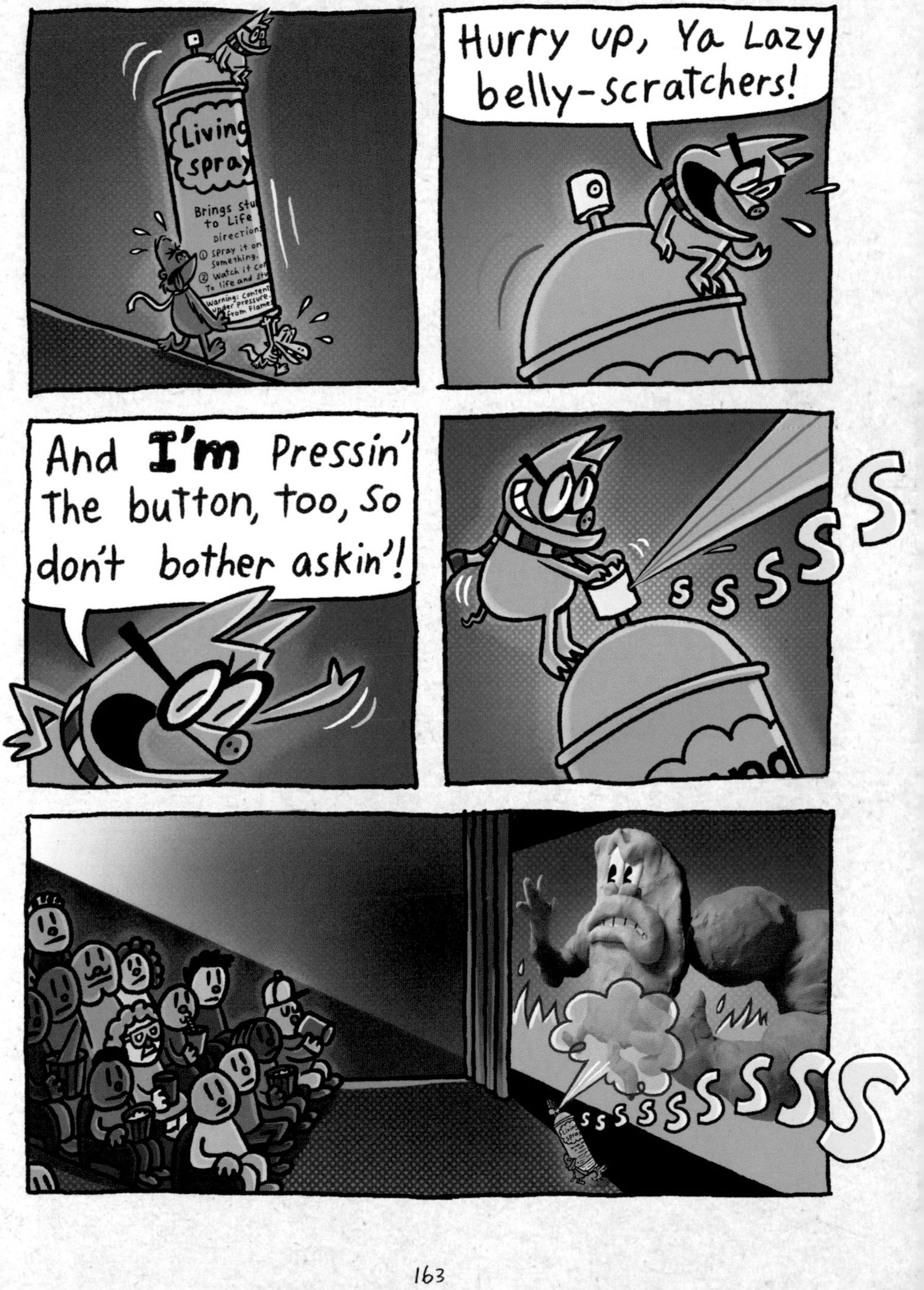

Living
spray
Hurry up, Ya Lazy belly-scratchers!
And **I'm** Pressin' The button, too, So don't bother askin'!
SSSSSS
SSSSSSSSSSS

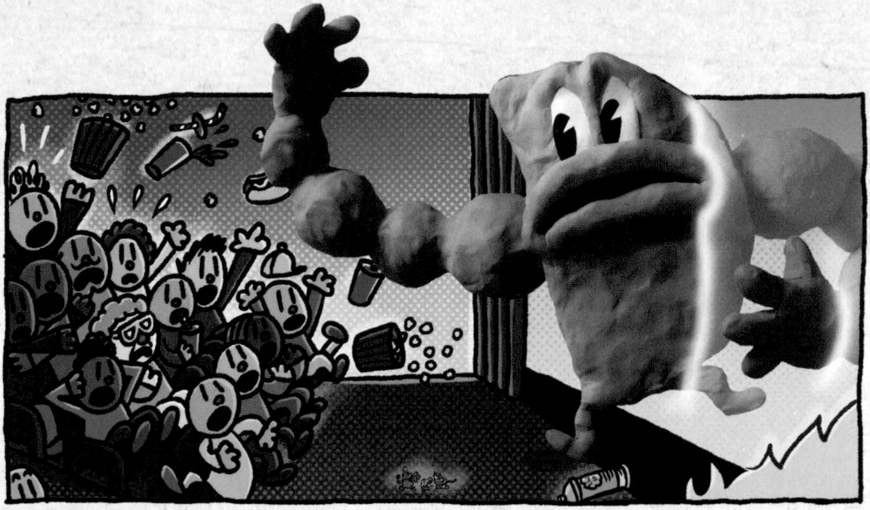

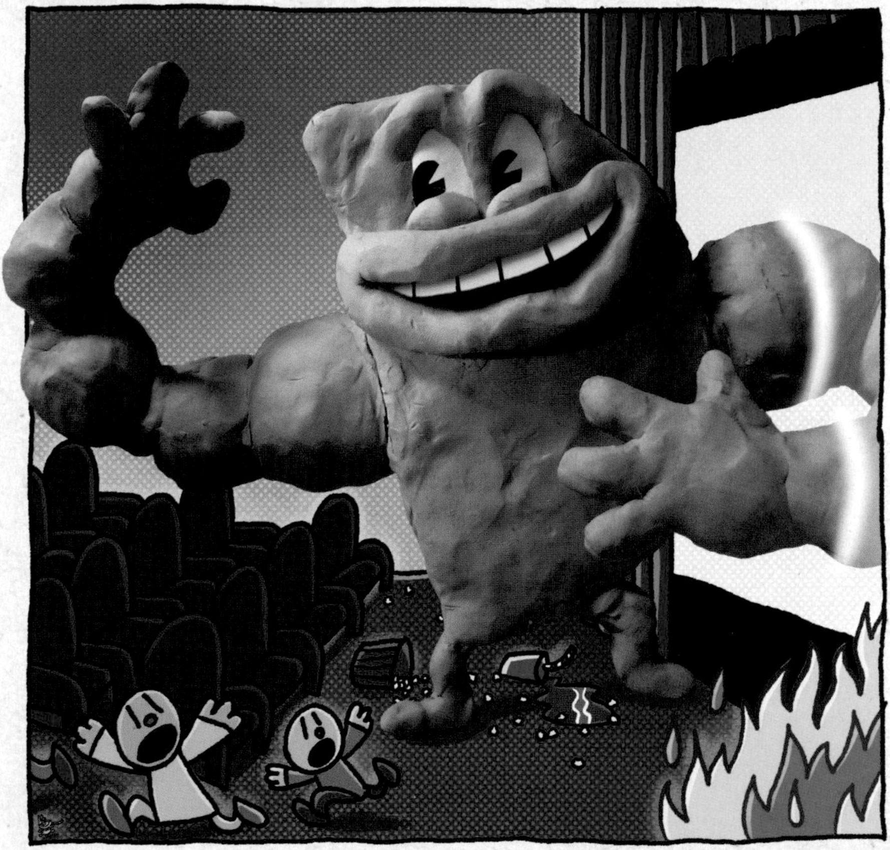

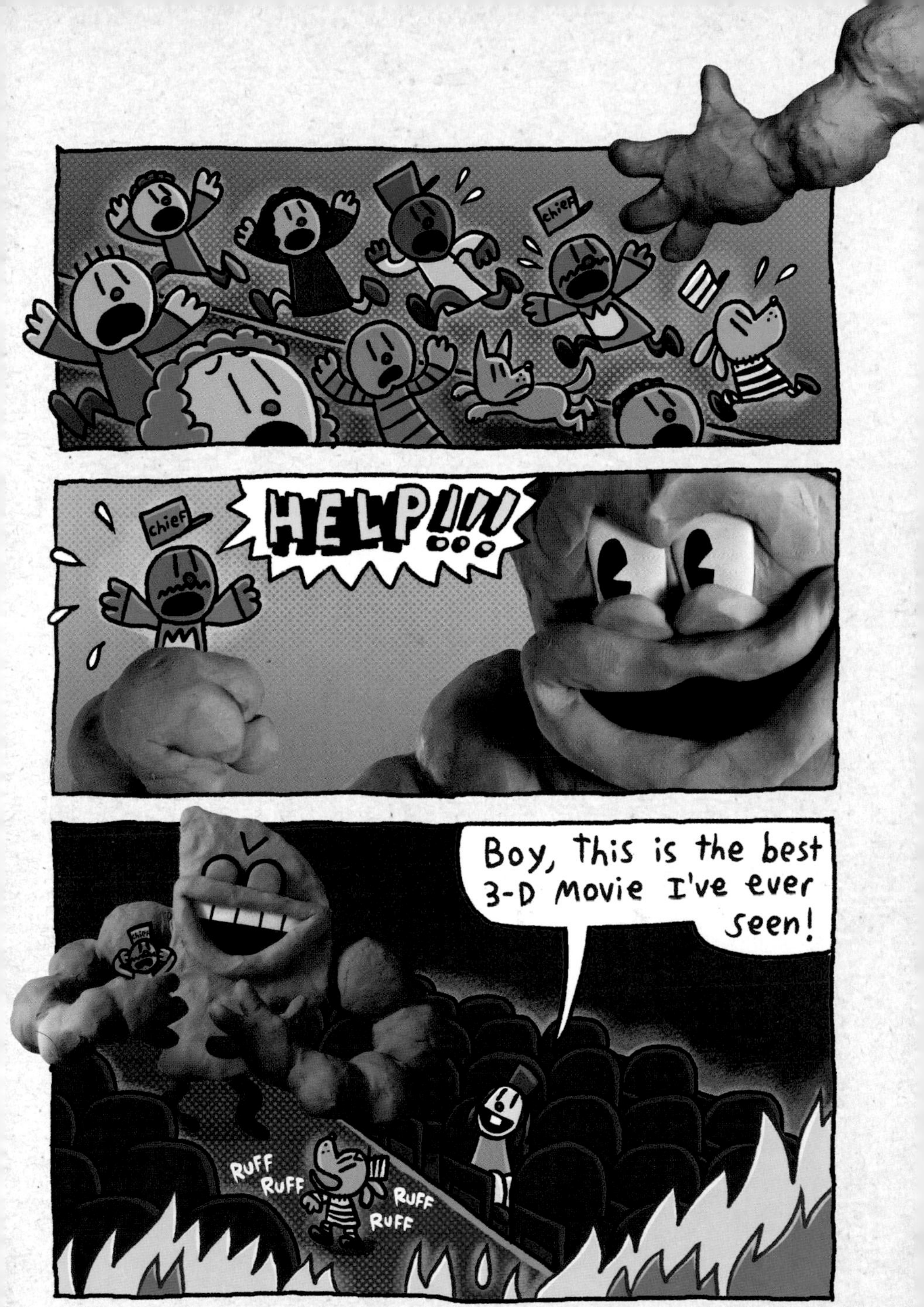
chief
chief
HELP!!!
chief
Boy, This is the best 3-D Movie I've ever seen!
RUFF RUFF RUFF RUFF

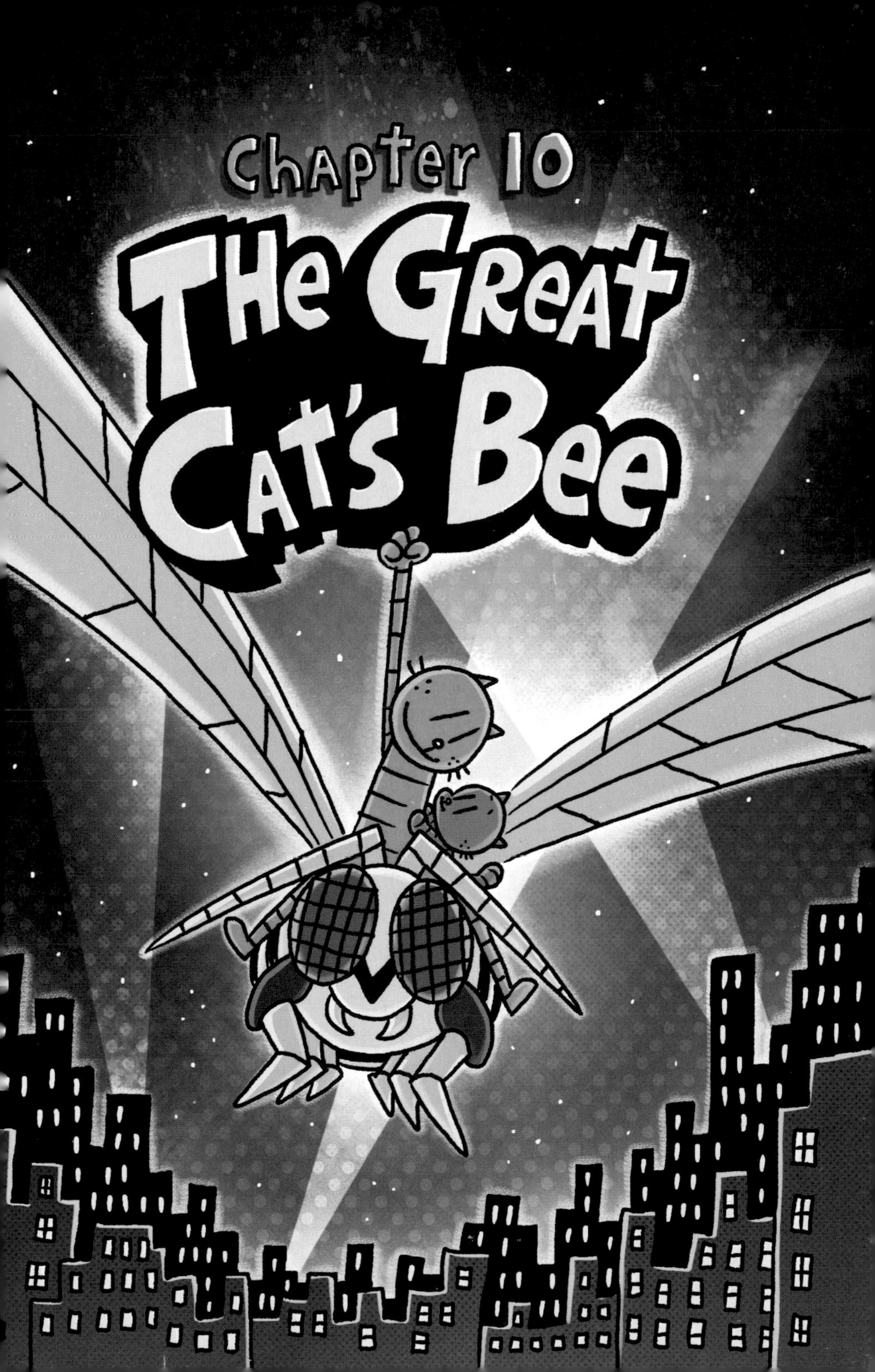
Chapter 10
The Great Cat's Bee

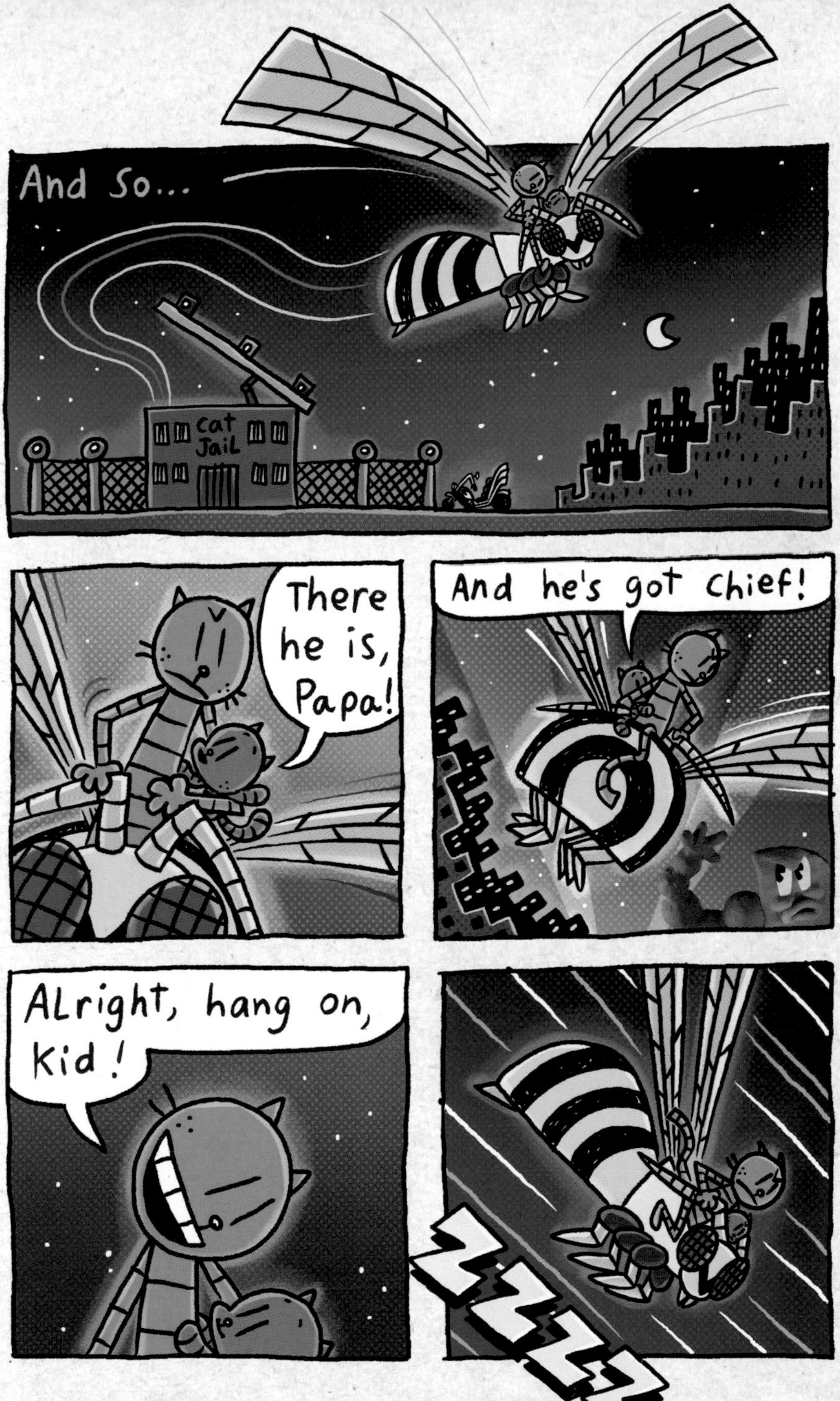
And So...
Cat Jail
There he is, Papa!
And he's got Chief!
ALright, hang on, Kid!
ZZZZZ

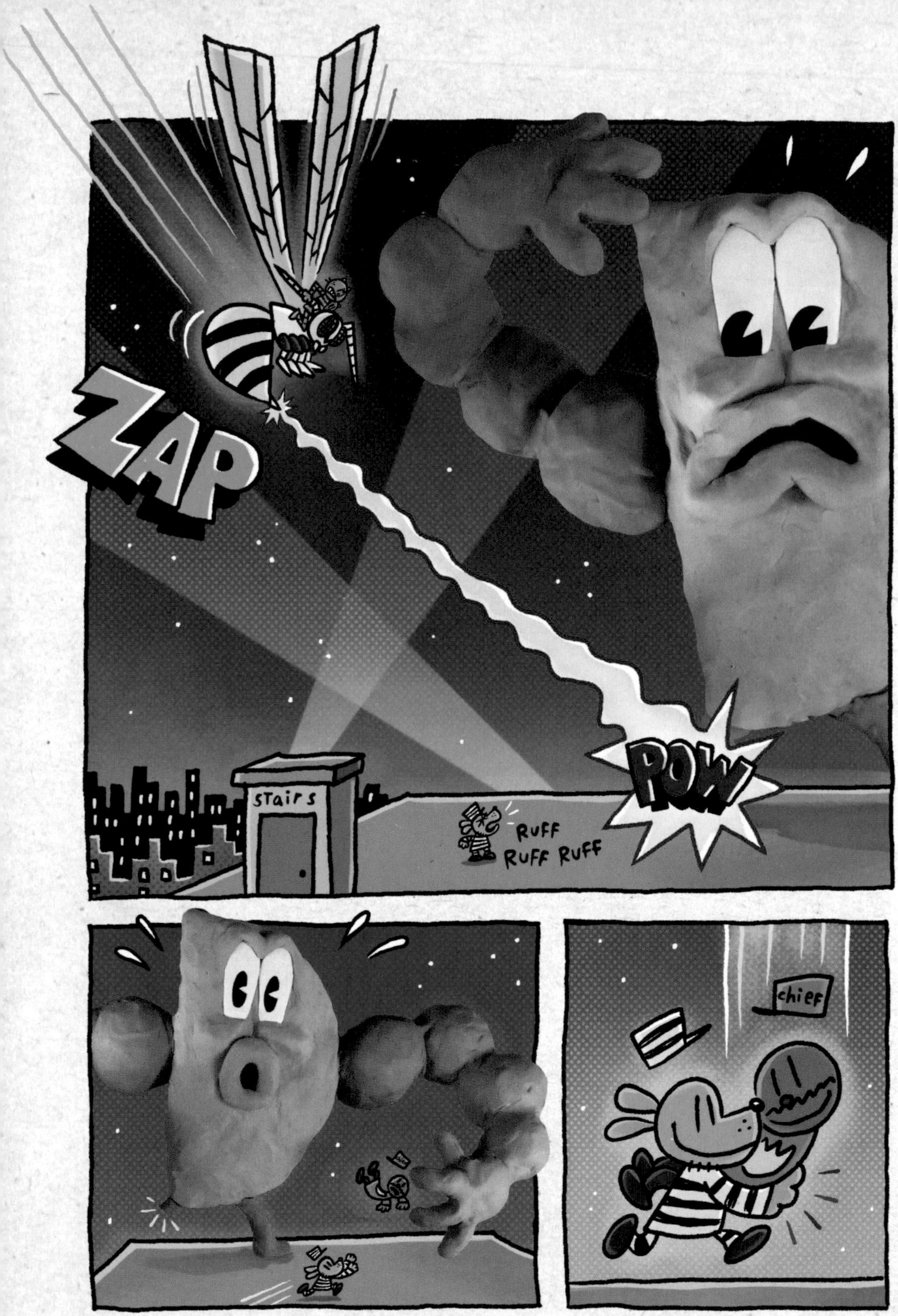
ZAP
stairs
RUFF
RUFF RUFF
POW
chief

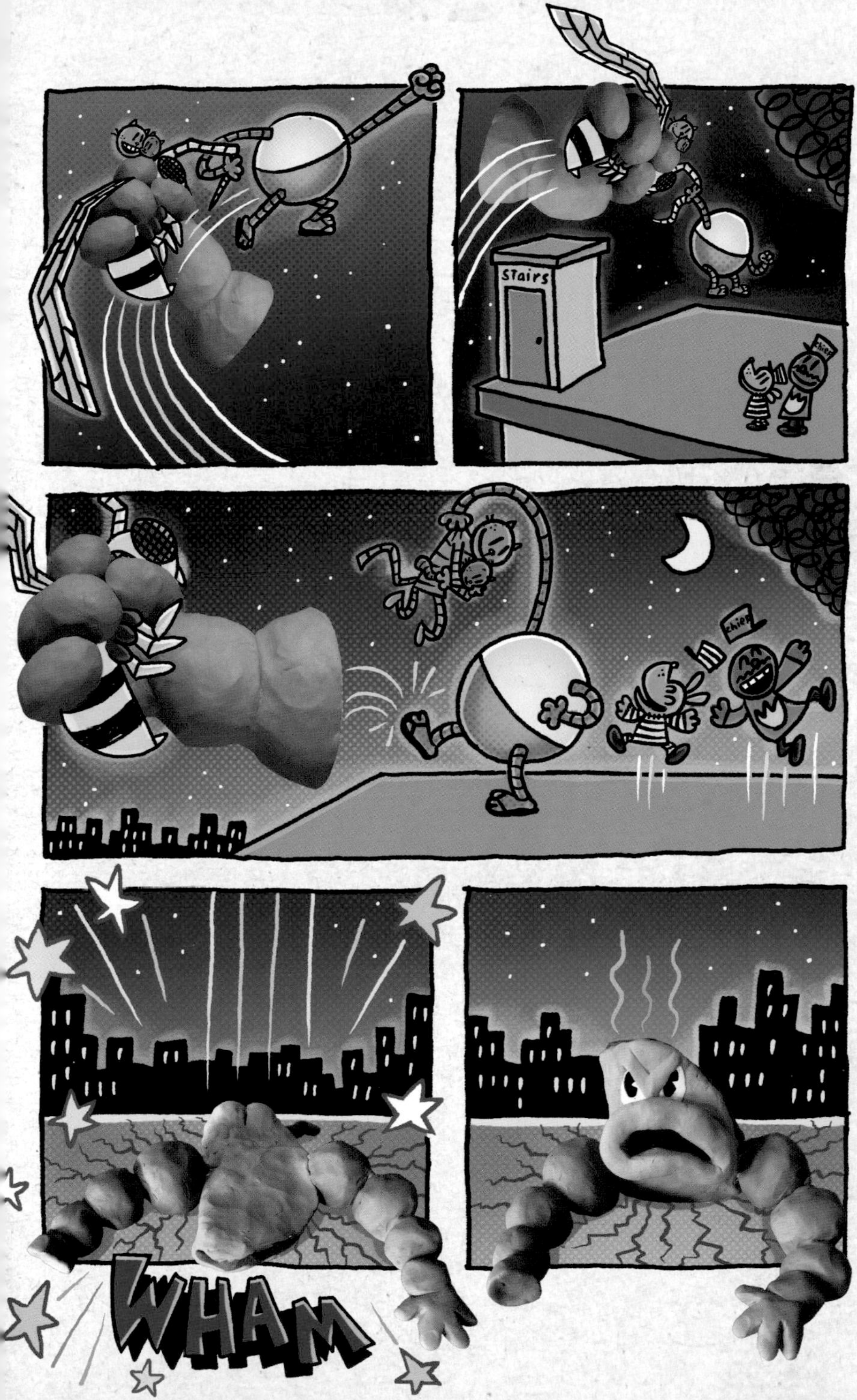

STAIRS
chief
chief
WHAM

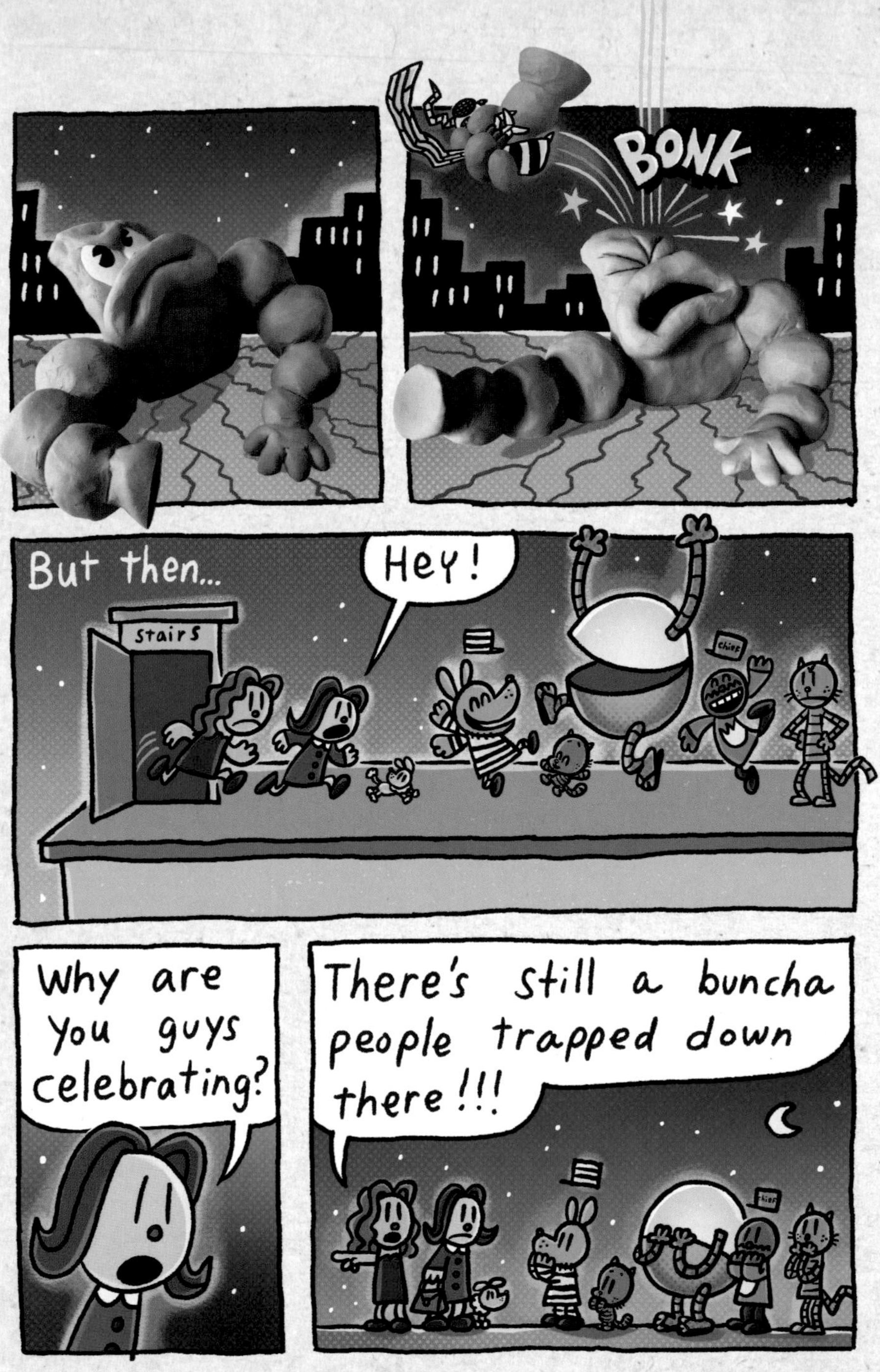
BONK
But then...
Hey!
Stairs
chief
Why are you guys celebrating?
There's still a buncha people trapped down there!!!

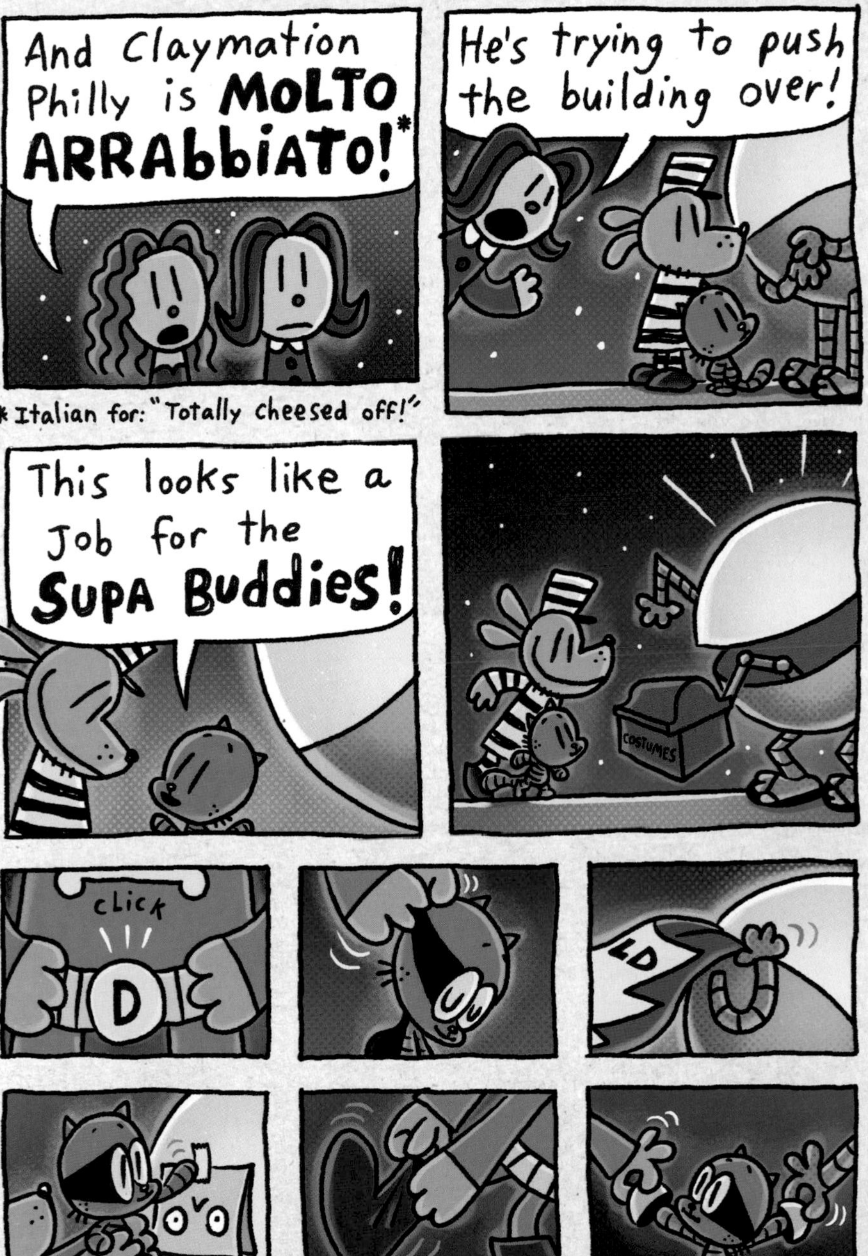
And Claymation Philly is MOLTO ARRABBIATO!*
*Italian for: "Totally cheesed off!"
He's trying to push the building over!
This looks like a Job for the SUPA BUDDIES!
COSTUMES
CLICK
D

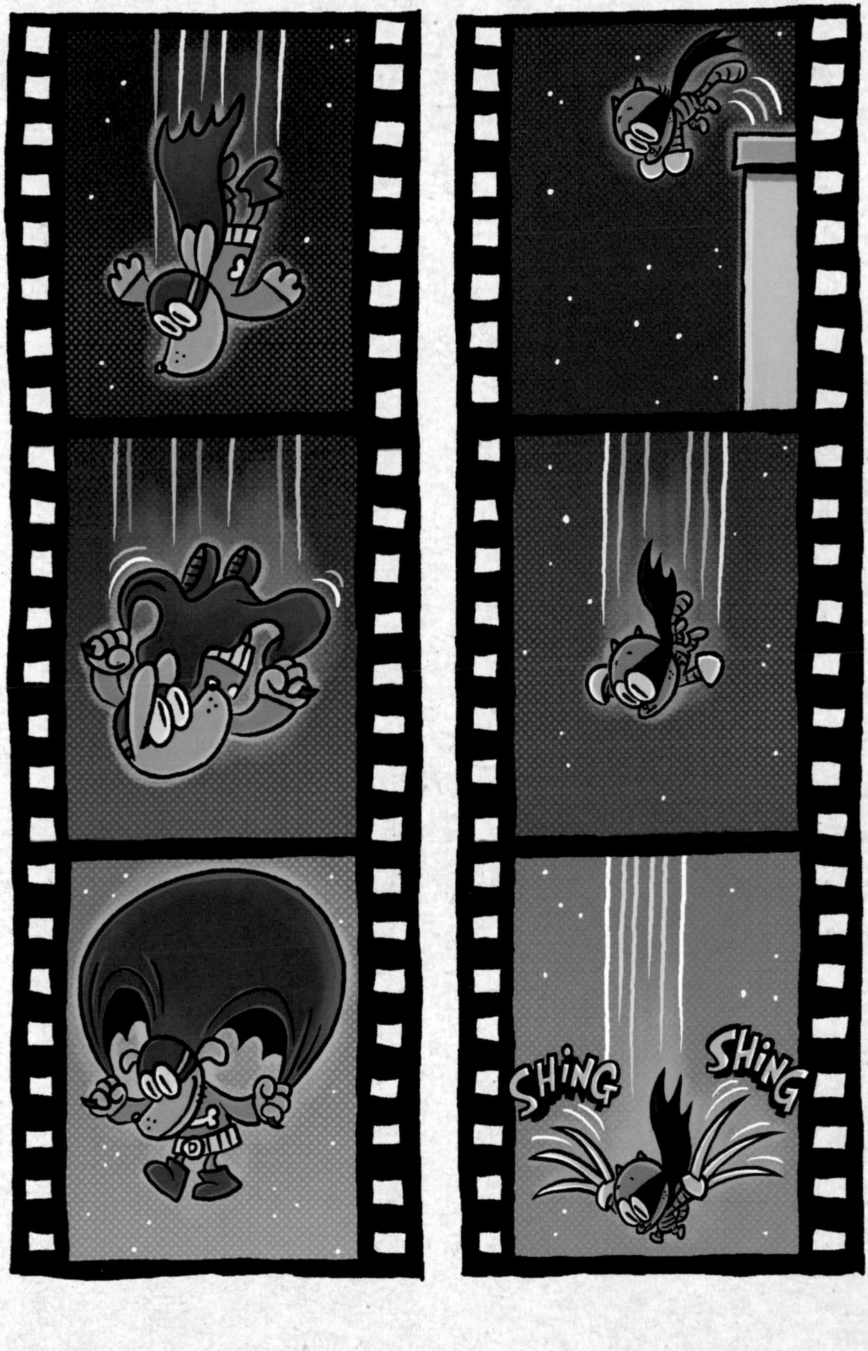
SHING
SHING

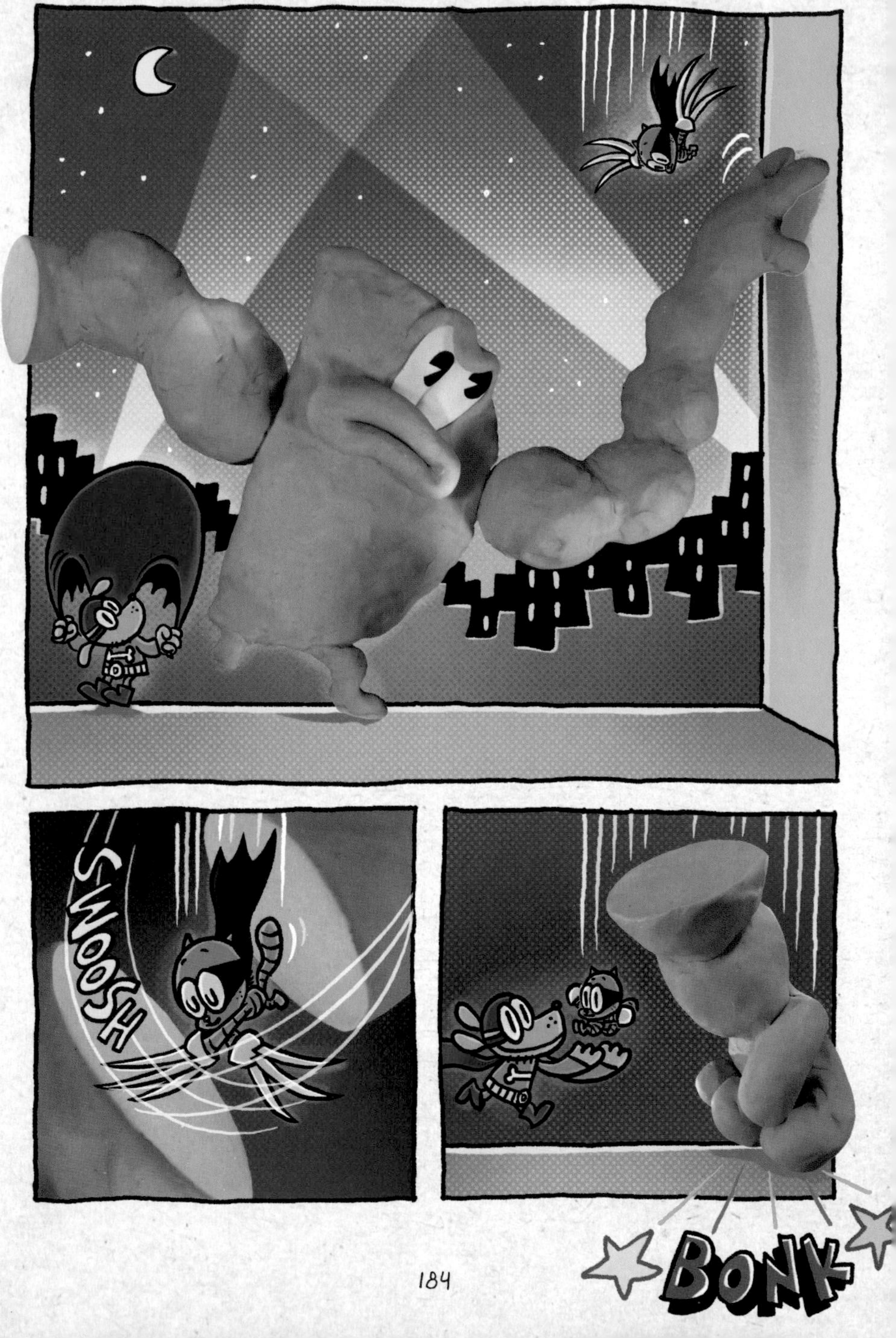
SWOOSH
BONK

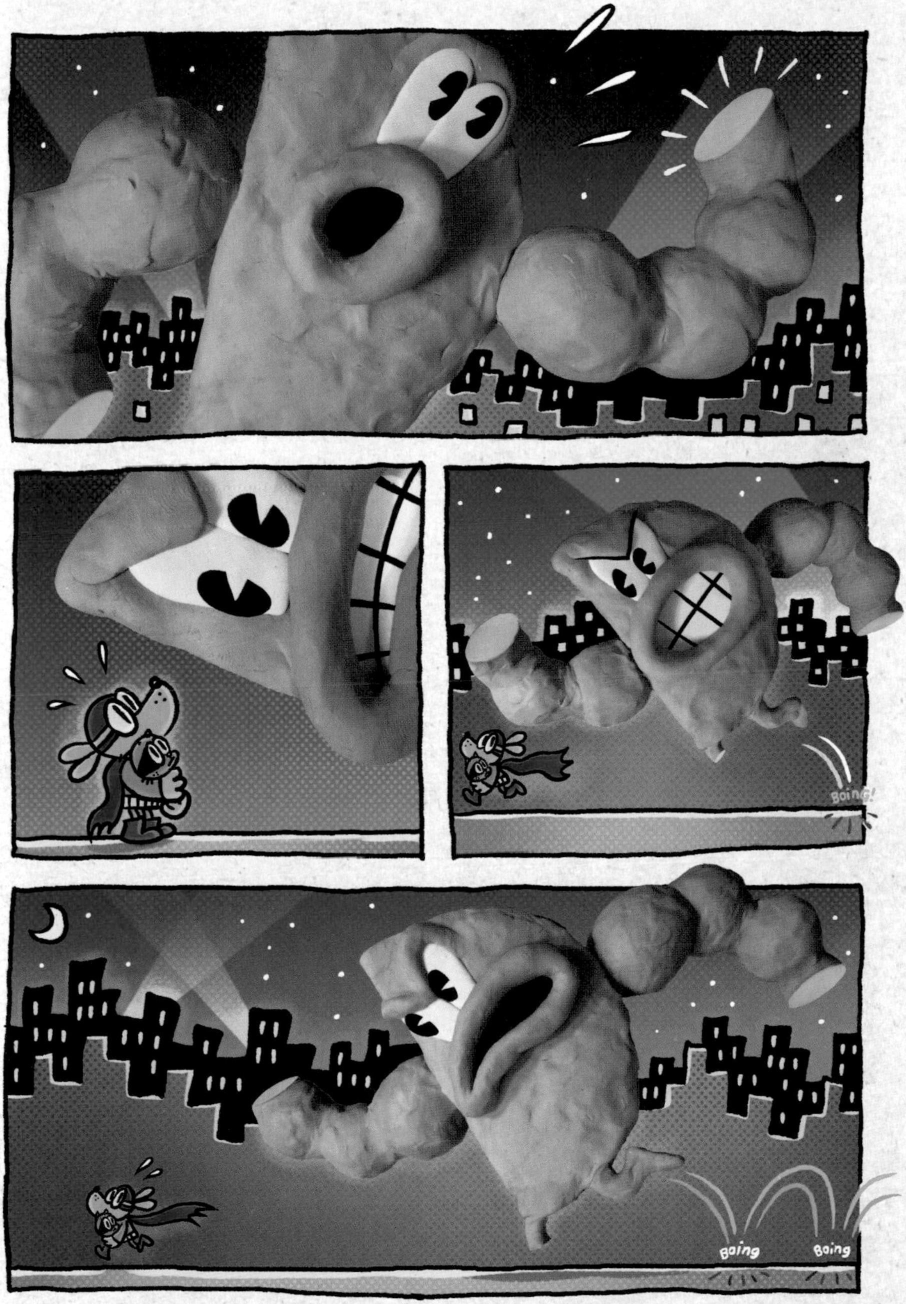
Boing!
Boing
Boing

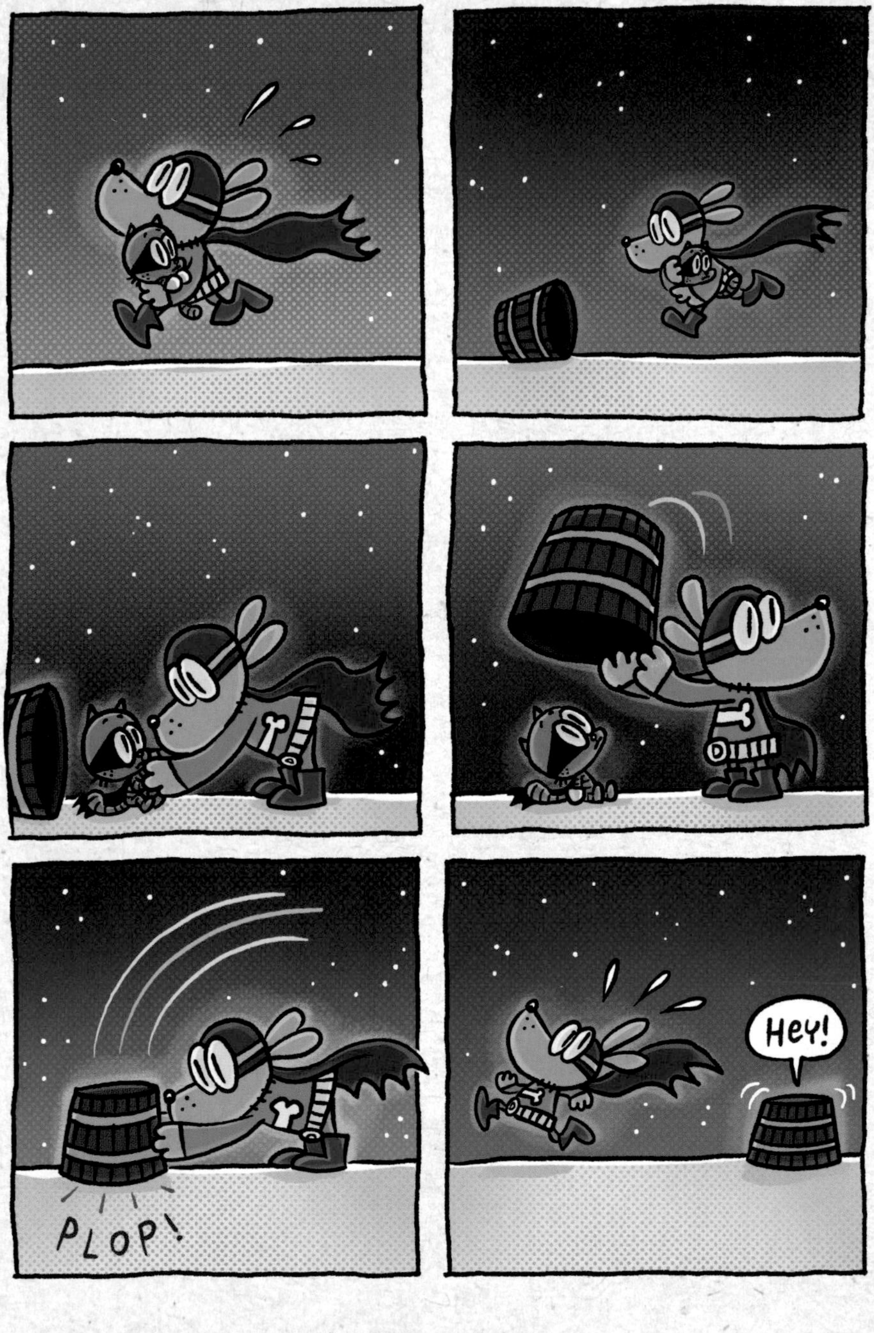
PLOP!
HEY!

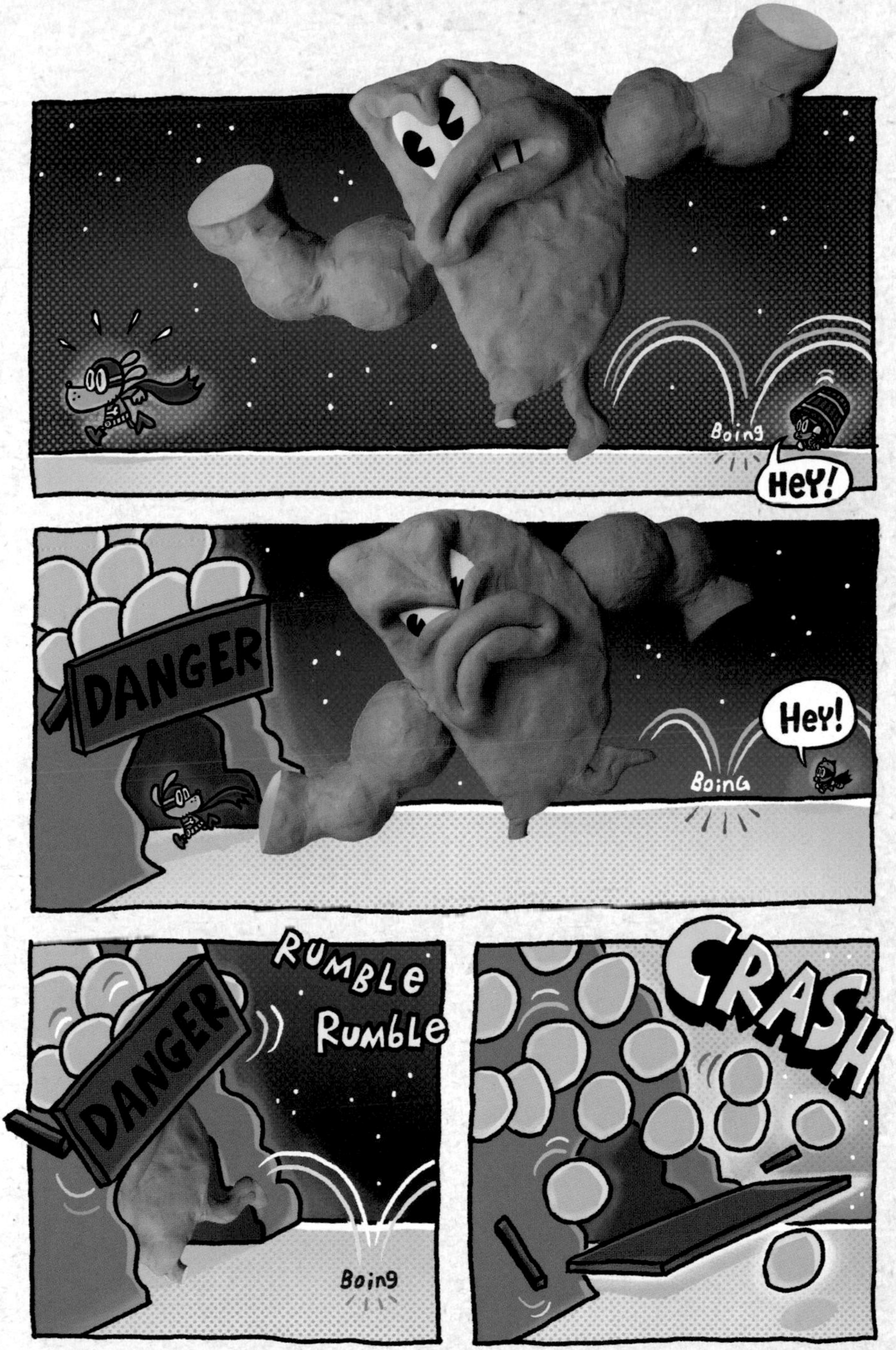
Boing
HEY!
DANGER
Boing
Hey!
RUMBLE
Rumble
DANGER
Boing
CRASH

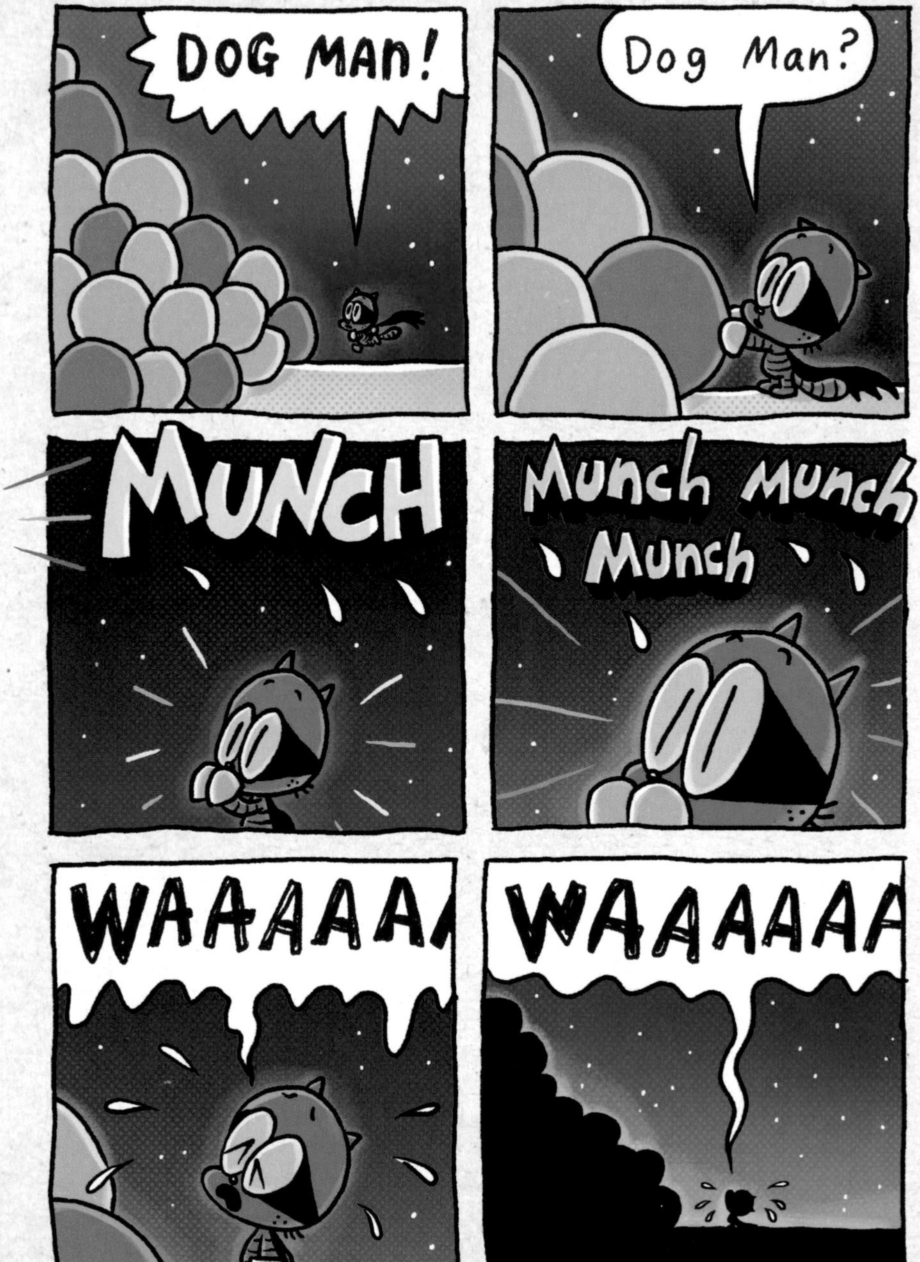
DOG MAN!
Dog Man?
MUNCH
Munch munch
Munch
WAAAAA
WAAAAAA

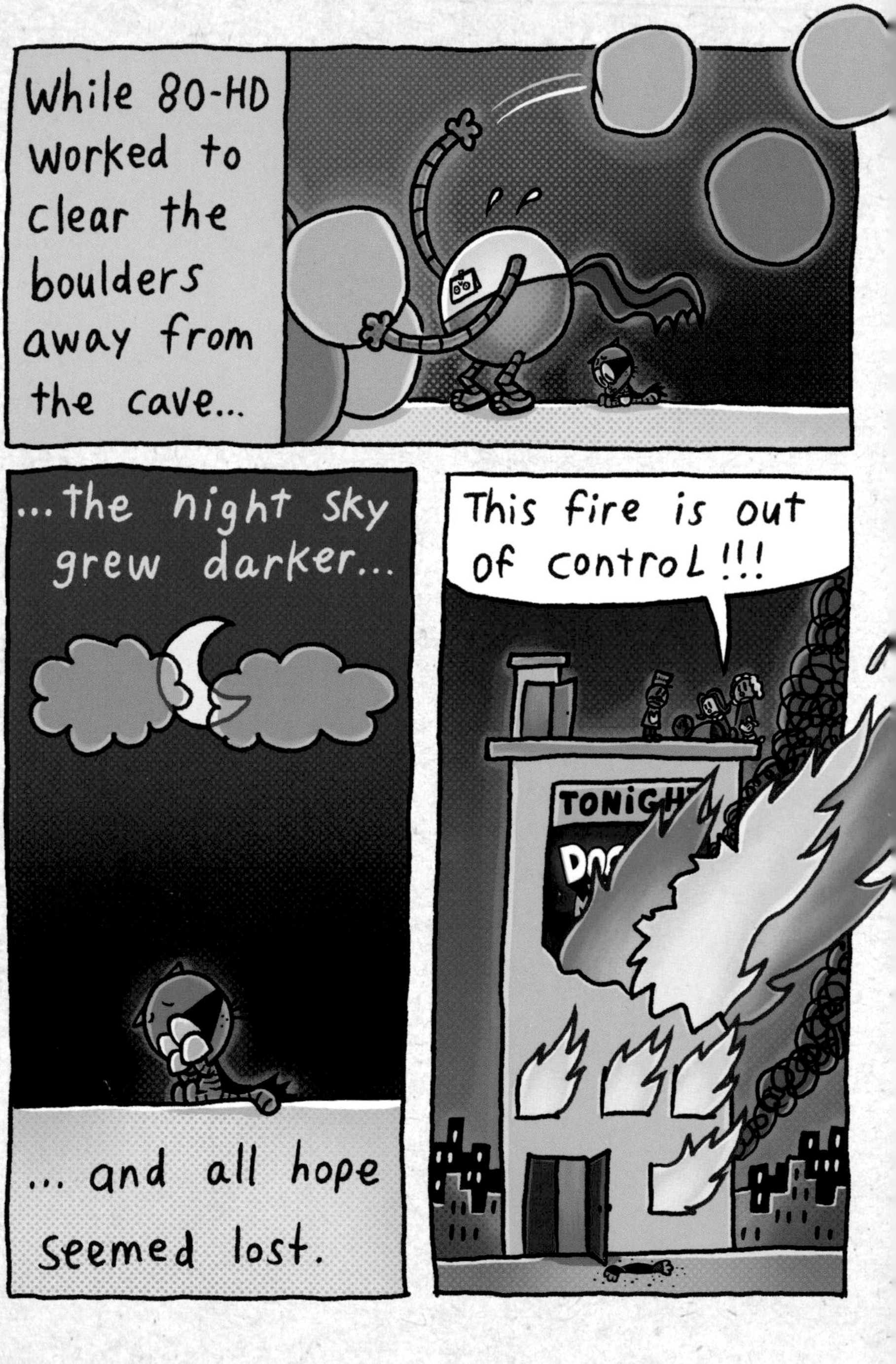
While 80-HD worked to clear the boulders away from the cave...
...the night sky grew darker...
... and all hope seemed lost.
This fire is out of control!!!
TONIGH

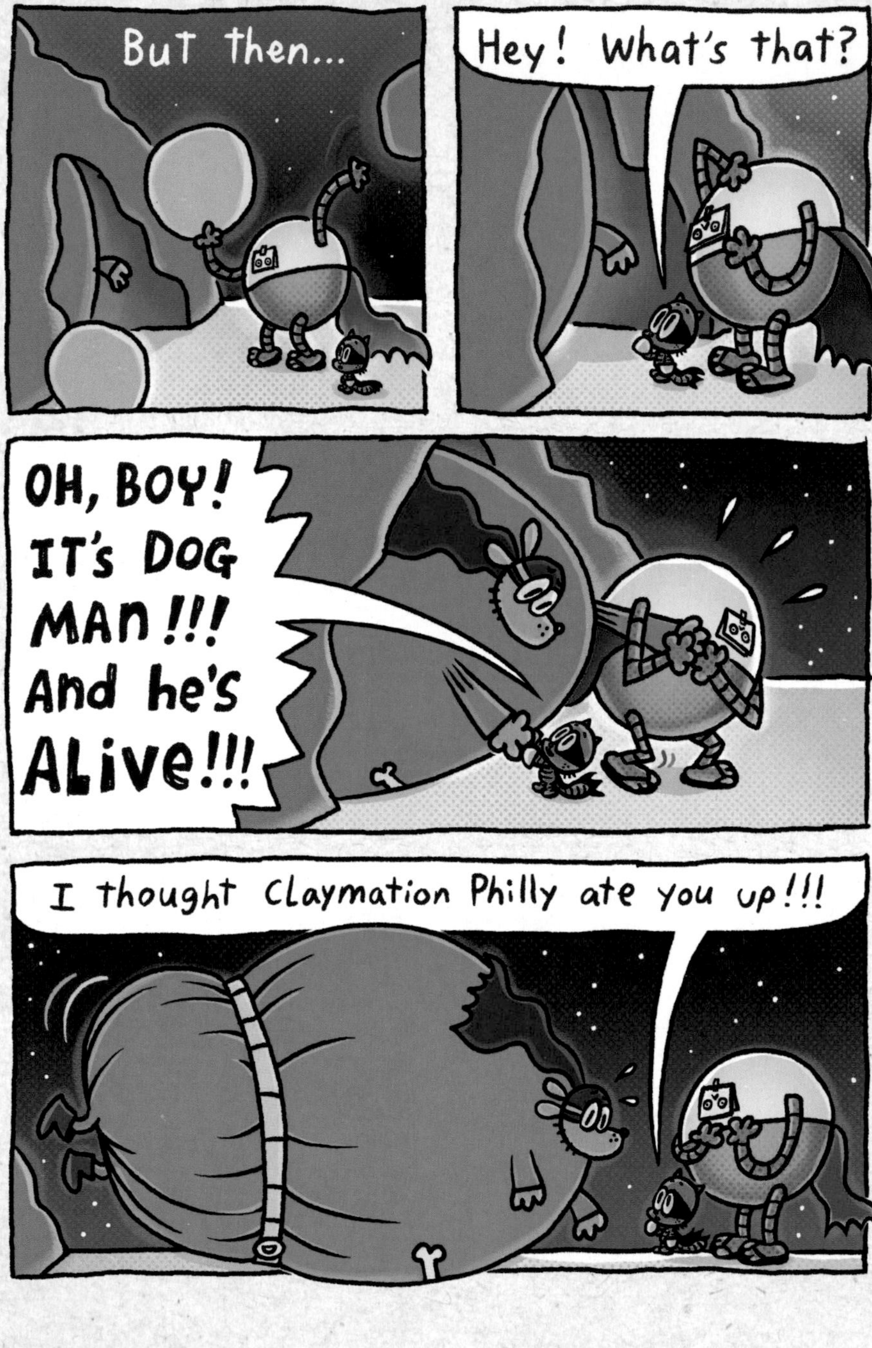
But then...
Hey! What's that?
OH, BOY! IT's DOG MAN!!! And he's ALive!!!
I thought Claymation Philly ate you up!!!

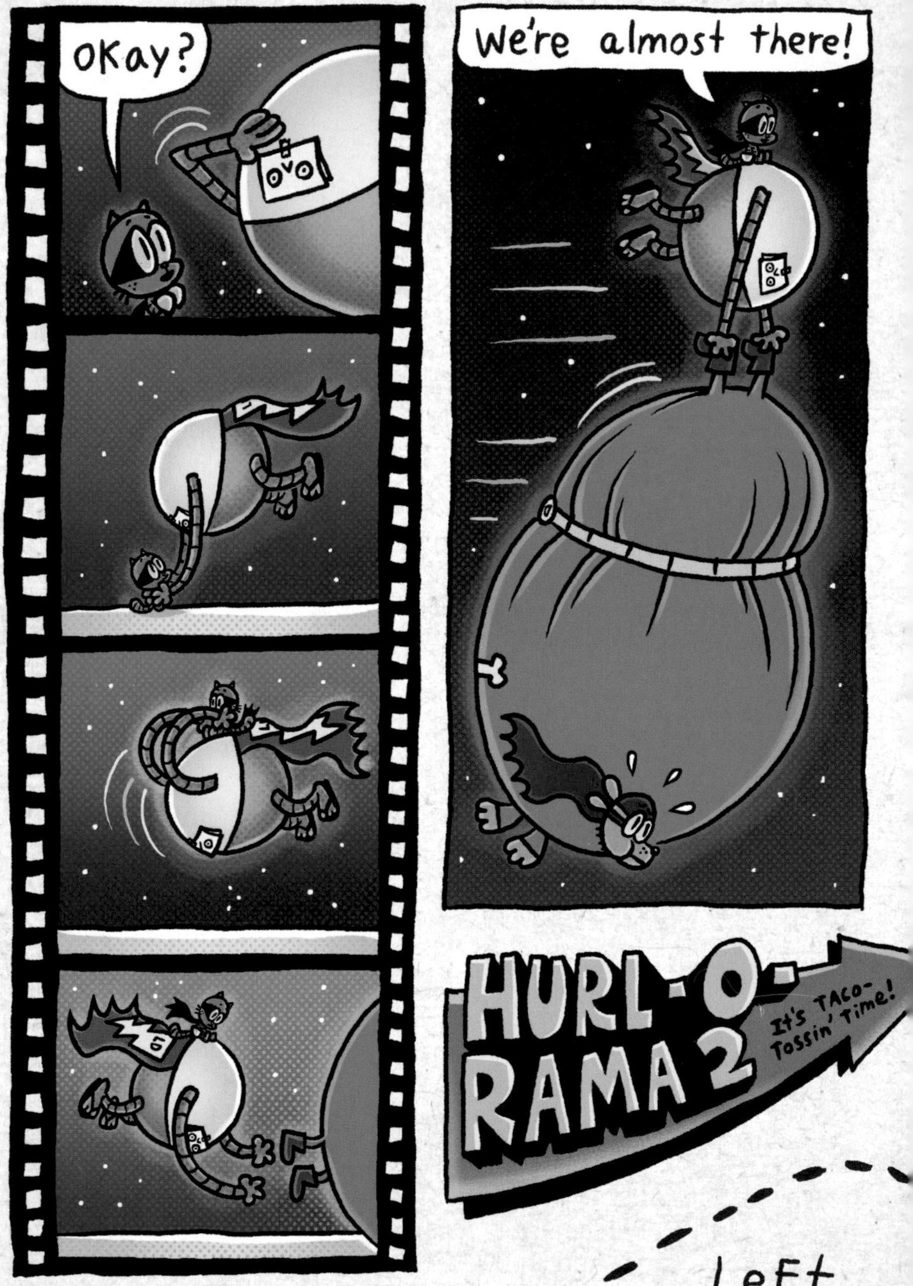

Left hand here.

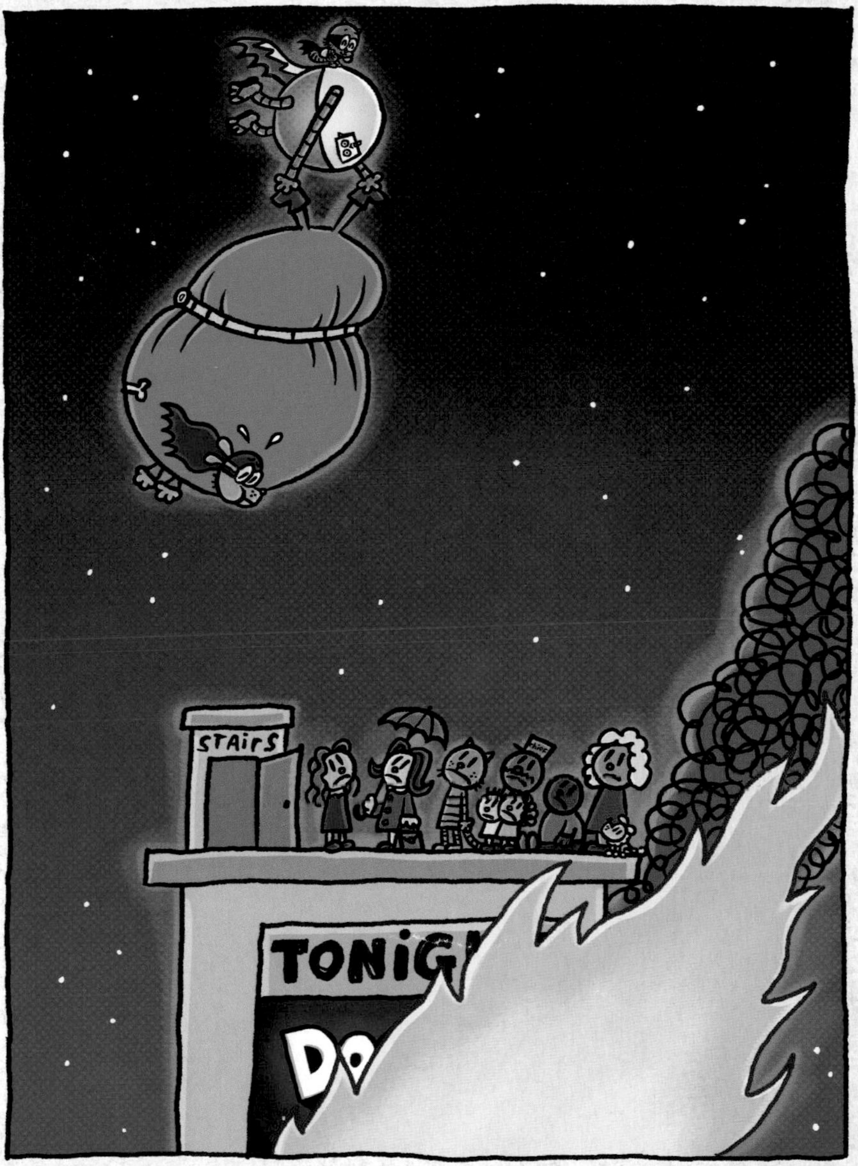
STAIrS
TONIG

Right Thumb here.

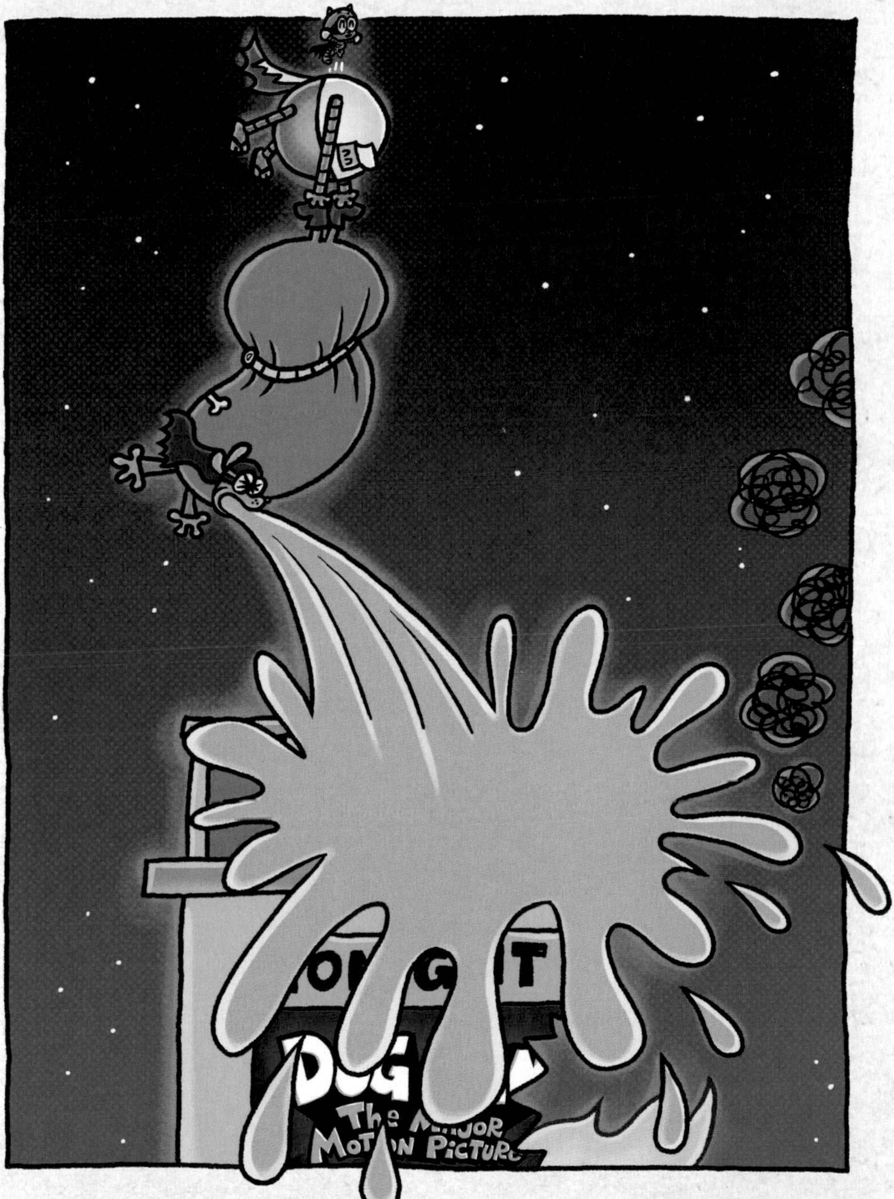

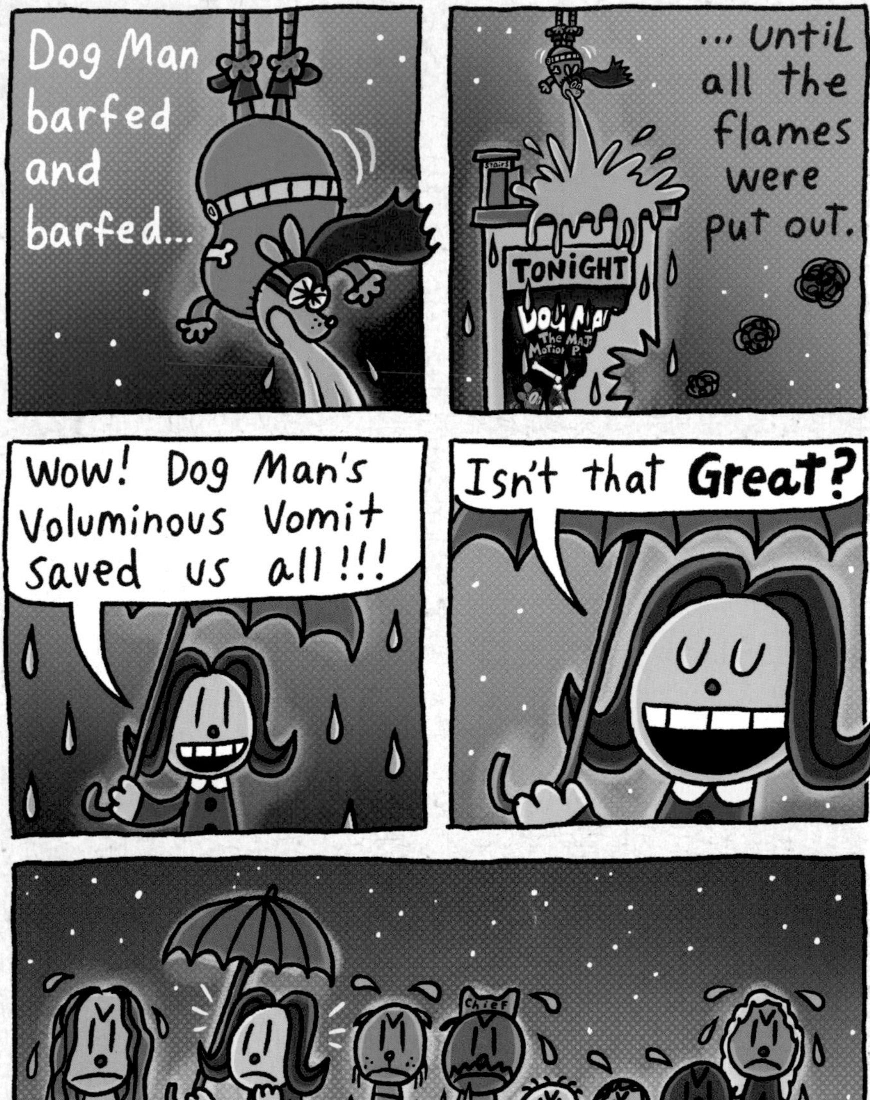
Dog Man barfed and barfed...
... until all the flames were put out.
TONIGHT
Wow! Dog Man's Voluminous Vomit saved us all!!!
Isn't that **Great**?
Chief

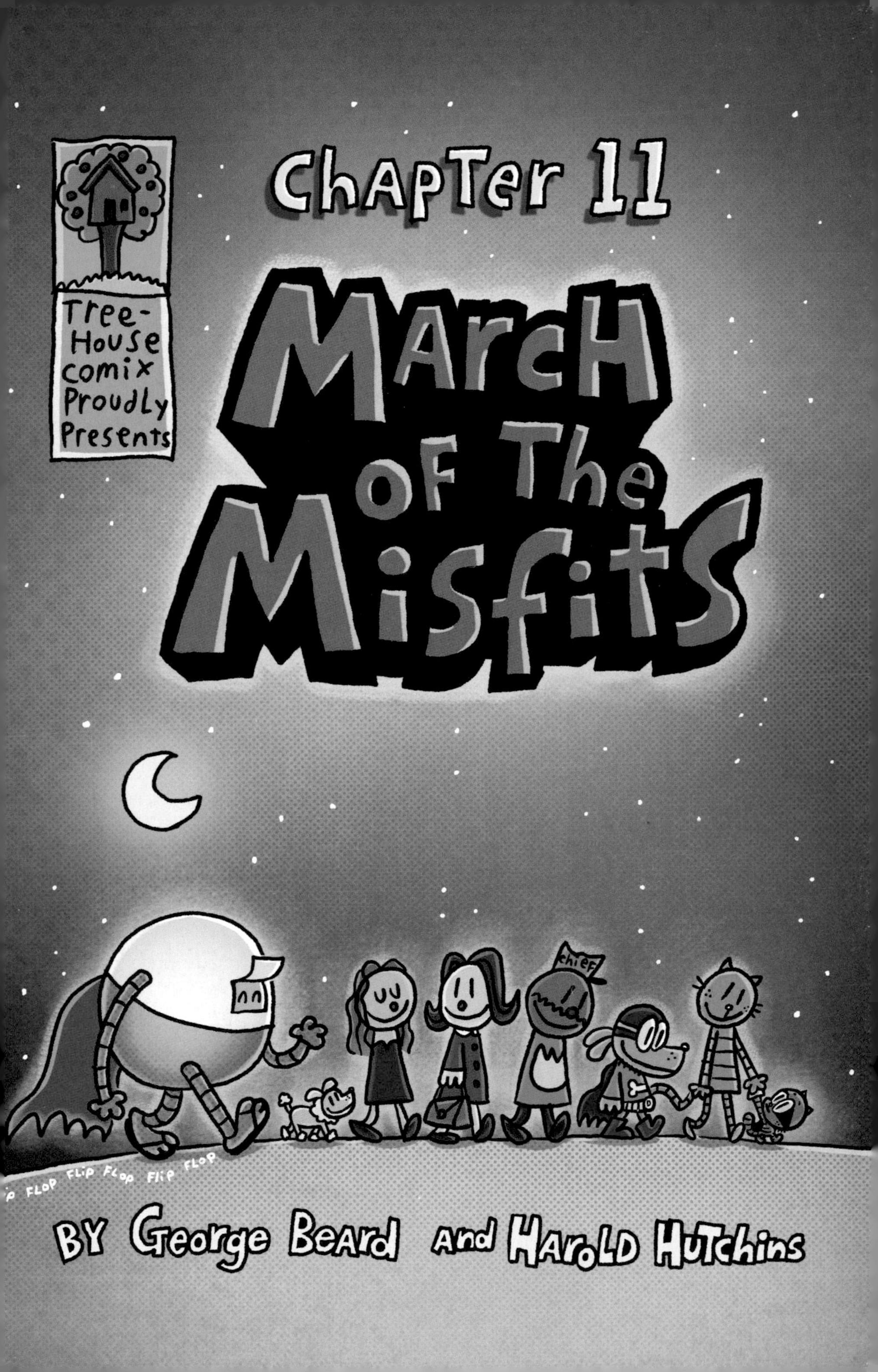
Tree-House comix Proudly Presents
ChapTer 11
March of The Misfits
chief
FLOP FLip FLop FLip FLOP
BY George Beard and Harold Hutchins

Don't feel bad, Dog Man.

I've never told anybody this...

...but I feel like a misfit, too.

HeY! So do **I**! Every day!!!

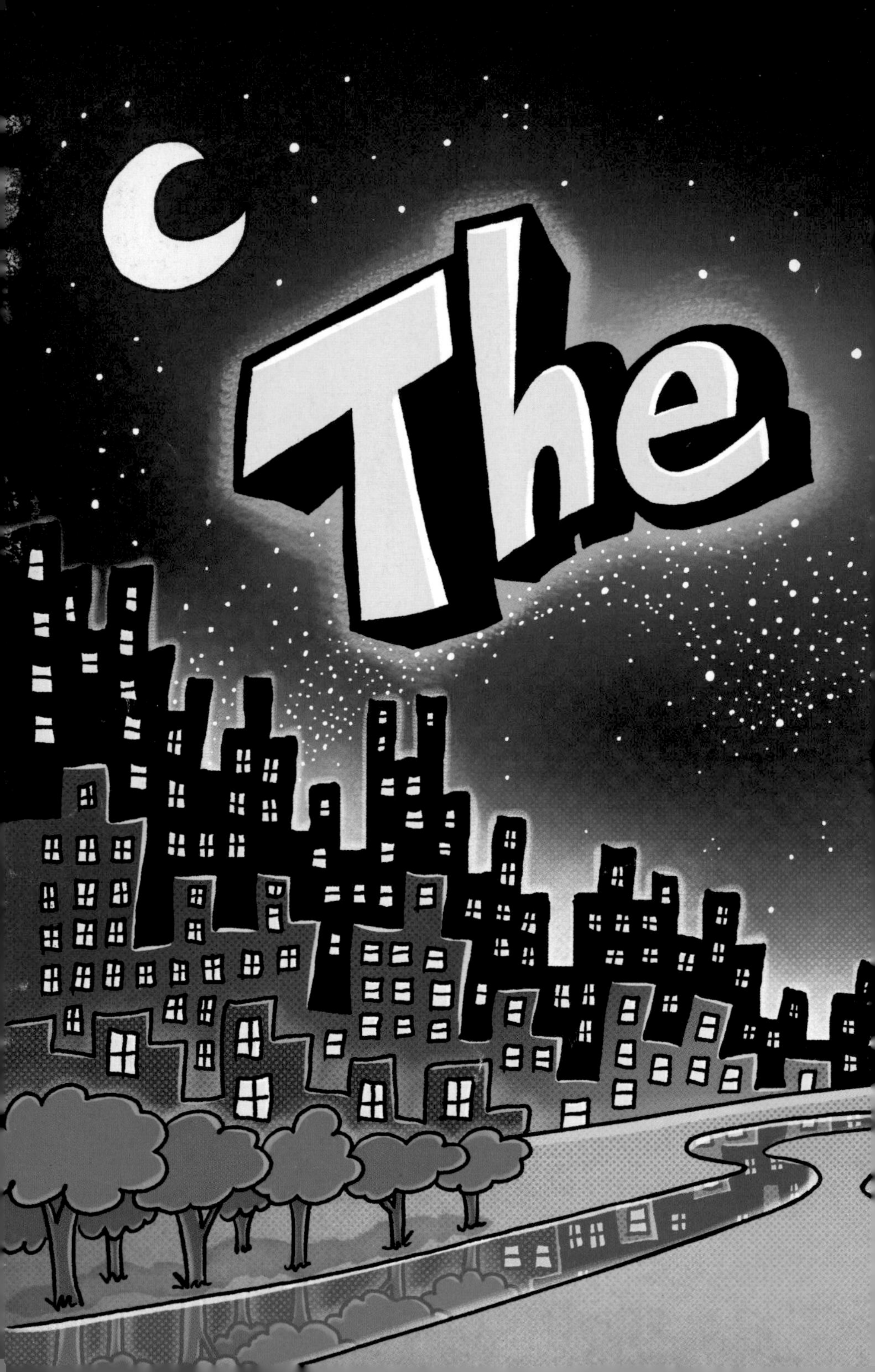
The

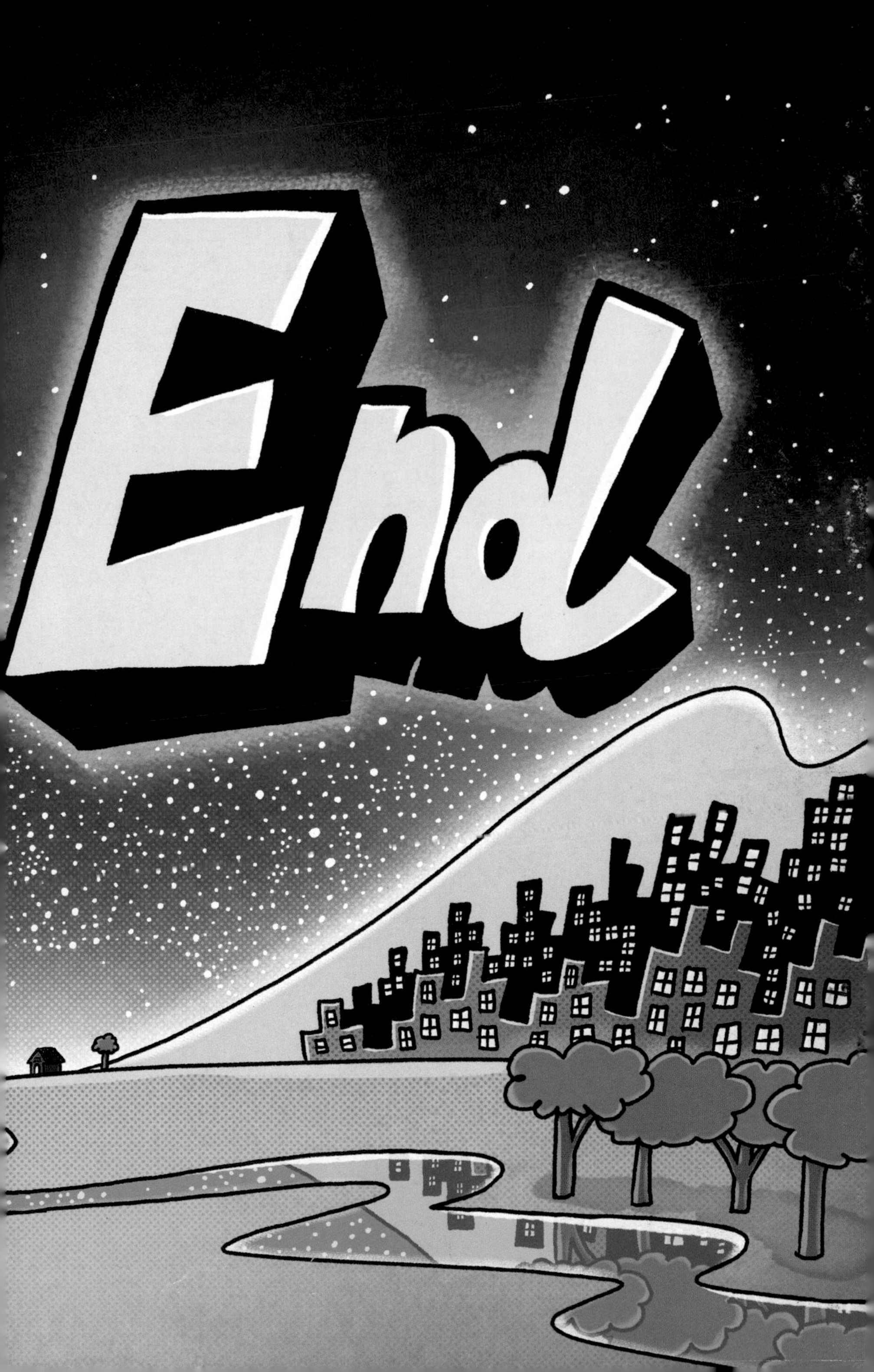
End

SUPA BUDDIES SAVE THE DAY:

The Supa Buddies kept everybody safe during last night's tragic fire. Cat Kid, the leader of the Supa Buddies, was sad afterward because he forgot to sing their theme song (which he made up) during the big brawl. "Next time I'll remember better," said Cat Kid.

THE FLEAS: WHERE ARE THEY NOW?

The FLEAS
(artist's depiction)

ey the Cat

Nobody knows the whereabouts of Piggy, Crunky, and Bub (AKA The FLEAS). They were last seen in the burning movie theater, but then they disappeared.

"I just don't know what happened to them," said Petey the Cat as he scratched himself inside his jail cell this morning. "They just vanished," he continued, scratching again and again. "Where could they be?" he asked again, scratching vigorously

Menu ≡

HERO DOGS FIND FOREVER HOMES

The seven former inmates at Dog Jail were pardoned this morning for being heroes at last night's fire. They were immediately adopted by a buncha nice families and stuff, and are living happily ever after and stuff.

COMEUPPANCE

This morning, three meanies were pulled out of a stinky hole in the ground.
During the rescue, the rope broke and they fell back into the hole a buncha times. It was awesome.

DOG MAN IS GO!

Reports are pouring in about an ALL-NEW Dog Man adventure that is coming your way. It will be available soon, but you should start bugging your parents, librarian, and/or bookseller about it now, just to be safe.
The title of this top secret book can now be revealed in this exclusive scoop:
The new book will be called DOG MAN !!! You heard it here first, folks!

HOW 2 DRAW CAT KiD

in 49 Ridiculously easy steps!

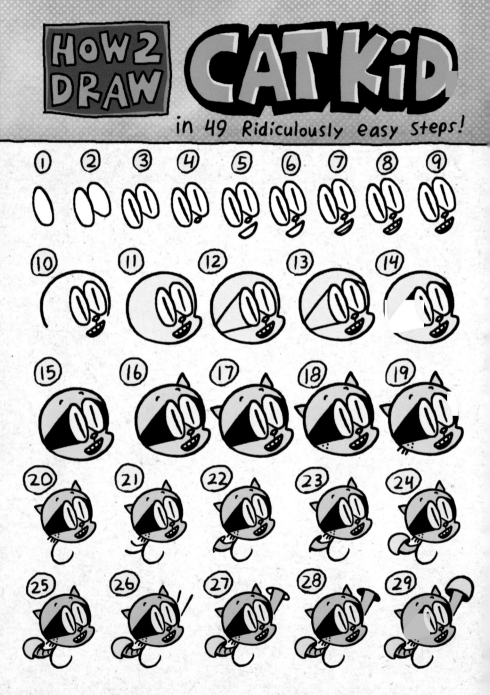

214

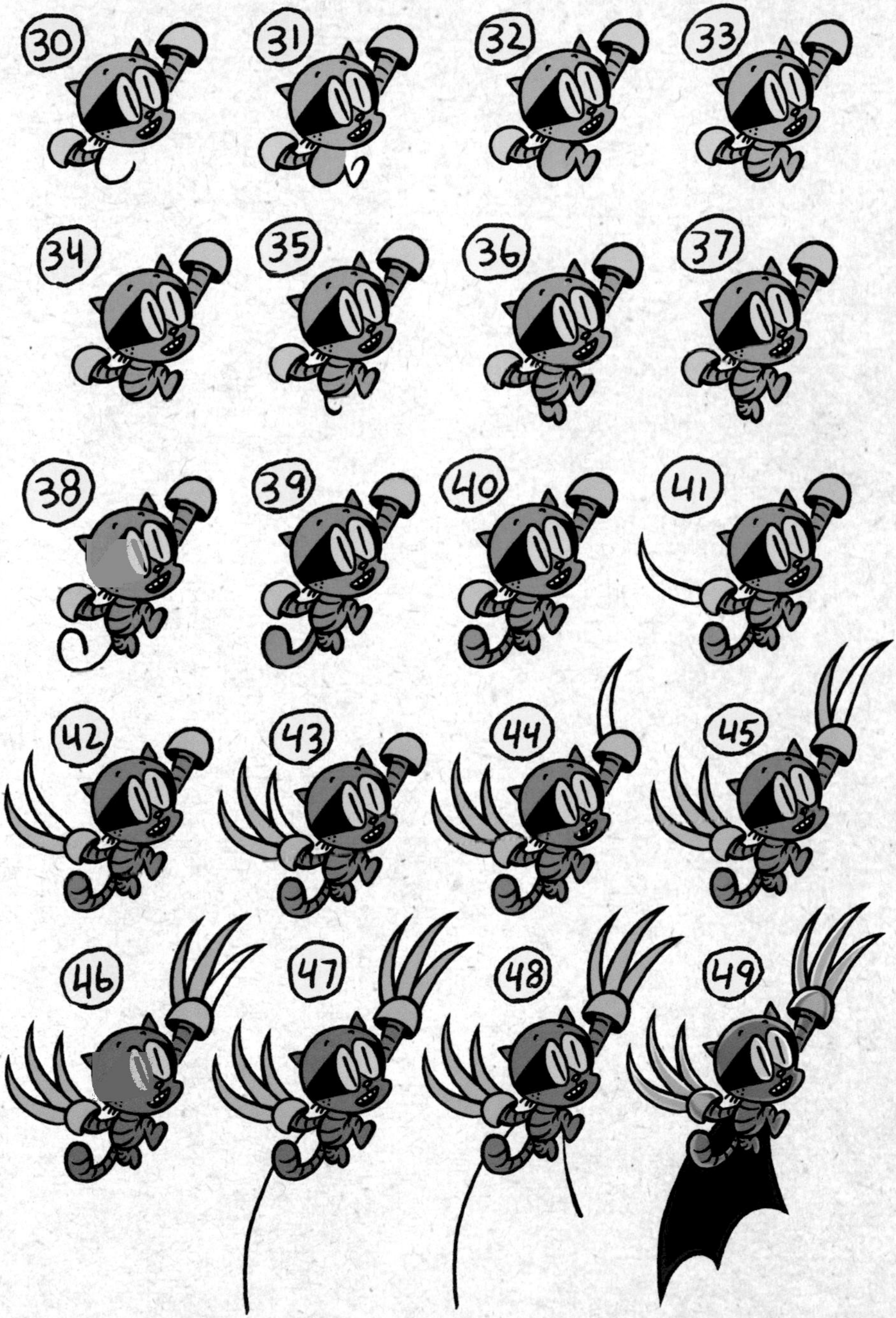
30
31
32
33
34
35
36
37
38
39
40
41
42
43
44
45
46
47
48
49

HOW 2 DRAW LIGHTNING DUDE

in 33 Ridiculously easy steps!

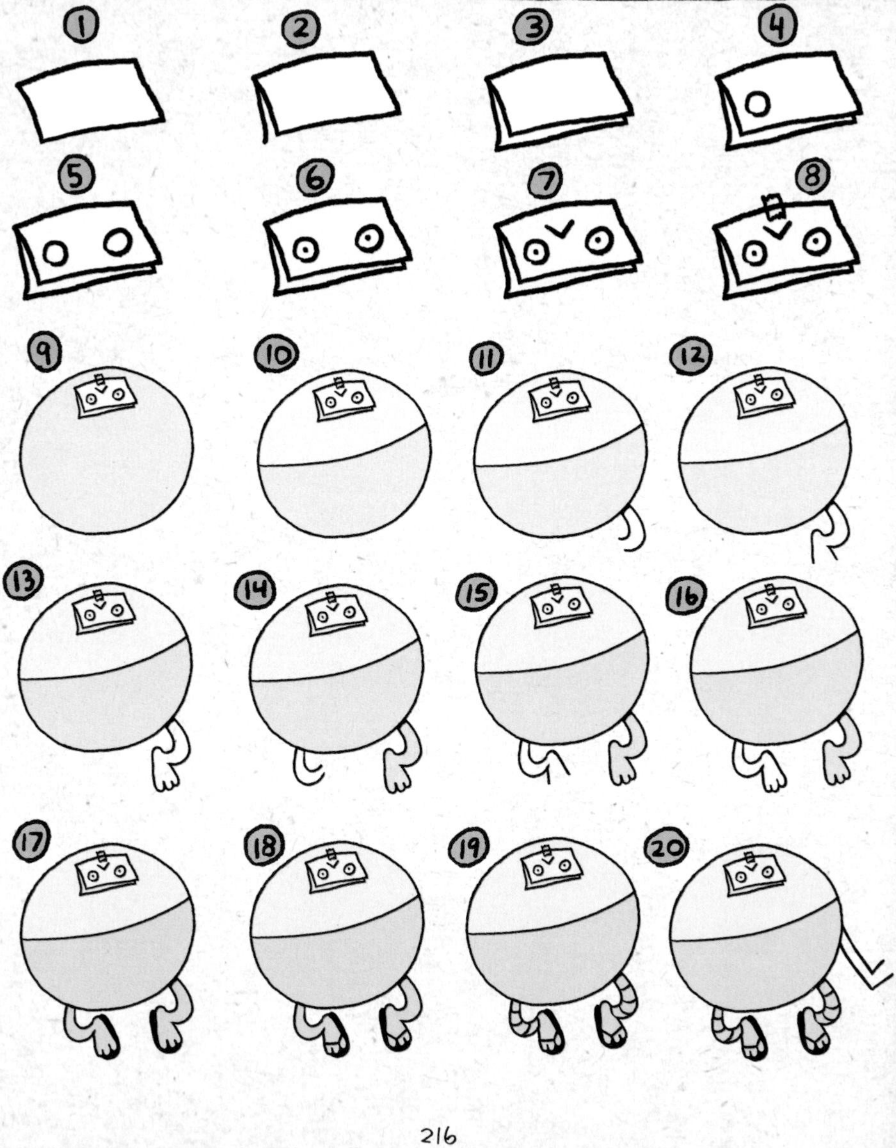
1
2
3
4
5
6
7
8
9
10
11
12
13
14
15
16
17
18
19
20

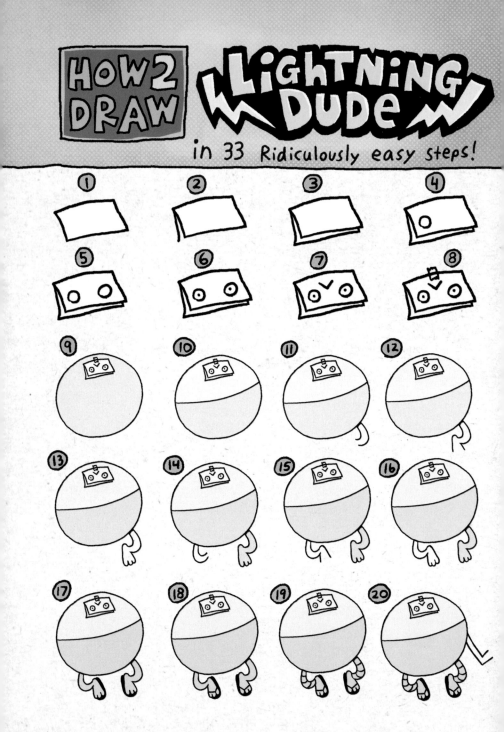

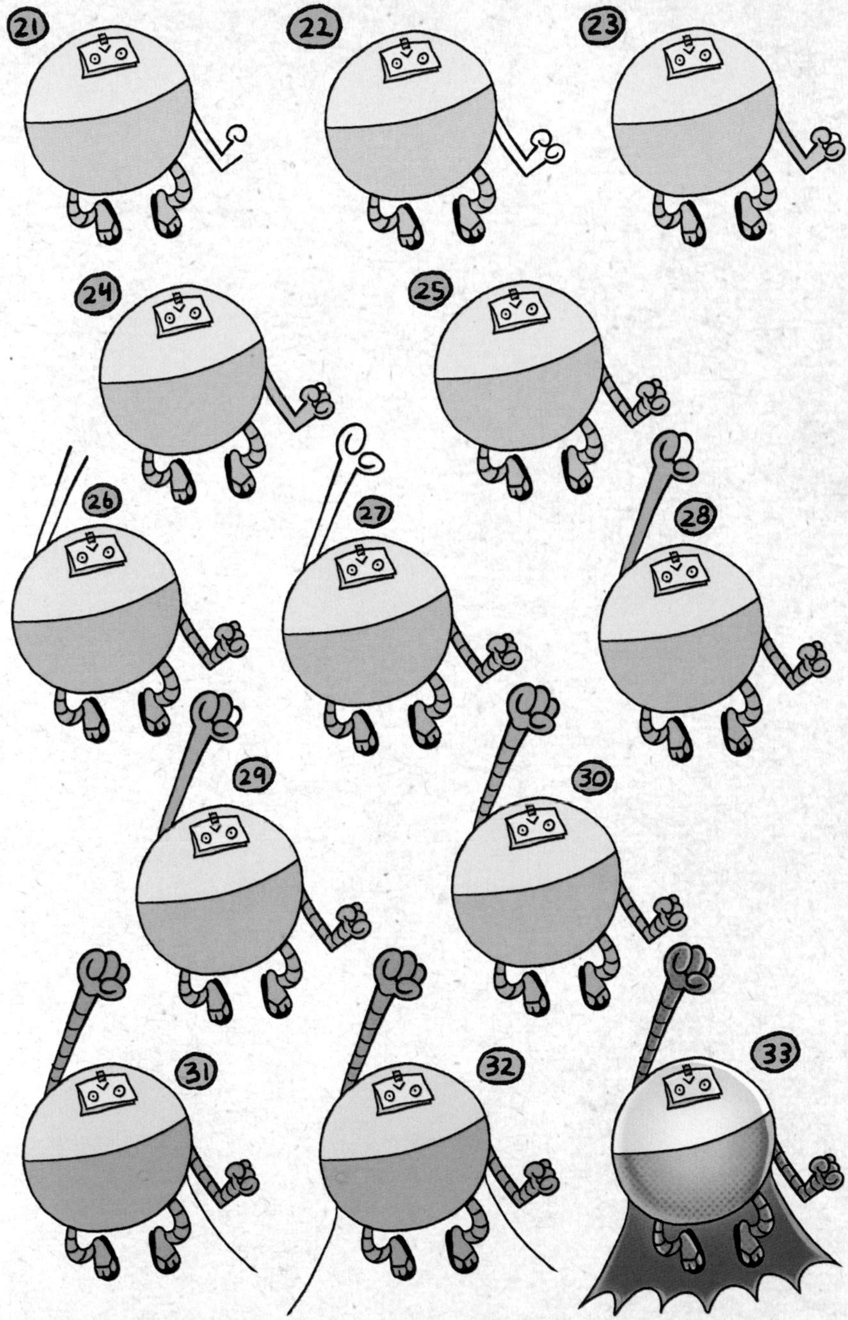
21
22
23
24
25
26
27
28
29
30
31
32
33

HOW 2 DRAW THE BARK KNIGHT

in 46 Ridiculously easy steps!

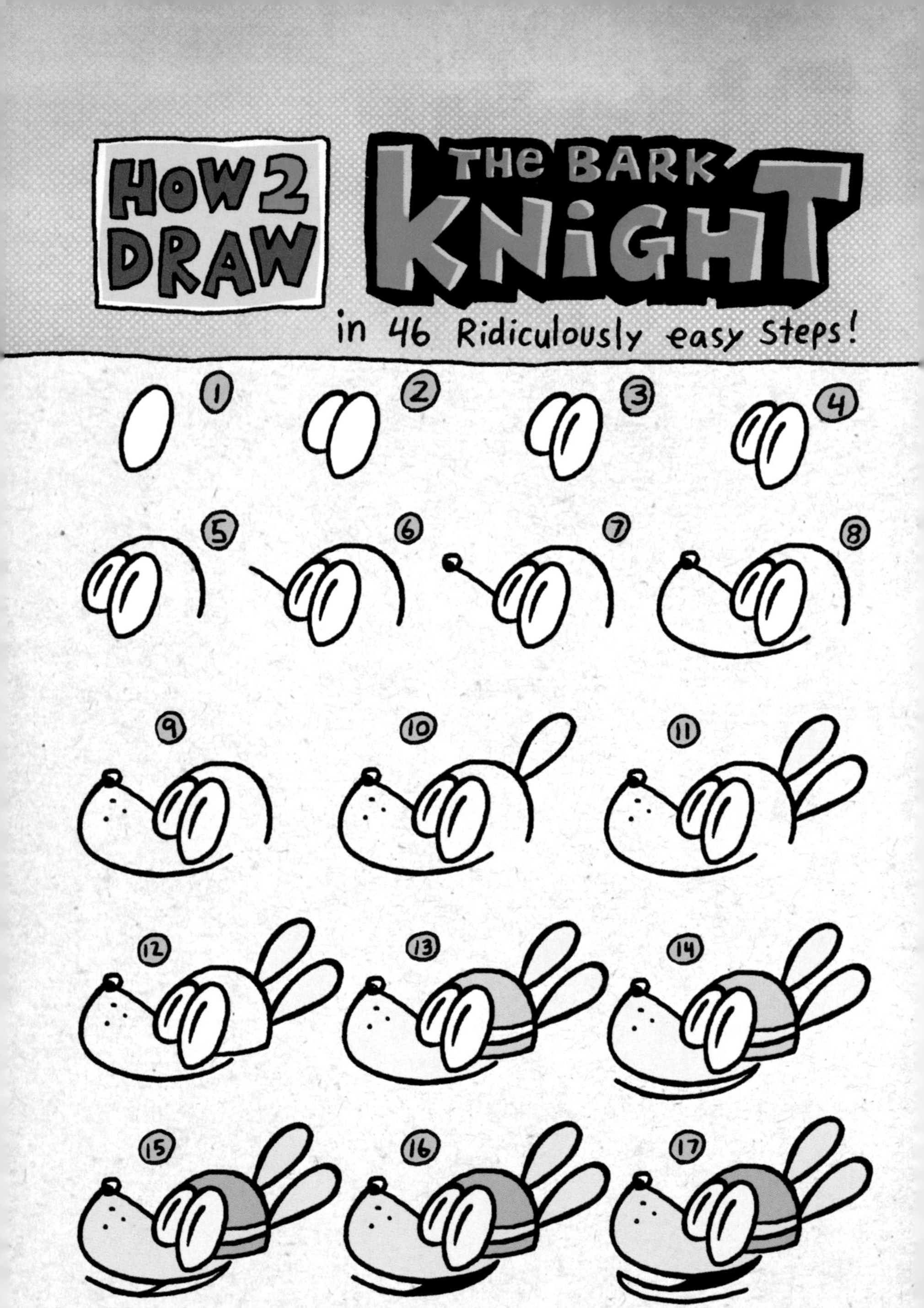
1
2
3
4
5
6
7
8
9
10
11
12
13
14
15
16
17

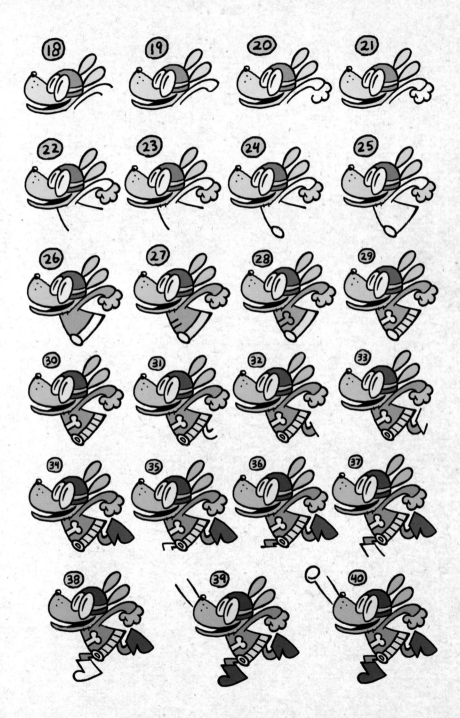

GET READING WITH DAV PILKEY!

"A fun introduction to chapter books."
— *SCHOOL LIBRARY JOURNAL*

ABOUT THE AUTHOR-ILLUSTRATOR

When Dav Pilkey was a kid, he suffered from ADHD, dyslexia, and behavioral problems. Dav was so disruptive in class that his teachers made him sit out in the hall every day. Luckily, Dav loved to draw and make up stories. He spent his time in the hallway creating his own original comic books.

In the second grade, Dav Pilkey created a comic book about a superhero named Captain Underpants. His teacher ripped it up and told him he couldn't spend the rest of his life making silly books.

Fortunately, Dav was not a very good listener.

ABOUT THE COLORIST

Jose Garibaldi grew up on the South Side of Chicago. As a kid, he was a daydreamer and a doodler, and now it's his full-time job to do both. Jose is a professional illustrator, painter, and cartoonist who has created work for many organizations, including Nickelodeon, MAD Magazine, Cartoon Network, and Disney. He is currently working as a visual development artist on THE EPIC ADVENTURES OF CAPTAIN UNDERPANTS for DreamWorks Animation. He lives in Los Angeles, California, with his wonder dogs, Herman and Spanky.